CHILHOWEE LEGACY

A Young Woman's Journey to the Truth

REBA RHYNE

Chilhowee Legacy

All Scripture quotations are taken from the KING JAMES VERSION (KJV): KING JAMES VERSION, public domain.

Cover by Ken Raney.

Editng by Sara Foust.

Special assistance by Mike Garner for clarity on final pages.

Thanks to Dawn Staymates, Kristen Veldhuis, and the crew at EA Publishing for another job well done.

Published by EA Books Publishing a division of Living Parables of Central Florida, Inc. a 501c3
EABooksPublishing.com

God keeps a file for our prayers – they are not blown away by the wind, they are treasured in the King's archives.

Charles Haddon Spurgeon

This book is dedicated to Tipton, Whitehead and Rhyne kin all over the world.

Contents

Foreword

I can remember my grandmother standing at the kitchen sink, the overhead fluorescent light shining on her gray hair. She stood washing the dishes and praying with tears dropping into the dishwater. In the solitude of her kitchen, this was her prayer closet.

I'm sure she learned this attitude of prayer from her parents who were prayer warriors, praying at any need or provocation. These utterances became a blanket hovering over their descendants, tapped into when illness, situation, or hurt arose without the receiver even knowing it. I call this phenomenon a legacy.

What is a legacy? Something handed down from one generation to another. Although we think of an inheritance usually as money or property, Noah and Nancy Tipton left a different one. Theirs was a spiritual legacy of prayers—prayers for their children and these children's extended families. I believe their perseverance in talking to God is still being felt today in their many descendants, who have come to acknowledge the God in whom the elder couple believed.

David sang in Psalms 61:5b, *thou hast given me the heritage of those that fear thy name.* Like King David, the Tipton offspring are overshadowed by a vast canopy of past whispered words which still keep them safe within this world. Just as Jesus Christ was God's gift to the world, Noah and Nancy Tipton were God's gift to their descendants.

This book is dedicated to Tipton, Whitehead, and Rhyne kin everywhere.

ALCOA, Alcoa, and Alcoa

This book has several words spelled the same but belonging to different meanings. So, I wanted to clarify their meaning before my reader gets confused.

1. ALCOA stands for the Aluminum Company of America — the aluminum smelting facility being built next to the City of Maryville, Tennessee.

2. Alcoa was the name given to a growing town on the Little Tennessee above Chilhowee, Tennessee while the ALCOA dams were being built. The name was later changed to Calderwood.

3. The third Alcoa was the new name for the city which sprang up around the smelting plant of ALCOA next to Maryville. When this town came into being, the name of the town above Chilhowee was changed to Calderwood.

❧ Chapter One ❧

Meet the Tipton's and Their Community

*By humility and the fear of the LORD are riches,
and honor, and life.*

Proverbs 22:4 KJV

Melva Lucinda Tipton looked out over the wide, river floodplain known as Chilhowee. From her vantage point near the top of a beech tree, she saw most of the open valley. This part of East Tennessee was her home and she loved every bit of it. It was Blount County, late autumn, 1911. Fallen, yellow leaves covered the ground and the bare, gray limbs left a clear view of her surroundings.

This wasn't the first time she'd climbed a tree, and this wasn't the first time she'd climbed this particular tree, although it was much taller now than her initial ascent. Years before, she and her brother had taken a hand saw and cleared excess limbs from the tree's trunk, making the way more open and easier to scale.

Usually, Melva's precarious perch resulted from a dare by her brother, Dwight Harley Tipton, or D.H. as the family called him.

But not today.

∾

The morning had started cool and crisp, but not cold enough for frost in the valley. The November sun had quickly heated the earth, and those inside buildings went outside to enjoy the last of summer's warmth.

Melva had finished sweeping the leaves off the front porch and stood looking at a lone robin which hadn't gone south for the winter.

"You'd better head to Florida, little bird. You'll freeze to death if you stay here."

"Are you talkin' to yourself?" D.H. came out of the house and promptly started sneezing at the dust she'd stirred up in the process of cleaning the porch.

"No. Just to a robin. It flew off when you sneezed."

"Let's sit on the porch and talk," D.H. suggested, looking at a disturbed line of comfortable rocking chairs, which Melva had just moved to sweep. He started putting them back in place.

Melva went inside the house to put the broom on its nail in the front closet under the stairs. When she returned the chairs were perfect, and D.H. was rocking in the one closest to the door. She sat in one next to her brother.

The porch of the Tipton's two-story, frame home stretched across the front of the house. In the summertime, the entrance was usually filled with guests, relaxing and debating the news of the day, especially after the heat of the afternoon.

Melva and D.H. sat to discuss the news from Maryville.

"Do you remember Carrie Stevens?"

"Wasn't she the woman who welcomed people into the bank and gave children a piece of peppermint candy?" Of course, Melva would remember her. She never turned down anything with sugar in it.

"The very same. She sent you something." D.H. dug into the pocket of his jacket and pulled out a small bag of the hard, pillow-shaped candy.

"Please tell her I said thank you." Melva shared with her brother and popped one into her mouth.

"Have you seen Ellie since she moved to Six Mile Community near Maryville?" Susan Ellen, or Ellie as the family called her, was Melva's older sister. Last month, she and her husband, Bill Garland, moved to several acres across the mountains from Chilhowee.

"No, I haven't had a chance. They came into the bank to invite me to supper, but I was busy on the night in question and couldn't go. Next time, I'll go even if I have to cancel an engagement. No one cooks like Ellie."

"Mother says if Bill Garland loves good cookin' and a clean house, they should get along well."

"Do you miss her?"

"Yes, but mother misses her more. Ellie was a good helper in the kitchen."

D.H. grinned, knowing that Melva wasn't much help in the kitchen at all.

Suddenly, the high-pitched, emergency bell of the Chilhowee Lumber Mill sounded in the distance, interrupting their conversation.

"Wonder what's goin' on at the Mill?" D.H. stood and looked upriver toward the mill's location, questioning if he should head there and lend a hand. "Can't see anything. We're too low here."

The unexpected bell continued to sound—a faint but shrill noise in the midst of the wide valley.

"Let's go find out. Meet you at our tree." He jumped off the porch and with a few steps, disappeared around the side of the house.

"Sure," Melva called after him, knowing exactly what to do.

Popping another mint into her mouth and pushing the paper bag into her pocket, she went through the front door into the parlor. She grabbed four large safety pins from her mother's sewing basket, pinning them to her blouse. Next, she opened an ornate wooden case on the upright piano and grabbed her father's spyglass, secreting it into another empty pocket. After closing the box, she headed through the double doors into the dining room and on to the kitchen.

Nancy Tipton, her mother, was starting the preparation for the noon meal. "Where are you going, Melva? I'll need you to set the table and help with dinner."

"Headin' up the path toward the springhouse with D.H.," she mumbled through the peppermint candy. "Won't be gone long." Not waiting for her mother's reply, she rushed through the screen door to the back porch. The door banged shut behind her.

Nan shook her head as her daughter left the kitchen. She huffed a sigh and walked to the door, calling after her offspring in a full, but smooth tone. She never raised her voice, but her children always heard her. "Since you're headin' in the direction of the spring, bring back the buttermilk and butter." All she saw was Melva's backside as she hurried up the dirt trail. "Be a miracle if she remembers," she murmured and returned to her hot woodstove.

Melva covered the trip up the well-worn path to the spring in record time. She jumped the trickle of water coming from the springhouse and hurried toward her brother. Pinning up her long skirt, she scrambled up the knobby beech tree, showing her shapely legs and skinning one of her knees. Blood trickled slowly down her exposed leg. Melva Tipton, an impulsive fifteen, sported flashing brown eyes and long, brown hair piled high on her head. She was a tall, slender girl with her own ideas.

"The bell's quit," D.H. stated, looking up at her and then north toward the mill.

She took out the spyglass and peered through it. "Yes. I guess the danger's over."

"Do you see the sawmill camp?" asked D.H.

"Yes," said Melva. "I see people movin' around. They look like ants they're so far away. Do you think this is another false alarm?"

"Could be, since that bell has a mind of its own— like you," he added and grinned, thinking it was interesting that a bell and his sister could be on the same level. He loved her, but she could be exasperating at times.

"Whoa!" A hard puff of wind moved the beech tree and rustled the leaves on the ground. Melva grabbed at a branch and clutched the spyglass more tightly.

"Be careful, Melva. Maybe you should come down. The wind's gettin' up." D.H. looked at the sky, trying to determine if rain was in the forecast.

White, puffy clouds drifted over the softly-shaped mountains, encircling the lowland farms along the Little Tennessee River. Beyond the bottomland owned by their father, the clear, cold river cut a path at the edge of the mountain on the opposite side of the elongated valley, and ended its journey at the Tennessee River several miles downstream. The noonday sun glinted on its surface.

"Just another minute." She didn't want to waste the effort she'd put into climbing the tree and continued to check out the people at the mill.

The fact that she could see anything so distant wasn't a tribute to her good eyes but to her father's handheld monocular or spyglass. This item, much cherished by Noah Tipton, was off-limits for his children to touch, much less use. Rumored to have been given to his great-grandfather by Andrew Jackson, it was a prized possession. When Melva snuck it out of the house in the pocket of her long skirt, she risked banishment to Africa or another of those faraway places she'd studied in school.

As she looked, smoke from the logging camp rolled upward, mingling with the blue sky.

"There may have been a fire, but it doesn't look serious." At that moment, the mill's fifteen-minute warning whistle sounded to announce the noon meal. "Dinner is served," Melva said.

"Better hurry, sister. Father will be headed to the house for his dinner. We don't want to be late," said D.H. looking up at her as she clung unsteadily to the swaying tree. Becoming dizzy, he looked at the ground, regretting he'd suggested this escapade. She might fall and break something, maybe her neck. He couldn't help but grin at the thought. His sister was tough as nails. Most likely, the ground would suffer a bruising quake.

Melva, intrigued at the scene she saw in the glass said, "I heard him tell Mother, because of the election, he'd be later than usual. So, don't get in a tizzy."

"I don't care. *Please* come on down." The word "please" usually worked.

Melva ignored her brother's wishes and continued to peer through the spyglass. She promised herself she'd never climb this tree again—or any tree for that matter. At her age, squeezing around and through the limbs was almost impossible, and her knee hurt. Anyhow, she was at a stage in life, when she needed to concentrate on adult things—like getting ready for marriage.

"Can you tell what's happening?" asked D.H., interrupting Melva's thoughts.

"No. Maybe we'll hear all the news at the dance tomorrow night. You're going, aren't you?"

"I didn't know there was one."

"Yes. At the Happy Valley Schoolhouse. I can't wait to see Betty Jo. Did you know she's seein' one of the clerks in the lumber mill office?"

"No, I didn't. Is it serious?" D.H worked in Maryville and came home less and less. The local news was provided by Melva or his father.

"Probably. She can't talk about anythin' else," said Melva who worried that getting married would end their friendship. Betty Jo was her best friend from grade school.

Girls in the mountains only went through the eighth grade at Big Cove School; something Melva already regretted. Some mountain girls married at fourteen and fifteen in the Appalachians.

Her father, Noah, didn't encourage his five girls to get married at such a young age. But mountain families were large, and one less mouth to feed was an attractive incentive, so girls married young and had babies while they were still children. Melva was in no hurry to marry. Although she'd been looking, she didn't have anyone in mind.

"You know better than to go to the dance. If Mom and Dad find out, they'll be so angry you'll be confined to the house forever. The Primitive Baptist Church doesn't agree with dancin' or drinking," D.H. warned, knowing he couldn't say too much, because he did a little of both in Maryville.

Melva wasn't worried about getting disciplined. If her parents penalized her for everything she did that they didn't like, she would never get out of the house. Not that she was a bad girl, but she was mischievous. She always skirted the edge of getting into serious trouble. She often saw a lurking smile as her mother or father reprimanded her.

"They won't know unless you tell them. I hoped you'd take me to Betty Jo's."

"We'll see." D.H. kicked at the beech tree leaves scattered over the ground, sending a pile flying in the wind. He looked up again. "Melva, come down."

"I'll come down in a minute." She quickly checked out the rest of the valley through the spyglass.

Directly below her, in front of her parents' two-story home, the dusty road snaked through the hilly land, heading upward toward the foot of the Great Smoky Mountains.

Almost across the road from her home, the white-framed Tipton's Mercantile Store, with the black and white sign hung over the door, welcomed many voters in today's special election.

"There's several horses and buggies in front of the store." Melva observed. "A bunch of men are standin' outside socializing." She could identify all of them. Some had traveled from Happy Valley along Mill Creek and passed Hill Cove School to get to the store. She recognized another who lived at Tallassee, a town on down the river.

"Since Father's conducting the election, I thought about goin' over to help him in the store." D.H. added, "but he said he wouldn't be waitin' on customers today unless there was an emergency."

"No. He didn't need me either." Melva usually helped on Friday. Her father was teaching her the workings of running the store.

Several years earlier, Noah had bought the store and moved the family from Cades Cove in the Smoky Mountains. Before the move, D.H. and Melva were both born on Rowan's Creek, a tributary of upper Abram's Creek in the cove.

Abram's Creek started in Cades Cove, continued several miles through the mountains, and emptied into the Little Tennessee a couple of miles above the Tipton home at Chilhowee. On this end, several families lived along its banks.

"Why can't women vote?" Melva put the eyepiece down and looked at her brother.

"What?" The question was unexpected.

His sister repeated the question, emphasizing each word. "Why can't women vote?"

"Melva, I don't know any reason they can't vote. You could certainly make a good decision on a candidate who's running, especially with all the politickin' that goes on around Father's store and our kitchen table. The law needs to be changed."

"Well, Brother. Why don't you change it?"

"Don't think it depends solely on me. All men and women need to get involved. There's already states in the mid-west lettin' women vote in their elections. It's coming, and soon." D.H. knew this discussion would never end. The sound of the train whistle stopped the conversation.

Melva put the spyglass to her eye. Behind the store building and running a short piece northeast, were the railroad tracks. At the end of the line, the Chilhowee Depot almost stood within rock-throwing distance of the store with a spur running to the sawmill site. An engine turntable turned the huge piece of machinery around and provided the quickest transportation back to Maryville, Tennessee, the county seat.

A necessary link to the outside world, the train brought the Maryville newspaper, Collier's and the Saturday Evening Post magazines, recently published books, and supplies which Noah sold at his business. The engine and a few cars sat parked on a side track.

From her perch, Melva recognized the engineer, oil can in hand, as he checked the gears and other mechanical parts underneath the train.

Secreting the spyglass in the deep pocket of her skirt, Melva started down out of the tree. A twig caught in her hair, pulling out a long strand as she jerked her head to free it. The brown lock hung down the side of her face.

D.H breathed a sigh of relief, glad to see her headed down. The gusts of wind had grown stronger.

Her attention turned to protecting her well knee from damage. Twisting and turning, she finally arrived at the bottom, jumping the last few feet.

She was breathing rapidly when she hit the ground and tucked the errant lock back into her tresses. "I'm sure Miss Annie Myers will be there," she said, rustling the leaves as she flounced by him down the trail, jumping the trickle of water and passing the springhouse.

"What are you talking about?" D.H. shook his head, confused by the rapidly changing subjects of conversation.

"The dance, of course. Annie will be there."

"You don't say!" D.H. responded in his resonant voice. Annie was his first girlfriend and his first kiss.

They walked down the path in silence.

Despite their age difference, Melva and he were best friends among the nine siblings. He had a slow, thoughtful way of talking, and blue eyes that locked onto yours and held your attention.

While he lived at home, they'd gone frog gigging on Tab Cat Creek, fished and boated in the Little Tennessee River, and hiked many miles in the mountains. Melva was always ready to try something new, even something she thought a little dangerous, especially if her brother suggested it. She trusted him and never doubted his words.

D.H. admired her spunk. Plus, he would never recommend anything to hurt his sister. At twenty-one, he was six years older than she, and would soon be returning to Maryville and his job as clerk at the local bank. D.H had attended Maryville Polytechnic School, a boarding school, from which he graduated three years ago.

For Melva, the few days D.H. remained home were like old times. They shared many secrets. This included an overlook in the nearby hills she called her *secret place*. With so many siblings at home and visitors in and out the door, Melva cherished her time on the hillside overlooking the calm and peaceful valley. But there was another reason she visited. When problems arose which she couldn't solve, she sat alone, spending time mulling over her troubles or maybe that was sulking over her minor skirmishes. Sometimes, she returned home with an answer, and sometimes she didn't.

Stopping on the path, she checked her knee. It had quit bleeding. She took the pins out of her skirt. "No reason for Mother to know what we were doing." Melva continued on down the trail.

"I agree." D.H. said, following close behind.

"Are you going to see Rita tomorrow night after you take me to the Boyd's?"

"Aren't you making a big assumption? I haven't said I'd take you."

"You will, won't you?" Melva turned around, hands on hips, and put her flashing, brown eyes on her brother.

"Whew! I think I will." D.H. decided, knowing he might as well or he'd never hear the end of it. He shook his head. "I need to see little James."

At seventeen, their sister Rita married James Gardner and the following year they announced the birth of a baby boy. Rita's husband owned land given to him by his father in Happy Valley.

"Is Rita well?" D.H. knew from letters he received from home that his sister had a tough time delivering the baby.

"Oh, yes. Mother says so. Rita's not sure she wants to have another baby, but mother said she would get over it. She says all expectant mothers develop a case of amnesia before they have another child." Nan had laughed as she told Melva this. Her daughter wondered if it was true.

Melva wasn't unhappy that Rita was gone. They always butted heads on everything, and Melva was a little jealous of her older sibling. Noah always said they were like two peas in a pod with a thorn between. Secretly, each admired the other.

As Melva and D.H. entered the house, the screen door banged shut behind them.

"Where have you two been? Did you bring the buttermilk and butter? If I'd known it was going to take this long, I'd of gotten them myself!" exclaimed their mother as the two trekked into the room with no milk of any kind in sight. Nancy Tipton bustled about the kitchen. Her last child, baby Joyce, lay sleeping in her small crib, totally oblivious to her mother's banging pots and pans.

"I declare your minds are so short. What were you doing?" Without waiting for an answer, she turned back to the stove.

"I forgot," Melva whispered to her brother.

"I'll run back and get them," D.H. said to his mother, exiting the dining room as quickly as he could, not wishing to incur more of his mother's wrath.

"Melva, I need you to set the table and help me here in the kitchen."

Setting the table was shared with her little sister. Lydia was six and at Hill Cove School today, along with her older brothers, Milton, who was thirteen, and eleven-year-old, Matthew.

"I'll be right back." Melva escaped upstairs to her bedroom to clean her knee with water that she'd remembered to carry to the pitchers in each room—one of her daily chores. Pouring water into a basin, she took a cloth, and carefully wiped around the cut on her knee. Taking an end of the fabric, she patted the area dry.

In the upstairs hall was a bottle of alcohol and a glass container of cotton balls on a small table. Obviously, scrapes and gashes were accidents the Tipton's knew well. Melva swabbed her knee liberally and blew as well as she could on the abrasion. It didn't hurt—much. This cut would soon be a scar and join all the others on her knees.

Turning toward the staircase, she rushed to help her mother. The spyglass banged against her thigh as she bounced down the stairs. She needed to replace it in its special box. She approached the parlor, avoiding squeaking floor boards. Luckily for Melva, the double doors to the dining room were partially closed, because she heard her mother in the next room. Replacing Noah's prized possession was accomplished without incident. Africa would have to wait.

"Melva is that you?" Nan called from the dining room.

"Yes, Mother. I'm coming."

As in most families, chores were divided between the children. However, since D.H. and Henry lived in Maryville, Henrietta and Susan Ellen were married, and Joyce was too young to help, that left only four Tipton children to share household duties. Melva was now the oldest girl child living at home.

As Melva entered the kitchen, delicious smells touched her nostrils—cinnamon, green beans with bacon grease, and boiling potatoes in butter. She wondered, would she ever be able to cook like her mother? If she had one weakness, pertaining to a future as a wife, it was not knowing how to cook. Sure. She could wash and peel vegetables, but the final preparation and addition of spices escaped her. She couldn't make a pie crust or a loaf of bread.

Nan Tipton busied herself with the final preparations for the dinner meal. She was at home here and totally in charge. In lots of ways, Melva took after her. But Melva was establishing behaviors of her own.

"Mother, I'll mix the cornbread," she said, reaching into the cupboard to get out a blue bowl with an intricate design. She loved this bowl and used it as much as she could to peel potatoes or apples. She got other boxes and tins she'd seen her sister, Ellie, use and placed them on the countertop. Mixing cornbread wasn't a chore she did often—actually never. But how difficult could it be?

"Good," said Nan, checking the stove's wood box and not paying attention. Nan's cast iron woodstove was much improved from those of her mother, Caroline, and grandmother, Susanna. She could regulate the air flow and amount of heat to areas on the cook top and oven. Her skill at cooking on the stove was routine. She made delicious meals effortlessly.

In her kitchen, cold running water came through a pipe by gravity from the concrete holding tank inside the springhouse. This small building was dug into the hillside high above the house. The buried pipe had enough pressure to fill a tank and flush the one commode built into a former clothes closet-pantry in the long hallway from the front door. A small tub and sink stand sat in one corner each of the tiny compartment. Hot water for a bath was boiled on the stove. More than one person in the family used the tub before the water got cold.

Noah always told Nan that every time a newfangled product was made, he had to tear up or out a place in the house to make way for the improvement.

He was willing to buy his wife a new electric stove, but Nan had clung to her cast-iron wood stove. When he'd suggested the new one, she'd said a firm, "No!" A deep pan with a dipper sat at the rear of the large stove's cooking surface. As long as the stove was fired up, Nan always had hot water for cooking and cleaning dishes.

She had agreed to electric lights, even though unsightly wires ran upstairs and down to provide it. The coal oil lanterns smelled and smoked after they were lit, and spills when filling them were common.

Bang! The slamming of the screen door from the back porch announced D.H.'s return. He deposited the buttermilk and butter on the countertop next to the sink. After hugging his mother and pinching his sister, he headed upstairs to his bedroom to clean up for dinner.

Melva placed the blue bowl on the countertop and poured fresh buttermilk into it.

Nan turned around just in time to check on her daughter's progress. "Melva, not the blue bowl, get the large white one,"

"Why, Mother?"

"Don't question me. Just do it," said Nan. She didn't have time to explain at the moment, and she was still irritated at her daughter's forgetfulness and late appearance.

Melva knew better than to push her mother. She got out the white bowl and set it down on the countertop. She couldn't understand why her mother always used the same bowl. She stared into its depths.

"What secret does the white bowl possess that makes better cornbread?"

Nan looked at her and gave a wry smile. How many times had this child seen cornbread made? Realizing she needed to help, Nan headed over to give her daughter proper instructions. She'd done the same thing for Rita and Ellie, but they could make perfect cornbread when they were the age of twelve.

"I'm sorry for being cross, daughter. Let me explain. There isn't any secret. Good mountain cooks know exactly how much of each ingredient to stir up for their recipes, because they use the same bowl each time to help with measuring." A pinch of this and a handful of that produced perfection when the meal was served.

Before Nan could stop her, Melva transferred the buttermilk to the puzzling white bowl. "No. You don't put the cornmeal into the milk," exclaimed Nan. "Pour it out and clean the bowl."

Melva did as told. Her mother watched, hands on hips, and then she helped her daughter mix the bread.

"Take this iron skillet," she pulled one from the back of the stove, "and put bacon grease in it to melt." The bacon grease, from the week's meat cooked for breakfast, was in a small Swift Leaf Lard can beside the skillet. She watched as Melva dipped from the can. "While you mix the bread, get the skillet hot on the stove."

Nan pulled a large, much-used, White Lily Flour tin from the back of the counter and opened it. It contained the family's own stone-ground cornmeal. Another tin contained White Lily Flour ground in Knoxville, Tennessee by Noah's friend, J. Allen Smith. Nan pulled a drinking glass from a cupboard and filled it twice with cornmeal. "Put cornmeal, some flour, a little sugar, baking powder, and a pinch of salt together in your bowl and blend. Add soda to your buttermilk and stir. Add two eggs, slightly beaten, along with your buttermilk to the dry mix." Nan watched as this was accomplished, lending a hand when necessary.

Not happy with her daughter's stirring the mix with a spoon, Nan took the bowl. Tilting it sideways in the crook of her arm, Nan stirred the contents with her hand. Setting the bowl on the counter, she rinsed the mixture off her hand into the sink.

Getting a potholder, hanging on a nail above the countertop, Nan took the hot, iron skillet from the stove and set it on a metal trivet. Melva stepped out of the way. "Add most of the hot, melted bacon grease." The cornmeal mixture sizzled and danced on top as she poured the hot, smoking grease onto it. "Careful don't get burned. Stir." A large spoon this time and then her hand. "Pour the cornmeal mixture into hot pan." The mixture sizzled again. "Place in the stovetop oven."

With the potholder on her hand, Nan walked over to her cook stove and placed the mixed cornbread inside the oven. "You keep an eye on it. Don't let it burn," she instructed Melva. "And, please set the table."

Melva's eyes were opened. She realized she didn't know much about cooking, but she vowed to learn. Her future man would be proud of her as a cook. From now on she'd watch more carefully. Learn everything her mother could teach her.

If her mother could have read her thoughts, she'd have agreed that at fifteen it was about time. Melva hadn't spent much time in the kitchen. She preferred outdoor activities, especially with her big brother.

Nan's small flower and vegetable garden, the one closest to the house, didn't have a growing weed, because Melva hoed and pulled any green stem that didn't belong there, and she kept the porches clean. She didn't gripe on wash day, using the new wringer washer like an expert, and hanging the clothes up to dry on the clothes line in the yard or on the back porch, if it was raining.

Ironing, well that was a different matter. This was an inside activity, done in the kitchen. Sometimes, Nan thought about setting the ironing board up in the yard, but heating the irons would have been impossible. Noah had suggested a new electric one, but after examining one in Maryville, Nan had decided against it.

Melva and D.H. carried the step ladder around the house and washed every window in the spring. No, Melva wasn't lazy.

∼

Known as a great cook to everyone in the Cove, Nan's friends and boarders raved about her delicious meals, especially her apple pies with cinnamon, and her chicken and dumplings. Today, both were on the menu and the smell which emanated from the kitchen would make anyone ready to eat, hungry or not. After her morning's forbidden activities, Melva's stomach growled. She was hungry.

~

Noah Tipton, Nan's husband, was successful in his business and a well-respected man in his community. His mercantile store serviced the Happy Valley, Tallahassee, and Chilhowee area. Even the people at the new town of Alcoa bought supplies from him.

Because it sat at the end of the railroad line, embarking or disembarking passengers usually visited his store. Until the railroad came to Chilhowee, supplies were brought over Chilhowee Mountain by wagon. Using a steep, dangerous road which passed through the edge of Six Mile and over the high Look Rock area, it came down the length of Happy Valley to his store. This trip took two days, and Noah always stayed a night with friends in Maryville. Sometimes, Noah paid a neighbor to make the journey.

The railroad made getting supplies easier and much quicker. Noah handed a note with a written list of supplies to the train conductor, Cal McMurray, and he delivered it to the wholesale supplier in Maryville. In return, the conductor ate Nan's dinner at no charge when he rode in on the train. This system worked out well for both men. After Noah installed his telephone, he called in his order.

Salesmen, tourists, and workers who visited his store were welcome to stay for dinner at Nan's table for a small fee. Noah sent someone over to tell Nan how many were coming for the noon meal each day. Lodging and meal prices were posted in the store. Visitors in the area always stayed with the Tipton's, unless they went north and stayed at the Howard farmhouse at Alcoa.

Nan kept many boarders, including the Primitive Baptist ministers, who held an associational meeting each year at the church in Happy Valley. Ministers stayed free of charge.

Because her facilities were clean and her food excellent, she wasn't surprised to find an extra dollar under a plate or pillow when she cleaned up — an exorbitant tip in those days. Noah kept the pay for her services in a small cigar box under the counter in his store. Every week he took the proceeds to her, and she used this money to buy whatever she needed. There were no restrictions on her purchases, as long as she paid for them in full.

Noah had no regrets about charging those who could afford to pay. This didn't mean he and Nan didn't extend a Christian hand to those in need. Vagrants, hoboes, and family friends who were down on their luck, could always count on them for a good meal. It wasn't unusual for Noah's horse and buggy to pull up to a home where a wife had just given birth or someone was sick with a box of food from Noah's store and some freshly cooked from Nan's kitchen. They always supplied food to a home where someone had died.

Noah, as a Christ-follower and honest man, was totally dedicated to his wife and family. Even tempered, it took a lot to make him angry. His motto, posted on the store wall in his handwriting, was, *"Stand for the right, even if you have to stand alone."* Melva heard him say these words many times. The Holy Bible determined right from wrong.

Like Nathaniel in the Bible, whom Jesus proclaimed as a man who knew *"no guile,"* Noah was an honest and trustworthy man. Not a deceitful or scheming bone existed in his body. He saw everything in black and white.

His job, as Squire and Justice-of-the-Peace (J.P.), made him the law of the area with authority to arrest and hold any lawbreaker he caught. Squire Noah Tipton, J.P., a well-respected man in his community, presided over today's special election.

～

Since this was a voting day, Noah opened his store early. Searching for an appropriate ballot container, he found a large shoebox and cut a hole in the top big enough to insert a paper ballot through the opening. Placing both under the counter, he welcomed the first voters and marked their names off his voting list.

Each day at noon, Noah headed home to eat. Election day was no different. With the election ballot box tucked carefully under his arm, Noah locked the door to his store. He stepped across the road and walked fifty yards down a path to eat dinner with his wife and children. Walking around Nan's small garden and flowers, he passed the cistern with its manual pump. He entered the house by the back-porch area, passing by the wringer washer sitting on the back porch. A clothes line strung several times across the porch's width allowed the clothes to dry in the fresh air, even if it was raining.

"Nan, I'm home," he called as he stepped through the door. He did not let the screen door slam shut.

While washing his hands at the kitchen sink, he placed the shoebox with the ballots inside on the counter beside him.

Nan appeared from the dining room. "Dinner's on the table, my dear," she said, kissing him on the offered cheek. She whispered something in his ear. He nodded.

The delicious smells in the dining area beckoned him to the table where he sat down to eat. "Hello, children."

D.H. winced at being called a child.

The salutation went right over Melva's head. She was hungry and already had her head bowed, eyes closed for the customary blessing.

"Let us pray," Noah said, eyeing his daughter with a smile. He blessed the food, his wife, and all his children.

"How's the election going?" D.H. asked as the dishes were passed and each scooped out the portion they desired.

Melva took her share and listened to them talk.

Since there were no guests this day, the family chatted about the election and other family matters as they ate. There was comfortable camaraderie as they spoke.

"Nan, Mrs. Gardner came in the store this morning, while her husband voted. She said the problem with her disappearing food is solved," Noah smiled. "The children's pet raccoon was the bandit. It learned to open the screen door and help itself." Noah laughed at the picture of the masked bandit munching cookies and biscuits on the Gardner's kitchen table. "She said the little beggar opened a jar of peanuts and ate all, but a pile of husks on the kitchen floor. They haven't found the jar yet." Noah sold the Spanish peanuts in his store for making peanut brittle.

"I'm glad it's nothing more than that," said Nan. The thought of a thief in the area wasn't one she wanted to entertain. In their close-knit community, everyone knew everyone else, and it wasn't acceptable that anyone couldn't be trusted.

Mrs. Gardner was Rita's mother-in-law.

"Did she say how Rita and little James are doing?" asked Nan.

"Yes. The baby's fine, except for the sniffles, and growing like a weed. We should go visit soon, if you're up to it," replied Noah. "Say, this cornbread is really good."

"Melva helped make it," Nan replied, smiling at her daughter. "A first, I think."

Suddenly, Noah jumped up from the table and hurried to the kitchen. Returning to the table he placed the shoebox next to his plate.

"I took an oath not to let this box out of my sight," he stated simply and continued to eat. "By the way Melva, Betty Jo's father said they're expecting you tomorrow afternoon around four. Are you staying the night with her?"

"Mother said she didn't need me, so I planned to stay if that's all right with you."

"I suppose D.H. will drive you over." The last sentence was more of a question than a statement.

"I'll do that Father," said D.H., "and also go on up to Rita's to see the new baby. That's if you don't need the carriage." The baby was about four months old and D.H. hadn't seen it. He'd brought a small set of wooden toy blocks for little James.

"Good," said Noah, not suspecting the horse and buggy might be used for purposes other than that stated or approved. "Son, why don't you come over and help me in the store tomorrow, since that will be your last full day with me until Christmas?"

D.H. hated to tell his dad that he didn't plan on being home until before New Year's Eve. He'd been invited to weekend in Townsend, a nearby valley, nestled in the foothills of the Great Smoky Mountains, which was rapidly becoming a tourist attraction, with houses and cabins sprouting along Little River. Some of his acquaintances intended to make Townsend their Christmas meeting place, and a certain young lady had requested his presence.

"I'll come over to help you. I noticed you have a new line of tools. Perhaps I can help you display them?"

Dinner over, Noah agreed and left the dining room for the store, shoebox tucked securely under his arm. When the election was over, he intended to lock it in the store's safe, until it was picked up by the election commission on Monday.

Melva helped her mother clear the table. Without her mother knowing it, she put a peppermint in her apron pocket.

Together the brother and sister washed the dishes, laughing and talking the whole time.

Nan shook her head and wondered how her dishes kept from breaking. And, how did they find so much to talk about? But these two had always been that way. Her children were growing up so fast. The nest was starting to empty.

∾

Now that the older siblings were gone from home, Melva slept in her own upstairs bedroom, and Lydia slept in the adjoining room. The two boys, Milton and Matthew, shared other second floor quarters. Three extra bedrooms were reserved for guests, paying or non-paying. D.H. slept there when he came to visit. Noah and Nan's bedroom was downstairs, behind the formal sitting room.

When entering the front door and the foyer, the sitting room, which was used for special occasions and special guests, appeared to the right of the stairs. Turning left, you walked into the parlor where the piano sat. The parlor connected with the dining room through a set of double doors, and the kitchen adjoined the dining room. The oak staircase, opposite the front door, ascended out of the foyer, which divided the sitting room and the parlor. A hall ran down the left side of the staircase, leading to the kitchen, downstairs bathroom, and Noah and Nan's bedroom. The family Bible rested on a small table in that hallway, with a rack for hats and coats over it. A container for umbrellas stood beside.

∾

After dinner, D.H. saddled a horse and rode toward the new town of Alcoa. He wanted to see the progress being made toward the extension of the railroad to the area. His boss in Maryville had specifically asked him to go check it out. He wouldn't be back until dark.

Melva went upstairs and opened the windows in her bedroom to let in cool air. She kicked off her shoes and stretched out on the bed. Intending to relax, she soon fell asleep and started dreaming. Dreaming about a dance. In a beautiful dress, she whirled around the floor with a handsome, tall man in a dark suit. Looking up into his face, she saw gray, blue eyes with flecks of brown. His long arms, hard muscles, and calloused hands told of tough manual work.

"I wore the suit for you," he said.

She awoke with a start, astonished and wondering at the meaning of the dream. Was this an alerting of events to come tomorrow or in the future?

The alarm clock on her side table said it was time to help in the kitchen. She didn't move, but shut her eyes. For another minute, she ran through the dream and danced a perfect turn in his arms.

Chapter Two

Dancing in the Dark

*To everything there is a season…a time to weep and
a time to laugh: a time to mourn and a time to
dance.*

Ecclesiastes 3:1a, 4 KJV

Saturday breakfast and dinner were routine. When
Melva could manage to leave the kitchen, she hurried
upstairs to her bedroom. Looking around the room, she
started collecting the toiletries to take on her trip to the
Boyd's. Gathering them didn't take long. Soon they
were lined up on her coverlet, ready to pack in her
cloth valise.

Next, she rummaged through her closet, looking
for the perfect dress to wear to the dance. Melva had
several dresses. Some were hand-me-downs from her
older sisters. Waistlines and weight seemed to change
with marriage and babies, but some of her dresses were
made just for her. She looked through those.

Usually, she completed her selection quickly. This
was a special occasion, and she planned to choose her
outfit more carefully. Ah, maybe this blue one. She
started to put the gown on.

Each time she changed, she walked down the hall to inspect the results before the tall, hall mirror. Checking out the reflection from top to bottom, she saw a tall, thin girl with sparkling, brown eyes, square jaw with pointed chin, and flushed cheeks.

Her excitement at visiting Betty Jo Boyd increased with each passing hour, especially after yesterday's dream. Would *he* be at the dance?

The Boyd family was small compared to the Tipton's brood of eleven. It consisted of Marlon and his wife; their children, Betty Jo and Edgar. What about Edgar? Was he the man in the dark suit?

Edgar and Melva's brother, D.H., were the same age and great buddies at Hill Cove School. Two years before, during a hunting trip, Edgar disclosed his admiration for Melva to D.H. Until then, it remained his own little secret. Her brother *made sure* Melva knew of Edgar's preference.

Since then, when Edgar carried Melva back and forth between the family's two houses, he'd never mentioned the fact that he cared for her. Even if he had, Melva didn't return his affection, but thought the relationship was interesting. She'd love to have Betty Jo as a sister-in-law, and as a husband Edgar was acceptable.

The question was should she marry for convenience, security, or love? Her heart told her she'd have to decide in the near future.

Melva didn't intend to end up an old maid or unclaimed jewel as an unmarried woman was often called in the mountains.

"No. That is not an option," she said to the girl in the mirror. What did she want?

In her dream world, a husband needed to be hard-working, dependable, and honest, like her father. He didn't need to be rich or famous. Decisive, someone who thought for himself and a one-woman man, that's what Melva desired—a man to respect, admire and love completely. Wasn't Edgar all of these?

"Oh. Shucks!" Melva pulled at a panel on the back of the blue wool dress. "No. This dress isn't any better than the last one. Somehow, the night doesn't lend to blue. I need somethin' eye catchin' and rememberable." She headed back to her bedroom, took off the dress, and put it back in the closet.

The truth was Edgar did fill her list of a good husband.

She sent the clothes hangers in all directions. Why couldn't she love him? She pulled out another dress as her train of thought continued.

Edgar loved hands-on work around the farm. When his father became ill, Edgar helped in the fields and with the cattle, performing many difficult tasks. Beyond cattle farming, his interests included sitting in the front porch swing and admiring the crops he grew. Melva knew she didn't want to do this for the rest of her life. Edgar would never leave Happy Valley or his father's farm.

"Edgar would be a hard-working husband." Melva nodded to the young woman in the mirror. "But, I don't love him, and that's that!"

The elder Mr. Boyd, a thin ghost at age forty-two, grew weaker each year, and those around him whispered that he wasn't long for this world. The Boyd's lived on Happy Valley Road about six miles from Noah's store and below Hill Top Primitive Baptist

Church, where both families attended on Sunday. Marlon Boyd was Noah's first friend at Chilhowee.

Noah's biggest concern, after he and Nan made the decision to move from Cades Cove to the Chilhowee area, was the lack of a local church. He went to Marlon with a proposal. If Marlon would give the land and oversee construction, he'd supply the lumber. Marlon agreed, the work started and the church quickly finished. Sitting on a knoll above his house, the church was visible from both directions when traveling Happy Valley Road. Standing in his yard and looking up at the church, Marlon often said, "We can't do anything against God's law, because He's watchin' over us."

Only a month later, the cemetery was started near the church.

Early and sudden death overshadowed life in the mountains. Epidemics among the young and elderly regularly ravaged the areas and added new graves at an alarming rate. Being young and robust didn't guarantee a long existence. So far, Melva's Tipton family hadn't been touched by death.

"No! This dress isn't the one either," Melva said beginning to feel impatient. "Why can't I make a choice?"

Disgusted, she went back to her bedroom.

As she tried on another dress, just as beautiful as the last one, she remembered a conversation Noah and Marlon exchanged about the cemetery.

Marlon didn't often go to the cemetery because it reminded him of his ill health. "I prefer not to visit the cemetery," he told Noah when Noah suggested a walk to see the burial place of a recently deceased Chilhowee resident. "Because it may not be long before I'll visit permanently, and you'll be paying your respects to me." Marlon would look at Noah with a slight smile on his face.

"Oh! Marlon, don't talk like that. What would I do without you as my good friend?" Noah had replied, feeling sad. "Besides, there's the machinery trip to Knoxville to see the new harvester we've heard so much about. I'm looking forward to our day in town."

Marlon always perked up when you started talking about farm machinery, and Noah always obliged him. Changing the subject always helped the sick man's mood.

On the way home Noah had confided to Melva, "I'm not a doctor, but he's growing weaker. The farm's responsibilities will soon be on Edgar's shoulders."

~

Melva stood before the tall, hall mirror, checking her outfit for the sixth time. "Oh," she said out loud, "the perfect one." The forest-green, velvet dress was adorned with heavy, cream lace around the neck and continuing down the dart on both sides of her bosom. Lace dripped off the end of her long sleeves. Her waist was accented by a green, satin sash, matching a smaller bow, sitting to the side of her stylish bun. An ivory brooch, given to her by her parents, was pinned at her throat. She looked older than her almost sixteen years. As the tallest of the Tipton sisters, she was a good-looking young lady but not particularly attractive.

Everyone noticed her brown eyes, without knowing the golden flecks embedded within caused them to be the most interesting part of her countenance. They danced in the sunlight or flashed in anger when provoked. Those eyes made her beautiful.

The thin mouth rested between two dimples in her cheeks. When she laughed, which she did frequently, she tossed her head back and gave vent to a delightful chuckle.

Melva did a pirouette in front of the mirror, sending her long full skirt billowing around her. Tonight was special. She knew it. Her heart was dancing along with her feet.

Melva didn't intend to dance at the party. She only planned to watch. The sweating boys, at least most of them, were so awkward and funny. The eligible girls were anxious, and most waited in anticipation of a boy asking them to dance. Few girls had steady beaus. Beaus didn't remain beaus long, if they were marriageable material.

"Melva," said Lydia, "you look beautiful!"

Melva didn't realize her little sister was standing in the hall.

"Do you really think so?" questioned Melva, glancing at her reflection another time. Tugging here and there.

"Yes." Lydia pulled her forehead into a frown and checked out her sister by walking around her. She was a little puzzled at Melva's fussing over her toilette. "Why are you so dressed up?"

"Oh, I'm not dressed up," Melva denied the obvious.

"But you've been dressin' and undressin' for hours," said Lydia, exaggerating a little bit on the time.

"I have not!" exclaimed Melva, staring at her little sister.

"Have too!" said Lydia, sticking out her chin.

Melva wasn't interested in sparring with her, so she quickly changed the subject.

"How was school this week?" She headed for her bedroom to take off the dress and put it carefully into a cloth bag her mother had made to transport her daughter's dresses. Lydia followed closely on her heels.

"Great. Johnny Webb fell off the porch and got a big bruise on his forehead. Teacher was scared to death. I thought she was goin' to cry," said a serious Lydia.

Melva shook her head. Trust Lydia to think of the worst possible happening.

"Was he okay?" asked Melva, making small talk as she put on her day clothes.

"Yep, except for the black eye the next day. He looked just like Rita's dog." Rita had a white stray with black and brown spots on its body. A black one was around its eye.

Melva grinned at the sight Johnny Webb must have made.

"Melva are you ready to go to the Boyd's?" D.H. called upstairs. He stood at the bottom of the stairs, warm coat on, and hat in hand.

"Coming." Melva headed for the stairs with her dress over her arm.

"Bye, sister," Lydia called.

"See you in church Sunday." At the bottom of the stairs, Melva put on her long cloak, grabbed her valise, and gathered a small traveling bag from the parlor couch as she passed.

A puzzled Lydia waved goodbye from the landing at the top of the stairs. Why would Melva dress up to spend the night with Betty Jo? Maybe there was something to the rumor that Melva would marry

Edgar. She'd overheard Melva and D.H. whispering about him. At least, that would explain her need to look extra nice. If she wanted to impress her beau, tonight she would succeed.

Lydia pondered her feelings about beaus. Every time someone managed to snag a boyfriend, they got married and left home. She wasn't ready to let her big sister go. She adored her. Besides, baby Joyce was too young to play with, and the boys ignored her, preferring their boy games.

～

The chilly ride along Happy Valley Road didn't take long, but D.H. let the horse walk at a leisurely pace. They passed Hill Cove School and Luke Boyd's. The elder Boyd was a brother to Marlon. The next house belonged to Tim Whitehead, whose extended family lived in several areas of Happy Valley, Cades Cove, and in Six Mile over the Chilhowee Mountains. Finally, they passed the Kirkpatrick's, a family new to the area.

Most of the families settling in Happy Valley were from Six Mile or Cades Cove, unless they came by rail for work in the area. During and after the Civil War, all cove families became suspicious of outsiders and intermarried with each other, seldom welcoming strangers. Most cove residents sided with the Union cause, like Noah's father, John "Jack" Tipton, who lived in Cades Cove.

Supposedly, their Union affiliation caused renegades from North Carolina to make regular pillages into the coves and other unprotected areas. Claiming to be Confederates, they took food, livestock and anything they could carry on horseback to the other state. Unaffiliated with either side, most were only scalawags or robbers who were too lazy to work. The war gave them a perfect cover to steal and sometimes murder. This was true in many areas of the South.

The early 1900's brought new enterprises and people who mingled with the long-established land owners. New names mixed with old familiar names and formed new alliances in marriage. Hence the Kirkpatrick's.

D.H. turned onto the short lane leading to the Boyd home. Coming from the barn, Edgar greeted them with his slow smile.

"Hello, D.H., Melva."

Betty Jo came running down the front steps of the Boyd house. "Melva!" she called, coming near and taking her friends overnight case and dress bag.

Edgar assisted Melva out of the carriage, holding her hand a little longer than necessary. Melva politely removed her appendage.

Like the Tipton's, the Boyd's were affluent in mountain standards. Marlon owned over two hundred acres of choice bottomland and hillside along Happy Valley Branch. When it was time for his son to attend boarding school in Maryville, Edgar's father suggested selling some acres to raise the money, but Edgar chose not to go.

"I thought Saturday would never come," cried Betty Jo, handing the dress bag over and giving her friend a hug. The two started sharing little tidbits of interesting Valley information. Engrossed in light-hearted conversation, just girlfriend stuff, they totally ignored Edgar and D.H. and headed for the house arm-in-arm.

D.H. looked down at Edgar who was left standing alone in the road. The younger Boyd glanced shyly after the two girls as they approached the house. He didn't quite know how to take Melva. Getting up the courage to speak to her, wouldn't be easy for him.

As time went by the urgency for his proposal increased. He dreaded asking her the question. Maybe, in his heart, he realized what her answer would be. Was it his destiny to be rejected? Or, as he hoped, was she playing hard to get?

D.H. tried to catch up on the area news by asking Edgar about their school chums. "How's John and Charlie Herrin."

Edgar half-listened and half-answered. "Just about the same. Put up their silage and dug the winter crops." He looked at the ground and tunneled a small trench with the heel of his shoe.

"Have you heard from George Hill. Did he sell his place and move to Missouri?"

Edgar mumbled something D.H. couldn't understand.

Okay, this conversation was going nowhere. As if there were a definite order for his sisters' marriages, D.H. mentioned, "Melva's the next in line to be married." D.H. was poking fun at him, but Edgar never caught his intention or even heard his words. Edgar's mind was a thousand miles away. No, it was only a few feet. He was suffering. Maybe tormented was a better word. Poor fella.

When Edgar divulged his interest in Melva, D.H. teased Melva with this information. But when she showed neither emotion nor anger, he stopped. Melva wasn't one whit interested in Edgar.

D.H. gave up. He said goodbye to his friend, who threw up his hand. Clucking to the horse, he turned the buggy around, and set off up the road to visit Rita.

Edgar went to help his dad tend a cow and her newly born calf.

∾

After going through the front door and down a hall, the two girls saw Mrs. Boyd who was cooking supper in her kitchen. She turned around to greet her visitor.

"Hello, Melva. Betty Jo's been excited and expectin' you for days." Mrs. Boyd grinned at her guest.

"I've been the same. Couldn't wait to get here."

That was the extent of their conversation. "Come on, Melva." Betty Jo rushed her friend upstairs to see her sixteenth birthday gift.

"It's from William's Furniture in Maryville," the new owner gushed, running her hand over the polished wood of the new dressing table. The gift consisted of several drawers in the cabinet area for storing makeup or treasures and three, long vertical mirrors attached to the back. The center mirror, unlike the two outside ones, did not swivel.

"Isn't it wonderful?"

Instead of answering, Melva sat down on the dresser stool to try it out. She turned her head from side to side and moved the mirrors to see the back of her hair.

"Wow! Betty Jo, this is great. You can see the back of your head without a handheld mirror." Taking out the green bow, which she had left in her hair, she repositioned it at the top of her bun.

"Does that look better?"

"Yes. But, pull the ribbon loops open a little more so it will stick up off your hair," said Betty Jo. She cocked her head from side to side and made faces at Miss Tipton's reflection in the mirror.

Melva moved the bow, and both girls looked to check the results.

"I think I like it better flat. You've got two ears on top of your head," laughed Betty Jo.

Melva patted the bow back down. She jumped up to get dressed and let her friend finish dressing. Betty Jo looked very pretty in a red velvet dress with a red comb in her hair.

"We'll be belles of the ball," said Betty Jo and both girls giggled, as they sat on the edge of the poster bed.

"Yes, our green and red dresses will remind everyone that Thanksgiving and Christmas aren't far away," said Melva. "When Robert sees you, he's going to sweep you off your feet, carry you out the door, and elope with you, you're so pretty."

"Oh, Melva," gushed an excited Betty Jo, "I really do love him. What would happen, if he had to go back to Maryville?" This was a distant but remote possibility. Melva leaned over and gave her best friend an affectionate hug.

"He's not going anywhere soon. The lumber mill will be here for years, and you an' Robert will have a houseful of babies before it ever closes down."

"Good gracious, Melva!" Betty Jo blushed under the face powder and rouge.

No one ever had to guess what Melva thought. Sometimes her mouth ran without her mind directing it, getting her into serious trouble.

Mrs. Boyd called from below, "Supper is ready."

After eating and washing the dishes, Edgar brought the buggy around to the front door. The two girls mounted to the upholstered seat. Betty Jo mischievously placed her friend next to her brother, knowing the anxiety this would cause him.

Secretly, she wished Melva would marry Edgar, making them sisters for life. She had, in fact, told Edgar that, but he hadn't replied. Edgar climbed up on the narrow seat beside the girl of his dreams. In his eagerness to go, he slapped the reins a bit too hard, scaring the gentle horse. The buggy went forward with a leap, almost throwing everyone from their seats.

"Sorry," an embarrassed Edgar apologized.

~

The frame schoolhouse in upper Happy Valley doubled as a community center where festivities, such as dances and spelling bees were held. Edgar, Betty Jo, and Melva heard the music from their parking place, two hundred feet down Happy Valley Road.

The square dance was literally in full swing when the three young people arrived. The school desks and chairs were lined up on either side of the room. Several young men were swinging their partners in the center of the floor. The other boys were congregated beside the refreshment table, totally absorbed or so it seemed, in the ham sandwiches, cookies, and lemonade. Single girls stood close to the door and down the wall leading to the door. Melva noticed several people were missing from the group—Betty's boyfriend, Annie Myers, and several of the Whitehead boys.

On the raised dais used for school functions, a banjo and fiddle player vigorously played their instruments. Mr. Razor from Cades Cove called the square dance, keeping time with the music by clapping his hands together. Others in the room were doing the same. D.H. hadn't arrived, but Melva knew he'd show up before the night was over.

"Hi, Melva."

This salutation came from a short, thin girl in a sky-blue dress, standing by her sister on the opposite side of the room. She walked across the dance floor and greeted Melva and Betty Jo. Clara Burchfield frequently visited Tipton's Mercantile where the beautiful blue material for her costume was purchased.

"Hi Clara," said Melva, noticing that Clara's long, red hair didn't have a strand out of place. "I love your dress. Didn't your mother buy the material at the store about a week ago?" asked Melva.

"Yes, she did, and I made the dress myself." Clara stroked the dress' folds. "I practically sewed day-and-night to get it finished," Clara was pleased to say.

"You did a beautiful job," said Melva. "I sew on a button now and then but haven't the patience to sit down and make anything." Besides, she might have said, life is too exciting to sit still a minute—except to eat. She didn't add this thought.

"Turn around so I can see the back of the dress." From the front, the bodice was rather plain. She and Betty Jo were amazed! They reached out to touch the huge ruffles, running horizontally from the waist, and down the back in an upside-down V-shape to the floor.

"Wow! Your dress is even more beautiful from the back. I love the ruffles. It looks like one I saw in Collier's Magazine." Each panel was lined with blue material. Attaching them to the dress required much patience and skill.

"My mother's been teachin' me to make patterns. I find it quite interesting," chimed in Betty Jo.

"I might start sewin' clothes to make some extra money." Clara offered.

"You'd certainly have my business," Melva exclaimed — not that she had any to sew at present.

The conversation continued for some minutes until Clara asked a question, taking the girls by surprise. "Have you heard that Rufus Boring proposed?" Clara rushed on, "We plan to marry before Christmas and move into the small cabin up the hollow from my parents. We've been fixin' it up, when Rufus has time."

Melva tried not to show her shock as she answered, "That's a lovely surprise. When did this happen?" Melva knew that Rufus Boring was on the rebound from another love, and this twosome seemed a bit quick. Somehow in Melva's mind, this betrothal boded future problems, but she shrugged off those feelings and showed a genuine interest in Clara's wedding plans. Mountain weddings weren't elaborate. This didn't take long.

"Clara," her sister called from across the room, motioning her to come.

"I'll send word about the wedding." Clara waved her goodbye and left to join her.

The schoolhouse door opened. Betty Jo's boyfriend strode through the door, looking for her. Betty Jo waved and walked toward him. Soon, the two were immersed in each other, and Melva was left to her own thoughts. She wouldn't be surprised, if there wasn't another wedding sometime next year. Her friend was obviously in love with this stranger to the valley.

Robert Ownby worked as a runner for the lumber mill. He picked up supplies and took materials to far-flung crews in the mountains. As the mill enlarged, the pick-ups were more frequent.

His job wouldn't last forever. Work depended on how long it took to clear the area of trees, supplying the mill with raw material to cut into lumber. Houses, being built around the new aluminum producing plant being constructed in the Maryville area, needed many board feet.

Several dams were scheduled to be built on the Little Tennessee by the Aluminum Company of America or ALCOA. They would produce electricity and control flooding downriver. Once the mountain land was cleared and the dams built, the mill's need would dwindle, and the mill would close.

Robert planned to move back to Friendsville, Tennessee, where he was born and raised. His folks were Quakers.

The mill hands and timber cutters boarded on the mill's property, taking their meals in the mess hall. The Boyd farm was one of the local farms which supplied vegetables for the company's large kitchen.

Mutual love-at-first-sight was the way Betty Jo described their first meeting. Robert had stayed longer than necessary to pick up fresh corn-in-the-shuck, tomatoes, green onions, and okra.

∽

"Betty Jo, let's go back to your house." Robert suggested since he came only to see her. In fact, he felt very uncomfortable here. Quakers did not attend dances.

"You mean you don't want to dance," she teased.

"You know I don't. We shouldn't even be here." He looked away from the twirling dancers. "Come on. Let's talk to Edgar."

"Melva and I came to see our friends." Betty Jo went on the defensive as they headed toward her brother. "Other than church, this is the only way we can learn what's happening in their lives."

Edgar said he'd go. "What about Melva?" he asked, looking in her direction.

"Let's find out," said Robert in total control. He let Betty Jo lead the way across the room. They skirted the dancers and acknowledged some other residents, stopping a bit to talk.

Betty Jo approached her friend. "We're headed back to the house, Melva. Do you want to ride with us? Edgar's goin' with us."

Melva didn't hesitate. Her toe was tapping with the music. "But we just got here. No. You go ahead. I'll come later with my brother." No way was she leaving, until the man in her dream appeared! She might be the last one to leave.

After they left, she walked toward Mr. Razor who owned Razor's Grist Mill in Cades Cove. He and his fellow players were taking a rest and visiting with the other attendees who were milling around waiting for the music to start again.

The last time she'd seen him was at Decoration Day at Cades Cove Primitive Baptist Church. Being a special day for descendants to remember those buried in the cemetery, the attendees brought blooms from their lawn, gardens, or fields in gallon jars or flower baskets. Some made multi-colored, paper flowers to decorate their family graves. The cemetery was beautiful at this time.

And dinner, after the long preaching service, was shared and spread potluck style under the huge oak trees at the front of the church. Preaching and singing filled the afternoon in the standing-room-only church — the music's harmony beautiful as it echoed in the room and outside the open windows.

John Razor didn't go there to church. He went because his family was buried in the cemetery. He and his wife attended the Missionary Baptist Church, which was closer to his home.

As she came near, he aimed tobacco spittle toward a brass can on the floor, making a loud *ping*.

"Hello, Melva. How's your dad?" he said, seeing her approaching. "The last time I saw him was in May at Decoration Day in the Cove."

Melva answered his question. "Oh, Father's working just as hard as ever. He monitored the special election yesterday with Buddy Whitehead."

"Did many people come out to vote?"

"I heard him tell Mother, at supper, they had less than a hundred who cast ballots. How about you? Did you have several?" Melva knew Mr. Razor's mill was one of the two places to vote in the cove — one in the upper cove and one in the lower cove.

"We had several more than one hundred, but less than our election two years ago. Our population has grown smaller since the last vote. Some people loaded up and left for Missouri, Texas, or Oregon, in search of the Promised Land, I guess," he laughed.

There were several grist mills in Cades Cove, including one operated by Noah's father-in-law, Isaac

LeQuire, on Rowans Creek, but John Razor ran the most successful and largest one in the Lower Cove.

His was an overshot mill. Forge Creek and Mill Creek supplied the water running through the wooden millrace. The weight of the water, which splashed into the cups as they appeared at the top of the large wheel, turned it slowly—clockwise. This engaged the grinding surfaces inside the building and reduced the wheat or corn into flour and cornmeal. A gate at the end of the millrace stopped the water and idled the wheel.

The Razor home was a large two-story, white frame structure like the Tipton's and Boyd's. The front entrance was shaded by a porch the length of the house. When John's business was slow, he could be found there, whittlin' and spittin' his tobacco juice out in the afternoon sun.

"Did you come over Cooper Road?" asked Melva.

"Yep. It's the shortest way." This old Indian trail, after being upgraded by Joe Cooper and tended by the men of the cove and valley, was passable by horse and buggy.

"How was the condition of the road?" Melva knew her father would be interested in this information. Every year after crops were in the ground, local men in Blount County spent a week working on every road. The Cooper Road repair started from each end, filling pot holes and clearing brush.

"Tolerable, if'n you drive slow and careful. Ridin' a horse, no problem. It's still too narry for me driving a buggy." John continued talking, mostly to himself. "I like ridin' the Parson's Branch Road and goin' by Henry and Tildy Whitehead's place. We always sit a spell and talk—catchin' up. The Branch Road is too far and snaky, if'n you're headed here to the Valley. Yep, Cooper Road's the best choice."

A commotion at the door caused them to turn and look in that direction.

D.H. walked in, followed by some of the unmarried Whitehead boys. Several other men came behind them, including Rufus Boring, who headed toward Clara. The men disturbed the whole room with a period of "Hello's," and hand shaking. The ladies, who were beginning to wilt, perked up and waited to be recognized.

Melva waved at her brother, and he headed toward her.

"Good to see you, Mr. Razor." He held out his hand.

Mr. Razor took it. "Good to see you, D.H. How's the bankin' business?"

While D.H. and Mr. Razor exchanged pleasantries, Melva looked over the men who'd just entered the building.

The Happy Valley Whiteheads were standouts from the crowd, taller than the other men but graceful in their lankiness. Alfred, Thomas, David, William, and Russell were familiar to Melva. They all came into her father's store. She could call them by name.

Three of the men she was sure she'd never seen before. *One stood out from the others.* Tall, with one wave in his brown hair, he was dressed in worn, but clean overalls.

Melva sucked in her breath, letting the air out slowly. He was the handsomest man in the room. She couldn't tell what color his eyes were from where she stood, but thought they would be gray-blue when she got closer. She planned to get closer.

As she watched him, he glanced over the room, as one who usually sized up the situation around him. Their eyes met briefly. Then he looked away.

D.H. said, "Goodbye," to Mr. Razor and headed for Russell Whitehead. Melva started to follow.

"Tell Noah I'll see him in January," John said to Melva as he stepped upon the dais. January was the next meeting of the county squires in Maryville. "Oh, and Melva, Jack's sick. Tell Noah that." John "Jack" Tipton was Noah's father who lived in the cove.

"I will," countered Melva. "Do you know what's wrong?"

"Nope. Some requested prayer for him Sunday. He may be well by now."

"Okay. I'll tell Father. See you next year." Melva hurried after her brother. He was in a group talking to Russell.

The music started again and couples formed in the middle of the room. John started the square dance, *"Bow to your partner. Bow to your corner — "*

Melva caught up with her brother. She whispered to him so the others standing nearby wouldn't hear. "You're late, D.H. Why?"

To D.H. this sounded like a complaint, although Melva didn't intend it that way. "No reason to be upset, sister. There was a ballgame goin' on as I passed Russell Whitehead's house, so I stopped to watch them play and then went on to Rita's."

"Oh, I see."

The Russell Whitehead ball field, where the men met, was worn from years of playing and designated solely for this purpose. The games played there were notorious for having the best players. Serious tournaments were played in the spring.

"Several men from the Mill, Happy Valley, and Tallassee were batting balls and running bases. I watched until they finished five innings. Then they decided to quit and jump in the creek to cool off and to get cleaned up for the dance. I told them I'd pick some of them up after I visited Rita. Then, I headed on up to see her."

"So, who won the game?" said Melva, making small talk.

"We'll have to ask Russell."

Russell stood close by. "The Six Mile team from the Mill was ahead when we quit." Russell pointed a finger toward the several newcomers. "They play and win when they're at home."

"They live at Six Mile?" Melva knew that this area was across the Chilhowee Mountain in the foothills — where Ellie lived.

"Yep," replied Russell. "If we'd kept playing, they were sure to win."

Melva certainly understood why they might win. Each had long, muscular arms and, being over six feet tall, could swing a bat with ease. This gave them a distinct advantage. Although Melva was taller than her other female siblings, the Tipton's and LeQuire's were fairly short people. None of them, men or women, ever grew over six feet, as far as she knew.

"Are the Six Mile men working in the area?" asked Melva.

Russell continued, "Yes, they work for the Bertrams. They're contracted to the Mill, surveyin' and loggin' for the new railroad extension to Alcoa."

The Bertrams, rich people from Maryville, supplied crews to work on area projects. They owned a large farm at Six Mile and several other businesses in the Maryville area. They were politically and financially connected and important to the county. If you were a good worker, your job was secure with this family group.

"The Bertrams also provide a ball field for the area workers on their farm at Six Mile—anyone can play," D.H. added.

"What are their names?" asked Melva.

"Who?" Russell asked.

D.H. looked at her inquiringly. "Melva, why are you asking so many questions?" he said and walked off to speak to other acquaintances.

Russell watched him go and turned to answer a question from someone else. With that, the conversation ended.

This gave Melva a chance to observe the wavy-haired one. She approached close enough to see that his eyes were gray-blue. He was talking to David Whitehead, but sensing someone nearby, he turned. His thin lips acknowledged her with a slight smile. Then, he went back to his previous conversation.

Quiet and reserved, an inner strength emanated from this man. She instinctively knew he could handle any situation he encountered. He appeared to be in his early twenties.

Melva's heart thumped loudly as she stood watching him. She wanted to touch him, engage him in conversation—anything to get his attention. Shyness was not one of her characteristics, but she stood rooted to the spot. She pulled in another lungful of air and released it in a rush.

Gathering her strength, she willed her leaden feet to move away from this man. Who was he? She needed urgently to know a name.

~

At last, D.H. was ready to go. Outside the school building, the bullfrogs in the distant creek and the crickets made the music as they left for the Boyd's home. D.H. didn't know it, but he was in for another question and answer session. This started as soon as the horse turned onto Happy Valley Road.

"How are Rita and the baby?" said Melva, bouncing off the seat due to a giant pothole that her brother didn't see in the dark and clutching anything substantial, including her brother.

When they'd resettled on the buggy seat, D.H. said, "Sorry about the cistern. I couldn't see it." He was smiling in the darkness. Melva could tell by the sound of his voice.

"Wouldn't one of those new-fangled inventions known as a flashlight be great tied to the horse's head?" she laughed. "Like the headlights on John Anderson's Ford car."

"You're fascinated by that car, aren't you?" D.H. laughed.

During a visit to Maryville, the car driven by Mr. Anderson chugged down the street before her. It did fascinate her. She mentioned the new, mechanical marvel to her father, asking him when he was going to buy one. Only a few people in Maryville owned them, and in rural Tennessee, autos were non-existent. The roads weren't maintained well enough for the fast-moving vehicles. You could steer a horse around the many potholes in the road.

"How are Rita and James?" said Melva returning to her former question.

"Rita's fine, bustlin' about the kitchen, while the baby squalled in his crib, which didn't help his sniffles. He's really got a set of lungs. She was gettin' supper ready to put on the table and couldn't pick him up. I walked him around the room, wipin' his nose and pattin' his back, trying to calm him a bit." D.H. paused, thinking, and then continued. "It seems strange to see her with a baby. She's so grown up. Not long ago, you two climbed trees together," he mused.

"I learned to climb a tree from her." Melva could have said there was no way Rita could get ahead of her. It was climb a tree or bust. "A baby always changes everything."

"I can't even think of you holdin' your baby," kidded D.H. He was smiling again.

Melva went on the defensive. "Why not? I plan to get married. Babies happen."

"You always preferred the outdoors rough-and-tumble to dolls and makeup."

"I'm beginning to use makeup, and I like beautiful dresses," Melva replied with a nod. She shook the folds of her green dress back in place.

"You did look really pretty tonight. I saw several of the boys eyein' you."

Now, Melva laughed. "Really? I wonder where Annie Myers was tonight?"

"I forgot to ask."

"By the way, Mr. Razor said Grandpa Tipton is sick. He didn't say any more than that. Will you tell Father?"

"Sure thing. First chance I get."

"He's the oldest person I know. We saw him on Decoration Day in May. He was in fairly good health, except for slowin' down due to arthritis. We walked arm-in-arm around the cemetery."

"Was he using his cane?"

"Yes. Maybe his bones don't work so well, but his mind is good."

"He always talked about being married twice. One wife buried in Shoal Creek, Missouri and the other in Cades Cove. Father's mother, Naomi, was much younger than Grandpa John Jack."

"I remember him admonishing me, *'Lassie, be careful and don't upset me.'* I'd put out a hand to help him over a small rock on the path. I was extra careful not to trip him but steady him on the rough ground."

D.H. continued, "He's a wonderful storyteller. How many times did we hear about his relatives and friends?"

"Many. Each grave was an invitation to recall stories from their lives."

D.H. threw out his hand and said, *"'Here's Russell Gregory, killed by rebels from North Carolina, during the Civil War. They come over the mountains, stealin', killin', and takin' our horses, food, and anything else they wanted. The men and boys who were left to protect the women, grabbed guns and horses and hurried for the hills, hopin' they wouldn't find them. Tryin' to save the two things they needed to stay alive.'* I can hear him sayin' that, plain as day."

"Yep, and Father always said that *they* were scalawags using the war as an excuse to rob the unprotected and innocent."

"You sure didn't say that to Grandpa. He wouldn't agree."

"I'll be sure and tell Father when I get home, if he's still up."

"I hope his sickness isn't —" Melva didn't finish the sentence, losing Grandpa would be hard to bear.

They rode in silence, each thinking their own thoughts about this respected elderly man. Melva changed the subject.

"I've never seen the Six Mile boys before."

"They're working with the surveying crew for the new railroad extension going north from Chilhowee to the old Howard farm at Alcoa. Their job is to cut wood on the proposed path, snake the logs down to Little Tennessee River, and facilitate floating them downstream to the Mill's holding pond. Three of them are brothers."

"Who's the curly haired one in the blue shirt?" Melva listened carefully for the answer to this important question.

"Which one?" asked D.H., not sure whom his sister meant. "Can you describe him a little better?"

"The one in the blue shirt," replied Melva. "He didn't talk much, just listened. He was taller than the others and had curly hair," she said, frustrated because she couldn't describe him better. "He wore overalls."

"Oh! You're talking about the three Whitehead brothers from Six Mile. There's Leonard, Willard, and Burl. Burl is the curly haired one, the tallest and the oldest. We've nicknamed him *'chimney knocker'* because

he struck a ball so hard it hit Russell's chimney,"
replied D.H. "The blow knocked some stones loose
from the top edge. They fell down the chimney. The
ball almost went behind them."

When Melva was silent, D.H. asked, "Why do you
want to know?"

They were approaching the Boyd's house. Robert's
horse was tied to a bush out front.

Melva remained quiet, thinking. Now she had the
information she needed. D.H. halted the buggy and
went to help his sister out on the other side. She
mumbled something almost under her breath.

"What did you say? I didn't understand."

"I said," Melva stated clearly, *"Because that's the
man I'm going to marry."*

D.H. stood, shocked to speechlessness. He watched
his sister approach the Boyd's front door and knock.
"God help him," whispered her brother, shaking his
head. He mounted to the buggy seat as Melva entered
the Boyd's door. "Now that's something I want to see,"
he said to the horse and flicked the reins.

~

When Melva was finally tucked into her bed
upstairs in the Boyd home, she had time to think. How
would she find out more about Burl Whitehead? He
nor his brothers ever came into her father's store, and
she never went to the lumber mill.

She couldn't ask Robert about him, because that
would alert Betty Jo to the fact she was interested in
him. Seeing this man again presented a problem for her
to solve. She would see him for sure. But how?

Melva snuggled deeper into the warmth of the
feather bed. Turning on her side, she hugged herself

and went to sleep. When the dream came this time, the man in the suit had a face.

❧ Chapter Three ❧

Cades Cove and the First Years

*A good name is rather to be chosen than great
riches, and loving favor rather than silver or gold.*

Proverbs 22:1 KJV

The electric porch light was the only one burning
when D.H. arrived back at Chilhowee. The moon lit the
way as he drove the buggy past the house and store,
over the railroad track, into the barn in the lowland
below. In the semi-darkness, he got out of the buggy
and stumbled over a galvanized bucket full of water,
disturbing the silent night with its clatter. The bucket
was used to water the horses when they were in the
barn.

"Oh, heck! Who left the pail in the middle of the
passage?" he complained as he unhitched the horse,
putting it in an empty stable. Stepping cautiously, so he
wouldn't hit something else, he went outside to the
concrete watering trough to fill the bucket. The water,
along with feed in a wooden bin attached to the side of
the stable, made the animal comfortable.

Turning, he left the barn and climbed the gradual
hill to the main road above.

The lonely call of a whip-poor-will serenaded him as his feet crunched the graveled road on the walk back to the house. A far-off hoot owl called an answer to his mate on the opposite side of the Little Tennessee River.

He stood for a minute in the cooler night air, looking across the corn stubble in the floodable bottomland behind the store. Smoke, from numerous fireplaces in the valley and beyond, hung in the river depression along with the developing dew and lowland moisture. The smell tickled his nostrils and made him sneeze.

The porch rockers looked inviting. He went up the steps, sat down, and started rocking. To him, this was the most enjoyable part of the day. The night was quiet, chores were done, and his mind could dwell on other things besides making change, cashing checks, or making loans at Blount Bank. Mr. Anderson had started him at the bottom, and he'd worked his way up.

He let his mind wander. What had Melva said? Grandpa John Jack was sick? *How sick?* he thought. At his age, over eighty-five, anything could be fatal.

Grandpa had lived in the Cove most of his life. There were two short trips to Shoal Creek, Missouri, to work and visit relatives. Because his wife had died in a terrible cholera epidemic while there, he'd come back and married Naomi Abbott. Naomi had birthed several children, including Noah Tipton.

D.H. got up from his chair. He'd call Mr. Anderson tomorrow and beg off next week. "I'll go with Father to Cades Cove," he said to the cricket, chirping under the porch. But, would Noah go tomorrow? Sunday was a day of rest.

~

Noah elected not to go on Sunday. No one had come from the Cove. John Jack was still alive. "We'll leave early Monday morning," he told D.H. "My pa may only have a bad case of the sniffles caused by the changing seasons. He's tough as a pine knot. Not much gets him down." Even though Noah said these words, his father's health was a concern.

D.H. thought pine knots ran in the family. Instead, he said, "It'll be good to visit the Cove and Grandpa."

"Are you going to church with us today? I'm leaving now. I have to welcome people this morning."

Nan came out the door, carrying baby Joyce. She was followed by Melva, holding Lydia's hand, and their two younger brothers. Noah turned to help his wife and children into the buggy.

D.H. was glad he didn't have to answer. He planned to sneak in later and sit in a back pew. His father didn't know he often missed going to church in Maryville.

~

Cades Cove nestled in the southwest end of the Smoky Mountains. The Calhoun Treaty of 1819 opened up the Cove area for permanent settlement. Land grants were issued at that time, through the State of Tennessee. Noah's Great, Grandfather William "Fightin' Billy" Tipton, born in 1761, was issued the first legal land grant under the Calhoun Treaty and soon owned much of the best bottomland. William gave or sold land to his relatives and friends from Carter Co., Tennessee. He never lived there.

William's son, Ensign Jacob Tipton, lived on several hundred acres of good, tillable land in the scooped-out valley. His son, John Jack, lived on part of this property in a big, white frame house, much like Noah's.

In 1911, Cades Cove was a secure, fertile valley with plenty of wildlife — a peaceful place.

"D.H., are you ready to go?" Noah called upstairs to his son.

"Yes, Father. I'll be down in a minute." D.H. finished stuffing his valise and snapped it shut.

"I still don't know why I can't go," Melva complained.

"You'll have to ask Father." He knew she had already asked their father, and he'd said no. He headed for the stairs with Melva close behind.

Noah stood at the bottom with his hand on the stair railing. He immediately realized the conversation which must have taken place. "Melva, we'll send for the family, if Grandpa's situation is dire. You need to help Buddy in the store. We'll be busy, since we weren't open because of the election, and you're the only one who can open the safe. Very important. They'll come today from Maryville to collect the ballots. Watch for the train." With that, Noah waved. He and D.H. went out the door and got in the buggy.

Noah slapped the horses' back with the leather straps of the harness and they were off. The two men were content to ride for several minutes in silence.

"Melva wanted to come." D.H. was grinning as he talked.

"Yes. She's a stubborn child. A good-hearted one, also." Noah chuckled. "I don't like to discipline her. Neither does her mother."

"Is that the reason she gets away with her tomfoolery?"

"Seems to me someone else got away with quite a bit of mischief, and he turned out all right."

"Thank you. I'm pleased you think so."

"Melva reminds me a lot of your mother at that age. She had a mind of her own. I couldn't have chosen a better helpmeet." Noah used a word from the Bible for a wife.

"Do you remember Melva's last year at school? She came home, and she was so excited. The teacher had talked about the subjects they'd be covering during the year. And I'd asked her to write them down." D.H. started laughing.

"Yes. We were eatin' dinner."

"She never was much good at spelling. She sounded her words out and wrote them accordingly." D.H. said each one and then spelled them. "Reading. Writing. Rithmetic. Arithmetic was especially problematic for her, but it was the last one—Boligee. She wrote it in big letters. When she held the paper up for us to see, it sent us older siblings into gales of laughter. Boligee! What's that?" D.H. continued to laugh as he remembered the episode.

"You know!" Melva had replied. "Teacher said it's the study of plants and animals."

"Henry said, 'It's Biology, sister. Biology, not Boligee.' We continued to hee-haw her. She jumped up, crumpled the paper, and threw it at me. She ran from the room. We heard her stompin' up the stairs two-at-a-time." D.H. wiped tears from his eyes. "I later apologized for our actions."

"She tries. She always tries." Noah turned onto the road to Happy Valley. He flicked the reins, causing the horse to pull the buggy a little faster.

"I haven't been on Cooper Road in some time."

"No. You didn't come to Decoration Day this year."

Noah's answers weren't very long as he drove the buggy. He seemed lost in thoughts of his own. A couple of miles later, he made a right turn onto Abram's Creek Road and followed a steep, curvy hill downward into the flat valley along the creek. Several homes were built on each side of the road running straight up the narrow valley and some hugged the hill across the creek. The aroma of wood smoke mingled with other smells in the morning mist.

"Somebody's cookin' a late breakfast," observed D.H., as the scent of bacon or fried pork hung in the air.

"Might be Mrs. Herren. It's just the children since her husband died. The neighbors and I've been takin' her food to help out. She's thinkin' about movin' to Maryville, where her folks live."

"What happened to her husband?"

"No one knows for sure. Looked like a runaway buggy. They found it and the horse without a scratch. He musta fell off and hit his head."

Noah maneuvered the horse to the right across Abram's Creek onto Cooper Road.

"I hope Grandpa Jack isn't too sick."

"He's a very old man."

"Eighty-five, Melva said. He's the oldest man I know."

"He's not the oldest Tipton in our ancestors. The first one to come to America from Jamaica was almost 100 years old when he died. But you know that story."

D.H. sensed his father's mind was on other things, probably the occupant of a white-framed house near

Rowan's Creek in Cades Cove. He tried again. "Who were the first settlers to the Cove?"

This was a story Noah loved to tell.

"The Jobe's and Oliver's settled there in the early 1800's. They were joined a little later by others, including the Tipton's. The first one's soon found out life included hard work and many of the newcomers didn't stay. They often left for greener pastures in Texas and Oklahoma. Some went to the newly discovered gold fields in northern Georgia or the lead mines of Missouri. The hardy souls that remained eked out a living by growing livestock, gardens, and orchards."

"Some did well and some didn't," added D.H., keeping the conversation going.

"That's true. The Jobe's left. The Oliver's and Tipton's persisted, establishing permanent homes in the cove. They flourished. My father loved gettin' up in the morning, lookin' down the misty valley, and checkin' out the mountain as the sun set in the west."

D.H. waited for Noah to continue. When he didn't, he asked, "How many people live there now?"

"About five hundred homes. At one time the census recorded over seven hundred households. John Razor says people come and go, but in the last few years, they mostly go."

A rough patch of road at Scott Gap caused the two men to hold on tight until it passed. The carriage crossed a small branch, bouncing into holes and around rocks where the dirt had eroded from storms. Once this was cleared, Noah continued up a short hill and turned the buggy onto a hard-packed and pine-needled mountaintop. This saddle afforded sights off both sides, and the view of mountain-on-mountain was spectacular. The riding was smooth for several minutes.

"Guess that's one spot the men need to work on," Noah commented when the road smoothed out.

"The creek always overflows there when it rains hard." D.H. observed. He continued his line of questioning. "Fightin' Billy was your great-grandfather, right?"

"That's true. America was in turmoil and fighting for its independence, when a young Fightin' Billy enlisted in the Revolutionary War. William Tipton, at seventeen, plunged into the midst of the raging battle. He was already shot twice, when another bullet broke two ribs."

D.H. held up his hand, interrupting the story. "Father, you need to write all this down. Our family will never remember the whole story, and truths always change over the years. That's why I keep askin' you to repeat it. So, I won't forget."

"I'll think about doing so—*in my spare time.*"

D.H. grinned. "You'll have more time when the rest of the children are gone."

"An empty nest. Somehow that saddens me." Noah loved his children, providing the very best for them, including a continuing education for his boys beyond Hill Cove School. He would've sent his girls except, the boarding school D.H. and Henry attended didn't take females until this year.

"I should think some peace and quiet would be welcome."

"Sometimes it is, but I'm used to the noise." Noah stopped the conversation again.

The pine forest they rode through covered thickets of rhododendron and mountain laurel, which grew profusely along their route. The quiet crunch of the wagon wheels in the pine needles, plus the creaking of buggy and harness, accompanied their thoughts. This mingled with the distant sound of cascading water from Abram's Creek and the soft smell of decaying leaves. If you could see, hear, and smell sadness, it would have been there, somewhere — with Noah or other long-gone residents.

"To continue the story. With so many bullet holes and not moving, William was left for dead on the battlefield at Savannah. The following day, he was found alive but very weak from the loss of blood. The soldiers loaded him on a stretcher, put him in a wagon, and carried him to Charleston, South Carolina."

"I bet that ride was painful."

"I'm sure it was, but he wasn't a quitter. He fought for his life, recovered enough from his wounds to be sent home to his father at Johnson City to mend. No more war for him. He was discharged shortly before he completed his two-year enlistment at almost nineteen."

"Wow, he'd already lived one lifetime at nineteen." D.H. realized his father had given him a shortened version of the history. "I can't imagine goin' to war."

"I hope you never have to go."

D.H. didn't feel very successful at diverting his father's thoughts from his sick father. He hoped the ride didn't end with what was on both their minds.

By now, the men had topped the crest of the mountain. The faint roar of Abram's falls could be heard off in the distance. They were headed downhill toward the old Elijah Oliver place. There they would connect with the road through the cove and end up close to John Jack's home. Noah made a brief stop at a spring flowing from an iron pipe in the hillside. The water was cold and clear.

Back in the buggy, D.H. asked, "William was a land speculator, wasn't he?"

"Yes, he was, but he wasn't the only one. His father, Colonel John Tipton, John Sevier and William Blount were other settlers who knew good land when they saw it.

In fact, all the Tipton's, from the first Jonathan who came to America, understood the value of owning and selling land. We'll talk about William again soon. There's lots of stories floatin' around about him."

Chapter Four

A Death in the Family

How much better is it to get wisdom than gold! And to get understanding rather to be chosen than silver!

Proverbs 16:16 KJV

When D.H. mentioned John "Jack" Tipton's sickness, Noah wished he could place a telephone call to his father who lived in Cades Cove. Wires for newfangled telephones were slowly springing up all over Blount County. He had a phone in his store. The rectangular box with removable receiver hung on the wall behind the counter. Telephone service interruptions were frequent due to storms and falling trees.

The cove had its own exchange, but it didn't reach to the outside world. There was only one thing to do—ride into the cove to check on his father.

He decided he and D.H. would go early on Monday morning.

Telling Nan not to expect him back until Tuesday night, and leaving the store in the capable hands of Buddy Whitehead, Melva, and his wife, Noah and D.H. left Chilhowee for Cades Cove.

A November chill was in the air as Noah and D.H headed up Happy Valley Road. Like D.H., he'd bundled up in his long, black coat, gloves and hat. Even so, the trip over the mountains would be a cold ride. The only warm place was where he sat on the padded buggy seat. Each breath was punctuated by a white mist and often a shiver to keep warm.

They passed Happy Valley Schoolhouse and turned down the steep hill into Abram's Creek Valley, curving back and forth until the flat land came in view. The gravel road following the creek was lined with walnut trees. The nuts piled under the barbed wire fence in small heaps told of children's imaginative games while they gathered the winter's supply. These would be picked up in baskets, thick outer hulls peeled off, hard shells cracked, and the delicious kernels lovingly removed. Brown, stained fingers and hands exposed what their owners had been doing. Nan baked them in cakes, cookies and pies—umm, their unique flavor made his mouth water just thinking about them.

Deeper into the valley, on the left side of the road, cultivated fields extended to the hillsides. Stubs of recently harvested corn, wheat, tobacco, and other crops told of the labor of the summer. On the right side, behind the houses, ran Abram's Creek. Its powerful potential to flood the whole valley caused the inhabitants much worry.

He and D.H. went by a favorite swimming hole. In the summertime, local residents spread old quilts and opened picnic baskets next to the narrow, sandy beach, where they swapped news of the neighborhood. The swim served as a daily bath. The cold water washing away the afternoon heat, along with the sweat and grime of the day's hard labor—nothing came easy if you lived in the mountains.

Today the laughter and squeals of delighted swimmers were silent, but a wire with crossbar, swinging from an oak tree testified to cannonballing into the river. Below the wire, the creek bank was bare where many feet had trodden. During the summer, young boys sneaked to the riverbank, carefully removed their clothes, and skinny-dipped in the cold mountain water of Abram's Creek.

Crossing the creek, Noah turned the horse onto Cooper Road. When D.H. wasn't talking, the forest was eerily silent except for the horse's hooves upon the path. A thick mist hung between the branches of the passing trees and dampened their exposed hair. Not a bird moved or sang. The squirrels did not chatter in the trees. It was as if the earth and its inhabitants were still asleep, except for the occupants of one buggy and someone cooking bacon behind them.

The slope of the trail was gentle but rising at a steady pace. This was a good place to let the horse walk. Noah was content to ride in silence, but D.H. asked questions to be answered.

In a rough place, the horse slipped on a loose rock, as Noah topped Scott Gap heading along the ridge to Coon Butt. The trail crossed Rabbit Creek and followed the creek for a short distance. Rabbit Creek drained the north side of Hannah Mountain and flowed into Abrams Creek. After leaving Rabbit Creek, the path dropped slowly into the lower end of the cove, passed the Oliver cabin, and came out close to John Razor's mill.

When they topped the hill and started the ridge to Coon Butt, Noah was ready for a quiet ride. He let his mind wander and nothing disturbed his thoughts — not even D.H.

Noah's reflections were on his father. He remembered the time he had, as a young, inexperienced lad, accidentally uncovered a nest of yellow jackets. These expert flyers had immediately swarmed him, stinging and stinging him. Noah started to run when all of a sudden, he was swept up into two strong arms and covered with his father's body. His pa's long legs quickly got them out of harm's way and took him home.

His mother, Naomi, applied a solution of soda and tobacco juice to the six swollen and painful stings on his arms and legs. This combination probably didn't do much to alleviate the situation, but it made Noah feel better. Noah learned to love his father because of his protection, fairness, and good judgment. He extended these qualities to everyone he met.

Patience and tenacity were virtues of Jack Tipton. Planting and harvesting demanded a good supply of these two characteristics. Plowing row after row of hard ground, tilling to cut up the clods, and harrowing to smooth out the fields were done each year. He loved the smell of freshly turned dirt and the look of a flat field ready to plant. Jack strode miles planting seeds in the furrows worked into the freshly prepared soil.

After the work was done and the rains came, he often walked the fields after supper, taking his boys with him. Holding the hand of the youngest, he checked out the progress of his plantings.

"Look-see the corn is comin' up," he would say in the early summertime. Reaching down, running his finger along a tender blade, and nodding, "It'll taste good in July when it's ready to eat, and the cows will like the dried yellow kernels to."

Or in early spring, "We're going to have a good crop of potatoes and peas. Look how high the plants have grown." All his older boys could think about was the work to harvest the corn, peas, and potatoes, taking away from their pastime of exploring the mountains, swimming in the local creek, and fishing their favorite fishing hole.

In December, he might pick some winter greens to take back to his wife to kill with hot bacon grease. There was nothing better, especially when his mother put chopped up boiled eggs, bacon and vinegar on top. Noah missed her.

Harvesting the fields of hay and wheat in the summer and fall was the most tedious and backbreaking job. Neighbor helped neighbor with cutting both grain crops. With the scythe's sharp, curved blade, standing and swinging it back and forth in the hot sun, Jack and the others cut down acres of wheat. A pitchfork moved the cut grain stalks into piles in the field and lifted the heaps onto a wagon bed. Then it was hauled to the cantilevered barn and pitched into the loft—backbreaking and hot work in the humid, summer sunshine.

~

After leaving Rabbit Creek and the ridges of the mountains behind, Noah headed downhill to the cove. He stopped the buggy, got out, and knelt beside a spring branch that ran beside the road. Cupping his hands, he drank cold, clear water coming out of a pipe. Taking a handkerchief out of his pocket, he wiped his wet mouth.

Looking into the small pool of glassy water made by the spring, he saw his own reflection. The sound of children playing filled his thoughts.

Noah smiled thinking of a time when his father knelt in this same fashion, lost his balance, and fell headlong into a large pool of water on Rowan's Creek. He was known for dizzy spells and the day was hot and humid.

"Come on in, sons," he exclaimed, laughing at his awkwardness and the shock of the cold water.

The branch wasn't very big, but his sons, large and small, were soon frolicking in the creek, fully clothed. Jack had the most fun of all.

Rowans Creek was a branch in the upper end of the cove, which flowed into Abrams Creek. Abrams ran straight through the middle of Cades Cove, into the swampy end near Chestnut Flats, and over Abrams Falls. From where Noah got out of the buggy, the waterfall was less than a mile away over Andy McCully Ridge. After rushing over the falls and traveling several miles, the creek cut a course through the mountains and rock. It came out north of Chilhowee where Noah lived and flowed into the Little Tennessee River. This was close to the Chilhowee Lumber Mill where Robert Ownby worked.

Not long after Noah rejoined D.H. in the buggy, he entered the lower end of the cove, where the cleared fields met the forested mountainside.

"D.H., let's take the trail behind Elijah Oliver's homeplace and make a stop at John Razor's. He may have news of Pa."

Noah forded Mill Creek at its confluence with Abrams Creek, it's clear cold water rushing around the hooves of his horse.

Turning onto the lane leading to the grist mill, Noah spotted several deer grazing in the field nearby. They appeared dimly, like antlered ghosts, in the mists of the morning. It would take the noon sun to clear away the heavy moisture from the air.

D.H. pulled out his pocket watch. "We been on the road for three hours, Father. Isn't Grandpa Jack's home about another hour away?"

"Yes. We should be there by noon."

D.H. added, "Unless we spend a lot of time at Razor's."

"No, son. We're just going to stop a few minutes." Noah let the horse take its time and rest as they continued down the well-used lane toward their destination. He pulled the buggy under the trees between the house and the mill.

"Hello, John," called Noah as he got down from the buggy. If John was near he would appear in the mill door and greet him.

"Hello back," replied John, who appeared from the area of the smokehouse next to his home.

Noah wasn't expecting his friend to be at the back of the house. He tied the horse's reins to the nearby rail fence.

"You aren't working as yet?" Noah asked walking toward his friend and shaking his hand.

"No. I'm late this morning at gittin' to the chores," replied John. "Hello, D.H."

"How's the family?" D.H. sat in the buggy.

"Well, that's the problem. Breakfast was late this morning. My Naomi's got a might of a cold and the children cooked at breakfast. She's still up and about but moving purty slowly," John said, as if she had a choice with eight children. "Thank goodness, the oldest offspring can help! Would you like some breakfast?"

"Nancy fixed food before we left this morning, but I appreciate the offer," said Noah.

Before he could ask about his father, John asked, "How's Nancy and the store business."

Noah went into a detailed description of the store and its customers, ending with Nancy's "hotel business" as he called it.

"She's doing quite well. Been able to purchase things for the house she needs and sometimes wants," Noah replied, putting emphasis on the "sometimes wants." He liked to tease his wife about being extravagant but was secretly pleased that she could have extra things. Early on in their married life, they had discussed the difference between needs and wants. Now that issue was no longer a problem, and Nancy could afford any item necessary or desired.

"Did you hear news of my father at church yesterday?" asked Noah.

"Ike Shields went over on Saturday to see him. Annie said he was asleep, so Ike didn't disturb him. Annie told him Jack was real weak, and his breathing was labored. He had a cold or somethin' and it went to his chest. She's worried about him. No wonder, at his age."

Noah visited a little longer with his friend and then continued along the road toward his father's house. He was anxious to find out for himself how his father was doing.

Just before arriving at Jack's house, he passed Isaac and Caroline LeQuire's log home. Isaac's gristmill was turning on Rowan's Creek, and a buggy sat outside the cabin. Wrapped in a shawl, Caroline and a visitor sat on kitchen chairs in the front yard. She waved as they drove by and helloed.

Annie was at the kitchen sink as he drove up. He could see the top of her bowed head through the window of the big farmhouse. She was his half-sister, the youngest child of John and his first wife who died in Missouri.

Noah got out of the buggy. "D.H. take the horse and buggy to the barn. You can leave the buggy under the overhang, and make sure the horse has feed and water."

Noah stood and watched his son's progress. Turning, he took a few steps and quietly opened the kitchen door.

"Annie!" exclaimed Noah

Annie practically jumped out of her skin and in the next second ran to embrace her younger brother. This was saying something since Annie was rotund.

"Noah," exclaimed Annie. She was the most exuberant member of the Tipton siblings. Rarely did you see Annie serious. She could turn the most profound moments into "a laughin' fit" her father always said in disapproval. Annie was sober now, and her face showed the struggle and strain of tending to her father, day and night.

"Did you read my thoughts? I've been wishin' and prayin' you'd come. Our Father's as sick as I've ever seen him." His sister had never married, preferring to stay at home after her sweetheart died of typhoid many years ago in Missouri. She had ridden back to Tennessee with Jack and her brother Nat after their mother died. Both of them decided they'd never return to Shoal Creek where Annie was born.

"John Razor told Melva about Father's sickness. I wanted to come and see how he's feeling. What's his problem?" asked Noah, sitting down at the kitchen table. He was tired after his long ride. "Has Dr. Saults been here to check him out?"

Annie was putting the finishing touches to the noon meal as she talked.

"Yes, Dr. Saults was here. He's concerned about pneumonia—galloping pneumonia," Annie said simply. "He thinks Dad had the influenza and you know how he hates going to the doctor. He's bad off, Noah. I don't know. I just don't know." And Annie's voice trailed off as she pondered the next possibility. Galloping pneumonia was a death knell to the elderly.

"Is he asleep?"

"He might be. He's been sleepin' a lot and gettin' weaker each day. He isn't breathing well." Annie looked straight at Noah and nodded. It was a go see-for-yourself kind of head movement.

Noah left the room and went down the hall toward his father's bedroom. He could hear Jack's raspy breathing before he stood in the doorway. Jack was in serious trouble. Noah was sure of that. He'd heard that sound before, when Buddy Whitehead's father had died of pneumonia.

The room he entered was the largest room in the house. It contained a poster bed, chest of drawers, and wardrobe for hanging clothes. One new item, pushed against the wall to the right as you walked through the door, was a cot for Annie or someone sitting with the patient. On it was a change of linens for the big bed and washcloths for the patient's bath.

He walked quietly to his father's bedside and sat down in a vacant chair, leaning forward to look at a familiar countenance he had known for almost forty-five years. His eyes touched each feature of the worn, weather-beaten face, including a well-known scar his father wore underneath his chin—the scar from an early morning milking session in the barn as a sleepy-eyed youth. Jack's father, Ensign Jacob Tipton, had said to his wife, "Gittin' kicked by an ornery cow was a lesson larned the hard way. 'Tis a good thing he didn't git a tooth knocked clean out."

It was strange, his father lying there in bed. Noah hadn't often seen him this way.

An overwhelming sadness touched his heart and tears welled in his eyes at the thought of losing his dad. He knew it would happen, but he wasn't prepared to embrace the prospect—not yet. He reached out and touched his father's arm as it lay on the coverlet. It felt hot to the touch, and there wasn't any reaction from the elderly man who owned it. Noah bent over and put his head on the warm arm, praying silently for his father's health. He wanted desperately to say "goodbye," to his beloved father. He asked God to let him do that.

Annie touched him on the shoulder.

"Come and eat, Noah," she whispered quietly. "You can't do anything here."

Annie's dinner was nourishing and tasty, as usual. A few bowls from the neighbors increased her supply of food. They sat for several minutes, talking about the cove and Chilhowee families.

While D.H. helped her clean the dishes, Noah went back to his father's room to sit by his bedside.

After placing the pots and pans back in the kitchen cabinets, D.H. and Annie came to check on him. "Noah, D.H and me been talkin'. We'll sit with Pa this afternoon. You can spell me tonight after supper. I could use a good night's sleep."

"Are you sure? I think I can manage to sit now and all night."

"Father, please let me sit with Annie. You always were the night owl when we were sick at home." D.H. was remembering the times his father sat with him when he ran a fever as a young boy. "Anyway, I think I need to do this for Grandpa."

"All right." Noah pulled in a lungful of air and let it out slowly. He stood from the chair and went to the front porch. Instead of sitting in the waiting swing, he walked to the barn to check on the horse and buggy. No problem there. Beyond the barn, the fields he knew as a boy stretched to the forest. Cattle grazed in a patch of land next to a stand of trees. A milk cow and calf nibbled at grass in a fenced area near the barn. Annie's small garden was the only reminder of the labor of his youth. She took good care of it, but today it had a few weeds growing among the rows. Absentmindedly, he started pulling them from the soil.

Walking slowly back to the barn, he needed to check on one more important thing. They were still there in a back corner on a work bench—sawn walnut boards from a large tree Jack had cut down years ago, to be used for his coffin.

~

Supper over, D.H walked up Rowan's Creek to visit a cousin, and Noah retired to the front porch as the sun started to set behind the Chilhowee Mountains. Beyond those tall ridges, Nan and the children, would be feeding the horses and cows, locking up the store, and cooking supper for their brood.

Noah thought about sending D.H. for his family but decided to wait. The telephone rang. He went into the house to answer it. He had done this more than once this afternoon. Church family and neighbors needed to know if Jack was better or worse.

The caller was Dr. Saults. "Noah, how's Jack?"

"There's no change. Annie's sittin' with him."

"I was hopin' he'd be better. I'll be over early in the morning to check on him."

"Come for breakfast at seven."

Placing the ear piece back on its hanger, he walked down the hall and looked in on Annie.

She held up her hand and said softly, "I'll sit until it's good an' dark. Come then."

He nodded. "Dr. Saults will be here in the morning. I told him to come for breakfast." The noise of Jack's breathing seemed different. "How is he?"

"I think he's taken a turn for the worse, but I'm no doctor. His breathing seems harder to me. Gotta be hard on his heart. Go on. I can sit 'till dark." Annie waved her hand, shooing him from the room.

Noah returned to the swing on the side porch. Jack had mounted his swing where he faced the lovely sunset, covering the mountaintop. Would his father see the sun go down again? The question really running around in Noah's mind was, would Jack survive the night?

The sound of horses' hooves disturbed the quiet of early evening. John Razor and Ike Shields rode up, tied their horses to the fence beside the road, and walked down the path to the porch.

Nice to have friends like John and Ike, Noah thought.

"How is he, Noah?"

"Not good. Not good at all," replied Noah with a long sigh. "Dr. Saults says it's only a matter of time. He was here this afternoon. Jack's not been awake since I arrived. Annie's sittin' with him now, and I plan on stayin' by his bed tonight. Annie's tired. Some of the neighbor ladies brought food for supper. She didn't cook. Nat and his wife will come tomorrow to help. He was here this afternoon for a while."

"I don't know what to say," replied John truthfully. "I'll send Daniel up to stay and run errands for you, if you want me to."

Daniel was John's middle son.

"He certainly would come in handy. Send him to help with the cows. If there's any change in Jack's condition, I'll let you know."

The three men sat quietly on the porch reminiscing about Jack's long life and mostly oblivious to the chill in the air. The sun touched the top of the mountain before John and Ike rose, shook hands with Noah, and said their goodbyes.

"I'll send Daniel first thing in the morning," John promised.

It was almost dark as they mounted their horses and rode down the lane. A full moon lit the path.

A kerosene lamps glow appeared in the window at the LeQuire's cabin. Across the fields, warm lights from other households shone in the shadowy night. The distant croaking of bullfrogs in the lowlands beside Rowan's Creek added to the peaceful atmosphere. All was well with the world — almost.

Noah went back to the swing. How often Jack rested here, after the day's long labor, *soakin' in the mountains* as the old timers often did. Granny Shields was noted for using this phrase as she sat in her front porch swing.

Noah thought he'd done a bit of that himself in the porch swing at Chilhowee. He shivered. Cold air had descended with the night into Cades Cove. Noah stopped swinging and went into the house to relieve his sister.

$\sim$

Noah had fallen asleep in the chair beside his father's bedside. He awoke with a start, realizing immediately something wasn't right! There wasn't a sound in the room — but the sound of silence.

Grabbing the lamp off the bedside table, he held it close to his father's pillow. He hadn't napped long, but long enough for Jack to enter another life, a life with the Father he'd read about in the Holy Bible. Noah felt his father's arm. It was still warm to the touch. He sat on the bed, rubbing the exposed arm. Leaning forward he closed his father's eyelids. He sat there for some minutes, still in shock at the swiftness with which death entered the room. Then he bowed his head and prayed.

"Thank you, Father for giving me this man as my earthly father. He has been a guide and an inspiration to

me — an example to follow. He has reflected You in his life for others to see. Now, accept him into Your kingdom and protect those of his family who remain, his sons and daughters, my wife and my children, until we meet again."

Noah got up from the bed. There were things to be done quickly, and he intended to take care of them. Annie needed her rest. He would not disturb her until he was finished. He found warm water on the stove, filled a large pail, and returned to the bedroom. Would he have the courage and strength to prepare his father for burial?

Those who died in the early 1900's were thoroughly washed, dressed in the best clothes they owned, and placed on a bed or other flat surface until a coffin could be delivered. This preparation was usually done by area women. Not this time. Noah would prepare his father for burial. This was how he would say, "goodbye." There was no need to hurry.

Noah placed his arms under his father and lifted him from the bed. Jack had lost weight and was lifted easily to the cot in the bedroom. Noah stripped the bed of its dirty sheets and managed to change the old ones, putting on the clean ones from the cot. Changing bed clothes was not a chore he did often, but he got it done. Then he placed another sheet over the made-up bed, lifted his father's thin body and positioned it atop.

After taking off his father's nightshirt, Noah carefully shaved him and trimmed his hair and beard — loving actions he had never done before. A dark spot on the sheet marked the falling of a tear as he tenderly washed Jack's well-used body. In the wardrobe, he found the suit of clothes his father had purchased at

Tipton Mercantile many years ago for this purpose. The outfit was a little big, but his father never looked better.

By this time, it was early morning. There was nothing else to do but awaken Annie, which he did gently. Annie looked at him. His eyes said it all. It was strange to see Annie cry.

When daylight came to the Chilhowee Mountains, John "Jack" Tipton had slept his last *"sleep of peacefulness"*. He had *"soaked in the mountains"* for the last time.

So many things needed to be done. Noah called Dr. Saults, and D.H. left for Chilhowee with the horse and buggy. Daniel came around eight o'clock. Noah sent him to Nat's home so he could contact the bell ringer at the Cades Cove Primitive Baptist Church. He called John Razor to tell him of Jack's passing and asked him to go by John McCaulley's house to tell him there was need of a coffin.

More than one person made coffins in the cove, but Jack had specified the McCaulleys build his. Young John knew where the wood was stored in the barn, and he'd build it on the spot. Most coffins were built old-style, with two narrow ends and a broad shoulder. The corpse was measured. Then the coffin was built to suit the person.

For Noah, there were two sounds he'd never forget that Tuesday morning. One was the sound of the hammer from the barn, driving nails in Jack's final resting place. The second, the bell's toll from Cades Cove Primitive Baptist Church. The bell rang first alike the call to church. Then slowly and methodically the reverberating sound of eighty-five years was tolled. Noah thought it would never end. His heart was sore, but he didn't feel it. After staying up all night, he was dazed from lack of sleep and with the shock of the night's happening.

Soon people began to arrive, bringing baskets of food and voicing their condolences. John and Ike came to tell Noah they would be in the group who dug Jack's grave. The LeQuires, Nan's kinfolk, across the road took care of the livestock. The Shields offered their large wagon to carry the body to the church. The Abbotts, Naomi's family, graciously straightened the house and served the food. Nat's family arrived, as did other relatives. Some of those would stay all night at the house. Elder Oliver came to discuss the family's wishes for the funeral. Everything would be ready for the services on Thursday morning. The funeral was a Cades Cove family affair.

"Thank you so much for coming." Annie kept repeating over and over as each family or friend arrived.

It was a good thing people lent a hand, because the next few hours became a blur in Noah's life.

Chapter Five

The Funeral, Engagement, and Proposal

*Two are better than one; because they have a good
reward for their labour. For if they fall, the one will
lift up his fellow: but woe to him that is alone when
he falleth; for he hath not another to help him up.*

Ecclesiastes 4:9-10 KJV

Melva watched her father and D.H. until they were
out of sight, wishing every minute she was going with
them. Monday at the store would not be nearly as
exciting as the drive over the mountains into Cades
Cove, no matter the reason. And it wasn't, until she
received a call from Chilhowee Lumber Mill that the
tedium of the day changed.

Robert Ownby was on the phone. "Melva, this is
Robert. Do you have any axle grease for wagon hubs? I
don't know how this was overlooked, but we need
some immediately."

"Robert hold on, and I'll check." Melva put down
the earpiece and headed for the back door of the store.
Outside, in a shed, she rummaged through its contents.
Several two-pound cans of axle grease sat next to
empty cans for carrying kerosene.

Back on the phone with Robert she said, "Yes, we have several two-pound cans. How many do you want?"

"Can you deliver four to the maintenance shed? I'd come and get 'em, but I'm leavin' to take a wagon load of supplies up to Alcoa. I'll be gone all day."

"Just a minute." Melva called to Buddy Whitehead, "Can you spare me for a few minutes? I need to run some material up to Robert at Chilhowee Lumber Mill."

"Go ahead. Write up a ticket for them to sign, and you can use my horse."

"Robert, I'll be there shortly." Melva hung up the phone, wrote the ticket, and tied the cans of grease in a flour sack for delivery.

Under a fenced lean-to attached to the store, Buddy's horse was saddled and ready to go. "Guess you're about as bored as me," Melva said as she hoisted herself into the seat with the bagged supplies Robert had ordered. She hung the sack over the saddle horn.

The ride to the mill took less than thirty minutes. The maintenance shed was on the far side of the mill and on a slight rise. A propped-up wagon with a wheel missing sat outside as Melva rode up. "Hello, there." Melva called and waited for a response.

"Hello, yourself," came from within the shed. "You got the grease?"

"Yes." When the voice answered her, Melva untangled the sack from the saddle. As she started to dismount, she looked up.

Burl Whitehead strode from the open door toward her horse. "No need for you to get down." His long legs covered the ground between them.

The man of her dreams was so unexpected, Melva obeyed his suggestion, and settled down in the saddle on the horse, gawking at him. She couldn't say another word.

Burl smiled at her with a friendly twinkle in his eye, showing his even teeth. "Thanks for bringing it." He took the sack from her limp hand, stood still, and waited for her to reply.

Melva nodded, thinking how silly she must appear.

Burl's smile faded. He looked at her and inquired, "Has the cat got your tongue?" He turned, shouldered the sack, and walked back toward the building.

Annoyed at his comment, Melva found her voice. "No! And you're welcome," she exclaimed to his disappearing back.

He threw up a hand and disappeared into the building.

Melva mentally kicked herself all the way back to the mercantile store. She shouted, exclaiming to the world around her, "What is wrong with you? Mr. Whitehead is goin' to think you're dumb as a box of rocks, and in my opinion, you may be worse." Throwing her hands in the air, she continued, "Couldn't you have at least said nice morning, isn't it, or the sun sure is bright today, or have you been working hard this morning? Or, how about, is that the wagon you're goin' to fix?" If she expected the horse to answer her, it didn't.

When she got off the animal, she realized the unsigned ticket was still in her pocket. She'd fumbled the whole transaction. No. She wasn't going back to make him sign it.

What on earth could she do to prove to Mr. Whitehead, she wasn't a clumsy, tongue-tied female? Surely there was a way.

~

On Tuesday before dinner, D.H. drove the buggy to the front of the store. Melva did not ask a single question. She knew Grandpa Jack was dead. Nan was in the house preparing a light dinner when the two banged the back door shut.

"Grandpa Jack's gone," she stated, looking at D.H.

"Yes, early this morning. They'll bury him on Thursday. Father said to pack clothes for four days and come to the cove."

Nan stood still, collecting her thoughts. "D.H., will you go to Hill Cove School and get your brothers and sister.?"

"I'm on the way." D.H. headed for the front door.

"Melva, go pack your clothes. Lay out clothes for your sister and some for your brothers. I'll come up and check on them as soon as I get mine packed. I imagine your father will need some also." She pulled in a lungful of air and let it out in a rush. "Go on. After we pack, we'll finish fixin' the dinner meal and eat it on the way."

When Nan gave orders, people obeyed. Before an hour passed, the children were home from school and in the buggy, valises were aboard, and the delicious odor of food made everyone's stomach growl.

"Are you ready to go?" Buddy Whitehead asked. He stood on the road in front of the house. Nan walked toward him.

"Yes. I locked the house. If there's any problem, you know where the extra key is in the store. I'm sure

Noah would like for you to keep the same store hours. We should be back Saturday or Sunday."

Buddy helped Nan into the buggy and stood waving goodbye as the horse moved the buggy forward.

~

When Noah and Nancy LeQuire Tipton were first married, they lived across Rowan's Creek from the LeQuire home in a small starter or "weaner" cabin. This two-room cabin was a temporary home where newlyweds started their married life under the guidance and protection of one set of parents. The Tiptons would remain there until Noah could afford to build a cabin of his own.

In the weaner cabin, Dwight Harley (D.H.), their first son, came to live in 1890. And in 1891, Noah Henry joined his older brother.

As it turned out, Noah didn't need to build immediately.

Years earlier, his grandfather, Ensign Jacob Tipton, had moved to Shoal Creek in Newton County, Missouri, after the discovery of lead at Webb City. The miners needed fresh food and feed for their animals. These could be sold at much higher prices.

Many letters came from the frontier, telling about the prospects of wealth to be made. Each letter pleaded with the men of the cove to move and join the others. Missouri was a land of plenty, well-watered, rich and forested. They would be right at home in a valley looking much like Cades Cove. They were assured of this.

Jack was persuaded and decided to move west with his wife and children to join his father. The family owned hundreds of acres on both sides of the only fordable part of the stream, Tipton's Ford at Shoal Creek. They could charge for wagons, horses, and people to cross in both directions. He stayed for several years, but Missouri could not make him forget Cades Cove.

The frontier was not without problems. An influenza epidemic and then cholera swept the area, and Jack's first wife died. His desire to come home grew. Giving his grown children, some married and some not, the option of heading back east or staying in Missouri, he returned to Tennessee with his daughter, Annie, and youngest son, Nathaniel.

After returning, a middle-aged Jack met and married Noah's mother, who was much younger than he.

Jack went back west another time, when his younger brother, Marcus, wanted to travel to Missouri. Jack knew the way, and his brother had no desire to go alone. The group of travelers would need to be in Missouri before the winter rains swelled the rivers to an impassable stage. October seemed the best month to do this. The harvest would be over and the roads easy to travel.

The year was 1892, when Jack packed his work wagon with some of his worldly goods and headed west with Marcus. Ensign Jacob, his father, died unexpectedly shortly after his arrival.

The Missouri frontier was expanding west into Kansas and Oklahoma where towns were springing up everywhere due to lead and zinc mining. Born not far from where Jack would settle, the future president, Harry S. Truman was eight years old in 1892. And

Jessie James the famous gunman and outlaw, had been dead ten years, shot at St. Joseph, Missouri by his cohort, outlaw Robert Ford.

~

The same month Jack left the second time for Missouri, The Noah Tiptons welcomed their first girl child, Henrietta June (Rita), and Noah assumed the responsibility of moving his young family into Jack's vacant house.

After a period of recuperation from Rita's birth in the LeQuire home with her mother, Caroline, Nan joined them in their new home. Letters coming from Missouri indicated Jack was satisfied with the move but homesick. He missed the cove and his friends, but most of all he missed the mountains. In Missouri, there were hills and valleys and a large creek, but behind the hilltops the silhouettes of the protective mountains didn't exist. He missed his *"sleep of peacefulness."*

Life in the cove didn't skip a beat. Noah was responsible for his father's fields. He did his best to farm the land as his father had done. His older step-brother Nathaniel was married and living across the cove valley not far from the Primitive Baptist Church. They usually saw each other on Sunday to catch up on cove news and almost as often at funerals of their friends.

Noah's family would pile into the two-seat buggy in their Sunday best and head across the valley to church. Sometimes the two families would go down by Abram's Creek with a picnic dinner. The children played in the creek catching crawdads or minnows or throwing rocks, and the adults sat on homemade quilts, nursing babies or just watching the clouds in the sky. Those were great times.

In February 1894, Susan Ellen was born. It was cold and cloudy that day. Noah went across the road to tell Caroline LeQuire to come quickly, because there wasn't time nor was Nancy able to come to her home. Susan Ellen was born in Noah's and Nancy's bed.

The snow started in the afternoon and by dark eight inches covered the ground. Turning away from the window, Caroline looked at her exhausted daughter and sighed. For women it was always this way—one child after another. Caroline stayed the night with her daughter and new grandchild, sleeping beside them in the same bed while fifteen-month-old Rita slept in the crib nearby.

Noah brought in a large piece of wood from the woodshed out back. It would be used as a backlog to hold the fire until the morning. Then Noah quietly climbed the stairs and slept with the children in their second-floor bedroom. Unaccustomed to sleeping with their father, D.H. and Henry snuggled close.

A cholera epidemic swept through Missouri in the summer of 1895. Jack wrote saying that Marcus and his nephew had died. The letters from Jack were discouraging. He had lost any desire to remain in Missouri, but he did not return immediately.

Melva Tipton was born in June of 1896, the same year that gold was discovered in the Yukon and the New Olympic Games were held in Athens, Greece. The flowers were in bloom, especially the day lilies around the cove houses. Daffodils, tulips, and daylilies were brought over from Europe, carefully packed in the trunks of families headed for America. Planted around pioneer homes, they brought comfort and color to the newly transplanted residents. This was also the first year of school for Noah's oldest son, D.H.

~

As soon as the buggy entered Cades Cove, Melva's thoughts about Jack were triggered by scenes around her. As a young girl, where he went, she went. It hurt inside to remember.

When the family arrived at the white-framed house, she had no desire to enter her grandfather's home. He always greeted her on the porch or in the parlor. He wouldn't meet her today or ever again. The sadness she felt wasn't describable.

She lingered on the front porch with D.H. and the other men folk, including Grayson Rowan. He was the first one to make her heart pitter-patter. They pretended not to notice her.

"Grayson, do you remember our first day of school?" D.H. stood, leaning on a porch post, talking to his friend.

"Yeah," Grayson nodded. "Your father took two, scared boys in the buggy as a celebration of the first day. You jumped outen the buggy, and the lid flew off your lunch pail. A red apple went rollin' onto the school yard." Both men laughed at the memory.

"Miss Myers was greetin' new students at the door. She hurried over and picked the apple up, put it in my bucket, and replaced the lid. She sure was pretty. I thought she'd be my girlfriend."

"You too." They laughed again. "She was purty," Grayson agreed.

"We solved a batch of problems on our mile walk to and from Upper School."

"We learned a bunch too. I always thought you'd make a good livin'. You knew your ABCs and numbers. You even could add numbers. It's no wonder you ended up at the bank. How do you like livin' there, in Maryville?"

"I like it—"

Before D.H. could answer further, Annie stuck her head out the front door. "D.H. or one of you, go over to Caroline's and see if'n she's got some extra salt an' sugar. Mine's 'bout gone."

"I'll go," Melva volunteered. She hurried off the front porch and down the walkway before anyone else could start. She wanted to get away.

∼

The LeQuire cabin was located by Rowan's Creek underneath large hemlock and oak trees and beside Cades Cove Road. This stream, normally a trickling branch in the summer, could become a raging torrent during spring storms. Isaac LeQuire's gristmill sat beside the creek.

The log cabin wasn't very big, having a living room, kitchen and two bedrooms downstairs, plus a pantry and woodshed off the kitchen. The first walls were covered with newspapers for decoration and to keep the wind out. Mixing flour and water to create glue held the paper to the log walls. The last layer was brightly flowered wallpaper which Caroline had picked out at Myers Mercantile in Townsend on one of her infrequent trips over Rich Mountain.

The loft was used by the children as a bedroom— the boys on one side of the attic and the girls on the other. A small window, within each of the gables, let in air from the outside and helped reduce the stuffiness in the confined area. Straw tick mattresses and little-to-no furnishings were upstairs. The straw was changed each spring when the weather faired up. The fresh scent of the bedding material reminded the sleepers that spring wasn't far away. The room was cold in the winter and hot in the summer. As a young girl, Nancy Susanna LeQuire couldn't decide which was worse.

Pegs in the log walls held the only clothes the family owned.

Being one of the oldest girls, Nancy shared the extra downstairs bedroom with her oldest sister, at least until Nancy married. Nancy's first child was born in this room.

Melva knocked on the door. She heard footsteps and her grandmother, Caroline LeQuire, opened the door. "Melva, come in. I'm sorry about your grandfather. I know you loved him so much."

Melva dropped her eyes. "I'll miss him. I'll—." The dam of suffering broke. The mental anguish she felt over her grandfather's death spewed forth in a waterfall of tears. She sobbed as Caroline drew her shaking body into the living room.

With her arms around her, Caroline held on tight until Melva was quiet. She pulled back and asked, "Do you feel better?"

"I guess I was holdin' the sadness in. Maybe if I didn't cry, Grandpa Jack would still be here."

Caroline smiled, "Jack's all right, Melva. He doesn't hurt anymore, and he's walkin' streets of gold. That's what the Bible says."

"I know. It's hard to give him up, and I'll never see him again." Fresh tears flowed.

"Melva, you just have to believe what he believed, and you'll see him again. Do you believe?"

"I'm trying to."

"Try harder." Caroline looked at her and added, "Did you come to see me, or were you sent for something?"

Melva remembered her errand. "Annie needs salt an' sugar, if you've got some."

Mountain people always had *some*, no matter the amount. Caroline left the room, and this gave Melva a chance to look around. The furnishings still sat in the same place. But Melva could remember a hurtful time when the chairs and couch were moved to other locations in the room and bedroom. This allowed for another coffin to be placed on the back wall.

～

When Isaac's great aunt, Martha Lincoln, came to live with the LeQuire's, she claimed the downstairs bedroom. She was the only survivor of that generation. Isaac LeQuire was her closest relative. As the eldest member of the family, he automatically inherited responsibility for the older members.

Caroline could not refuse to take Martha into her home. This wasn't done in the pecking order of families in the mountains. The unwritten mountain code said you took care of the elderly or sick within the family unit. There wasn't anyone else to do it.

Martha was bed-ridden with crippling arthritis. A crotchety and downright mean old maid, the children were scared of her. They dreaded to hear her call, because she was demanding and always wanted her requests without delay. "Right this minute!" or "Hurry!" were her two favorite comments. The children tried to sneak past her open door, hoping she wouldn't see them.

"Isaac, I'm worried about the children." Caroline wanted Isaac to know about Martha's bluntness to her children and grandchildren. "She threatens them to get them to attend to her wishes."

"What can you do?" questioned Isaac, putting his arm around his beleaguered wife. "They're children. They'll survive."

"I wish she were a little less demandin'. I try so hard to make her comfortable."

Isaac just shook his head. What could he say? He couldn't go into Martha's bedroom and demand she leave his house at once. She had nowhere else to go, and anyway she was family.

"Do you want me to speak to her? I'm not sure anythin' I say will help, but I will if'n that's what you want," said Isaac. Maybe he could ask her to be gentler to the children.

"Would you please," pleaded his wife. Whereupon Isaac marched into Martha's bedroom and carefully explained his concern over her dealings with her nieces and nephews. He called out her shortness of words, the roughness of her actions, and her demand for immediate attention. Aunt Martha immediately started crying, making Isaac feel less than a worm, but she promised to be more thoughtful in her actions.

Her thoughtfulness turned out to be more calculating and devious activities in hiding her hateful ways from Caroline and Isaac. But nothing was hidden from them.

A young Melva, especially, despised her. "I hate her," she'd say out of her mother and father's hearing.

Of course, she had a reason to hate or dislike Aunt Martha. When the elderly woman learned she couldn't boss this young urchin around easily, she threatened to harm Melva's younger brother. Milton still slept in the family cradle. Melva loved her little brother and with much resentment did the bidding of her aunt.

"Good! I'm glad she's dead," was her only comment upon hearing of the great aunt's death. Nan Tipton had quickly pulled her aside and scolded her headstrong child for her words.

"I don't ever want to hear you say that again," she had exclaimed, giving Melva a small shake to go along with the scolding.

"But Mother," Melva tried to explain. "She threatened little brother," said the six-year-old.

"I don't care what her problems were. We are to respect the dead," and Nan left, turning in the door to say, "Remember what I said!"

But Melva wasn't the least bit sorry for Aunt Martha's passing.

Each time she went near the wooden casket on the back wall, she would mutter under her breath to the deceased woman, "I'm glad," but not so her mother could hear. Melva wasn't afraid of the dead, but she was afraid of her mother!

After the funeral service, Martha Lincoln was buried in the family cemetery across from the LeQuire home in a pasture field. Two large trees sheltered the spot. This wasn't far enough away for Melva. She had never gone back to the spot.

∼

Melva returned to her grandfather's home with the salt and sugar in small Mason jars. She gave the items to Annie.

"Thanks, child." To Annie, they were all children.

Tomorrow was the funeral. She headed down the hall to the bedroom where Grandpa Jack lay in his coffin. After releasing the flood of tears at her grandma's, she could say goodbye.

The room was full of people.

When Noah saw his daughter in the door, he said, "Why don't we let Melva have some time alone with her grandfather?"

Noah shooed the people from the room. He stood outside the door as Melva approached the coffin.

～

Two weeks had passed since Jack Tipton's burial. Noah needed to make sure the gravestone was in place.

On Wednesday before Thanksgiving, Nancy and Noah loaded their brood into the buggy and headed for Cades Cove. D.H. and Henry would ride horses from Townsend across Rich Mountain to join them. Rita and Ellie would visit their in-laws and not be present.

The trip with his youngest children, two boys and three girls, was a happy one for Noah. There was plenty of banter amongst them. The air was still cold, but the ride was cheerful with the chattering of his children. Silently he vowed to be a fine father to them as his father had been to him. With nine children, he hoped his quiver was full.

Nancy sat beside him on the front seat of the buggy, holding baby Joyce. His youngest looked like an Eskimo, with only her eyes and tiny nose showing in her blanket.

Lydia nestled against Melva, who wrapped a blanket and her arms around her sister to keep her warm and steady her in the bouncing buggy. A woolen scarf kept Melva's ears warm.

Beside Melva and Lydia, the two boys bounded from side to side afraid one of them wouldn't see something the other saw. A large basket filled with Nan's cooked delicacies rested under the front buggy seat.

Noah turned onto Cooper Road and began the slow climb to the top of Hannah Mountain.

A few minutes later, Matthew exclaimed, "Look Milton, there's a bear behind that tree."

Milton immediately jumped to Matthew's side of the buggy, tripping over Melva's feet. She grabbed Matthew's collar to keep him from falling to the ground.

"Careful, Milton!" Nan cautioned, "You almost pushed your brother from the buggy."

"I'm sorry, Mother."

Matthew, still excited at seeing a bear, pointed. "See! There."

A subdued Milton answered, "Yeah, I see that old bear tree trunk."

Milton's brother had a vivid imagination, seeing animals in the clouds, soap suds, and even tree stumps.

"No, Milton," exclaimed Matthew. "There's a bear across the creek. See it moving behind the holly tree. There! There!" The boy jabbed his finger to accompany his statement.

"It's late in the season for a bear to be moving about," Noah commented, but he looked anyway. He was wrong! Matthew was pointing in the direction of a moving animal.

Noah halted the buggy. Everyone watched the bear's movements, including the horse. The horse was not happy. Snorting at the strange scent and becoming nervous, the animal turned its head and stared uneasily in the direction of everyone else.

The bear was foraging for food. Ignoring the audience, the black animal was across the small creek under several large oak trees, grunting and scratching around in the leaves. Ready for hibernation, it was large, as were most black bears at this time of year. Why it wasn't in a cave or den, Noah couldn't imagine.

The family sat for several minutes watching the animal hunting for acorns. Finally, disturbed by the strange contraption and human presence, the bear disappeared into the dense underbrush. Noah slapped the reins and continued down the road.

"Do you remember the first time we travelled this road?" Noah asked Nan.

She nodded. "Your father had sent a letter saying he was coming home from Missouri. He was there for Melva's first birthday in 1897."

"We moved out of his house and rented our own. Our sixth child, Milton Andrew, was born in 1898 and Matthew Laurence in 1901. This was the same year we thought the world was coming to an end, because President McKinley was assassinated and Teddy Roosevelt took over."

"You were never happy being a farmer."

"No. Raisin' a crop was interesting, but I didn't want to do it the rest of my life." He and Nan had had a long conversation about their prospects and decided to save money for a future investment. "Then the chance to buy the mercantile store in Chilhowee became a possibility. At first, you weren't too happy about my idea, Nan." He put his gloved hand on hers.

"No, I wasn't. I remember you and Elder Herron talkin' at church about the store." She'd felt a sudden surge of anxiety as the two men spoke. They would leave everything familiar to them and have no family support if they moved out of the cove. Nancy's mother, Caroline, was a great help with the children. Frankly, Nancy would miss her and her help.

"'What do you think, Nan-Nan?' I had asked you after we came back from church. 'Do you think I should go and check out the store?'"

She'd pondered his question. This might be the very chance they had hoped for and should be checked out. "Yes, I think you should go," and that was the end of the discussion.

Noah, realizing he had no competition, decided this would be an ideal chance to have a business of his own.

Rumors floating around the area said there was interest in building dams to harness the power of the rivers to produce electricity. This would mean cutting timber and the establishment of a saw mill. Because the river was undependable, the railroad would come to carry the timber to the outside world, and the need for men to work meant more people moving into Chilhowee's surrounding area. The possibility for the business to increase was endless, at least for a few years.

Noah considered the drastic change for days. When he finally made up his mind and told his father, the elderly gentleman gave him his blessing. John "Jack" Tipton would miss his son and grandchildren but knew Noah couldn't pass up this chance. He gave him a small amount of cash to help him get established.

Noah soon found that moving a household with seven children wasn't easy and required many trips out the lower end of Cades Cove. Every curve became familiar to him as he moved possessions and family. Only eighteen miles of curvy mountain road separated the families, but it might as well have been one hundred.

Noah's plans were to build a house across the road from his store, and he needed to do this soon. Nan was expecting their eighth child, so the first move into the valley to a smaller house was hard on her.

Melva was six years old when she saw the last of the family's possessions loaded onto the buggy for transport to Chilhowee. The new frame house was taking shape, and her father was now an established merchant with his own business. Leaving their Cades Cove family was the hardest of all. Each year, they would return on Decoration Day, which was the last Sunday in May, to put flowers on their ancestors' graves and at Thanksgiving. Not long after the move, the family celebrated their first Christmas and New Year's Day in their newly built home.

Noah found that running the store was something he enjoyed. He instinctively knew how to exhibit and sell merchandise and set about rearranging and restocking the shelves displaying the items for easy finding and pickup. His business prospered and Noah was content.

When Noah left Cades Cove, another venture was booming to the north in Tuckaleechee Cove on Little River. The gold in the hills surrounding this area was green, and being tapped. This green gold would change mountain lives and mountain forests for many years.

In the near future, the Little River Lumber Co. would become part of his extended family's lives. But now, he was moving away from it.

～

Annie was expecting Noah to come for Thanksgiving, but he had a detour to make on the way to her house.

From the lower part of the cove, the northern section of the Cades Cove Loop Road passed the Missionary Baptist Church and the Methodist Church before arriving at the Primitive Baptist Church. Nathaniel Tipton's house was on Tater Branch, just before the Baptist Church, where he sometimes preached on Sunday. Noah had business to discuss with him and decided to stop there before heading to Jack's gravesite. He needed to see Nat before returning to Chilhowee. Their arrival was just before dinner.

The family coon dog stood on the front porch barking his head off.

Noah's older brother came out the door to greet them, followed by his children. "Shut up, Queenie," he yelled at the dog, using the tip of his boot to push the lazy animal off the porch as he descended the porch steps to the buggy. "Hi, brother. Come in an' visit a spell."

Noah dismounted the buggy and shook his brother's offered hand. "I'm ready to be on solid ground and out of the shaky buggy." Turning around and reaching up, he took baby Joyce and let Nat help Nan down.

The other children jumped from both sides of the buggy, eyeing their cousins. "We saw a bear on the way," Matthew stated, eager to relate the sighting. Bear stories became the discussion with each child trying to outdo the other.

"Come on in the house." Nat led the way up the steps and held the door for the family. Queenie ran in before he could catch her. "Confounded dog!"

A warm fire greeted them. Noah went to warm his hands at the fireplace. Most of his family joined him. "It's cold today."

"Yes, I think winter has arrived. We had a skiff of snow on Monday morning. By noon, the white stuff turned to drizzle. Are you headed to Annie's for Thanksgiving?"

"We are, but there's something I need to discuss with you, and now's a good time." Noah took off his long coat and put it on a wall peg. He pulled some sheets of paper from his suit pocket.

Talking about anything in the room with so many people chattering didn't seem possible. "Children can't you find something to do?" Nat asked, thinking. "Boys, why don't you show your cousins the tree house you're building in the woods. And I'm sure Melva would like to see the newborn lamb in the stable," he suggested.

Whether Melva wanted to see the lamb or not, Lydia certainly did. She grabbed her sister's hand and followed the girls from the room.

"Don't ruin your clothes," Nan called before the front door slammed shut.

Nat's wife, Martha, came into the parlor with a pan of apples recently picked in their orchard and stored in the cellar. "Nan come with me to the kitchen. I have a cradle for the baby. We'll make apple pies."

"Oh, thank you. I'd be delighted." Nan got up and prepared to leave. She didn't get to share time with Martha often.

Martha looked at Nat and then at Noah and Nan. "Join us for dinner? We have plenty for everyone."

"Yes, of course." Nat nodded. "I don't know what I was thinking."

Noah looked quizzically at Nan, who nodded and accepted the invitation to eat with his brother. The two women left the room.

"Annie doesn't expect us until supper," Noah explained to Nat.

Now, Noah and Nat were alone, except for the old coon dog who was too lazy to get up and join any of the groups leaving the room. She lay on the hearth, nose down, and eyes closed.

"Coon dogs aren't worth a dime unless they're hunting," Nat observed. "What did you want to talk about?"

"I have Jack's will. He left it in my business safe, when he bought his burial suit." Noah handed the papers to Nat, who opened them and leaned back in his chair.

"I wondered where his suit came from. Jack always thought of everything." He started reading the pages.

The will was very straightforward. Annie would remain on the farm during her lifetime. When she no longer needed the homeplace, the land was to be sold and the proceeds divided between his children — those who were still alive. Until that time, his sons and daughters were asked to farm the land and use the money for their necessities but give Annie a good supply to meet her needs.

"I don't have a problem with this." Nat gave the papers to Noah.

"It's the last part I wanted to discuss, deciding on an amount sufficient and even more for Annie." He planned on talking to Annie tomorrow, and he wanted to assure his sister there was no need to worry.

He and Nat came to an understanding. Annie and Nat were the only two children from Jack's first family who lived in the Cove, and none of Noah's brothers lived there.

"I'm in agreement, that you and I must take care of her. I'll supply Annie with fresh food from my crops and garden and enough for her to put up for winter."

"You know I'm not a farmer, but she'll need money to buy other necessities. My business is good, so I'll give her cash to meet those needs. She should have plenty." He didn't tell Nat, but he already had an envelope with one hundred dollars inside to support her. The two stood and shook hands.

After their meeting, Noah and Nat went outside. They walked around the farm, inspecting his growing orchard and new addition to his barn. The children were not in sight but yells and laughter from the woods behind the barn meant they'd be easy to find. Soon a "come-and-get-it-bell" rang from the back porch of Nat's home. Food was on the table. It didn't take long for everyone to assemble.

～

After turning off the main road, the family was silent on the short ride down the secluded lane to Cades Cove Primitive Baptist Church. The buggy passed under the leafless skeletons of majestic oak, hickory, and maple. The white pine and brooding hemlock trees maintained a somber and dark-green presence in the forest. Two beautiful red cardinals few across the road followed by their small flocks of less showy females. Their colors more striking because the leaves were off the trees and grays and greens filled the forest.

The white frame church appeared around a long curve, framed in a cozy clearing. Noah made a long sweep with the buggy, ending up heading back out toward the main road. He alighted from the buggy and tied the horse's reins to the rail provided for that purpose. The boys immediately jumped out of each side of the buggy.

"Milton, come and hold baby Joyce, while I help your mother out."

The two lads were heading for the iron gate entrance to the cemetery, oblivious to anything except their own little world of boy thoughts and deeds.

Melva was already out and helping her sister Lydia down to the ground. Once Nan was afoot, the family headed for the cemetery. This walk was different for each family member.

Since the land for the church was given by William Tipton many years earlier, it was as much their family cemetery as any in the cove.

The first church consisted of wooden logs and was much smaller. The church the family walked by today was white-frame with several steep steps leading to the front door. The bell tower atop the roof was positioned at the front over the church entrance. Inside there were wooden floors with wooden benches sitting on each side of the center aisle. The simple pulpit and potbellied stove stood alone at the front. Noah and his family attended here until their move to Chilhowee ten years ago.

Jack was buried at the back edge of the cemetery beside his second wife, Naomi. There were many graves to pass before reaching his. Lydia raced ahead down the cemetery path while Melva took her time reaching her grandfather's grave.

Some of the granite tombstones were elaborate, but there were those of simple slabs of slate. The slate ones broke easily, and with weather changes and years passing, these graves would soon be lost forever.

Melva loved reading the epitaphs on the various granite tombstones. She and Grandfather Jack had walked by them every year at decoration. "Gone but not forgotten," "Though lost to sight – to memory dear," "Love lives on," or "They live with us in memory and will forever more," were those she loved the best. She knew exactly where she could find these, because the cemetery was so familiar to her.

The words spoke to her heart. They told of ties of love which cannot be broken even by death. She wasn't sure she knew this kind of love, but she yearned for it.

This was the first time Melva had visited the cemetery since the burial, and she was dawdling. Her feet felt like lead. Her heart trembled as she got nearer the forest beyond the gravesites. She acknowledged the fact that Jack wouldn't be around to swing with her on the front porch, or tell her stories of the family, but seeing the mound of earth over his grave would make it real.

For the second time, her heart mourned his passing, and she sobbed over his grave. Human love, when touched with loss, involves great sadness. This was a new awakening, a new feeling for her. Noah put his arm around her shaking shoulders. Melva turned around to be comforted in the shelter of her father's arms.

Lydia cried because her big sister cried.

~

The last days before the new year, 1912, were hectic days in the Tipton household. The Primitive Baptists did not believe in the celebration of Christmas. Therefore, Noah eschewed store-bought decorations for his family, but he loved bringing the outdoors inside the house. Everyone made pilgrimages to the mountains collecting items to use in decorating its interior.

Holly with its red berries was intertwined with pine and draped over the upstairs banister and the handrail down the stairs to the foyer. The pine aroma filled the parlor, where the greenery was used on the mantle with pine cones and the soft glow of candles. Electric lights were turned off.

Each night, Nan popped corn and every-one crunched the white kernels. The odor of the popped corn added to the festive atmosphere of the year end. Collecting berries to make berry ropes was like picking blackberries in the summer. Each child was given a container and sent to the woods, returning with their contribution.

December became a family affair, much like a picnic in the woods or Decoration Day in the Cove.

Visits from Melva's sisters and brothers filled the house full to overflowing. Laugher and goodwill dominated the scene. Susan Ellen, expecting one of her own, hovered over Rita's infant, while baby James' contribution was crying at the top of his lungs at the noise around him. Baby Joyce wasn't the only one vying for Nan's attention, and in her almost two-year-old world, she was a bit jealous. The amount of work was overwhelming and tiring. All shared in the task of making the others comfortable, and the upstairs bedrooms were crowded with people and belongings.

Finally, Noah closed the store early on the Saturday afternoon chosen for the family gathering, and everyone waited expectantly for him to come home.

"He's on the way," Lydia announced from her post at the parlor window. She headed for the back door, with Milton and Matthew following her.

It was cloudy and cold, and in the air was the smell of coming snow. Noah carried a paper bag full of candy canes and oranges from the store. The back door flew open as he pulled on the screen door.

"Father," Lydia, Milton, and Matthew greeted him at the door. "We've been waiting on you." And sure enough, they had.

He walked down the hall, and as he entered the parlor, he saw the Bible on his chair. The three young ones went to their seats on the floor, sat down, and followed him with their eyes.

"Hello, everyone." He was greeted with a chorus of welcomes.

Pulling out the contents of the bag, he carefully placed the candy canes and oranges amongst the pine boughs on the mantle and in the pine boughs on the Bible table in the hall. After supper, these would be eaten by all as a treat.

Chairs came from every room in the house. The youngest of the bunch, sitting on the floor, leaned forward with expectation at the story or maybe at the supper or goodies to follow. Nan, along with Ellie and Rita, stood or sat in the doorway to the dining room. Slipping out, they could tend the cooking food without disturbing the listeners. Melva, wrapped in a red shawl, made herself small in a corner.

Noah took the Bible and sat down in his chair. It was time to read Luke's account of Jesus' birth and lead a discussion the family had participated in for years.

Noah opened the King James Version, adjusted his glasses, and started with Chapter Two. At verse eight he read, *"And there were in the same country shepherds abiding in the fields, keeping watch over their flock by night –"* He stopped and looked around the room. He had the attention of all.

In the candlelight, he could almost imagine the night he was reading about was here—in this room. This was his flock. He and Nan were the two shepherds tending it. He looked over at Nan, who held baby Joyce, and around the room at his other children—eight of them, two with husbands, and one grandson. Had he and Nan taught biblical principles, prayed enough, and conveyed the excellent way this flock needed? He pulled in a rugged sigh, and tears glistened in his eyes as he continued. The burden of raising children in a Godly household was great.

Noah read on. The scripture told of a special baby's birth in Bethlehem — Christ, Emanuel, God with us. The shepherds who watched their flocks were visited by angels, and a beautiful star guided them to the stable where others came to worship a babe.

Noah closed the Bible. Normally, he would go ahead with his question-and- answer session, but tonight he felt led to say his prayer first.

"My Father, You are the God of the universe. God of every person who has lived, who lives now, and who will live in the future. Because You love us, You give us the freedom to choose You as our Heavenly Father. It is my prayer that my children will choose You over the other influences in this world. I thank You for a prosperous year and for keeping my family safe.

Thank You for Jesus' birth and for the sacrifice of His life. Because of His death on a cruel cross, we'll see our loved ones again and live forever with them and You in Your heavenly kingdom. Bless our fellowship together and give this family another year of good health and safety. In Your Son's holy name. Amen.

Noah removed his glasses, pulled a handkerchief from a back pocket, and wiped the tears from his cheeks and eyes. In this sacred moment, no one said a word, but more than one eye glistened with tears.

Noah cleared his throat and leaned forward, "Why was there a bright star in the sky, the night Jesus was born?" he asked.

"Because Jesus was born," piped up Matthew.

"Uh, that's true Matthew, but what was the importance of the star?" Noah asked again. "Why would God place a star in the sky?"

Milton held up his hand, and Noah pointed at him. "The coming of Jesus' birth in Bethlehem. The star foretold Jesus' birth," said Milton. "Once Jesus was born, it stood over His home so the shepherds and wise men could find the manger where He lay."

"Exactly," Noah agreed. "Where did the shepherds find Jesus?"

As the question period continued, Nan motioned for Melva to come from her corner. She pulled her into the dining room. "Would you set the table?" Nan whispered. "Ellie and Rita can help me." Melva and her shadow, Lydia, started taking the china from its cabinet. The other women left the room to finish preparing the food for the evening meal.

～

New Year's Day fell on Monday in 1912, and the following Saturday, Betty Jo sent for Melva to stay the night. Melva was ready to go. She wanted a change of scenery. She was exhausted, and the house was quiet after the holiday's festivities ended.

Betty Jo came with Edgar to pick her up on Saturday afternoon. The sky was full of low-lying, gray clouds. A light snow fell lazily from the sky, touching their cheeks, and whirling in disarray behind the moving buggy. Melva and Betty Jo caught the flakes in their gloved hands as they rode along. Just being with Betty Jo lifted Melva's spirits after the letdown following the family's activities.

When they arrived at the Boyd's house, Edgar stopped at the flagstone walk and helped Melva out first. Then he assisted his sister. Edgar drove in the direction of the barn to take the harness off the horse.

The girls headed for Betty Jo's upstairs bedroom. Coats, with gloves and scarves stuffed in the pockets were hung in the clothes closet built into the wall. At that moment, Melva noticed a flash from Betty Jo's left hand.

"Betty Jo," exclaimed Melva, "Is that what I think it is?"

Betty Jo started laughing, "Yes, it is. Robert asked me to marry him right after he came back from the holidays in Friendsville. I wanted you to come, so I could surprise you! So, you'd be the first to know."

Melva grabbed her friend's hands, and they went twirling around the room. "Surprise me you did! I'm so happy for you. Where and how did he ask you?" Melva wanted to know all the details.

"We'll be married in April, and I want you to stand up for me at the wedding. Will you do that?"

"Of course, I will," said Melva, "I'll be there with bells on."

Betty Jo hugged her best friend and continued telling her about Robert's proposal.

"While he was home in Maryville, he bought the ring and a small box of chocolates. He placed the ring inside with the candy. They were sitting on the buggy seat when he came to pick me up for a drive up to Look Rock." Betty Jo stopped to get her breath. She was in such a big hurry to tell her friend every detail, she didn't stop to breathe.

Look Rock was on top of Chilhowee Mountain. From the upper end of Happy Valley, it was possible to look up and see its rocky outcrop on the mountain side. The road, leading to the bluff, was a series of steep switchbacks which topped out there, before going over the mountain to Maryville. Anyone going from the valley to that town, either took this road or the railroad.

From Look Rock, a traveler was afforded a good view of Happy Valley and its serene pastureland.

"After arriving at Look Rock, Robert suggested eating some of the candy. We had gloves on. After taking them off, I opened the box. The first thing I saw was the ring."

Melva took her hand and examined the ring.

Betty Jo continued, "He said, 'Betty Jo, I love you and I want you to be my wife.' He took the ring out of the box. Holding it in his hand, he was ready to place it on my finger. 'Will you marry me?' I just stared at him. In my daydreams, I envisioned this moment, and now it was happening."

"What happened next?"

"I said 'Yes! Yes!' I flung my arms around Robert. He took advantage of the moment to exchange our first kiss."

"You'd never kissed him before?"

"No. For some minutes, we sat entwined on the buggy seat with the beautiful vista below, oblivious to the cold air moving around us. Finally, Robert said, laughing, 'I think I need to put this on your finger.' He was one happy man as he slipped the ring on my finger. 'We'd better head back down, it's gettin' cold and I need to talk to your father about something very important,' he teased me. We sat close to each other on the drive back down the mountain."

"I guess your father was happy at the prospect of Robert as a son."

"Yes. After Robert left, he said I was gettin' an honest and dependable man. He gave us his blessing."

Betty Jo had been pacing the room as she talked. She plopped on the bed, exhausted. "I'm just so happy,

Melva. I hoped Robert would ask me, but until he did, there was always a question of his affection and intention. Now I don't have to worry anymore, and we can make plans for the future. Isn't that exciting?"

Melva nodded. Yes, it was exciting.

Supper at the Boyd's was filled with talk of the wedding plans. Later that night, when the girls were in bed, Melva asked Betty Jo to come and stay with her the next weekend.

"Robert won't have so far to ride, and he can come to my house to see you. We'll talk weddin' plans."

Below, unbeknownst to the giggling girls upstairs, Edgar paced the floor in his room. Melva was more beautiful tonight than he had ever seen her. His heart ached for her—had for years. He decided it was now or never. He needed to know her answer.

Church the next day was routine for Melva but not for Betty Jo. All the young, single girls wanted to see her ring. Most engagements in the mountains did not involve the giving of a ring. There was a circle of excited women around her.

Three inches of new snow fell overnight, blanketing the ground. The sure-footed horses pulling the buggies to church never faltered, but church attendance was down. Even Noah, Nan, and the children arrived a little late. In fact, the whole church service was late getting started.

Elder John Hall spoke on each member's responsibility of staying on the straight and narrow path during the new year, the one spelled out in the Holy Bible. Before the service was over, several people dedicated themselves to walk that course, going forward and kneeling at the altar. Noah and Nan were the first ones to step out and go down the aisle.

Finally, after a long prayer by Elder Herron, the service was over, and each family headed home for dinner. Elder John planned to eat with the Tipton's and leave on the afternoon train. Melva was returning to the Boyd house for Sunday dinner, and then Edgar and Betty Jo were to take her home.

The threesome stood in the kitchen after washing the dishes. "Betty Jo, I'll take Melva home. It's messy, and a cold wind's blowin' outside. There's really no reason for you to go."

Betty Jo protested, "But we planned on goin' together."

Edgar held up his hand. "No. I'll go." He left to hitch the horse to the buggy.

Melva went upstairs to gather her things. When she came downstairs, Edgar stood before the front door.

"Betty Jo, I'll see you next Saturday."

"Yes. I'll ride my horse down to your house."

Melva did not notice Betty Jo looking questionably at Edgar. Nor did she see Edgar turn his head, not acknowledging his sister's gaze.

Betty Jo knew that Melva didn't gush about Edgar like she gushed about Robert. Still she wished some miracle would happen and Melva would fall madly in love with her brother. A double wedding in April would be wonderful.

～

Usually Melva shared a comfortable, friendly ride with Edgar to Chilhowee. Today, the ride was cold, strained and, for some reason, uncomfortable. Melva wondered why. She would soon know. About halfway there

Edgar reached over and took Melva's gloved hand. He did this more to steady himself than show his affection for her. Melva was so shocked at his touch, she didn't move. She sat looking at his gloved hand on hers.

"Melva, I need to say something to you." Edgar was practically stuttering and not because of the cold.

"Please, Edgar, don't." Melva didn't want him to say anything. Not today! He was going to ruin a wonderful weekend. She pulled her hand away.

"No! No! I have to say this. I have to say it now." Edgar finally had the courage to tell Melva how he felt. He would never find the courage to speak again.

Holding the reins loosely in one hand, he let the horse find its own way. Melva looked down at her feet, afraid of what was going to happen. Edgar sat searching for the right words. He faced her and continued.

"Melva, you've known how I felt about you for some time. D.H. told you. I've never said anything to you before, because it was never the right time, and I was afraid too." At least he was honest. "I need to share these feelings with you now and hope you feel the same way. Melva, I really like you. Would you think about being my wife? I would be a good husband to you." Edgar was silent. Had he bungled the whole thing? He waited for a response.

There was no "I love you."

Melva sat dumbfounded. It had happened! Now, she must kindly reject him. But should she? Here was a man who wanted her for his wife. She might never have another offer this good.

Should she base her future life on Burl Whitehead, a man she didn't know, and had seen only twice? It seemed strangely silly and unwise to do so. And yet, it wouldn't be fair to Edgar to accept him and not love him as he deserved. How could she tell him and tell him firmly so he could look for another—the wife he needed?

Melva never mentioned to Betty Jo her statement about the Whitehead boy. And that was strange because they shared every secret. The possibility that Edgar would share his feelings and her response might affect her friendship with Betty Jo, probably explained her silence at speaking about Burl.

Anyway, she didn't know Mr. Whitehead and had no idea she would ever see him again. Who was she kidding? If there was a way to know him, she would find it. She'd set her cap for him, as the old-timers often said.

Melva had sat for several minutes with thoughts chasing each other in her head. She placed her hands on either side of her face, closed her eyes and tried to erase the scene and words from her mind. This wasn't happening!

"Melva, I'm sorry if I upset you. I only wanted you to know how I feel," said Edgar, thinking she was angry at him.

"No, Edgar, I'm not upset with you. You've honored me by asking me to marry you. You're a fine man and worthy of a good wife, I'm just not the one you need. I don't care for you like that. I like you for a friend, a very good friend."

Melva paused for a minute, thinking Edgar might respond.

He was silent.

"I'm sorry," she continued, "but I haven't given you reason to think otherwise. At least, I've tried not to." Now Melva was being truthful.

She was silent. The horse continued down the road during their strained conversation, and Melva was glad it had. They were nearing her home, and getting there wouldn't be a bit too soon.

"Melva, lots of people get married and learn to love each other. Don't you think we could do that? You would never want for anything, because I can provide anything you need. The farm is established and flourishing, and one day it will be mine."

Edgar was pleading with her. He made an awkward attempt to put his arm around her and draw her to him.

This wouldn't do! Melva bolted from the slowly moving buggy, which Edgar immediately halted.

Turning to face him Melva said, "I tried to tell you gently how I felt. Now let me state it plainly. I can't be your wife, because I don't love you. I think marrying a man I don't love would make us both miserable. You deserve better." Melva started walking in the snowy slush beside the road. She could feel the cold wetness coming through her shoes, wetting her stocking feet.

Holding up her hand in anticipation of the next question Melva said, "No. I don't have other prospects." Melva might have said it would take a stronger man than he for her to respect. Edgar was a man who needed someone to constantly lead him, instead of leading. Being strong-willed, Melva would soon loathe that situation. Melva wanted a mutual respect built on love. Love, then, involved a deep respect. Now Melva understood why she couldn't marry Edgar. She didn't have the respect for him that a woman should have for a husband.

Melva was home. Her feet were wet with snow.

Looking at Edgar's downcast face, she said, "I'm sorry." She turned and hurried into the house before he could respond.

Seeing her flushed face as she went up the stairs to her room, Nan wondered if she might be catching a cold. She must check on her later. Right now, she had guests to entertain.

Melva flung herself on her bed and cried from frustration and anger. Her mind was filled with questions. Why did Edgar ruin a perfectly wonderful weekend? Why couldn't she accept his proposal? How would Betty Jo feel about her rejection of her brother? Nothing would ever be the same with the Boyd family. Under no circumstances could she be comfortable in their home again. Before long, she was asleep.

Later in the afternoon, Nan checked on Melva. She was still asleep. Her wet shoes and hose were on the rug beside the bed where she had taken them off. Melva's exposed feet and legs were cold as ice. Taking an afghan from a nearby chair, Nan gently covered them up.

What ailed the child, she wondered? Melva never slept in the afternoon. Nan went downstairs and placed the shoes next to the stove. Tomorrow morning, they would be dry and toasty for her daughter. She washed the hose in the sink and hung them on the small clothes line on the inside porch. She must remember to ask Melva what happened.

⚜ **Chapter Six** ⚜

The Flood and the Meeting

*Pleasant words are as an honeycomb, sweet to the
soul, and health to the bones.*

Proverbs 16:24 KJV

The next day after Edgar's proposal, Nan had
expressed concern over her daughter's appearance the
previous day, and Melva was ready to share her heart.

"I wasn't sick, Mother," she said. "I thought Betty
Jo was coming, but at the last moment Edgar decided to
bring me himself. I had no idea he wanted to speak to
me privately."

"I see," said Nan. She was mixing apple pie spices
at the counter. The aroma of nutmeg and cinnamon
floated in the room.

Melva continued. "I was stunned when he asked
me to think about being his wife." There she had said
it! It was like being in a dream—a distant dream.

"He what!" exclaimed Nan, putting down the
cinnamon and the teaspoons and turning toward her
daughter. In her wildest thoughts, this was the last
thing she would have guessed was wrong with her
daughter. Nan had no idea Edgar even liked Melva that

way. She'd never observed any special intentions toward her daughter.

"I can't believe this. Are you sure you heard right?"

"Oh, yes. I heard him plainly. I like Edgar but don't love him. He's my friend. Mother, I haven't given him any reason to think otherwise. I told him I couldn't accept him." Again, Melva felt the confusion of the previous afternoon.

Nan sat down in a chair at the kitchen table. She was flabbergasted! She could hear the emotional turmoil in her daughter's voice. What should she say to her about this turn of events? Edgar and Melva — they would've made a good-looking couple, she thought. The Boyds — Oh! Marlon and his wife — .

Melva continued, "I was nice to him, trying not to hurt him, but I felt I needed to be firm. I didn't want him to hope I might change my mind."

Nan's mind was racing. Noah must go to Marlon and explain Melva's feelings and even talk to Edgar. There could be no misunderstanding between their families.

"Mother, I'm afraid Betty Jo will be upset. We had such a wonderful weekend. She's engaged to Robert at the Mill. I don't want anything to come between our friendship." Melva's words were tumbling out of her mouth.

"I'll have your father go and talk to Marlon. He may want to talk to Edgar also. I understand how you feel about Betty Jo, and she may feel hurt for a while. If she's a real friend, she'll get over it."

"But what if she doesn't?"

"Then there's nothing you or anyone else can do. You say she's engaged."

"Yes, to Robert Ownby from the Mill. They plan to marry in April. She asked me to stand up for her at the wedding. I promised her I would."

What a strange turn of events, thought Nan. Betty Jo was engaged, and Edgar asked Melva to marry him. She wondered if the engagement triggered Edgar's proposal. Nan's main concern was for her daughter, who obviously was disturbed because she'd turned down her best friend's brother.

"Let's wait and see what the next few days bring," she encouraged Melva. "You have no control over Betty Jo's feelings, so try not to worry about your decision. If you don't love Edgar, you made the right choice. Your father and I wouldn't want you to marry for security or because of age." Hadn't Noah's and Nan's marriage based on mutual love been rewarding and successful? She wanted that same relationship for all her children. There was no other reason to get married!

Nan looked at her daughter's downcast face. She got up from the table and tenderly put her arms around her distraught child. This time she spoke more forcefully as she tried to reassure her. "You made the right decision. Let's see what your father says when he comes home to eat. There's one other thing. Your father wouldn't approve of you getting married at your age. You do realize this, don't you?"

Melva nodded.

Nan held Melva at arm's length and looked into her eyes. "Everything will work out for the best." Leaning over, she kissed her daughter lightly on the forehead.

Nan went back to making her pies and with Melva's help started to fix dinner.

Noah arrived at his usual time, unaware of the dilemma he would face. Seeing the faces of his womenfolk, he knew something was brewing. Instead of asking immediately, he washed up and went to the head of the table to say grace. After that the floor was open for discussion which started straight way.

"Noah, I need to talk to you about a problem concerning your daughter and Edgar Boyd," said Nan.

"What's happened!" exclaimed Noah, dropping his fork and looking quickly at Melva.

"Oh Father, nothing bad," said Melva quickly. "In fact, Edgar honored me by asking me to be his wife. The problem is I don't feel that way about him. He's my friend, and I can't marry him. I don't love him. I told him that and terribly disappointed him, I'm afraid."

"I've never noticed any interest by Edgar in your direction," thought Noah out loud, reflecting on the words he was hearing and echoing Nan's sentiments.

"That's what I said," observed Nan. "Evidently, he's been harboring a secret desire for her for some time. Do you think you should go talk to Marlon? I don't want hard feelings between our families."

For several seconds, Noah sat there, fork in hand, with a smile on his face. He would've laughed except he knew Melva was upset. He could tell by her face. He was sure Edgar was in the same shape. Marlon wasn't the type to get upset over such a thing, but it wouldn't hurt to follow up, just to make sure.

"Let me think about it. This is quite a surprise." That's all Noah said. He continued to eat his dinner.

Melva knew her father would come up with the right solution. She felt better but not close to being cured.

~

The difficulties following her rejection of Edgar were immediate and extended to Betty Jo, who decided not to come to Melva's house for the planned weekend.

How could their friendship decline so rapidly? She thought the feelings they had for each other were deeper, on more solid ground, and harder to tear down than this. They laughed, giggled, and had a camaraderie most friends didn't share. Devastated, Melva grieved their predicament. Time might take care of the problem, but it didn't take care of the unease Melva presently felt.

~

January was one of the months the Blount County Quarterly Court met during the year. As an elected Squire, Noah was required to be present. He decided to take Melva with him on the trip into Maryville.

The plan was to board the train at Tipton's Mercantile and arrive in Maryville late afternoon. D.H. had decided to pick them up at the train depot and take them to eat supper at John Anderson's home.

Melva was glad for the distraction. After Edgar's proposal and subsequent events, the trip was a welcome relief from the last hectic days. It seemed to her the emotional blows of the last months were too close together. She didn't get over one before another hit her. Boarding the train would be a welcome breather from the current scene at Chilhowee and a time to think through everything happening in her life.

~

Melva sat on the padded seat, enjoying the afternoon train ride from her home to the Maryville Depot. Riding the train was a special treat for her. She watched the Little Tennessee River or as the locals called it, the Little T, as they rode along. The stream, a silver ribbon, weaving toward the tracks and then away, cut through empty fields of last year's harvested corn planted in the lowland.

This spring-fed river started as a trickle deep in the mountains of Georgia. Then it did something strange. It flowed north into North Carolina and west into Tennessee before heading south to the Tennessee River. Its watershed involved thousands of square miles. The cold-as-ice waters were preferred breeding grounds for rainbow trout, as fishermen from many states could attest.

Once a favorite passageway of the Cherokee's, they canoed the river like a highway, traveling to Indian villages along its length. Putting a boat on its waters took you to the Gulf Coast via the Ohio and Mississippi Rivers, through quiet deep pools, marshland, and rugged shoals.

The river where Melva lived was wide and deep and the smooth, blue-green water moved swiftly downriver with the decreasing elevation. At one time, steam boats plied its waters going upstream from Niles Ferry and the train Station at Upton to Chilhowee Landing. There the passengers disembarked and freight was unloaded and loaded. With the extension of the railroad spur to Chilhowee, boat traffic almost disappeared, except for fishing enthusiasts.

Melva leaned forward to catch the first glimpse of the railroad trestle crossing the river. The spur ended up at Babcock Lumber Co. in Tellico and Etowah. Babcock lumbered the section on the other side of the river. Melva was looking for an interesting phenomenon. If the sun was at the right angle, there was a reflection on the rails which followed the shiny metal and flashed across the river.

"Father, are you watching for the flash?"

Noah was busy talking to the train conductor, Cal McMurray.

"You look for it," he said. "I really couldn't see it from here."

At that moment and for a millisecond Melva saw it. This trip was going very nicely, she thought.

At this juncture, the main line of the Tennessee Carolina Southern Railroad left the riverbank and headed inland for several miles. It ran through forested hills and small rural communities. Several stops were made at platforms serving as depots along the main line.

Melva kept watch out the window as passengers loaded onto the train. A sharp hissing sound came from the front of the train, as the train pulled out of each station. The sharp jolt of cars starting to roll down the tracks meant she was closer to town and her new adventure.

Melva looked over at her father who sat on the inside seat of the passenger train. He was still talking to Cal McMurray, the conductor. Noah was the wisest man in the world, at least in her world. He was dressed in a fashionable navy-blue suit with vest and hat. His ironed shirt was as white as snow due to Nan's efforts and bleach. Clean-shaven, he wore round, wire-rimmed glasses. Distinguished, dependable, and serious were three words she could easily apply to him.

After boarding the train, he'd known instinctively she'd prefer the window seat. He motioned her into it and placed their suitcases in the overhead compartments. When Cal came by for their tickets, he pulled them out of the inside pocket of his coat. Her father was the most organized man she knew. He ran his business the same way.

Looking over at Melva, he smiled and said, "Daughter, we're going to enjoy ourselves on this trip. Would you like to visit some of the downtown Maryville stores? You can check out the latest fashions and eat at the Café."

The courthouse was only a short walk to downtown, and they were staying at a hotel across the street.

"I think it would be safe for you to go alone from the courthouse. In fact, you could walk down the street to the bank and invite your brother to lunch."

Melva realized her father was treating her as an adult when she replied, "Thank you, I'd love to do that. Do you think we could visit Ellie while we're in town?"

"We might have time. I don't know what's on the agenda for this court session. When I see the list, I'll decide. In the meantime, here's some money to spend however you wish."

"I've some of the money you pay me for working at the store. I brought it with me. I really don't need more," replied Melva.

"Consider this a bonus for being such a good employee," her father said smiling. He continued, "I think you'll like John Anderson and his family. He has several girls and I believe one of them is your age."

Just at that time Cal came by again. Noah turned back to talk to him.

~

D.H. was waiting with John Anderson's Model-T Ford at the station. Remembering Melva's comment to her father about Mr. Anderson's car, D.H. had asked to borrow it. Mr. Anderson would drive his guests back to the hotel after supper and take D.H. home.

From the depot, D.H. pulled onto Washington Avenue and drove a short distance to the intersection with Broadway Street. He turned left.

A few horses with buggies still lined the dirt streets of downtown Maryville. Badgett's Store, the Café, Caldwell's Hardware, Blount State Bank, and many other businesses were located along the length of this street. As they drove west, they passed the turn for the Courthouse. A block or two beyond this turn was the newly renovated, three story, Pride Mansion, turned into West Side School. Most of the residential district started after passing the school.

The Anderson mansion was a two-story, colonial house on West Broadway. It had running, heated water, electric lights, telephone and inside plumbing. Spacious, even for a banker's house, it suggested affluence and influence. The circular drive in front was surrounded by extensive landscaping and the white, sculpted columns were imposing as D.H pulled up to the front entrance and parked behind another vehicle.

A laughing John Anderson came bounding down the steps toward them and extended his hand to Noah who shook it warmly.

"Noah, I'm glad my car made it back in one piece," he said, eyeing his young employee, and still shaking Noah's hand. John had three interests in life, taking care of his family, making money, and laughing. He laughed at everything.

"I'm glad to see you, old friend," said Noah, who patted John on the back.

"And who's this?" said John looking at Melva. "Not Melva. I haven't seen you in years. Why you were only twelve or thirteen then. My you've sprouted up."

"Yes, this is my daughter Melva. I decided the trip to Maryville would be a change for her—an adventure." Noah was walking up the steps with his arm around his friend's shoulder. "Who does the other car in the driveway belong too?" asked Noah.

"Do you remember W.B. Townsend from Pittsburg, Pennsylvania? His company is developing the timber reserves above Tuckaleechee Cove, or should I say Townsend. Can you believe they named the town after him?" John laughed.

"Yes, I met him at some of our court meetings a few years back." Noah and John proceeded into the house with Melva and D.H. standing on the steps behind them.

Melva's brother extended his arm to his sister who looked at him incredulously.

"And what am I supposed to do?" asked Melva, drawing back in mock astonishment, but knowing full well what was expected of her.

D.H. didn't answer, but reaching down, he grabbed Melva's gloved hand, and placed it on his arm. "You're in society now," he teased. "Act like it."

So, Melva put on her best societal air, and held her head high. She sashayed up the steps with D.H. and disappeared into the house through the massive front door.

Inside, the house was huge, much like the one she lived in, but on a much grander scale. Downstairs, the ceilings were twelve feet high. Wood floors were graced with Persian rugs—bought somewhere besides Maryville. The parlor stretched across the front of the house with the customary stairs opposite the front door.

Three young girls were lined up looking over the upstairs banister at the entering guests. Melva smiled and waved at them. They reminded her of the days when Ellie, Rita and she did the same thing at Chilhowee, when guests filed in the entrance below.

A large grand piano and a music stand sat in the room to the left. Comfortable chairs were everywhere with settees appropriately placed amongst them. She could imagine impromptu recitals and people clapping to the pieces being played or sung.

Several people sat in the main parlor to the right. Noah and John headed there, and she and D.H. followed.

Among them was an impeccably-dressed, distinguished, middle-aged gentleman with thinning, brown hair and expressive green eyes. His prominent nose was softened by a bushy mustache. He was the most handsome man Melva had ever seen. His air was important, and yet, she instinctively knew he could be warm and gracious to his intimate friends.

Mr. Anderson introduced him as W.B. Townsend of Little River Lumber Co. A partner with several other gentlemen from Pennsylvania, they built the railroad to Townsend to support their timber cutting efforts. Another gentleman was Arthur Justin Fisher, Sr., or A.J., part of the Schlosser Tannery at Walland.

"Noah, I'm pleased to see you again," said Mr. Townsend. "I believe the last time we talked, the county was in the planning stages for a new courthouse. I'm not sure how I got involved in that project, but I was glad when it was over," Mr. Townsend turned his attention to Melva, who fidgeted under his gaze.

"And who is this young lady?" he said.

"This is my daughter, Melva. She's the oldest child left at home. Two other daughters are married, and you know D.H. One of his brothers, Henry will graduate from Bill Joe's Academy this year. The others are younger."

"I'm pleased to meet you, young lady," said Mr. Townsend. "This is my wife, Margaret."

Melva had never seen such an elegantly dressed woman. She wore a beautiful blue velvet dress that matched her eyes and blue combs in her hair. Beautiful topaz earrings dangled from her pierced ears, and a topaz necklace set in silver graced her long neck. The flashes from her hands said diamonds, wealth, and upper-class.

Margaret Townsend was both of those, wealthy, and upper-class, but she was not arrogant. She was friendly and open. "Melva, I love your brooch. Is it a family heirloom?"

"Oh no, Ma'am." Melva's hand went to her brooch. "My mother and father gave it to me after finishing school." The brooch was the same one she'd worn to the dance at Happy Valley School. "I wear it often." Melva made a mental note to ask Mrs. Townsend about her pierced ears, if she got the chance.

At this moment, Mrs. Anderson came into the room with her daughter, Juliet. She was obviously the daughter spoken of by Noah on the way to Maryville. She had beautiful, naturally-curly blond hair cut fairly short. She looked at Melva, and Melva looked back. They decided to be friends.

Mrs. Anderson announced, "Dinner is served."

Supper was interspersed by business conversation. Melva soon learned that Mr. Townsend originally came to the Maryville area in the winter of 1898. This trip almost cost him his life. "Yes, my good friend here," he patted Mr. A.J. Fisher on the back, "almost got me killed."

"Hey. How did I know it would come a blizzard?" Fisher responded.

"At this time, A.J. was proposing a tannery at Walland, Tennessee. We were surveying in the mountains, looking at cutting timber for a future sawmill, and to supply bark for his business. The air was downright cold, freezing, and snow started to fall. Our group got caught in a horrific snow storm, but we managed to hike out in deep snow. Later, we heard some in other parts of the mountains were not so lucky."

∼

Because of his proposed larger scale of operation, Mr. Fisher's future business required a steady and large supply of tree bark. Local suppliers would not be able to keep up with his demand—he hoped. He'd traveled north in search of men who were interested in inspecting the timber resources in the southern Appalachians.

During a social gathering of his northern friends, Mr. Fisher was introduced to men within the state of Pennsylvania who were currently in the lumbering business. This is where he met Townsend and their business relationship started.

W.B. Townsend and his partners owned Clearfield Lumber Co. and had a large timbering operation in the local area. They'd been looking at expanding into other areas, such as Ohio, and were interested in his proposal. This interest had almost cost Townsend his life on his cold, snowy hike in the Smokies.

~

"Tanning wasn't new to Blount County or Maryville." Mr. Fisher stated. "Wild animal skins and cattle hides were processed in the lower Appalachians, starting in the late 1700's. In fact, many of the skins came from the coves of the Smoky Mountains, and even the Cherokees sold them to local small tanners."

John Anderson added, "Tanned hides supported the making of saddles, clothes, and shoes using different grades of leather produced locally. These men were small entrepreneurs. The banks in the area knew of them."

Noah added, "Timber was also harvested on a smaller scale for housing and fuel for fire. We have numerous small sawmills at home, and our Chilhowee Lumber Mill is running from dawn to dark."

Townsend nodded at Noah's comment. "In our company's case, the prospect of cutting timber on a large scale within the southern area was made more attractive, because Fisher would be an immediate customer, and there was an extensive network of railroads. Getting sawn wood to the market place by rail was less expensive, and the product moved to its end customer faster."

"The mountain people of Tennessee provided an inexpensive and plentiful labor supply with a strong work ethic." Anderson gestured to those at the table. "W.B. and especially his wife, Margaret, have returned the worker's faithfulness by making sure Townsend has good schools, churches, a community market place, and activities they otherwise wouldn't have."

Townsend shook his head. "I couldn't say anything negative about the beautiful Great Smoky Mountains. This area was full of virgin timber with magnificent trees. By 1901, we constructed the tracks of Little River Railroad from Walland to Tuckaleechee Cove and beyond. We bought up thousands of acres of mountain land, built the lumber mill, hired a crew, and started cutting timber. Fisher's Schlosser Tannery opened in 1902 with a good supply of bark."

"The rest, as they say, is history," laughed John Anderson, interrupting his friend's commentary.

Fisher added, "Our mountain wood has been shipped to the major capitals of Europe. Cherry, walnut, oak, and hickory are in some of the most famous buildings in the world. I wish I could say that about our tanned goods."

"Yes," replied W.B. "and we've completed the railroad bed into Elkmont, where we're cutting timber for the mill at Townsend. You must visit someday, Noah, and observe the operation. It's impressive." Mr. Townsend continued, "Have you been to Townsend?"

"No. My store keeps me busy at home."

"Please come. The process involved building a dam across Little River to hold the logs, the mill pond, the entranceway into the cutting operation, and the circular sawing of wood. I'll take you up to Elkmont on the new spur and treat you to dinner at the Wonderland Hotel. D.H., you're welcome to come also," he added as an afterthought.

Mr. Townsend was impressed with D.H. although he mainly dealt with John in his bank dealings.

The meal was over. Its participants adjourned to the extensive parlor. The men, still talking business, sat by themselves to the right of the staircase, and the women occupied the other half which contained the piano. Mrs. Anderson asked Juliet to play a song for everyone. The conversation was light and cheerful.

Melva positioned herself next to Mrs. Townsend. After playing the piano, Juliet came and sat next to her.

"Do you enjoy living in the mountains?" Melva wanted to know Mrs. Townsend much better, and she wasn't afraid to ask questions.

"Yes, I do. But I travel by train to Pennsylvania quite often."

"I've been in the state of North Carolina," said Melva. "I'd like to travel all over the world, but I probably never will."

"I didn't think I would either, but sometimes situations change. I married W.B., and he has included me on many of his trips. I've been to England and France on sales trips with him."

Melva had never met anyone who had been overseas. She was anxious to hear about Big Ben and the Eiffel Tower. The conversation continued for several minutes on Mrs. Townsend's overseas trips.

Finally, Juliet asked Melva what she was going to do the next day.

"Father has said I may go shopping. Would you like to come with me?" asked Melva turning to face her new friend.

Juliet looked at her mother with the question in her eyes.

"Yes, Juliet. I suppose you may go," said her mother. "Will there be a chaperone along, Melva?"

"No. Father thinks I'm old enough to go by myself. It's only two blocks from Blount Hotel."

Mrs. Townsend spoke up. "Girls, I'm remaining in town overnight, let me pick you both up and take you shopping." Turning to Mrs. Anderson she added, "Stella go with us."

Wow! thought Melva. Things were looking up.

After the final arrangements were talked through, Juliet was allowed to go with Melva and stay all night at the hotel. Mrs. Townsend would stay at the Anderson home, and both women would drive over to pick up the girls the next morning after breakfast.

The two girls bounded up the stairs to Juliet's bedroom to pack her small bag. A few minutes later, they were out the door and riding to the hotel.

～

The car arrived the next morning, making all kinds of weird noises. Noah opened the door and helped Juliet and then Melva into the back seat. He stood on the boardwalk of the hotel and waved goodbye before crossing the street to the courthouse.

"Melva, we're taking the scenic route," Mrs. Townsend said over the noise the car was making.

She circled through the grounds of Maryville College, coming out at Washington Avenue. "If you turn right, Melva, you're headed in the direction toward my house." Mrs. Townsend was having a hard time turning left, because the car was hard to steer.

Melva looked in the direction Mrs. Townsend indicated. All she could see was a dirt road heading into the forest. In the background, the hazy Smoky foothills were visible above the trees.

The road, like the train, headed toward Townsend generally following Little River. The train track going east and west was across the road from where they were turning. "How far is it to your home?" asked Melva.

"It's about sixteen miles from here. I usually ride the train into town and pick up the car at the depot." Mrs. Townsend completed turning left onto Broadway.

"Do you have another car in Townsend?" asked Melva.

"Yes, I have one to drive around in the area, but most places I walk.

Townsend had many stores, but none of them were built of brick like the Maryville stores. Much of Townsend was exposed to flooding, because Little River ran through it.

Broadway, on the other hand, ran north-south along the top of the hill. Because the stores were built on a hill, they usually had three floors. The top two were dedicated to merchandising or rental as apartments or businesses. The bottom floor was used as storage or for small shops, even cafés run by the businesses above.

Mrs. Townsend stopped in front of Badgett's, the only large department store in Maryville. Horses pulling buggies looked white-eyed at the strange, noisy contraption pulling in beside them. This car was the only one on Broadway. Melva had a strange urge to get out of the auto and put its reins over the hitching rails provided for the horses. Of course, cars didn't have reins.

"We're here. Everyone out," Mrs. Anderson said.

Badgett's was a forerunner of a more modern department store. The women's section was on the entire main floor, and the men on the upper. A wide staircase allowed customers to access the upper floor. The basement contained items both sexes would purchase like watches, a shoe department, and sale area. Bargain basement certainly described a large part of this floor.

Some sections on the higher floors contained a concentration of different sets of items such as hats, jewelry, or clothes. Dress or suit racks were built into the side walls and ran the length of the business. The ladies headed toward the racks and started searching through the different styles and colors. Dress hems were shorter this year exposing shoes and ankles.

Although not primarily someone who needed lots of clothes, Melva was enjoying her first shopping trip. She and Juliet looked at large furry, hand-muffs, on a stand near the center aisle—something any girl would love.

"I like this white one. It would look great with most of the colors I wear, especially my green and blue velvet dresses," said Juliet.

Melva usually stuck her gloved hands in the pockets of her coat, but she could see a natural brown one with her brown coat. She must choose wisely because her money wouldn't buy much.

"Juliet, I need dress shoes for Sunday." Melva put down the furry muff.

"We need to take the steps to the basement. Badgett's has a good supply of shoes—all kinds." She grabbed Melva's hand and headed for the back of the store. "Mama we're going to look at shoes."

They headed downstairs, Juliet in the lead. Most of the shoes Noah carried were serviceable, work shoes. He didn't have a line of dress shoes, although they could be ordered out of the store's catalogues.

Melva was thrilled by the different kinds of heeled shoes that Badgett's stocked. Walking through the extensive display of paper shoe boxes, she was drawn by some black patent heels. She sat on a small stool while a salesman measured her foot with a metal contraption.

The salesman left for the stockroom, returning with Melva's shoe size. He knelt in front of her and placed the shoes on her feet. They were lace up so he tied the black strings, and she stood up.

"I think those are nice," said Juliet. "I have a pair almost like them which I wear during the spring and summer."

Melva checked out their looks in a small mirror sitting on the floor. They were perfect. She bought them.

"I love your shoes," Juliet said as soon as Melva received her written receipt and took the paper bag with her purchase inside. "Let's go back upstairs and look at dresses." Juliet was an outgoing young woman who never slowed down.

Melva followed her up the stairs to join Mrs. Townsend and Juliet's mother.

A new dress was something she desired but didn't necessarily need. She looked at them anyway, picking out a two-piece, coral-colored one which had a hip-length but light, weight coat.

Mrs. Townsend said the two-piece dress suit was worn everywhere in the north. It was a new design by one of the famous New York designers. Of course, his idea was copied by many clothiers, and soon everyone had their version in the department stores.

"Melva, you will be right in style!" exclaimed Juliet when she appeared in the new dress to walk in front of the tall mirror next to the dress racks.

"She's right. You look lovely," Mrs. Townsend agreed.

Actually, Melva would be right out of style in Chilhowee, but she entertained the prospect for a moment, deciding against it.

"Mrs. Townsend, I've been looking at your pierced ears. Where did you have them done? I think I would like to do mine." Melva was really interested.

"My Pennsylvania doctor did mine. He used a needle to make the hole and put my gold earrings in immediately. I had to turn them and use alcohol swabs for several days. I'm told you can do them yourself with ice and a large needle."

Melva decided she would wait before starting that adventure.

"Ladies, I think we've had enough shopping, and I'm getting hungry. Does anyone else want to go eat?"

Mrs. Anderson smiled and picked up her purchases. "Margaret are you ready?"

"I am. Let's go."

Shopping was over, and lunch at a small restaurant not far down the street was on the agenda. The girls walked ahead chattering away.

After lunch, Melva and Juliet decided to walk back to her hotel. Juliet was to stay the afternoon, and her father would pick her up after work. They made a detour to Blount State Bank where her brother worked. He was behind the cage and saw them enter the building.

"Madame's, may I help you," he said in his best clerical air as the girls approached his window.

The girls giggled. Melva spoke up. "Father told me to lunch with you tomorrow. I wanted to make sure this was okay."

"If it isn't fair lady, I will cancel all unimportant appointments and indeed have lunch with you." Melva looked around to see why he was showing off. Only men worked the cages.

"Is noon the best time?" inquired Melva.

"Perfect," said D.H. coming around the counter. He offered an arm to each young lady and escorted them to the front entrance, bowing as they left.

Outside, Juliet couldn't contain her laughter while Melva just shook her head. Her brother, the showoff! He was charming, she had to admit.

Noah needed one more day to be present for his meetings, since not much business was on the docket this quarter.

On her second day in town, Melva was in no hurry to get out of bed. Her toilette was longer than usual, but finally she graced Maryville with her presence. She took a short walk down Broadway before joining her brother for lunch. The hardware store looked inviting, so she went inside to look around. The variety of merchandise available was extensive, making her father's gadget and tool area small indeed.

Back out on the boardwalk, she stopped at the theatre and read each poster on present and future attractions. She looked at pierced earrings in the jewelry store window and passed a music store. A sign advertised a local beauty parlor, and she had just enough money to get her hair done. She decided against it. Her father was a man who taught restraint. He didn't believe in spending your last dollar and neither did she. Besides, she wanted to take her mother and Lydia some candy. This trip wasn't all about her. The headline on the paper in the newsstand outside the local drugstore read, *New Mexico Becomes the 47th State.*

Abruptly, she realized she hadn't thought about Edgar or Betty Jo since arriving in town. She felt a little bit guilty.

Lunch with her brother was always special. Afterwards, he took her to The Candy Kitchen where she bought handmade chocolates to take home on the train the next morning. D.H. planned to eat supper with them at Blount Hotel that night.

The train ride home was *almost* uneventful. Cal McMurray helped Noah with their suitcases and purchases, stowing them overhead. Her father carried a rather large box as they entered the passenger coach. After they were comfortably settled in their seats, Melva's father laid the box in her lap.

"Open it," he said.

When Melva opened the box, the lovely, coral, dress suit appeared beneath the tissue that was covering it. She was so excited. Leaning over, she kissed her father and gave him a huge hug, knocking his glasses awry on his nose.

Noah laughed, pleased that his daughter was happy.

Upon arriving home on the train, Melva found out she had the sniffles. The sniffles turned into a fever and her lungs felt like they had rocks in them. She was so sick. When she opened her mouth, she croaked like a frog until she came down with laryngitis and couldn't make a sound. She didn't go to church for two Sundays and her mother stayed home to take care of her needs. She felt so bad, she wasn't sorry she didn't get to dazzle everyone with her new dress suit.

~

Melva and Betty Jo had a patched-up relationship. Their bond was never the same again, and they didn't sit together at church on Sunday. Melva never spent another night at the Boyd's. When Betty Jo was married the first day in April to Robert Ownby, Melva went to the wedding and wished her friend the best. She avoided Edgar like the plague.

Robert and Betty Jo settled into quarters provided by the Mill and became involved in the Mill culture, participating in the activities provided for their employees. The marriage further distanced the two friends. From time to time, Betty Jo took time to stop and see Melva at the store.

~

On April 12th, it started to rain. The sky opened up and poured water out of buckets for two days.

On Sunday, April 14, 1912, the night the Titanic hit the iceberg off the coast of Newfoundland, Chilhowee was bracing for a terrible flood. Church was cancelled since water covered the train tracks from Maryville, and Elder Hall couldn't get there.

Noah's store was on higher ground, but it would not be safe if it kept on pouring rain. The railroad was at risk and the lumber mill was in crisis. The water crept over Noah's bottomland farm. His barn looked like it floated on the water surrounding it. The livestock and horses were moved to the Boyd's in Happy Valley. From her upstairs bedroom, Melva viewed the impending disaster.

Noah, Nancy, Melva, Milton, and Matthew worked steadily to place the store's merchandise out of harm's way as best they could. Using the countertops and built-in shelving, they furiously stacked the merchandise sitting on the floor onto higher resting places. The water lapped at the road in front of the store as they walked across the street to their home. Within one hour, it was completely covered.

The Tipton house across the street was susceptible but not as much at risk as the store. The house sat about four feet higher than the business, requiring steps to descend to street level. Surrounded by trees and a picket fence with gate to the road, it would be protected from flotsam on the waters, should the river rise that high.

"This looks like a bad one," Nan said, opening the door so the others could walk into the house. The exhausted family sat down in the parlor. Noah went to get the Bible off the hall table. After all, it was Sunday, and today especially this family and the others within the flood's path needed God's protection. He turned to Psalms 23 and read the first two verses. *The LORD is my shepherd; I shall not want. He maketh me to lie down in green pastures: he leadeth me beside the still waters.*

And then he prayed.

Melva did not remember much of the short prayer but this, *"Father, you are our comforter and help, our only help in time of need, and we need you now. Keep my family and the others in the Cove who will be affected by these waters safe. I pray for the still waters of restoration and peace during this time of crisis. You are LORD of this family and praised in all things."* Noah continued but Melva didn't hear another word. She wondered what her world would look like tomorrow.

Sunrise on Monday morning revealed the extent of the water's coverage. It was at the top of the last step into Noah's store. It covered the railroad rails and the road. Sawn lumber from the lumber mill floated atop the broad lake outside and huge logs floated by. The mill pond containing hundred's of logs was flooded. The timber was lost down river. It would be days, if not weeks before the mill would open to cut more product. Houses in the lowlands, along the river and up the coves leading to the Little T were flooded, some were washed away and others collapsed.

Milton and Matthew hung out on the picket fence around the house, looking at the lake formed by the flooding waters. Each hour they entered the house and gave a blow by blow description of the scene around them.

Nan spent her time cooking, cleaning, and darning clothes. Noah read a new book written by Zane Grey called *Riders of the Purple Sage*. Because he had relatives in Missouri, he was interested in the west and all things western.

Melva couldn't figure out what to do with herself. She was outside, inside, playing games with Lydia, looking at old magazines, and pacing the floor. Tomorrow couldn't come too soon for her.

In the early afternoon, on her last trip outside, she came back with good news. "Father, the water's receding."

Noah jumped up to look. "Thank you, Lord!" The water did not get into the store.

～

The Tennessee River was notorious for great floods. Water rushed down the extensive Tennessee Valley watershed and flooded the city of Chattanooga. This city was at the lower end of the valley, situated on Horseshoe Bend where the famous Civil War battle took place.

The proposed Alcoa's dams would control the flooding for the valley and cove residents along the Little T, and building them was in the near future. The one saving grace about flooding in the Chilhowee area was the water didn't stay in flood stage very long. It would go down as fast as it came up, and this rush of water added good soil to the inundated Tennessee Valley flatlands.

On Tuesday morning, the river was almost back within its banks.

A thin layer of mud and debris was everywhere. The outside world seemed to have turned reddish, or dirty-brown.

Other areas were flooded, including Cades Cove, but Chilhowee and its surrounding neighbors were hit the hardest. Happy Valley suffered the least damage, and the waters did not reach the Boyd's house.

Most Abram's Creek homes were devastated, because the run off from Cades Cove and the watershed of Abram's Creek flooded the area. The main part of the water was slower to reach their secluded cove, giving them more time to remove the furniture from the houses in the area.

Those who weren't in harm's way soon appeared in the area that was. Bringing mops, hoes, shovels, other tools, and cooked food, they went to work helping their neighbors dig out of the mud. Soon the smoke from multiple fires was seen in the lowlands as trash, ruined furniture, mattresses, and other debris burned in heaps.

That wasn't the only way the fortunate participated. Seeing the needs of those they were helping, they emptied their own homes of items they could spare, giving them to those whose homes were inundated—amazing what came from barn lofts and sheds.

After breakfast on Tuesday morning, Noah organized his family to help. Nan and Lydia would open the store and serve sandwiches, coffee, and water to the people who were flooded out—as long as supplies lasted. He, Melva, Matthew, and Milton were to start up the railroad tracks with tools and cleaning supplies. They'd help the first family they came to, cleaning their home, or any other task the folks needed done. Donning their galoshes, Noah and his little crew headed out, leaving four sets of footprints in the newly deposited mud.

A widow, Mrs. Lindsey, lived in the first small house. She lived above the railroad tracks which ran to the mill and traded at Noah's store.

"I hope she's safe," he told Melva, when he was in sight of her house. Before the water went down, he had no way to find out, since he didn't own a boat, and the water was too high to walk to her house.

Multiple tracks in the mud outside her house relieved his worry.

"Mrs. Lindsey," he called. "It's Noah Tipton. Please open the door. We've come to help you." No response.

"Mrs. Lindsey," Noah called louder. "Are you alright?"

The crew was startled when she appeared from the back of the house. She was covered with dirt and much disheveled. She carried a bag in her hand.

"Noah," she exclaimed with tears in her eyes. "Thank God you've come. I been trying to clean up the back porch, but things is such helter-skelter and so heavy. I don't have the strength for nothin.'"

"We'll help you. Are you all right?"

"I do look a mess. I'm doin' purt well, since I slept on the hill yonder." She pointed to the one back of the house. "I took my treasures in a tow sack with me, 'cause I was afeard the water would go into the house. Don't have much stuff to worry about."

Noah followed her in the front door. Most of her belongings, although still sitting in their normal places, were covered with a thin layer of mud. Assessing the situation, Noah felt he could leave Melva in charge of helping this small, fragile old lady. There was work for them to do before he could move the largest pieces outside. Some items looked damaged beyond repair.

He and the boys went on to the next home, promising they would be back to move the heaviest things.

Melva looked at the impossible task before her. She walked around the yard and through the house. The water had risen to the tops of the low windows but hadn't invaded the attic.

"Mrs. Lindsey, we need heat." The sun felt good when they were outside, but inside the house was chilly and damp. The rain had brought cooler temperatures. "I brought some rags for cleaning," Melva indicated a canvas bag in the parlor. "Do you have a bunch of old rags we can use to wipe the stove—and how about wood?"

"Wood's in the shed, and I toted two buckets of water from the spring. It's on the back porch."

The two women were soon swiping the kitchen cook stove, removing the old ashes, and even moping the floor underneath. The shed outback provided enough dry wood to start a fire, making the next work more pleasant, starting the drying process within the whole house.

Melva looked around the rooms. Since the water had only come to the tops of the windows, everything above them was clean, including the ceilings.

Melva suggested they start with cleaning out the kitchen. "You could sleep and eat in this room, while we work on the bedroom and parlor."

"Yes, I'd have all I want in this room."

"We'll need more buckets and water."

"Come here." The buckets were on the back porch. Clean water would have to be carried from the spring behind Mrs. Lindsey's home. "I'll get the water."

"No. Let me." Melva tried to take the buckets from the elderly woman.

"Melva, I can tote water. You start taking the dishes outen the cupboard, so it can be moved. Thar's dishpans under the sink and a large one on the back porch. It's possibly clean."

Melva watched her walk along a well-worn path to the spring. She turned and entered the kitchen. Bending over, she pulled the wet cloth covering the opening under the sink. The pans were full of muddy water. Carefully, she lifted each container and going to the back porch emptied its contents—hanging each on nails driven into the cabin walls.

Everything in the house was covered with a thin layer of mud except the dishes stored above the waterline. Melva got the large dishpan and a rickety step stool from the back porch. Mrs. Lindsey came just as she was starting to pull plates, cups, and saucers from the shelves.

The stool wobbled as Melva got down. "Here, let me help you. We need gallons of hot and cold water."

They cleaned one of the big pots, filled it with water, and placed it on the stove to heat. Another dishpan was cleaned and the remaining water was poured into it as rinse water.

"We have a lot of work to do," Melva said, pulling in a sigh and looking about the kitchen. Mrs. Lindsey didn't answer.

Melva looked around at her. Mrs. Lindsey's eyes were moist with tears.

"I'm so sorry this happened to you." What else could Melva say?

The elderly woman started to shake and then sob. Melva took two steps and put her arms around her, holding her tight until she was quiet. She was vulnerable and frail when faced with the task before them.

"Oh, Melva, so many times in my long life I've asked the question, 'Why?' Sooner or later, I'll know the answer."

"I'm here, and we'll get this job done. I won't leave until you're comfortable and I'm sure my father will never quit until you are safe and contented."

When Mrs. Lindsey could talk she said, "The Lord works in mysterious ways, doesn't He? Everything happens for a reason. Don't you think so, Melva?"

"I certainly do," she assured the elderly lady. But, did she?

The spell of crying was over. "Let's roll up our sleeves and get to work."

Melva couldn't help but smile as she looked at Mrs. Lindsey's clothes. She had an idea. "Where are your clothes and linens?" This seemed like a dumb question compared to what needed to be done. "We'll wash them and put them on your clothes line in the back yard so they can dry."

Soon clean pans filled with hot water sat on the dirty kitchen counter. The two scrubbed Mrs. Lindsey's clothes and bed linens, placing the wet items on the back clothes line.

Melva went into the house to finish removing the dishes from the cupboard, and Mrs. Lindsey left for more water.

She was working intently at her job, standing on the rickety stool and noisily, stacking glass plates in a round pan.

With her head stuck in a cabinet, she didn't notice a shadow at the open front door, nor hear footprints on the floor behind her.

"Ma'am, let me help you move that," a male voice said.

Melva almost jumped out of her skin. The stool gave way, and she sat down flat on the muddy floor, the round pan containing Mrs. Lindsey's dishes caught firmly in the hands of the man towering over her. She turned slightly and looked up into the gray-blue eyes of Burl Whitehead.

Chapter Seven

Getting to Know You

*The voice of my beloved! behold, he cometh leaping
upon the mountains, skipping upon the hills.*

Song of Solomon 2:8 KJV

It's strange how things happen, thought Melva.

It was early summer, and life after the flood was back to normal or at least it was normal for some of the cove residents. Because of the April flood, it would never be normal for her again.

～

The Chilhowee Lumber Mill was the first place to flood. When it became obvious the Little T would overrun its banks, Betty Jo and Robert Ownby's small company home located on the Mill's property was in harm's way like the rest of the mill's operations. Edgar brought the farm wagon and helped them stack their belongings onto its bed. The newly married couple hadn't been in their new quarters but days. They moved most of their possessions before the main flood and stored them in Marlon's barn.

Realizing the pending disaster, Burl Whitehead and the other men started clearing out their living quarters at the Mill. Cots, sleeping pads, food, and other housing needs were packed out by horse drawn wagons, mules, and on foot before the camp flooded — the last loads in ankle-deep water. Once the buildings were cleaned, the residents could move back in with much the same belongings as before. Their thoughtfulness saved the company hundreds of dollars.

Barns of local residents were loaned as sleeping quarters. In the lofts, the men reclined on sweet-smelling hay with their worldly possessions in sacks at their feet. After two nights spent in the safety of these haylofts, the men were ready to help. On Tuesday morning, the waters still covered the lowest bottomland, including most of the mill. Burl Whitehead and his brothers set out down the railroad tracks looking for someone in charge. This is where they ran into Noah and his sons who were walking toward them.

"Good morning, I'm Burl Whitehead, and these are my brothers, Willard and Leonard. We work on the surveying crew for the Bertrams. How can we help?"

"The task is great," said Noah shaking his head. "We can use your help. I'm Noah Tipton. I run the store at Chilhowee. My daughter, Melva, is down at Widow Lindsey's," he pointed to a small house one-half mile away. "If you can go help her, I'd appreciate it. Your brothers can come with me. They're needed to help with other homes which are close by."

"I'll be glad to do that," said Burl who was sure he remembered the mentioned young lady. He bid his brothers goodbye and promised to be back to their shelter by dark.

Noah watched him stride confidently toward the small house, his long legs making short work of the distance.

Noah guessed that Leonard probably wasn't over seventeen. But he was wrong. Later, he found out Leonard or Len as Willard called him was twenty. He just looked younger. In fact, Willard was younger at eighteen than both brothers. Noah turned around and headed for the next creek bed. Several families lived up this hollow.

It didn't take long for Burl to cover the ground to Mrs. Lindsey's. He walked up the porch steps and peered within. For a few seconds he did not see clearly. His eyes needed to adjust to the darkness inside. Then he picked out the form of a young girl on a stool, trying to hold a pan full of dishes as she pulled others from a shelf in front of her.

And that's the way Burl Whitehead ended up at Widow Lindsey's and into the world of Melva Tipton.

∽

After her initial shock, Melva got up off the floor helped by the man of her dreams, who extended his hand in her direction. Her prince wore overalls and a blue shirt.

"Name's Burl, Burl Whitehead," said the tall, curly-haired one. Sorry, I didn't intend to scare the livin' daylights out of you."

"Guess there's no reason to worry about the mud on my clothes," she said, grabbing her skirt and giving the cloth a shake. "They'll wash." No longer tongue-tied, she felt free to talk.

"Your father sent me to help you clean up. What do you want to do first, Miss Tipton?" asked Burl.

"First," replied Melva, "call me Melva.

Then she explained her plan to clear out the house. "We decided to clean the whole kitchen area. Mrs. Lindsey can use this room for sleepin', cookin', and eatin' until the other rooms are ready to move into. From there it's take out the furniture, wash down the walls, and clean the floors. Next, each piece of furniture needs to be cleaned and replaced in its previous position in the house."

Burl was agreeable. "Do you want the kitchen table moved?"

"Yes, and the chairs. I have some rags, if'n you can clean them."

Mrs. Lindley came through the back door. "Who's this handsome feller?" she asked smiling. "One of yer friends, Melva?"

"No, ma'am.   Burl answered. "We've seen each other a couple of times."

Melva was rummaging in the rag box. Wow! He remembers me.

"I'm here to help you and carryin' water is one of my chores after I put the table and chairs wherever Melva wants them."

Melva looked around to find him watching her. "I think the front porch. The sun will make cleanin' them there a warm job."

Moving the table and chairs didn't take long. He left the house with two five-gallon pails in the spring's direction. Melva stepped to the door. She watched his long stride as he disappeared into a hollow behind the house. She smiled. He *was* a handsome man.

She and Widow Lindsey packed items to be moved from the kitchen in anything that would serve as a container. Finally, everything was gone except the empty dish cupboard.

Burl put his latest buckets of water on the floor. "Do you want me to move the cupboard to the front porch?"

"Yes," Melva said. "I'll start washing down the walls. Do you mind helping me with that? As soon as they're washed, we'll scrub the floor."

The three worked together to get the kitchen clean.

"Do you ever eat a noon, or maybe it's afternoon meal now, Melva," Burl asked. He said her name easily. He had gone to the front door to look out. "The suns probably in the two o'clock position."

"Oh! I'm so sorry," exclaimed Mrs. Lindsey. "I don't have a thing to offer except some dry crackers an' canned tuna. Can you eat that?"

Her fare probably wouldn't fill up Mr. Whitehead's holler leg, but Melva knew where food could be had. "Don't worry. If Burl doesn't mind a short walk, my mother has sandwiches and drink at the store. Maybe he'll go get our dinner?"

"I'll get two more buckets of water and be on my way."

Melva wrote a quick note to her mother. Burl took the note with him.

After he left, the two women used the broom and mop on the last wall. "If'n the walls was dry, I'd get some paint outen the wood shed and give 'em a goin' over."

"Maybe we can do that tomorrow or the next day."

"He's a right, good-looking feller, isn't he?" Mrs. Lindsey looked at Melva when she made the statement. "Is he eligible?"

"Yes, to both questions."

"I think you like him?"

Melva's smile was wide. "Maybe I do."

～

When Burl came back, he was loaded down with all kinds of supplies, some of them she hadn't asked him to bring.

He placed a paper bag on the counter and started pulling out the contents. "Thought we might need candles, bread, peanut butter, and here's the mat you wanted, to make a bed in the kitchen floor for Mrs. Lindsey. Your mama sent a sheet and blanket. They're rolled up in the pad. She said to tell the widow *'don't worry about sending them back.'* Just to keep them."

Melva looked into the picnic basket. "There's enough food in here for dinner and supper and even some eggs. Mrs. Lindsey you can have eggs and toast for breakfast!"

The older woman smiled and took the eggs, handling them as if they were gold or silver. "This'll be the best mornin' meal I've ever had," she said, putting them on the counter. "I turned my chickens out of the pen so they wouldn't drown. Haven't seed 'em since."

Burl laughed. "What a load." He stretched his back and arms. "See if'n I volunteer to go get eats again. I'm surprised the kitchen sink isn't in there."

Melva was smiling at him. She didn't have to tell him everything. He could think for himself.

"I did tell your mother if we had to work until dark, I'd walk you home."

What a statement! Dark, huh! Melva was grinning inside. Dark it would be.

The three of them walked up the hillside behind the house and sat on a rotting log. They ate the bologna sandwiches and pickles Nan served to anyone coming to the store.

"Did Mother say if others were coming for supplies?" asked Melva.

"Not many. It seems most of the helpers brought enough supplies for themselves and the people they were helping. She said kerosene was sellin', because people needed a way to start a fire with wet wood. Others are buyin' supplies and takin' them back to restock the homes of those they're helping." Burl got up and went for the water buckets.

Melva sat in the warmth of the sun, her face tilted upward, and her eyes closed. She didn't want to move. Her body was starting to ache. She breathed deeply, pulling in a bunch of air and letting it out slowly. She heard movement on the hill. When she opened her eyes, Burl was standing with his hand held out in her direction.

"Let's go back to work," he said simply. On arriving at the kitchen, he poured out his full buckets and headed back toward the spring. Melva watched him go. Her heart was smiling.

By the end of the day, the kitchen was clean, top to bottom. All the can goods were scrubbed and placed in the cupboards including the can of tuna and box of crackers. New supplies that Nan sent with Burl were placed alongside.

Burl built the fire up in the stove until it was almost glowing. The extra heat started aggressively drying out the kitchen and the parlor.

"I think we should clean the couch and put it in the kitchen. The cloth and horsehair will dry fast."

"Yes. We could pull the dust cloth off the bottom and expose the springs and underneath first, drying the top last." Melva suggested.

After the three took soap and water to the cover and wood legs, Burl hefted the couch to his shoulder and carried it close to the stove. He tilted the divan until Melva could grasp the dust cover and remove it. They placed the piece of furniture on two extra buckets with the underside open to the stove.

"We'd better keep checking on it. Don't want to let it get too hot," Melva said, touching the wood and cloth.

"Have you two thought about the mattress on the bed? Don't you think we need to check and see how bad it is?" Burl asked, heading for the bedroom.

The three pulled the mattress off the bed and stood looking at it.

"Don't think its salvageable, Mrs. Lindsey. Maybe we can find another one."

Burl rolled the tick up, took it outside, and placed it on the roof of the wood shed. They were washing down the walls of the parlor when Noah returned and entered the house.

"You've made real headway," he observed, walking around. "The kitchen is useable. There's still a lot of work to do. Guess we'd better quit for today and start in again tomorrow."

"Father, we want to work until we get the walls done in the parlor."

"It's almost dark now, Melva. I—"

"Mr. Tipton, I'll walk her home when we finish."

Noah looked at Melva. "I'm tired, but if she wants to stay longer and you'll walk her home, I'll not object. I think the boys are exhausted too." Noah walked down the porch steps and headed toward Chilhowee. He turned around and came back. "Burl, thanks for helping today. Without your assistance, Melva wouldn't have gotten as much done." Noah held out his hand and Burl leaned down from the porch and shook it. "Your brothers said they'd meet you at John Hill's barn."

Melva wondered if she would see Mr. Whitehead again. He answered that question in his response to Noah.

"There's still much to be done. If it's okay with Melva and Mrs. Lindsey, I would like to work with them tomorrow and until the job is done." Burl said this looking at Melva who was looking at her father.

"Melva, what do you think?" said Noah.

"I'd like to have Mr. Whitehead help us tomorrow."

"Then it's settled. Good night, Mrs. Lindsey."

For another two hours Mrs. Lindsey's crew labored at cleaning the walls of the parlor. Finally, they turned the couch over and sat down on it to eat their supper. The seat was warm and toasty.

The afternoon sun had set behind the Chilhowee Mountains as Burl walked Melva home. He carried a candle to illuminate the road. On the way, Melva asked him about the Mill and where he and his brothers were staying.

She stopped at the picket fence. "Thank you for bringing me home, Mr. Whitehead. I'll see you tomorrow."

"Melva, my name's Burl," he said. "That is, if you want me to help tomorrow."

"Thank you, Burl. See you tomorrow."

She opened the gate, walked through, and closed it. She took a few steps toward the house. The porch light was on. Turning, she went back to the picket fence. She could make out the candle as he headed back toward Mrs. Lindsey's. Its golden glow softly exposed his walkway as his long legs carried him away.

What was it Mrs. Lindley had said about the Lord working in strange—no mysterious ways? Was this His working in her life? Did she believe in Him? Melva was too tired to answer these questions, and she could no longer distinguish the candle.

She walked up the steps to the porch and opened the door. Climbing the stairs took effort. She was aching and tired. She cleaned off with a wash cloth and warm water from the upstairs stove, put on her nightgown, and went to bed. Burl had proved to be someone she could respect and love. Tomorrow, she would get to know him even better.

~

During the next two days these two new friends became comfortable with each other, and their friendship deepened. When the work was over and it was necessary to go home for the last time, Melva lingered on the front porch. She didn't want to say goodbye, but she knew she must.

Mrs. Lindsey looked from the front window, smiling at a budding love between the two young people.

"I hope to see you again, Burl," Melva said lamely. "I work in the store on Friday's." There, she'd given him a day to visit. Then she impulsively stood on tiptoe and kissed him on the cheek. Her face immediately felt hot. She was blushing at her impulsiveness.

Burl could not have been more startled if a rattlesnake had bit him. He was the tongue-tied one now. No one kissed him but his mama.

He stood smiling at her. "I, uh—we'll be cleanin' the Mill, and then it's back to cuttin' timber. Guess we'll be rushed since we've lost work with the flood and all."

Melva realized he wouldn't have much time to socialize or come and see her. It might be months before she'd see him again. Her heart hurt just thinkin' about this fact. She wanted to see him tomorrow! She walked down the steps to the road and headed in the direction of Chilhowee. She felt like crying. Instead, she turned and waved at Burl and Mrs. Lindsey.

Mrs. Lindsey, on the other hand, instinctively knew there was an attraction between them. It was the little things she observed as they helped each other. The unexpected touch, the quiet eye contact, and the intimacy of their close work alerted her to this. She invited Burl to come by and see her again. She would cook for him. And being the matchmaker that she was, she decided to ask Melva at the same time.

~

When the train started to run again, Nan was glad.

"There wasn't a shred of bologna or loaf of bread in Noah's store," she told everyone laughing.

On Wednesday, Peter Hall, plant manager at the Mill, finally managed to return to Chilhowee. He inspected the damage to the mill and realized much work must be done to start the factory again. The lumbermen were capable of helping with this process and the cleanup started. He praised them all for their quick action in saving the companies possessions. Within four weeks the mill was in full operation and sawn timber was moving down the rails.

In May, Noah expanded Melva's hours to three days per week. She worked on Thursday, Friday and Saturday unless her mother needed her help with boarders. Melva enjoyed her interaction with Noah's customers, and they liked her willingness to help. Working was a good way to keep her mind off her PROBLEM, and with the extra money, she bought things for the hope chest she'd started.

"That's your hopeless chest," kidded D.H on one of his few trips home. She'd proudly shown him the cedar wood box with the growing number of necessary items for her future home.

"Well at least I have some hope!" said Melva. "How about you? You're becoming the perennial bachelor."

"Oh, I don't know about that. There are some prospects out there. I just have to decide which one. Get it, which one!" said D.H.

He meant that Melva hadn't many suitors while he, on the other hand, had women falling all over him.

"Well one thing's for sure," said Melva, "I won't have any trouble making up my mind." What else could she say?

She secretly thought her future life might be taking shape, but she hadn't seen Burl since the flood when they both helped Mrs. Lindsey. She comforted herself with the thought that the crews were busy making up for lost time.

She was sure he felt the connection she felt, but why hadn't he visited her. She had shown her interest in him. She kept reliving every moment and everything that was said. Maybe she'd acted too hastily. Her mind kept turning the possibilities over and over. There wasn't any way of knowing.

On June 23, 1912, Melva would celebrate her sixteenth birthday. Sweet sixteen and she'd never been kissed. She walked up to Mrs. Lindsey's to invite her to come.

"Melva, it's so good to see you. Come in."

"Good morning, Mrs. Lindsey. How're you doing?" She gave the elderly woman a hug and looked around at the freshly painted room. "Certainly looks better than the last time I was here."

"My, that was a lot of work, wasn't it?" said the widow, referring to the flood in April. "I hope we never have another one like that again."

"Father says if ALCOA hurries and builds the dams on the tributaries of the upper Little T, flooding will be eliminated."

"I pray they'll hurry." Mrs. Lindsey was speaking from the kitchen. She appeared with milk and cookies.

"Have you heard anything about the surveying crew?" Melva meant Burl but just couldn't admit to Mrs. Lindsey she hadn't heard from him.

Mrs. Lindsey knew exactly the question she asked.

"I saw Burl briefly," she smiled. "He was headed across the mountain to Six Mile. Seems the Bertrams had an emergency on one of their farms. They sent for him and he was hurrying to get there. I invited him to come soon for supper. He said he would, but that was over a month ago. He hasn't come by yet."

"I wonder why he didn't stop to see me," questioned Melva.

"I don't know dear."

"I thought we were good friends," Melva's smile was fleeting as she admitted her feelings. She looked down at her feet, not meeting Mrs. Lindsey's eyes. Looking up she said, "I want to be good friends and..." Her voice trailed off. She wasn't sure what she thought.

"Hmm, I think the first trip to see you will be the hardest, after all this is a boy-girl friendship and that's different." She paused a minute thinking or remembering. "He reminds me of my husband. Frank was not one for jabbering away. When he said something, it was important. He always weighed every decision, you know the *fors and againsts* as he called them, to make up his mind. But when he decided on a course of action, nothing could deter him. Maybe Mr. Whitehead is the same way. He's making an important decision in his life. When he makes it, nothing will change his mind. Mark my words!" Mrs. Lindsey was waving her finger in the air and nodding emphatically.

"You like him a lot, don't you" the widow said.

Melva smiled and simply said, "Yes."

For several minutes the two sat in comfortable silence.

"Will you tell him I was asking about him if you see him?" asked Melva

"You can count on it," said the little old lady, a twinkle in her eye.

Realizing she hadn't accomplished her reason for visiting, Melva asked Mrs. Lindsey to come to her party.

"I'd be delighted," the widow said.

Melva left and headed home.

Mrs. Lindsey lingered on the front porch and watched her as she trudged along. She remembered another time when she waited for her future husband to make the first move. The uncertainty of the situation was the hardest part. If Burl Whitehead didn't show up soon, that young girl would go looking for him. Ah, young love! For a few moments she was sad.

Because Melva's birthday was on Sunday, the Tipton's decided to celebrate it on Saturday night. When the morning train rolled into Chilhowee Depot, Melva's two older brothers were aboard. Henry was now a clerk at Blount State Bank, joining his older brother.

D.H. grabbed his sister, whirling her around saying, "Happy, Happy Birthday, Sister." Henry was much more reserved.

The talk around the table at noon was of the Republican National Convention held in Chicago during the week. William Howard Taft, the 27th president of the United States was nominated to run on the ticket again. His potential opponent was Woodrow Wilson on the Democratic side, but they would not know for sure until around June 25 when the convention convened in Baltimore.

The other fly in the Republican ointment was Theodore Roosevelt. The rumor mill said he would start a third party, the Progressive Party, if he wasn't nominated at the convention. Everyone was waiting to see if this happened.

Melva was glad when the meal was over. Most politics didn't interest her.

Her brothers left with Noah, so she was relieved from this day's store duty. She helped her mother clear the table.

Melva washed the dishes, and Lydia stood on a stool to reach the counter so she could dry them. Soon they were clean and stacked safely into the cupboards.

"Lydia," she asked, "How about going for a walk?" Lydia was more than ready. The two girls didn't have much time to interact as sisters. When they did, Lydia followed Melva around like a puppy dog. Sometimes her adoration wore on Melva's patience. There were times when her mother admonished her for leaving her sister behind, especially when Lydia was younger.

'But mother, she gets under my feet and slows me down.' Whereupon her mother gave her a no back-talk stare, and Melva took her sister by the hand.

Melva went out the back door of the house. She and Lydia walked up the hollow and passed the springhouse built into the side of the hill. To Lydia she pointed out the bird's foot violet, its purple petals standing up proudly in the forest. Closer to the top of the hill, the saintly passion-flower grew in profusion on the bank's side. It's beautiful frilly purple and pink design was the Tennessee State Flower. The small green protrusions growing along its length looked like shriveled apricots. These would become the size of lemons and they were edible fruit in the fall.

Melva pointed out spiderwort.

"Does it give spider's warts?" asked Lydia.

"No." laughed Melva.

"Would I get warts if I touched it?"

"No, you wouldn't.

"Melva do frogs and toads make you have warts?" Lydia was on one of her question and answer sessions.

Melva and Lydia turned left and cut across a ridge on the hilltop heading south toward Tallassee. The trees sheltered them from the sun, which beat down on the forest canopy. Three hundred feet beyond, the trail came out on a bluff cut by the railroad into the mountainside.

This was Melva's *secret place*. From there she and Lydia could see across the cove to the mountains on the far side. They sat on the pungent pine-needled ground. The sun-warmed smells of the pine forest surrounded them. Melva was at peace as she watched several crows sailing above the fields below.

These were the fields where Noah planted acres of corn to harvest for silage or take to the mill to be ground into corn. It was starting to tassel. Up the valley, the barn was filled with the first cutting of winter hay for the cows Noah kept to milk. The herd milled about in ten fenced-in acres to the south of the building. Six horses munched grasses next to the river keeping a watchful eye on a boat downriver. Looking up the valley, she could see houses and smoke from the Mill in the distance.

"Look Lydia, there's Mrs. Lindsey's house. I helped clean it after the flood."

Lydia was peering into the distance, but she couldn't see a house. She did see the train belching steam, preparing to head back to Maryville.

"Melva, I want to take a train ride. Do you think father will take me someday? I want to go shopping like you did and stay at the hotel."

"Of course, he will. You'll need to be a little older to enjoy shopping. What would you buy?" said Melva making conversation. She was amazed Lydia remembered her trip.

Lydia sat for a few minutes in thought. "I'd buy the most beautiful doll in the world, with golden hair and blue eyes. I saw one in the store's catalog like that."

Melva smiled, "I see. What color of dress do you want on it?

"The color of the one you wore to Betty Jo's, green velvet with white lace. You were so pretty, Melva." Lydia turned adoring eyes upon her sister.

"Why don't you go to Betty Jo's now?" The question was unexpected.

Melva explained to Lydia about marriage and that Betty Jo did not live at the Boyd's, but she lived with her new husband in his home.

"Will you get married someday?" This question caught Melva by surprise. Lydia had no idea how much her sister was thinking about this very subject these days.

"Yes, I certainly hope so," said Melva. "I don't want to be a spinster."

"What's a spinster. Is that like someone who spins thread?"

"No silly. It's someone who never gets married," grinned Melva.

"Will you move away when you get married?" Melva detected tears in Lydia's voice. "I might miss you."

"If, and when I get married, I will have too. But that's a long time away."

Lydia was thinking again. "I don't think I like husbands."

Melva was laughing. "You may change your mind about that someday. Look, Lydia! There's a boat on the river. Someone's fishing." Melva hoped this would change the subject.

"I don't like fish. They are too wiggly. One of the boys at school got a fishhook in his finger. I saw the scar," said Lydia.

"He wasn't very careful, was he?"

"No. Look! The man's caught one." Lydia stood up, watching the fisherman pull in his catch.

"I'll bet it's a brook trout and he's going to cook it over his campfire tonight. What do you think?" said Melva, looking up at her. People who could afford to vacation came to the mountains to fish, hike and camp. Many camped on the river bank and cooked over a campfire.

"Maybe so. It may fall off into the fire and burn up."

"Why do you say that?"

"Don't you remember? Mama was roasting some meat over a spit papa had built out back of the house. The meat fell into the fire. Mama said the chunk burnt to a crisp."

Melva laughed. "It's time we head back to the house." She stood up. Lydia continued to watch the boat on the river.

"Where do you think they come from?" asked Lydia.

"I have no idea," replied Melva. "He may be a rich man from Knoxville, a lawyer or doctor, who lives in one of the new cabins by the river."

"I think I'll marry a doctor or lawyer," stated Lydia.

"I hope you do."

Melva and Lydia headed back to the house with Lydia leading the way. It was time to start preparations for the birthday party.

After supper, Melva's hopeless chest continued to be filled with the gifts she received. Her parents gave her a family Bible and a four-place setting of stoneware. This was tableware Noah carried in his store, so she could add more settings at any time.

There was a crocheted doily from Lydia. Melva knew she was working on something important. Each night she'd retire to her special corner and work furiously before going to bed. The stitches weren't quite right, but Melva told Lydia who was sitting at her feet it was perfect. The practical Henry brought an iron skillet for making muffins. Mrs. Lindsey gave her a green, glass bowl that Melva had admired when cleaning her home.

"I'll cherish it," said Melva. "Thank you."

She saved D.H.'s gift for last. The box was flat and not thick at all. She turned it over and over. She had no idea what was inside. It didn't rattle.

"Open the box, Melva," said D.H. and Lydia at the same time.

"Can't I savor the moment?" she said and then she ripped into the package. The gift was the most impracticable one she received but the most wonderful. It was a print of the famous *Blue Boy* oil painting by Thomas Gainsborough in a golden frame. A copy of the painting hung in the Anderson's parlor and Melva instantly loved it. D.H. must have heard her comments. She never thought she would have a copy.

Suddenly a tear fell on the glass. Her birthday would've been perfect if one certain person was there. He wasn't. Where was he?

Nan served her famous pound cake with whipped cream and everyone sat around sharing the events of the day. Finally, Milton and Matthew got up to escort Mrs. Lindsey home. Melva went to wish her a goodbye. They walked out the sidewalk to the steps leading to the street. Mrs. Lindsey hugged Melva and whispered in her ear.

"He'll come. I feel sure of it."

Melva wished she could be as sure.

"Love requires patience, my dear," said Mrs. Lindsey.

❀ Chapter Eight ❀

The Whiteheads

In the morning sow thy seed, and in the evening withhold not thine hand: for thou knowest not whether shall prosper, either this or that, or whether they both shall be good.

Ecclesiastes 11:6 KJV

Burl was in a quandary. He was haunted by two brown eyes that sunk deep into his soul. He couldn't deny his attraction to the Tipton girl, as he started calling her, because that seemed more impersonal and not so intimate. He just couldn't figure out what to do about it. He'd managed during the years after puberty not to get entangled with any woman. It wasn't that he thought the opposite sex was unattractive. He had other more important things to do, like learn to grow vegetables, shoe horses, and blacksmith. His lot was with his father, doing man things, which he learned well.

Burl was twenty-two years old and the eldest son in the family. His father was an expert blacksmith. He found it hard to care for eleven children, so Burl and his other brothers worked to help support the family. The eldest girl child was married. The others helped their mother with the babies. The youngest, a boy, was two years old.

Yes, Burl was in a predicament. He couldn't turn to his brothers. They would only laugh at and tease him unmercifully. It was well-known to them that he shied away from women.

He might talk to Mrs. Lindsey. She seemed understanding and motherly.

He knew a polite call on the Tipton girl wouldn't raise too many eyebrows, but he didn't know if he could resist her charms. He wasn't ready to settle down and marry, so he decided to do nothing.

When the Bertram Brothers sent a message asking him to come back to Maryville, he was ready to go. Putting distance between the Tipton girl and himself might lessen and finally get rid of his attraction and fascination with her.

No. He was not running away, he kept telling himself. He had never run from anything in his life, much less a woman.

But he couldn't keep from stopping at Mrs. Lindsey's to tell her goodbye. Was he hoping she'd get the message to the Tipton girl about his going? He passed close to the Tipton Mercantile Store on his way to Happy Valley. He didn't know it, but Melva was inside waiting on a customer.

When Burl left Chilhowee, he rode one of the Bertram's excellent steeds. The red mule, Johnny, as he was called, was a gelded mule. While working in the field for his employers, Burl was in charge of the animals' upkeep, plus helping the surveying crew. At sixteen, he was employed by the twin brothers, Josten and Jorge, and he had their complete trust. He shod horses using his blacksmithing skills. His patience with even the most ill-tempered horses and mules was well-known.

The brothers always had a good laugh, remembering a time when Burl was training another gelded mule. The brothers had driven to Boone, North Carolina in their Model T to pick him up. Jorge drove the car back, and the big red mule rode in a train boxcar with Josten.

The mule's name was D. Boone. And he did not take kindly to being moved from his home state of North Carolina. On arriving at the Bertram's farm, he was led into the barn. Burl was examining the head of the mule and leaned over to inspect his unshod hooves. At that moment, D. Boone decided to take out his frustration and anxiety on Burl. Boone laid his ears back, indicating he was irritated, and bit Burl on the shoulder.

"You son-of-a-gun," said a startled Burl, whose first inclination was to draw back his fist, which he did, and give that old mule a whack up the side of his head, which he didn't. Mules never forget. If Burl had struck him, Boone would've remembered and waited for him. The next time, the assault might have been more severe. At the very least, it would be humiliating.

While Burl stood there rubbing his smarting shoulder, the Bertram's stood there hee-hawing, excuse the use of the term.

But Burl, who recovered quickly, led the mule to his new quarters. He hadn't been bested by a horse or mule yet. He would win the mule with kindness, and he eventually did.

Even today, a whistle would bring D. Boone ambling across the field so Burl could scratch behind his ears — a favored place for loving on a mule.

The Bertrams always made it clear that he was welcome to use any of their fine stable for his personal use. The red mules were his favorites.

～

It was late May as he rode out of Chilhowee. He stopped at Look Rock to look down into the peaceful valley. This was the same place where Robert and Betty Jo became engaged to marry several months ago. A V-shape in the distance with the far mountain behind was the entrance to the Little Tennessee River Valley and Chilhowee — where she was. They already seemed so far away. He shook his head. What did that matter? He was going home to Six Mile.

He rode along the top of the ridge where he could see on both sides of the mountain. The sun beat down on the old felt hat he wore. The wind sighed through the pine trees and blackberries bloomed in the dry hollows.

"Whoa, Johnny," he said, stopping the red mule at a place where he had a good view of the valley at Six Mile. What a perfect day, he thought.

Looking down over the rolling hills and deep ravines, he saw a road coming from the city of Maryville. It ran as a snake through the forested lowlands until the foothills of Chilhowee Mountain erased its passageway.

"Gitup," he nudged the mule gently in the ribs.

The old Indian path where he was riding ran along the top of Chilhowee Mountain. If he kept going west, he would come out at Tellico Blockhouse on the Little

Tennessee which was only a few miles from the Tennessee River. This blockhouse or fort was built by John Sevier the first governor of Tennessee. To go further west, he would have to swim the Little T or take the ferry at Morganton further down the river.

If Burl turned around and went east along the ridge, he'd come out at Walland where the Schlosser Tannery operated. Here he might cross the railroad and Little River then turn northeast to Townsend and the Little River Lumber Company or if he went southeast he passed through Sunshine, Hubbard and Union Communities before arriving in Maryville.

This morning, Burl was looking for a little-known trail. It was the old Whitehead Trail leading into a hollow and out into the valley where his mother and father lived. This pathway was a well-known shortcut to him. The Whitehead Trail crossed the old Indian path and linked the kinfolks in Cades Cove, Happy Valley and Six Mile.

He found it and turned right heading off the ridge and down into the valley below.

The hollow he rode through might as well be called Whitehead Hollow since it was full of them and their kin. Freshly plowed ground, what could be turned over between the hills, was ready for planting at many of the white frame houses and log cabins. When the earth warmed up, vegetables would be planted or dropped seed by seed into laid-out rows. A good-sized stream ran out of the valley to Six Mile Creek. His father's farm was on the bigger creek, the house situated beneath huge oak trees.

His family didn't expect him, so he decided to stop and see his mother and father. They'd need to know he'd be staying at home and working at the Bertram's farm. His youngest sisters and brothers came running out to greet him, at least those who weren't working the fields.

"Where's your mother?" he asked Raymond who was seven years old.

"She's in the house," replied Tom as he was called who pointed in the direction of the kitchen. How they ever got Tom out of Raymond was a mystery to Burl.

Burl handed Tom the reins of the mule to hold, while he visited with his mother, Sinda. He wouldn't have done this, but he knew the mule was gentle, and would only nuzzle Tom to death.

At least one of the Whitehead sons who worked in Chilhowee managed to get back over the mountains per month. He was responsible for picking up their work money and taking it home to their parents, keeping only a little back for their needs on the surveying crew. The Bertrams furnished everything the crew needed, contracting with Chilhowee Lumber Mill for lodging and food.

"Mama," cried Burl as he entered the house. There were no frills inside. The family couldn't afford them.

Sinda appeared in the kitchen door glad to see her eldest son. She'd birthed a boy older than Burl, but he'd died early in life. Burl was her third child. Lula, her first child, was married and no longer lived at home.

"Son, I'm glad to see you. Nothing's wrong with Leonard and Willard?"

"No. They're fine. I'm back to work at the farm for some reason. I won't know why until I ride on out there," replied Burl.

"It'll be good to have you home. Are you hungry? I have biscuits from breakfast, and I can fry some eggs," said his mother who picked up a newly washed iron skillet ready to start the process.

"I'm really not hungry. Where's dad?"

"I think he went down to the barn to fix one of the hinges on a door. I'm not sure which door." Sinda turned around and kept washing the dishes. She added more hot water from the stove. Dishwater tended to cool quickly, and she liked it steaming.

"Do you need me to carry some water from the spring?"

"No. I'm using the water out of the cistern. We only carry drinking water from the spring. You had quite a flood in April at Chilhowee. Heard the Mill got flooded," said Sinda.

"Yes. If we hadn't moved our belongings, our crew would've been sleeping in a puddle of water. They couldn't operate the mill for days. I suppose our crew might have gone back to work surveying and cuttin' timber, but many people were hurtin', and we decided to help out. I helped clean a widow lady's house, and Leonard along with Willard helped with others. How's dad doing?" asked Burl, changing the subject.

When Willard came over the first of April, before the flood, his father was in bed sick with the flu. Alford never stayed in bed for any reason except to sleep.

"The flu laid him low, that's for sure. I've never seen him that sick. But after three or four days, he was up plowing with Old Spot. He refuses to quit, and I guess that's a good thing with all these young'uns to feed."

"Think I'll go around and see him a minute," said Burl, getting ready to go out the kitchen door.

"Well, let me give you a hug," said his mother. "I'm glad you're home," she said, grabbing him around his broad shoulders with her dripping hands.

"You be good today. You're still not too big to whip," said Sinda. This was his mother's standby phrase. It covered up the emotions she felt.

Burl was pretty sure that her statement wasn't true.

His father was hammering away. He could hear the noise from the back of the barn.

Cool, dark corners greeted him as he entered and stepped to the opposite end. He passed a sign his father had tacked on a stall door. He used it as a teaching tool for his sons. It read, *"A small person can carry a big grudge."* He always said, "Forgivin' is a lot easier than carrying a grudge."

James Alford Whitehead was working on the door on the last stall. He glanced up as his son approached.

"Dad, how are you," asked Burl. "Can I help you with that?"

"Yep, you can hold the door steady so I can nail easier," replied his father. "Old Spot's been gettin' out and feasting on the neighbor's winter lettuce. It's a wonder he doesn't just take a long hike down the road and see the world." Alford wasn't laughing but you could hear it in his voice.

For a few minutes the hammering of nails and testing of the door's swing occupied the two men.

"Are you home to collect your wages?"

"Yes I am, but the Bertrams want me to stay awhile. I don't know how long, and I don't know why.

Guess I'd better head on over that way and find out," said Burl.

"You're welcome to stay here. I'll have Sinda fix up your room."

When you moved out of a room at the Whitehead house, the other urchins moved right in.

"Guess I could stay here in the loft. Old Spot and I are good friends," said Burl. That way he wouldn't disturb the pecking order.

Sleeping in the sweet-smelling hay wasn't a bad idea. If his mother had an extra tick, he wouldn't mind doing just that. He'd wait and see what shook out.

"I'll see you later, Dad. I need to get going."

His father walked him out to Tom and the red mule.

"He's real friendly," said Tom.

"Yes, he is." said Burl, giving Johnny a pat on the rump. He mounted the animal, waved to his dad and Tom, and rode in the direction of the Bertram's farm.

The lane leading into the farm was lined with a white-washed fence typical of those around horse farms. The main house sat on a knoll within a grove of trees to the left. Burl passed it on the way to the barn. Or maybe that was barns. There was a barn for the horses, a barn for milking the cattle, a smaller barn for the various fowl found on the premises and one for the farm machinery and tools. If barns were a symbol of wealth then the man who owned this sprawling acreage was a rich man. The Bertram's extensive holdings allowed them the luxury of doing whatever they wished.

Jorge Bertram wouldn't be at the house. Since Jorge was a man who loved farming, horses, and cattle, he'd be at the barn.

Burl headed in that direction. He rode up to the horse barn and dismounted. There didn't seem to be anyone around. He walked down the rows of stalls, calling each animal by name as he headed for Dark Queen's stall. She was a prize-winning Tennessee Walking Horse shown by the Bertrams.

When she first came to the farm, Burl was her groomer. She liked Burl, and he loved her gentle nature. The chestnut mare with black mane and tail was the most beautiful animal Burl had ever seen. Her long neck, sloping shoulders and smooth gait won the heart of this tall, lanky mountain boy.

The Tennessee Walker was an all-around horse. It could be hitched to a plow, ridden comfortably for long distances, or trained for show.

Before he got to the end, Mr. Bertram appeared from her stall.

"Burl, am I glad to see you," he said closing the distance between them and shaking Burl's hand.

"The Queen's limping, and she won't let anyone touch her. We hoped you might be able to examine her and get her to stand still till we can help her."

"How long has she been limping?" asked Burl. He didn't like to see any animal in pain and this horse especially. She couldn't afford to have foot problems.

"Jake first noticed a problem about five days ago. At first, we didn't think anything about it, but she's gotten worse," said Jorge.

Burl heard a low whinny from the stall. That was her *I recognize your voice sound*. He opened the stall gate and went inside. Going to Queen's head he rubbed her silky nose.

"What's wrong, girl?" he said softly. "What have you been in to? Are you showing a female tendency to be ornery? You should let these men help you. They only want to find out what's wrong." All the time he talked, Burl was rubbing her nose, between her ears and her long neck underneath her black mane. At the same time, he stepped a little farther into her stall.

Dark Queen's head followed Burl's movements and another low whinny said, *I'm warning you don't go any farther.* So, Burl stopped and turned around. He wasn't going to push her. He needed to get reacquainted and build up the mare's trust.

"Jorge, Dark Queen and I need to reestablish our bond, so I'll start feeding and watering her. I'll keep her stall clean, and if you don't mind, I'll probably just sleep down here with her. That's the only way I can think of to quickly build up her confidence in me. We need to check her hoof as soon as possible so she won't have permanent damage," said Burl closing the stall door behind him. There was a small bedroom next to the tack room and running water outside at the watering trough.

"Mind you, she's not a happy horse," said Jorge.

"I realize that. I'll be careful." Even as he said this, Burl knew he must trust Queen, or she would never trust him.

"I'll bring you some supplies and bedding. You must come up to the house to eat your meals." Jorge was already heading in the direction of the house.

"I'd rather eat here, and I can wash up down at the springhouse." Burl called after him. There would be privacy in both places.

Jorge stopped walking, turning he said, "No. I insist. The cook can prepare your meals as you need them. Eat in the kitchen, if you must. There won't be a schedule. And there's a bathroom on the back porch. It's my own personal one that I installed last year. I'm ordering you to use it. Do I need to send Jake to your Dad's house and tell them you will be staying here?" As usual, Jorge was covering all the bases. This was one of his best traits. He was a great organizer.

"Thank you. And yes, send Jake," he said as Jorge continued his walk toward the white house on the knoll.

Burl turned back to Johnny. He unsaddled the red mule and walked him to the pasture behind the barn. "I'll give you a good brushing later," he promised.

Returning, he placed the saddle and bridle in the tack room.

On his way back to Queen's stall, Burl ran through many scenarios connected with her foot problem. She might have thrush. This was an infection on the bottom of the foot, but cleanliness of her stall and her hooves was an obsession with Jorge.

There was founder, or bog spavin, or splints, all painful problems with the legs and hooves. Founder might cause her hoof to become deformed. In that case, she would never be shown again. When Burl thought about each of the possibilities, nothing fit. She has to let us look at her leg and hoof, he thought. He walked back to the barn with a determined step.

Jake came riding down the lane at that moment. They talked several minutes about her condition, and Burl wrote down her feeding schedule.

"I'll take care of her for the next few days," said Burl.

"I don't mind if you do. I'm at my wit's end. I haven't been home for three days," said Jake. And then, "If anyone can touch her leg, you can." Jake Jones was Burl's pupil.

Jorge appeared with the supplies he promised.

"I have confidence in you, Burl." That was all he said.

The next three days, Burl fed Dark Queen, watered her, cleaned her stable and brushed her coat. He rubbed the muscles in her legs and taped the ankles without a problem. Slowly she let him approach the offended area. He could now say with certainty the problem was her hoof.

"You, big baby," he said quietly. "Can't you stand a little pain? You're worse'n Samuel Duggan." Sam was the surveyor on Burl's crew. "He yells if'n you look at him cross-eyed. You don't want me to put you in the same class with him. Do you? That would be embarrassing." Burn kept up his spiel, softy praising one moment and cajoling the next. Dark Queen listened carefully. Her big eyes staring at him intently.

Each night he put his mattress in her stall, and they slept head to head.

On the fourth morning, Burl ate breakfast with Jorge and his brother, Josten.

"I think she may let us look at her hoof this morning. I was close yesterday but didn't want to push her."

"Okay. When do you want us to come down?" asked Jorge.

"Let me run through her routine. Keep watch, and when I start rubbing her legs come then. I hope we'll be ready," said Burl.

After nine days of limping, Queen let the men examine her hoof. She had a deep cut at the back with a rock lodged inside. A few more days and it might have festered enough to come out on its own. But this way, she would heal faster with less scaring. A soft brush cleaned up the area and a healing salve applied with a linen boot would keep out dirt.

"She'll be alright now, Burl. I'm glad it wasn't worse. Do you want to continue staying here in the barn?" asked Jorge. "You could go home to sleep now."

"I'll stay here but in the bunk room. Sleeping with a horse is okay in an emergency, but I wouldn't want to make it permanent," and Burl laughed. He was relieved that Dark Queen was on her way to recovery.

Each day as Burl entered the barn, he was greeted with a low *I recognize you whinny*. And each day, Burl cleaned the hoof and changed the dressing. After three weeks, the cut was healed but the spot was tender. Exercising in the ring and the pasture would take care of that.

First, she needed to get used to the soft dirt of the ring. Jorge and Josten often came to sit and watch her from the fences top rung. Some days they would take over and put the Queen through her paces.

Finally, Burl put her in the pasture. She started to run across the green expanse and thought better of it.

The foot was still tender but improving greatly.

The day Queen ran for the first time in the pasture, Jorge told Burl that he and Josten had purchased two new red mules and wanted him to train them. He wouldn't be going back to the surveying crew for at least three or four months.

Burl went out to the pasture and gave two distinct whistles. From the distance D. Boone and Johnny ambled their way toward him.

Burl had promised Johnny a good brushing. It was time he kept his promise.

Johnny stood still as Burl used the currycomb first, lifting out dirt which flew in all directions. Mules liked to roll in the dirt. As dirt was removed, body oils surfaced. A mane and tail comb straightened out hair tats in these areas. Finally, a good brushing with a body brush removed the dirt and dandruff loosened by the currycomb and made the red mule's coat shine. By this time, Johnny was in mule heaven, and Burl was tired.

"I can't afford you to be jealous, D. Boone. So, you're next." Burl repeated the brushing steps with him.

As Burl was finishing up Boone, Josten Bertram joined them in the pasture.

"George Washington was the first breeder of mules in America," he said.

"I didn't know that," said Burl. "How'd that happen?"

"The best jackasses in the world were raised and bred in Spain, and George wanted a team of them. The Spanish protected their strain by refusing to export to other countries. When the King of Spain found out George had inquired about his Andalusian breed, he offered to send him two of his prize jacks as a gift.

George called the first one to arrive, Royal Gift. Seems his Royal Highness didn't want anything to do with George's "plebian mares" until a year later. Then George successfully bred all his mares and the mules became famous at Mount Vernon."

"George swore that they were stronger, worked longer and stayed fat on pastureland. He found out they lived longer and withstood heat and cold much better than a horse."

"And you don't have to shoe them," said Burl, giving D. Boone a love pat on the rump, signaling that he was done. "That's some story."

"George got the last laugh. His jackasses were in such demand that George sent them on a tour of the eastern states. So much for the Spaniards protected strain. I suspect Boone and Johnny have a little bit of Royal blood in them."

Burl watched the two red mules as they walked back to the pasture.

"That wouldn't matter to me. They'd still be two of the best red mules in the country, royal or not," he said.

Chapter Nine

Melva Becomes an Entrepreneur and Burl Returns

Trust in the LORD with all thine heart; and lean not unto thine own understanding. In all thy ways acknowledge him, and he shall direct thy paths.

Proverbs 3:5-6 KJV

The months of June, July, August, and September went quickly by. Burl settled down into his routine of training the two new red mules, shoeing horses, and grooming his growing stock. After Dark Queen's recovery, he slept at home and ate breakfast and supper with his family. These times were special to him, interacting with his brothers and sisters while helping his father around the farm. He was still learning the intricacies of blacksmithing and farming from his father.

Melva waited on customers in her father's store and continued to add to her hopeless chest, as she was calling it now. The beautiful chest seemed more hopeless as the weeks dragged on. Rita brought down little James who was taking his first steps. Baby Joyce looked and looked at him. She could walk circles around James and was starting to talk.

When Burl and his brothers came to help the victims of the flood, they were just days away from moving their belongings to the new construction site at Alcoa on the old John Howard farm north of Chilhowee. When Chilhowee Lumber Mill cranked up after the flood, it started sending most of the sawn lumber to Alcoa where construction on the company homes and men's barracks was progressing nicely. Many of the completed ones had families living in them. Noah's store was the closest place to buy supplies, and his business was booming.

The surveying crew moved its base from Chilhowee to a house on Strawberry Hollow. Since the first dam to be built up the Little T was Cheoah, they needed to keep heading up the Little T, staking out the railroad bed. The crew's job below Alcoa to Chilhowee was done. The grade was set and the railroad was ready to be extended.

During the summer of 1912, Melva met the president of the Aluminum Company of America or ALCOA when he came to inspect the progress at the base of construction operations in the Tennessee and North Carolina mountains. He got off the train at Chilhowee, expecting personnel from the town of Alcoa to meet him. They were late, and he was thirsty. The best thing he could do was go over to Noah's store to pass time until his transportation arrived. Arthur Vining Davis, at forty-five and newly married, wore a business suit, and a hat, and carried an umbrella.

"How are you, young lady?" he said politely. "I could use a tall glass of water."

Melva had no idea who he was, but she knew that any water she could give him would be hot and not very drinkable.

"Would you mind going to the springhouse with me? The water will be cold and refreshing," she said, willing to go the extra mile for this well-dressed gentleman.

Noah was gone to deliver food to a local family, so she called in a young clerk from out back to watch the counter.

"Mrs. Lindsey's eggs are under the counter in the shoebox, and she'll bring four cakes for us to sell. We swap out with her so no money will be exchanged," she told the young man.

Melva took the gentleman in tow. They walked the fifty yards to the back of Noah's house. Melva went in to get a clean glass, and then she and Mr. Davis, who had introduced himself, walked up to the springhouse.

Melva chattered away asking about the new town being built on the Howard's old farm. "The gossip is that two hundred houses will be built there," she said.

"There may be," said Mr. Davis. "We'll build whatever we need. But, we're making progress on building barracks for the single men."

"What's a barracks?" asked Melva.

"Oh," he replied, "It's a rather large building housing several men, maybe three hundred or more. It can be as long as needed. We plan on building several."

"How many people will you employ?" Melva was thinking about a building holding over three hundred men. She had never seen anything that large.

"Hundreds, for sure. Probably thousands."

There weren't a thousand people living in all of the coves in the area! "Where will you get so many employees?"

"Probably from Mississippi and Alabama — out of state. There's lots of men looking for jobs in the south. We may hire Negro men too. We'll bring them in by train. After the dams are built, the new aluminum plant in the Maryville area will hire most of them. Some may go back home. We already have several men at Alcoa. Do you want a job?"

"Do you think there might be something I could do?" questioned Melva, who had never thought about working for anyone but her father.

"There might be."

"When will the railroad be extended?" asked Melva. "My father is sure there will be a company store, and his business will be affected."

She went into the springhouse and came out with a glass of clear, cold water. Mr. Davis drank the whole glass.

"I think that's the best water I've ever tasted. Could I have another?" He held the glass out in her direction.

"Sure," said Melva.

After the second glass, he answered her question.

"We're having problems getting the line extended, but it'll happen one day in the near future." They were walking down the path back to the house and then the store.

Mr. Davis asked her name. He was impressed with this young lady. She asked good questions.

"I'm sorry. I should've told you. It's Melva," she said. "Melva Tipton."

"Miss Tipton, thank you for a glass of cold water on a hot summer's day. I'll be coming back periodically to check the construction that's going on. I'll stop by for another cold drink, and we can chat again," he said bowing slightly.

Mr. Davis walked back to the depot, his ride was waiting on him.

Melva didn't know exactly who Mr. Davis was until her father saw him departing on the afternoon train. His picture was often in the Maryville paper. Then she told Noah about their morning walk and talk. Her father was impressed.

On October 15, Melva's father came to dinner telling them that Theodore Roosevelt was almost killed by an assassin's bullet the day before. Noah read from the newspaper, "John Schrank, a German immigrant and saloon keeper from New York, shot Roosevelt as he was preparing to give a speech. Roosevelt's steel glasses case and his speech papers, fifty pages worth, saved his life. Later, Mr. Roosevelt mounted the stage, and told the crowd, 'I don't know whether you fully understand that I have just been shot; but it takes more than that to kill a Bull Moose.' Mr. Roosevelt delivered a ninety-minute speech, although at times he could only whisper."

"What do you think of that? He's tough, isn't he?" said Noah, his voice showing admiration. Mr. Roosevelt had formed the Progressive Party, also known as the Bull Moose Party, after he wasn't selected as the presidential nominee at the Republican National Convention. He was the chief Bull Moose. It was during his campaign in Wisconsin that he was shot.

∾

The town of Alcoa increased in size. Each day the train brought more workers, engineers, clerical staff, and experts of all kinds. Some came by Noah's store on the way to the camp, so Melva met many of its new residents. Some were families with children, going to live in newly built homes. There was so much traffic going to Alcoa, that a permanent road crew was sent to upgrade and maintain the road. The six miles of road saw large freight wagons with huge wheels. These came daily to the train depot to pick up building supplies, metal parts and increasingly large amounts of food supplies. But the end of the railroad didn't move.

And Burl didn't come, but Mr. Arthur Vining Davis did, again.

In September, he walked into Tipton's Mercantile and told Melva, "I'd like to get another glass of cold spring water." When Melva looked up, she recognized him and smiled.

"Hello, Mr. Davis. Are you ready to walk to the spring?"

"Yes, and I want to talk to you, Miss Tipton. Is your father here?"

"Yes. He's over at the house talking to Mother. Do you need to speak to him? And, please call me Melva." Now Melva's curiosity was aroused.

"Let's walk over that way, so I can talk to you both at the same time. I'd like another glass of the best water I've ever tasted."

Noah had never met Mr. Davis before and graciously invited him into the house, leading him to the dining room, through the kitchen.

"I'm afraid you're seeing the area where most of the work takes place in this house. My wife is known as an excellent cook. Have you had dinner?"

"Come to think of it, I haven't. This has been a busy morning, but I don't want to interrupt your wife's routine."

"You don't know my wife. It'll be her pleasure." Noah went to the bedroom to get Nan, who'd put Joyce down for her afternoon nap. "We have a visitor. The president of ALCOA, and he's hungry, he wants to eat." He teased his wife. "No. That's not true. I invited him to eat since he hasn't eaten dinner today. Is that all right?"

Nan gave her husband a light kiss on the cheek. "I feed hoboes and beggars, so why not the president of ALCOA." Nan laughed as she headed for the kitchen.

"No, Nan-Nan," said Noah. "You must meet Mr. Davis first." Noah said this as he steered her down the hall to the dining room. Nan took off her apron on the way.

As Mr. Davis ate dinner, he outlined a plan for Noah to set up a store at Alcoa until the railroad was built to the site. Then he couldn't promise Noah any further business, because a company commissary would be constructed for the enlarging community.

Melva was all ears.

Mr. Davis continued, "The post office will be established by the end of September, and I'd like you to maintain it until you leave. So, starting your business quickly is crucial. Once you leave, the post office will remain in your building."

"Your proposition is very interesting. What about a building?" Noah was turning the possibilities over in his mind as Nan joined them at the table. She had heard the conversation from the kitchen. She poured more tea into the glasses on the table.

"We need you to come. So, I'll rent you an end of one of the barracks for one dollar a year. We'll put a partition between the sleeping quarters and the store and give you storage room for stock. You'll haul your merchandise from here or put it on one of our supply wagons, if there's room." Mr. Davis' plan was growing more attractive.

"How long do you think it will be before the commissary is built?" Noah was interested in the length of time his second store would be open. The way Mr. Davis was presenting his plan, there'd be no investment except stock.

"I can't say with any certainty but probably two or three years, maybe four. I don't plan on building a commissary until the railroad spur is in Alcoa."

"Okay, Mr. Davis. You've got yourself a store, that is, if Nan agrees," said Noah who looked over at his wife.

Nan nodded yes. My! She thought. Life was changing again.

"Now there's one other stipulation," said Mr. Davis. "I want Miss Melva here to help managed the store. I'm much impressed with her abilities and spunk."

Melva was startled when Mr. Davis mentioned her name.

Noah replied, "I think that can be arranged. Is there any question about her safety, since there'll be so many men around?"

"None whatsoever. We have our own security in place. Somehow, moonshine makes its way into our camp. Saturday nights and Sunday are the worst, but so far, no one's gotten hurt."

Mr. Davis, or Arthur as Noah was now calling him, asked Noah to accompany him to the town site. There he was shown the exact location where the outlet would be placed. Mr. Harmon who was the construction supervisor joined the two men.

Turning to Mr. Harmon, Arthur said, "We'll have the back walls up and shelving built by this weekend. I think there are extra counters at one of our buildings in Maryville. We over-ordered when we established our offices at the new plant's construction site. I'll send them up." Turning back to Noah he continued, "Do you think you could start moving supplies next week, Noah?"

"Whew! That's short notice." Noah thought for a moment. "Yes. I think that's entirely possible. We'll do it."

Part of Arthur Davis' enthusiasm rubbed off on Noah, who could see why he was president of ALCOA. Mr. Davis was a take charge and let's get it done yesterday kind of man.

By November, Melva was working five days per week at their new location in Alcoa. Because Monday was the least busy day of the week at the Chilhowee store, Noah worked at Alcoa and Melva worked Tuesday through Saturday.

One of Noah's concerns was Melva's ride back to Chilhowee, which was along a deserted road much of the time. That's the reason she closed the store before dark to head home. She rode sidesaddle on one of her father's horses. Her father insisted that proper young ladies did not sit astride a horse.

Late October and the month of November were glorious with fall colors. The dogwood trees, first to bloom in the spring, were the first to dress themselves with crimson in the fall. The ride to Alcoa in the morning was sometimes heavy with a cold fog. And to home in the afternoon, it was filled with yellow beech, fiery-orange maples and crimson sumac bathed in the warm, golden glow of the setting sun. Oaks added brown leaves to the mix.

Hummingbirds flew in the hollows after the sweeter nectar of autumn's red blooms, preparing for their flight south. Geese honked overhead as they flew to warmer weather, and bees made honey in the honeycombs in their hives. God's creatures in the mountains prepared for winter.

Melva loved her new job; the smell of new wood and paint, stocking the shelves, and meeting new people. She stayed physically active rearranging her supplies for sales impact, dusting shelves, sweeping the floor, and delivering groceries to women with new babies or a family whose parent was sick.

Each afternoon the mail, which arrived on one of the big construction wagons, was sorted. She soon learned the names of many of the people she served and recognized patrons of her father's Chilhowee store. The population was mostly men, who worked out in the mountains or on projects in Alcoa. These men were busy during the day and came into the store before it closed. Several of the single men flirted with her, but she remembered her father's warning and kept them at arm's length.

About thirty houses were complete and that many more were soon to be constructed. Already, several families lived in these new homes. The children went to school at Big Cove School, until the Alcoa School was built. Each day, the huge supply wagon transported them down the curvy road to Chilhowee and picked them up in the afternoon. On these trips, Noah sometimes sent back stock for the Alcoa store.

The men whose families hadn't joined them here at Alcoa lived in long barracks. Each barrack housed several men who were double-bunked inside, one bunk over the other.

Construction was continuing at a frantic pace. Houses seemed to appear overnight. Logging on the hills to clear the forest for more construction could be seen out the windows of Melva's store. Each day more of the sky appeared until the loggers reached the peaks of the hills. Melva was so absorbed in the activity around her and so busy, she hardly thought of Burl.

Well, almost never.

In November, the men who came into the store were engrossed in politics. The death of Vice President James Sherman on October 30th left William Howard Taft without a running partner. The election on November 5th was less than a week away.

When the newspapers were delivered from Tipton's Mercantile in Chilhowee on Wednesday afternoon, November 6th, the headlines read, 'Teddy Splits the Republican Party—Wilson Wins.'

Afraid they wouldn't get a copy, several men were milling about inside Melva's store waiting for the newspapers. Brought in the back door by Noah's young clerk, Melva averted a stampede by letting him help sell the issues. She didn't sell completely out. There would be some for the crews working in the mountains when they returned.

She was bent over checking the safe under the counter when she heard, "It seems I never see you unless you're bent over or tending to something."

She knew that voice. She thought her heart would leap out of her body. For a minute she couldn't breathe. At least she didn't sit flat on the floor.

Slowly she stood, looking up at the broad smile of Burl Whitehead. He looked two feet taller than when she had last seen him. Her heart raced in her chest. Did he know she was here?

"I didn't know you were back in Alcoa," she said lamely.

He was looking at her intently. If five months had erased those brown eyes from his memory, it took only one look to put them back.

"I arrived this afternoon. I could've come on Monday, but I stayed to vote in the election at Six Mile yesterday. I haven't settled in or seen my brothers yet. I came by to get a newspaper. Someone said they were sold at the store. I didn't expect to see you here."

So, he hadn't known she was here. He had only stopped to get a newspaper. Somehow this took the wind out of Melva's sails. She turned into a store clerk.

"I have a few left. They're a nickel each," said Melva crisply.

Burl dug into his overall pocket and came up with the money, holding it out to her. Melva folded the paper and handed it to him.

Somehow, he had offended her. He sensed it.

"Have you been well? How's your father? I stopped by to see Mrs. Lindsey for a few minutes. She's doing well. Has her house fixed up real nice. She didn't mention you were here." Burl would win her with kindness. She couldn't be any harder than D. Boone, he thought.

Wow! Burl didn't know anything about women. It's a good thing Melva wasn't privy to that thought. Being compared to a mule—

Burl unfolded the newspaper and read the headlines. He looked disappointed.

"Didn't the election go your way?" asked Melva who didn't answer Burl's previous questions, totally ignoring them.

"No, sure didn't." He voted Republican as did most of East Tennessee. "Teddy shouldn't have started another group. The Bull Moose lost the election for the Republican Party."

"My father won't be pleased, either." Noah was a staunch Republican. He always ran as a Republican when his term was up for Squire.

"How long have you had the store here?" asked Burl.

"Only a little over four weeks. We're planning on running it until the railroad's completed to this point. Then we'll go back to Chilhowee."

"Do you work every day?"

"I don't work on Mondays. My father comes up and works that day. We've been really busy since we opened up. But Monday is a slow day here and at home. I'm glad for the day off," said Melva. "You've been gone quite a while." This was a question for Burl to answer.

"Yes. The Bertrams had a sick horse. They wanted me to come and work with it. Then they bought two new red mules that needed to be trained. Training red mules takes several months. But I'm back, at least for now," said Burl tucking his paper under his arm.

"I'm glad to see you." Melva stood looking at him. The store door opened and two customers walked through it.

"Guess I'd better go see where I'm supposed to sleep tonight." He was smiling again. "I'll be back to see you," said Burl, and Melva knew he would.

Thanksgiving came and went.

Burl frequently stopped by after he finished work for the day just to say, "Hello." They laughed and talked, and he helped with keeping wood in the stove. Sometimes, he even found a broom 'to fit his hand.' After he saddled her horse, he helped to lock up the store and stood on the boardwalk, waving goodbye.

On the last Saturday in November, he rode with her to Chilhowee. It was cold that day. Melva looked like an Eskimo. She was bundled up in a long coat, gloves and hat pulled over her ears. The road leading down into the Little T valley was steep, full of curves, and today it was a muddy, rutted mess. The two riders had to be careful not to let their mounts slip on the slick road. This caused the ride to take longer than usual.

Burl didn't intend to stay for any length of time after they arrived at her house. He only wanted to accompany Melva and make sure she arrived home safely.

When they got to Tipton's Mercantile, Noah was locking up the store. Melva and Burl rode on past the house to where he stood.

"Mr. Tipton," said Burl, "how are you?" Burl dismounted his red mule and shook Noah's hand.

"I'm going to take my horse down to the barn, unsaddle and feed him," said Melva as she rode in that direction.

"That's a fine red mule. Is it the Bertram's?" asked Noah.

"Yes, he is. He's one of a matched set that I trained to skid logs in the mountains. Johnny's so gentle anyone can ride him." Burl was watching Melva as she approached the barn. If it weren't for Noah, he would ride down and help her with the horse. He thought better of it and continued to talk to Noah.

"I've heard that mules are easy to keep and have more stamina than horses," Noah replied. He'd brought up a subject that Burl knew well.

"They sure are easy to keep, and on the trail there's almost no limit you can ride, and you don't have to shoe them." Burl reached down and raised one of Johnny's hooves so Noah could examine it. "I keep them trimmed and even."

"I was gettin' ready to go home to eat supper. Come on in and eat with us. You haven't eaten, have you?" Noah took the reins to Burl's mule and started toward the house. Burl guessed that he couldn't say no, since Melva's father headed in that direction. Anyway, he had the reins to Burl's ride. "Melva will be along in a minute."

When Melva entered the house, Burl had cleaned up and was sittin' in the parlor talking about the election with her father. He smelled of fresh soap as Melva walked by to the kitchen.

Noah introduced him to Nan, Milton, Matthew and Lydia as they appeared in the dining room and from upstairs. Joyce toddled in from the kitchen area. Milton and Matthew asked several questions about using his mule to skid logs off the mountain. They were fascinated by the logging business.

"Could I come and help one day?" asked Milton.

"Loggin' is a dangerous business. Accidents can happen. But if your father will let you come, I'll take good care to see that you don't come to any harm." Burl was looking at Noah.

"We'll see," Noah replied. His comment was neither a yes or no.

Nan appeared from the dining room. "Are any of you men ready to eat?"

Burl whispered to Milton as they went to the dining room, "I'll ask again closer to next summer. You'll be out of school, and it'll be warm. Is that all right?"

Milton's eyes shown as he nodded, "Yes." Burl had a new friend.

Burl made short work of Nan's country ham with red eye gravy, mashed potatoes, green beans, and cat's head biscuits. For dessert, he had a piece of apple cobbler. Everything he ate, the Tipton's grew in the garden or the field. Their orchard supplied the apples for the pie.

"Mrs. Tipton, that was really good. I miss my Mama's home cooking," said Burl. "Food's good at work, but it's not like what my Mom makes."

"Mr. Whitehead, you'll have to come back and eat with us again," replied Nan.

"Thank you, Ma'am. I'd love that."

"Let's go into the parlor so Nan and Melva can clear the table," suggested Noah as he pushed back from the table.

"I can't stay long. I need to get back to Alcoa. The road will be freezing and more dangerous in the dark," stated Burl as he settled into a chair. "My brothers will be wondering where I am," He'd told Willard and Len he was going to the store. They still didn't know about Melva. He glanced up and smiled as she came into the room.

"Melva, fix up a lantern for Burl to take with him on the ride home."

"Thank you, sir. Didn't think of it when I told Melva I was seeing her home. I'll prepare better next time."

Both Melva and Noah heard the next time part. "Where do you go to church, Burl?" asked Noah as his daughter went for the lantern.

"When I'm at home, I go to Six Mile Baptist with my parents, but up here I haven't been goin' anywhere."

"Come up to Hill Top where we go to church. We'd be glad to have you. Services start at ten o'clock on Sunday mornings. We don't have evening services, because Elder Hall rides the train home to Maryville in the afternoons. Then you could come and eat Nan's Sunday dinner."

"I probably can't this Sunday but maybe next week," said Burl. Burl didn't have many clothes and all that he had was dirty. He guessed that overalls would have to do even if he did come on Sunday. He needed to save money for a suit so he would be properly dressed.

"Mr. Tipton, I thank you for your hospitality, but I really need to head back." Burl arose from his chair and headed for the door. He saw the family Bible on the hall table. "I'll try to come to your church next week," he promised.

Melva appeared with the glowing lantern, while Milton and Matthew followed him out the door. They wanted to see his red mule.

Melva handed him the lantern and said goodbye at the door. She was emotionally and physically exhausted, but happy. Burl seemed to fit right in with her family.

~

Sunday week, he came to church. Noah invited him to sit with their family. He looked a little strange, this tall, lanky, handsome man, sitting with Milton, who was now his best friend. All the elders and their families came around and shook his hand. Some lingered long enough to ask a few questions.

After the altar call and prayer, the Tipton family headed for home. Burl went with them. He stayed until the afternoon train left, and then he bid them all goodbye and headed for Alcoa.

"Noah," said Nan, "That's a really nice, polite young man."

"Yes, he is," was Noah's reply. "He seems to be a hard worker too." Noah was sure he knew the reason Burl came to church. He noticed Melva's face glowed when he was around. Noah wondered how much these two liked each other. "Guess I'll have to ask him," said Noah to himself.

❦ Chapter Ten ❦

Christmas Gifts, Family Changes and "The" Questions

One generation passeth away, and another
generation cometh: but the earth   abideth for ever.

Ecclesiastes 1:4 KJV

Each Monday, after Burl got off from work, he made it a point to go and help Noah in his store. Burl didn't realize how much he missed his family, especially his father when he was on work assignments. Working with Noah kept him from being lonely for his family. He and Noah had long conversations on politics, business, mules, horses, and church. Their camaraderie was much like that between a father and son.

And yet, Noah wasn't anything like his dad. Alford was physically minded, preferring his horse shoeing and blacksmithing tools to Noah's interest in stocking shelves, waiting on customers, and operating a smooth-running business. Alford's interests ran to church and family. He didn't have time or money for anything else. Noah's interests included church and family, but extended to include the greater good of the community and politics. Alford could be funny. Noah was mostly serious, a reader, and a deep thinker. Each man was good at listening. Burl reckoned that was their best trait.

On December 20th, the Bertrams sent word for their crew to come home for Christmas. On Saturday, at noon, Burl walked briskly to the Alcoa store where Melva was working. This was one goodbye he did not look forward to. He stood outside the door with his hand on the knob. She was waiting the counter, and there was someone picking up mail. He opened the door and entered. Melva waved. He found the broom behind the postal counter and started sweeping. Anything to keep his mind off the word goodbye. After the customer left, she walked around the counter to greet him.

"You came early today. Is everything all right?"

Burl usually waited until afternoon to come so he could accompany her to Chilhowee. These days he stopped at Mrs. Lindsey's, who fixed him supper, rather than go on to Melva's home. Since he usually ate dinner at the Tipton's on Sunday, he didn't want to wear out his welcome.

"I wanted to tell you, we're heading home for Christmas, and we'll be staying until the 5th of January." Burl saw the disappointment in her face. "I'm sorry I won't be here for those days. I'll...I'll miss you." Never had Burl said anything like that to her before.

She'd looked forward to their first Christmas together. She nodded. "Of course, you want to spend the holidays with your family. When are you leaving?" asked Melva who hadn't missed the "I'll miss you."

"We're already packed and ready to go. We'll ride out within the hour. I'd wait until later and accompany you to Chilhowee, but we'd be so late gettin' home."

Burl was uneasy as he told Melva goodbye. He wanted to give her a hug. No! he wanted to give her a kiss. He settled on a handshake.

"Have a wonderful Christmas and New Year's. You'll be coming back, won't you?" Melva was afraid she might not see him for several months like before.

"As far as I know. The Bertrams have many irons in the fire. They're still committed to the project here." He held out his hand.

Melva grasped it, put her arm through his, and walked to the door with him.

"I'll miss you too," she said looking up at him with those liquid brown eyes, melting his heart. "Thank you for all you've done to help me these weeks."

"I'll be back to help in January. I guess I'd better go now," and Burl opened the door, preparing to leave.

Melva continued to hold his hand. She decided he wasn't leaving without some show of affection. She was insisting on this.

Burl stood rooted to the spot, undecided on what to do.

Melva would have kissed him on the lips, but didn't. Instead, she put her arms around his neck and kissed him on the cheek. To his and her amazement, he kissed her back.

Then Burl was gone.

～

Christmas went by quickly and was so calm and peaceful that Melva was shocked at its passing. Rita, pregnant again, came down with the two James' and spent part of the day. She left after dinner to visit his parents. Ellie and Bill could not come for Christmas but promised to be there for New Year's Day. D.H. and

Henry rode the train from Maryville, arriving on Tuesday around noon. Melva was glad to see her brothers. She couldn't wait to get D.H. aside and tell him about her life. Since Christmas was on Wednesday, she would have several days to fill her brother in on the details.

On Thursday morning, D.H. wanted to ride up to Alcoa to see the new city he'd heard so much about. Several of the bank's new customers were employed by ALCOA in their temporary offices on the outskirts of Maryville. Their comments had piqued his interest.

At first, Noah was to take him. Then Nan learned of the death of one of Noah's customers and she insisted he take food to the bereaved family who lived down river in the opposite direction. So, Melva was given the nod.

She and D.H went to the barn to saddle their horses. They waved to Milton and Matthew as they passed the house.

"Those boys are almost inseparable, aren't they?" They were so much younger than D.H., Matthew wasn't much more than a toddler when D.H. went to boarding school.

"Yes. They're growing up. It's a shame no one else lives close by. They do have playmates at school but at home it's pretty much just them." Melva changed the subject. "It's hard to believe 1913 is just around the corner."

"I know. I've been so busy this year. Mr. Anderson wants me to go to Chicago with him for a business meeting in March," said D.H. matter-of-factly.

"That's wonderful," said Melva, missing the possibilities associated with this opportunity. "I'd love

to travel to Chicago, or New York, or Nashville."
Nashville was closer and probably more realistic.

"How long will you be gone?"

"We'll be gone a week."

"You'll have to bring me back a souvenir," said
Melva.

"I'll try to remember to do that. I hear the wind
blows constantly in the city. I guess I'm looking
forward to going." D.H. was a home boy at heart. He'd
be happier when he got back. Seeing Melva's
enthusiastic response, he didn't want to say this.

"I want to hear all about it when you return."
Melva was envisioning skyscrapers, cars, and cabs.
She'd heard about big cities. Her friend Juliet, John's
daughter, had told her about them. Juliet had been to
New York City. Melva never expected to visit one.

They rode in silence for a while.

"How do you like working at Father's new store?"

"Oh, I like it very much. It's not really hard work,
stockin' shelves and greetin' customers. Father says
we're doing well."

"Do you work six days a week?" D.H. knew his
father would never open on Sunday. This was church
day and a day of rest.

"I work from Tuesday through Saturday. Father
goes up on Monday. We have a safe under the counter
where we put the proceeds of the day. He doesn't want
me carrying money back and forth, so he carries it
home in a bag on Monday afternoon."

Melva started to tell him about Burl but thought
better of it. They had arrived at the store. She would tell
him on the ride home.

The new store was impressive with built-in shelves stacked and stocked to the ceiling. Every space was utilized. The post-office area was to the left of the front door. Melva could get behind the slotted front and place mail in from the back. She sold stamps and shipped parcel post, carrying the boxes to Chilhowee in a bag slung across her horse.

The huge wood stove sat in the middle of the store. Those days when it was cold, Melva lit the fire to warm up the area by bringing in wood from the side entrance. Today, there wasn't any fire but the heat from the adjacent barracks kept the room and its contents from freezing, that is, unless the temperatures were in the teens. Then they gave a local teenager, the son of a worker, a dollar to come and start a fire to heat the room. He was responsible for keeping it going during the day and night. So far, they hadn't any problem with the cold.

"Aren't you afraid someone will break in and steal the safe?" said D.H. after seeing where it was located.

"We haven't had any trouble here in town, except for a few drunks. Moonshine is readily available despite efforts to keep it out. Mostly the trouble starts on the weekends after I get home."

Melva was remembering Burl telling of collaring a drunk before he fell into the water of the Little T. He knew the man and dragged him by his shirt back to his barracks, leaving him on his bed. The man was so drunk he didn't remember Burl saving his life or how he got in bed. Burl never told him. Burl and his brothers didn't drink.

D.H. and Melva walked outside and several feet down the boardwalk. They passed a barbershop and tack store. Horses needed new harness and harnesses needed repaired. The tack store stocked supplemental horse food. Horses could survive on only so much hay, and then they needed other food to keep them healthy, especially these animals. The horses and mules of Alcoa worked long, hard days in the mountains.

The two siblings turned around and walked back to where their horses were tied. Mounting, they rode up to Strawberry Holler to see the new homes being built by Alcoa. Turning off the road they passed through some of the new construction and stopped at the end of a newly graded road.

"It looks like they plan on several thousand employees," said D.H. who was at an advantage point high on a hill surveying the site.

"Mr. Fisher said hundreds, if not thousands," replied Melva.

"Which Mr. Fisher are you talking about?" asked her brother.

"ALCOA's president, Mr. Arthur Vining Fisher."

"How do you know him?" D.H. was mystified.

"He likes our spring water."

"What!" D.H was laughing. "I know there's a story behind this."

Melva proceeded to tell him about Mr. Fisher's two visits to Tipton Mercantile and his offer to her father. "And part of the deal was for me to work at the new store."

"Did he realize how old you were?"

"I've helped Father long enough to know the ropes of the store business." Melva bristled at her brother's comment. She was upset that her brother thought she wasn't old enough to wait a counter. Maybe he didn't think she had a brain!

"I'm sorry," said D.H. contritely, giving her a slight bow. "I have no doubt you can handle the job. You are old, very old, very, very old for your age." He was teasing her.

Melva drew back her hand as if to throw something at him, and D.H. ducked playfully.

"What's the building about halfway down the hill? Looks like a church." He pointed to a structure under roof, but not complete.

"It is. Won't be long until Alcoa residents will be havin' meetings here at Strawberry Holler. I think there'll be more than one church, but this is the first. The cemetery will be on the side, lookin' toward the town.

They were headed back down the curvy road to Chilhowee. Now was the time to tell him.

Melva drew a deep breath and said, "I have a new friend."

"Really, what's her name," said D.H. as innocent as a babe.

"She's a he," said Melva with a twinkle in her brown eyes.

Her brother pulled his horse to a stop and looked at her. Melva couldn't keep from smiling. Sure enough, he'd seen this look on other girls' faces. Melva was in love.

"Well, I'll be a toad frog!" exclaimed D.H. as they started riding again. "When did this happen?"

"It didn't just happen, it's been happening for some time," said Melva.

"What's the lucky guy's name?"

"You know who it is," said Melva.

Now D.H. was baffled. He had no idea who she was talking about. Suddenly a thought came to him. "Edgar! You've realized what a swell guy he is at last and —"

"No!" Melva cut him off. "It's not him."

"Well, who is it?"

"Don't you remember the Whitehead boy who was at the dance at Happy Valley School? He had curly hair. You told me his name was Burl, Burl Whitehead."

D.H was thinking as he rode. The dance happened over a year ago.

"Is he the one you said you were going to marry?" asked D.H.

"That's him," said Melva simply.

After the shock wore off, D.H. threw back his head and started to laugh and laugh. "You did it. He's going to marry you," he stated, looking at her in amazement. He shook his head. "I can't believe this."

"No, silly!" said Melva. "He hasn't asked me, but I think he will, and if he does, I'll say yes."

"Well, sister, I'll dance the polka at your wedding." D.H. was still smiling. The polka was a new dance just introduced this year. D.H. had tried it out at socials in Maryville.

"No use in going that far," said Melva dryly.

"Does anyone know how you feel?" asked her brother.

"No. They may suspect something since Burl comes to church each Sunday and sits with us. But I've never said anything to anyone but you. I wanted you to be the first to know."

They were back at the barn dismounting their horses.

D.H hugged his sister and gave her a kiss on the forehead.

"I'll keep your secret, and if I can be of any help let me know," he said.

Melva was glad someone else knew about her feelings for Burl. At present, she didn't want to share them with anyone else.

They spent the rest of the week knowing they had a secret.

~

Noah never got to travel to Knoxville with Marlon Boyd. Marlon grew weaker and weaker and died on December 28 in his sleep. No one ever knew what was wrong with him. Edgar was heartbroken at his funeral, which was attended by every member of Hill Top Primitive Baptist. Melva wanted to comfort him but knew she could not. In lieu of a church service on that Sunday, Elder Hall conducted a funeral service. Marlon was buried in the church cemetery with the wind blowing so hard that Melva thought she would freeze stiff. There were no flowers since it was winter and cold.

Noah looked grim as he helped carry his friend to the open grave, his long overcoat whipping in the breeze.

The women of the church served the noon meal at the Boyd's. D.H. and Noah ate with the family. Melva, Henry, Lydia, and the boy's road home with family friends, and Melva fixed leftovers for dinner.

~

D.H. had much to ponder on the way home to Maryville, especially Melva's admission of her love for the Whitehead man. This had taken him by surprise. The marriages of his other sisters hadn't affected him, because he was their brother not their pal. He and Melva were pals. He and Melva loved each other, but their attachment was one of well-wishing and camaraderie. He wanted the best for his sister. No! He coveted the best for *this sister*.

Even so, if he wasn't careful, he might be a little jealous of this Burl Whitehead. He wished he knew the man better. He might ask around and see what he could find out about him. He had contacts. It was time to use them.

~

Tuesday and Wednesday, the last two days of 1912, were the most tiresome days Melva had worked at Alcoa. They were tiring because there was little to no traffic at the store. Most of the town residents went home for the holidays and those that were left didn't need supplies or were in no mood to buy anything. Wednesday couldn't come too soon for her.

The year, 1913, dawned clear and cold. Melva had no plans for the day. She did for the rest of the year. Whether any of them panned out would depend on the man she loved with all her heart. In many ways, she was ready. In other ways, she was nervous, anxious, and waiting expectedly.

On January 5, 1913, which was a Monday, Noah rode to Alcoa and opened the store. He felt sure his business would be slow since this was the first day back for the working men of Alcoa. The store was cold, so Noah's first priority was to build a fire. The day went gradually by. He was thinking about closing early, when Burl walked in the door.

"Hello, Burl, how was your first day at work?"

"Just about what you'd expect. In the cold, the mules and men were sluggish. Tomorrow will be a better day," said Burl. "I was even rusty."

"Today was very slow here. I'm gettin' ready to head home. I don't think the men are thinking about supplies today. They're probably penniless after the break." Noah was preparing his bag with the store's cash, except what Melva would need to open the store in the morning.

"Do you mind if I ride partway with you?"

Noah cocked his head and looked at Burl. "Why, no. You're welcome too. I'll need to get my horse."

"You go ahead and get ready. I'll get your horse saddled and bring him around." Burl was already headed out the back door. Noah's horse was in the community corral about fifty yards away. The area was shaded by trees with water continuously supplied by gravity. Saddles rested under a lean-to by the fence.

Noah finished totaling the cash and got ready to lock the front door. He checked the stove and added a couple of pieces of wood. He didn't want it to get too hot. He wondered what was on Burl's mind. He thought he knew.

Burl came in the back door. "We're ready to go," he said to Noah.

Noah mounted his horse, and Burl mounted his mule. They made an interesting pair as they rode out of Alcoa.

The two men talked until they reached the top of Strawberry Holler and headed down the steep grade toward Chilhowee.

Noah decided he would save the young man the anxiety of starting the conversation. "Burl are you interested in my daughter, Melva?"

Burl looked at Noah with astonishment. That was exactly the next words out of his mouth. Noah beat him to it.

"Yes, sir, I am. I was just gettin' ready to tell you that. I'd like to get to know your daughter better with the idea of her becomin' my wife. I'd like to tell her that, but I wanted you to know first how I felt. I've stayed away from women, because I wanted to learn my father's skills and get good at them. I don't have much money, but I'm a hard worker. If you will give your blessin', I'll make her a dependable husband." That was the longest speech Burl had made about a woman in his life and probably not the best one.

"Burl, how would you take care of her?" Noah wanted to ask a few questions.

"Well, I have some money saved up. I know horseshoein' and blacksmithin', so I would always have a job doin' them. I'm good at logging and training horses and mules," said Burl simply. He added, "And I'm not lazy. I'm not a quitter. And, Melva knows I can use a broom." Burl grinned at his last statement.

"Sounds to me like that's a lot to offer. Where would you live?" Noah knew there were many men who didn't have the drive Burl had. Their Monday afternoon conversations were enough for Noah to know that Burl was honest, dependable, and patient. These three virtues were important to Noah.

"That's a hard question to answer. We'd live here at Alcoa until my job is up. There's housin' available, and then we might move to Six Mile. Since I work for the Bertrams, I work at their pleasure. I'll go wherever the work is, and my family will go with me."

"Will you take Melva to church and be a God-fearing man?"

"Yes, sir, I will."

"Well then, I don't have any serious objections to you talking to Melva. She's always been a spirited child and young woman. Do you know what you're gettin' into?"

Burl grinned. "I think so, sir. Melva has a mind of her own and doesn't hesitate to use it. That could be a plus, if I work away from home much of the time. She'd have to run the household" Burl was at the edge of feeling relief but not quite yet.

"By all means speak to her, but I'd rather she not marry until she's seventeen. I'm adamant about that!" said Noah.

"We'll honor your wishes. I still have to talk to her. She may turn me down." Now, Burl was relieved. The first hurdle was over. He still had to approach Melva.

Noah smiled. "I don't think she'll turn you down. I think she loves you too. Are you riding to the house?" asked Noah.

"No. I'm going back to Alcoa." They were at the last curve before the road leveled out into the valley. Burl halted his mule.

"Son, I'll see you at church Sunday." said Noah. That was the first time Noah called Burl, 'Son.'

"Yes sir," Burl called after him and turned Johnny around for the ride back home.

~

On his return to Alcoa, Burl *thought back* to his Christmas vacation. He had decided to tell Alford and Sinda about his feelings for the Tipton girl. He knew they would be shocked because he never mentioned a woman or the possibility of getting married.

The opportunity came on the Sunday after Christmas, the same day that Marlon Boyd was buried at Hill Top Primitive Baptist Church. The children had scattered in all directions, each going to their friends' houses to play. After church, Willard and Len had gone hunting with friends from Montvale Springs. They planned to stay overnight and come home the next afternoon. It was a cold, bitter day and the wind was blowing fiercely.

Resting after the week's festivities, Sinda and Alford sat in the living room. Burl entered the room and stood with his back to the radiating heat from the stove.

"Dad, Mama, I'd like to talk to you about a personal matter." Burl started and then continued. "I know I haven't said anything before about gettin' married, but I've met a girl who lives in Chilhowee, and I'm thinkin' about doing just that."

You could've knocked Sinda and Alford off their seats with a feather. A pending marriage by Burl was the last thought in their minds. Alford recovered first.

"Well, Son, it was bound to happen sooner or later. You're old enough," said Alford who didn't know what else to say. Burl was the eldest son and at, twenty-three, mature enough to marry.

"What's the girl's name? Do we know her? Does she live up Abram's Creek?" asked Sinda, always the practical one. They had distant relatives who lived there.

"Her name is Melva Tipton. Her father runs Tipton's Mercantile in Chilhowee. We've known each other several months now, and I think she likes me too."

"She's going to get a good man for a husband," said Sinda. "That's all I can say."

"I haven't asked her yet, and I need to talk to her father. She could say no."

"She'd be a really silly girl to say no to you," said Sinda, going on the offensive. Her son was the handsomest, most hard-working young man she knew. This girl had better be amazing. Her son deserved that. "Well, I'll be. I just can't believe we're havin' this conversation," she said in wonder.

"Son, there's something your mother and I need to tell you." Alford looked at Sinda, who nodded her head at him.

"Your mother and I have been savin' the money you've been givin' us. If we needed some, we used it, but there's several dollars saved up."

Sinda got up and went to the kitchen, coming back with a fruit jar stuffed with dollars. She handed it to Alford.

Alford handed it to Burl. It was his time to be astonished.

Alford continued, "I don't know how much money is in there, but I think there's enough to start a household."

And buy a new suit, Burl thought.

There was something else he wanted to buy with it — a gift for Melva. It would be her engagement gift.

"This is wonderful," exclaimed Burl with a big smile on his face. He would ride into Maryville tomorrow and buy both.

Alford and Sinda sat talking about when they were first married—how they struggled to make a crop in newly plowed fields. At first, Sinda helped, until the babies started coming. They were both young and strong and with a determined spirit they eked out a living for themselves and their children. No, there were no frills, but the family was never hungry. And clothes were sometimes patched, but functional. And most important, after several years and thirteen children, they were still very much in love. Alford put his arm around his wife and drew her to him. They were often affectionate with each other in front of the children.

"All I got to say is she's a very lucky young lady, and I hope you and she are as happy as your mama and me. Next year, it'll be thirty years since we said I dos."

~

Burl went to Maryville the next day. He bought a suit and a new felt hat. It was his conviction that a real man wore a hat. He didn't feel dressed up without one. Then he went to the jewelers. He'd passed the store on his way to buy the suit. In the window, he saw something he thought she would really like. Not a ring, because he was limited by money. If she said "yes," he'd save up and buy that later.

Telling his brothers was as hard as telling his parents.

"What! Burl the uncatchable is caught!" exclaimed Willard and guffawed.

"Well, who caught you?" asked Len, who was amazed. Burl hadn't said anything about a woman. Burl confessed his trips to the Alcoa store had an ulterior motive. He wasn't only buying a newspaper.

"So that's why you went every afternoon," said Len.

"You went to see that pretty girl who waits the counter." Burl nodded his head at Willard's comment.

〜

On January 6, 1913, which was a Tuesday, Melva went back to work at Alcoa. She knew she would not see Burl until the late afternoon, and she anxiously awaited his coming. What would their relationship be now? Their feelings for each other had become evident with their holiday goodbyes. She pulled in a lungful of air and let it out in a rush.

If Burl didn't express his feelings, what was the problem with sharing hers? Why did the man always have to go first? That was perfectly ridiculous!

At dinner she wasn't hungry. She picked at the leftovers her mother had sent to eat. The day dragged on as the pressure of the future meeting grew. Her feet were like lead weights on her legs.

Melva waited on customers and placed the afternoon mail in slots. Finally, it was time for Burl to arrive. Melva thought she would explode. Where was he? Why hadn't he come? Anticipating his coming, she paced up and down the store. She was waiting on her last customer when she saw his tall, handsome frame through the store windows. He opened the door so the customer could leave. Then he entered and came toward her, placing a small box on the counter. He smelled of soap.

"Hi, Melva," he said smiling broadly, wondering how she would greet him.

She didn't. She couldn't. Her feet were heavy. Instead she calmly, too calmly, moved around the counter in a daze and opened her mouth to say, "Hello."

Suddenly, the anticipation she'd felt all day caught up to her. She gulped air and grabbed the counter. She was speechless. Her brain didn't work. She just stood there looking at him, trying to steady herself.

"How was your Christmas? Did you have snow last week?" asked Burl, looking at her with a frown. "Are you okay? You don't look so good."

Everything started to dim. Was she was going to faint?

"Melva?" He sounded like he was in a cave, far away.

Burl caught Melva as she fell, and lifted her off the floor. He held her in his strong arms, but there was no place to put her. He remembered a person who fainted should be placed flat on something. He looked around. Every counter was full of saleable merchandise.

A chair sat by the woodstove. He walked over and sat down with the woman he loved held in his arms. What now? If she were Dark Queen, he'd rub her arms and legs.

Melva closed her eyes. Be quiet. Be still, went through her thoughts. Several minutes lapsed as she struggled not to faint. When she opened her eyes, he was there.

"Don't move," he said. "Just be quiet and still until you feel better." He was rubbing her free arm, concern and love showing in his eyes and face.

"I'm sorry. I felt faint for a few seconds. I am feeling much better now."

She sat up, still testing her ability to stay upright. It dawned on her where she was—*in his lap*. She jumped up, smoothing down her dress. Now she was embarrassed. She had never done anything so silly in her life!

"Are you alright?" asked Burl, genuinely worried.

"Yes." She put her hand to her head. "I need a little water."

"I'll get some." Burl hurried out the back door with a glass he pulled from under the counter. While he was gone, she sat down in the chair, breathing in large amounts of air. Her head cleared.

The water was ice cold as she sipped it. She wet her handkerchief and wiped her face. She was much, much better now.

Burl stood before her. Melva wasn't well. He wondered if he should say anything to her. Still, maybe the gift would make her feel better. He went to the counter and retrieved it. Coming back, he hunkered down and held the box toward her.

"I brought you something from Maryville. I hope you like it."

She took the box. It was wrapped in pink paper with a jeweler's sticker on the top. She opened it. Inside, wrapped in pink tissue, was the most beautiful piece of ceramic pottery she'd ever seen. It was for your dresser top and held jewelry, or hair pins or anything you treasured. The body shape was unusual and pink and the removable top was adorned with one red rose, a bud and four green petals.

"Melva, I don't know if this is a good time to tell you. I know you don't feel well. I don't know how to say this to you, except the saleslady said a red rose stood for love. I think that's how I feel about you. I love you."

It's a good thing Burl stood up, because that's as far as he got. Melva jumped from the chair and flung herself into his arms—deliberately this time.

"What took you so long? I've been waiting on you to tell me those very words. I love you too," she said. Then, standing on tiptoes, she kissed him squarely on the mouth.

Later, Melva couldn't remember all they talked about as they sat near the woodstove. He told her of his talk with her father. Noah had given his blessing, but they must wait to get married until she was seventeen.

Melva had nodded at that. She'd be seventeen in June—not long at all.

He told her of telling his mother and father about his feelings for her. Of the money they had saved for him out of his pay. How his brothers had laughed.

Burl rode home with her to Chilhowee.

Realizing he hadn't properly asked Melva to marry him, he stopped Johnny in the road and dismounted. On that cold January day, he took Melva's hand and said, "Will you marry me? I'll make you the best husband in the world."

Of course, she said, "Yes."

❧ **Chapter Eleven** ❧

Burl's Loss, The Wait, The Marriage

*Trust in the LORD with all thine heart; and lean
not to thine own understanding. In all thy ways
acknowledge him, and he shall direct thy paths.*

Proverbs 3:5-6 KJV

When Burl and his brothers came to Hill Top Primitive Baptist the following Sunday, they sat with Melva, Milton, and Matthew. There wasn't room for anyone else in the pew. Much to Melva's surprise, Burl was wearing his new suit and hat.

"Very nice," she whispered to him as the service got under way. He was the most handsome man in the room. After church, the Tiptons and the Whiteheads headed home to Chilhowee to eat dinner. They made a good-looking group riding down the road.

This was the first time Willard and Len had seen Noah since the flood.

The dining table was the biggest piece of furniture in the house. Twelve people could easily sit down its length and today it was almost full. After serving the food, Nan and Melva joined them. Melva took a vacant seat next to Burl, while the brothers and sisters snickered at the sight. Nan sat at the opposite end from Noah.

~

With memories crowding in her mind, Nan looked around the table. The sound of male voices filled the room, much like the days when D.H. and Henry were home. She missed her oldest boys.

Nan was amazed at how much schooling and marriage had changed her family. When D.H. went to boarding school in Maryville, it didn't dawn on her that he wouldn't be coming back home. Then Henry joined his brother. Their departure left a big hole at the table. She missed their lively discussions and help around the house.

After the boys left, the sounds of women's voices were dominant at the table, because the next three older children were girls. When Rita and Ellie married and left the household, much of the noisy busyness of the household left with them. In the silence, the differences really hit home.

Because of the vacant chairs in the dining room, Nan had switched her place, sitting closer to her husband. Everyone else seemed to gravitate to Noah's end of the table, leaving the other end empty.

Now, Melva was leaving. Over half of her children would be gone. The last five years had made a lot of difference.

Reaching over, she pushed the hair out of Joyce's three-year-old eyes. At least, she wouldn't be leaving for several years. That was a comforting thought. At forty-four, Nan did not intend or expect to have more children.

~

Earlier in the week, Noah prepared Nan for Burl and Melva's announcement, which they planned to make that afternoon after dinner. An air of expectancy overshadowed the whole meal. Everyone knew that something important was about to happen—actually everyone already knew of the engagement. The announcement itself was anticlimactic.

After the Sunday meal, life settled down to normal in the Little T valley. Twice, snow blanketed the ground, making the trees droop with the white cover. Melva rode her horse up the white pathway to Alcoa through the pristine and quiet forest. Until the horses and freight wagons stirred the snow into mud, she felt like a princess in a wonderland.

Noah kept working on Mondays at the Alcoa store, and Burl always stopped by to help in the afternoon. The respect they had for each other continued to build.

Melva worked the rest of the week, and Burl came by after his workday in the mountains. They talked about their future, deciding they would marry in July, the month after Melva turned seventeen. Then, Burl saddled Melva's horse, and he rode his mule to Chilhowee. They kissed goodbye at the last curve, and he rode back to Alcoa while she proceeded on home. Five o'clock would come early the next morning, and Burl needed to get into bed soon.

Sunday was church day along with dinner at the big house in Chilhowee.

Mondays, they didn't see each other. This was a day to do personal things such as wash clothes or tidy up their living quarters. Melva helped her mother around the house and in the kitchen. On Tuesday, when Melva returned to Alcoa, she always carried the apple, peach or cherry cobbler her mother baked for the Whitehead boys. It lasted exactly two days. In this way January and February went by.

In March, three weeks after Woodrow Wilson was sworn in as President of the United States, Jake came from the Bertram's Six Mile farm to get the three Whitehead men. There was an emergency. James Alford Whitehead was sick and they should come home at once.

"Do you know any details of Dad's problem?" asked Burl.

"All I know is that he has a pain in his stomach and each day he gets worse. Your brother, Tom, came over and told us the doctor said to come and get you." Jake knew a little bit more, but he didn't tell them.

"So, they don't know what's wrong?" asked Willard.

"Don't seem too. But I don't know everything," he admitted.

"We'll get ready and come immediately. Are you headed back now?" Burl was already putting his clothing in a sack. Willard and Len followed his example.

"Yes. Jorge said to come on home as soon as I told you. I've been over there, helpin' Sinda since he took to his bed."

"Could rain on you going back," Burl observed, looking out a window at the gray, leaden sky.

Jake nodded. "Sprinkled as I came over. Guess I'd better go." He went out the door of the barracks.

"Tell Mom we'll be there before nightfall."

It took about an hour for the men to get their belongings ready and inform the construction superintendent. Then, Willard and Len went in search of Sam Duggan so they could tell him about their father's sickness. Burl went to tell Melva.

"I don't know how bad it is," said Burl after he arrived.

"Will you let me know when you find out?" asked Melva.

"I'll try, but that may be hard to do. Don't get upset if you don't hear anything for a few days." Burl knew Melva would jump to the worst conclusion if she didn't hear from him. He would try, but he couldn't promise it would happen.

At that moment, Willard and Len arrived. Burl kissed Melva goodbye and she walked out the door behind him.

"I hope your father will be okay," said Melva to the brothers. "Burl said he would try to get word to me on his condition. You'll help him do that, won't you?" Melva thought if she could enlist their help, the possibility of hearing was better.

"Sure," said Len. And then they were gone.

At Look Rock, it started to rain. The Whitehead Trail into the hollow would be too bad to use. It turned into a muddy morass, a creek unto itself during a rainfall. They would have to go the long, curvy way. The road was down the face of Chilhowee Mountain by Montvale Springs, and then turn left on Six Mile Road. By the time they got to the intersection it was dark.

The ride was miserable and cold. Water ran off man and horse alike as they plodded down the muddy road. A warm light radiated from the windows of the

Bertram farm as they passed by the entrance. The sight of the Whitehead's white frame house couldn't come too soon for the waterlogged men. At least the rain had stopped by the time they arrived. Riding into the open barn, the men dismounted.

"Len, you go on into the house, and tell Mama we're here. We'll unsaddle the horses and be in shortly." Burl was in quiet control as usual.

As Len disappeared in the direction of the house, Burl called after him, "Take off your shoes on the back porch."

Willard gave a slight chuckle. "One day he's going to take off your shoes on the back porch."

"You may be right. But if I didn't remind him, mud would be tracked over Mama's kitchen. You know how she feels about her floors, and she doesn't need that right now." Sinda had her hands full if Alford was sick. He hoped his father was better, but there was a nagging feeling that once he entered the house, his world was going to change.

Willard and Burl left their shoes next to Len's on the porch. Several other pairs were lined up with theirs. Muddy shoes were one of Sinda's pet peeves—one way to get on her bad side fast. Even Alford's shoes sat there close to the back door. He had deposited them in their place of honor by the cane-backed chair. He'd taken them off the last time he entered the house.

Burl drew a long breath and entered the kitchen. He dreaded what he would find beyond the door. His two-year-old sister, Grace, and five-year-old brother, Wayne, were playing there, attended by their fifteen-year-old sister, Flora. Since Ida married in February,

Flora was the eldest sister left at home. When Burl married, he would be the first Whitehead son to marry.

Flora stepped forward to greet her brothers.

"Mom will be glad to see you. She and J.A. are in the bedroom sitting with Dad. Elmer and Tom are over at Mrs. Simerly's house. She insisted they come and stay with her." Mrs. Simerly was a Christian sister from Six Mile Baptist Church. She was a widow and often had one or the other of the boys over to stay the night. Since she was childless, they kept her company and helped her with chores.

James Alford, Jr., or J.A. as the family called him, was only thirteen. Struggling with his dad's illness was a tremendous responsibility at his age. When his eldest brothers appeared in his father's sick room, he was relieved.

Sinda jumped up and greeted her sons with hugs. "I'm so glad you're here. I know your ride was miserable. I'll get some towels so you can dry off."

Sinda reappeared with the towels. She continued to talk while they dried off. "Dr. Kerr was here earlier this afternoon. He's not sure what's wrong with your father," she whispered before she sat down again. "He told me he was a family doctor who delivered babies, set limbs, and stitched up wounds. He's afraid to diagnose Alford's problem. He said we need to take him to Maryville to a surgeon. Alford was adamant about not going."

Alford smiled weakly from the bed. His face was ashen and filled with pain. He didn't attempt to speak.

Burl went over to his bedside. "Dad, I'm here to take care of you."

Alford nodded his head ever so slightly, his eyes closed.

"Willard, would you get some chairs so you can sit down?" asked Burl. He sat in the one J.A. willingly vacated next to his mother Sinda.

"What else did Dr. Kerr say?" Burl kept looking at his father.

Sinda whispered again, "He doesn't like the way Alford's keeps gettin' worse. He thought maybe it was something he ate, but now he doesn't think so. He mentioned the word appendicitis, or gallbladder, or ulcer, or possibly an inflamed liver. Seems there are a lot of illnesses that start in the abdomen. He's going into Maryville to see Dr. Lincoln to get his opinion. He'll be back in the morning."

"There's no use in Dad being stubborn. If he needs to go to Maryville, we need to take him." Now Burl was adamant. He whispered, "From the looks of him, I doubt he could protest."

"How did this start?" asked Willard.

"Pain in his abdomen which moved to his right side. He's not eating, has a slight fever and has been nauseous, but not throwin' up. That's the reason he lays so still, and the pain has gradually gotten worse." Sinda looked lovingly at her husband. She felt helpless. "I've been prayin' he'd get well."

"How long has he been in bed?" asked Burl.

"Five days. I didn't send for the doctor until two days ago. Alford wouldn't let me. You know, he's never been this sick a day in his life. He thought he could best it. Dr. Kerr's been coming every day since."

"Mom, you go on and do whatever you need to do. Willard and I will sit with Dad tonight." Burl wanted her to get out of the room and do something different.

"Have you had supper?" asked Sinda.

"No. We hurried over as soon as we could find Sam Duggan and tell Melva. We didn't take time to eat. We probably need to change into dry clothes soon before we get our death of cold." Burl looked around. "Where'd Len go?"

"I sent him to change into dry clothes. When he comes back why don't you take turns changing your clothes? I'll go fix you boys a hot plate of food." Burl nodded and Sinda left the room just as Len appeared. He sat in Sinda's vacant chair.

"Brothers, I don't like the looks of this. Tomorrow, if the doctor says Dad needs to go to Maryville, we will load him up and go. What do you to think?" asked Burl.

"I'm all for it." Willard was in shock at the sight of his father.

"I'm ready to load him up right now," said impulsive Len. "But I know that's not the best plan. I'll help you load him in the wagon tomorrow."

Alford groaned from the bed as he moved ever so slightly.

Sinda went to the kitchen. After sitting with Alford so long, she ached all over. Moving around felt good.

She went to the cupboard where the cooling food from supper was kept. People in rural areas cooked only what they could eat at two meals. Storing or saving food for long periods of time wasn't safe or practical, unless you had an icebox. She couldn't afford to buy ice, so she didn't have a box. She pulled out several bowls and put as much food as she had on three plates. These she placed in the oven that was attached over the stove. The warmth of the heated air inside would warm the food where it would be more appetizing. Sinda was a practical but good cook, as you could tell by looking at her children.

Burl, Willard, and Len took over the duties of sitting with their father. He rarely spoke but lay with his eyes closed — a painful look on his face.

When Dr. Kerr arrived the following day, Alford's temperature was higher and he wasn't rational at times. Burl and Sinda stayed in the room as he examined Alford. When he pushed on the spot that was earlier identified as sore or painful, Alford groaned and writhed in agony. Burl and Sinda both noticed the red streaks on his abdomen. They exchanged knowing glances. Red streaks meant blood poisoning.

"Dr. Lincoln thinks the diagnosis is appendicitis. Now, I think I agree with him. There is an operation known as an appendectomy, but Alford needs to travel to Maryville immediately. I'm not a surgeon, but Dr. Lincoln is a good one. I think he's Alford's only chance. There's a good possibility we may be too late for surgery. When he became worse the day you called me, I think his appendix had already ruptured. Now the infection has spread into his abdomen, and gangrene has started in his stomach area. You can see the redness indicating blood poisoning. There aren't any worse complications."

"Okay, Doctor. We'll load him up and take him right now." Burl was giving orders to Willard and Len to get the wagon ready. Sinda he sent to get bedding.

They would need a bed mattress or two to place on the bottom of the wagon. Burl intended to lift Alford on the sheet he lay on, carry him out the front door, and as gently as possible, place him on the wagon bed. He felt that was the least painful way of moving his father.

"Dr. Kerr, are you going with us?" asked Sinda.

"Yes, I am."

Sinda was thankful the sky was clear, even though it was cold.

The ride into Maryville was best forgotten. Burl drove the wagon, and his mom sat on the seat beside him. Willard and Len rode in the back on each side of their dad. They attempted to steady him in rough places. The pain was severe. Alford passed out. That was the only blessing of the whole ride.

They stopped only once—at the Bertrams. Burl ran to the back door of the home. Jorge answered his knock. "What's wrong?"

"We're taking Dad into Maryville. Will you see that Jake takes care of the place and that the children are fed? We don't have any time to lose."

"You go on. I'll take care of the house and children." Jorge gestured with his hands to send Burl on his way.

Burl hurried back to the wagon, got in, and slapped the reins on Spot's back.

～

Dr. Lincoln immediately dismissed his other patients and prepared for surgery. After examining Alford, he called the family into his office and told them that this operation would cure him or would take his life, but this was his only option.

There was no hospital in Maryville in 1913. Several surgeons had rooms in their offices where minor surgery was performed and one of these rooms was where they wheeled Alford. There was no time to waste.

Anesthetic was administered by Dr. Lincoln's nurse, who also assisted with his tools. Dr. Kerr decided to observe.

Appendectomies were being perfected in the 1890's, and twenty years later were routine for most doctors and patients, especially if the problem was caught early. Alford's stubbornness put his life in great jeopardy.

Dr. Kerr was the first doctor to appear after the surgery. His face said it all.

"We were too late. He's still alive, but it's only a matter of time. If he had let us bring him in earlier, Dr. Lincoln might have saved his life. The key word here is might. As it is, we need to make him comfortable. With morphine, he will feel no pain."

Alford didn't last through the night. Dr. Lincoln sat up with the family until there was no need to. He gave Sinda and her boys the use of his office to prepare Alford for his trip home.

The last time Burl walked down the Maryville streets, it was to buy himself a suit of clothes and a gift for his future bride. On that happy day, he never dreamed the next time he bought a suit it would be for his father — one in which to bury him.

On the morning of March 31, 1913, James Alford Whitehead, Sr. was buried at Six Mile Cemetery. He was forty-eight years old. The afternoon before his internment, Jake rode to the Tipton's to tell Melva and her father about the funeral plans. Guided by Jake, Noah and Melva came the day Alford was buried and attended his funeral. Later, everyone ate the dinner prepared by the ladies of the church at Six Mile.

Telling Sinda, Burl, and the children goodbye, Noah and Melva rode back to Chilhowee. Melva rode behind her dependable father. Never had she appreciated or loved her father more than on the trip home.

After dinner, when the house was empty of well-wishers and friends, the Whitehead family sat down to discuss Sinda's situation.

Burl started the conversation, "Mama, I know you need some time to grieve and understand the drastic changes our family's undergone in the last few days. But you can't stay in this big house with young children and tend the farm. Willard, Len, and me would feel more comfortable if you moved closer to us. Then we could help take care of you. There's work at Alcoa for several more years, and good wages working for the Bertrams, so we don't plan on going anywhere else. Our idea is for you to move into one of the houses to be rented in Alcoa or even on Abram's Creek."

He continued, "Or you could move in with other relatives of your choosing, but we've talked, and we feel moving closer to our work is the best idea. We'll keep paying your bills for the present time. Still, it's your choice," said Burl.

"When you decide what to do, send Tom to Jorge Bertram and tell him. He will get a message to us. We will help you, whatever you decide. There's no hurry."

The next day was Tuesday, April Fool's Day.

Burl went out to the porch to put his shoes on. He sat down in the cane-backed chair outside the kitchen door and looked around. There next to the chair sat Alford's old boots. He picked one up and pulled at a leather shoelace. He turned it over. The grooves were caked with mud—mud from the last time his father walked on his farm. He put the shoe down.

Burl quickly laced up his boots and left the porch. The sight of those old shoes brought tears to his eyes, and grown men didn't cry. He swiped the water from his eyes. From then on, Burl placed his shoes on the back steps and sat there to lace them.

Until Sinda made up her mind, Alford's shoes remained in the same spot.

Alford's sons stayed until Wednesday, helping around the farm and teaching the youngsters new responsibilities. Then, Burl, Willard and Len went back to Alcoa. A month passed by and then two.

On June 1st, Jake came with the boys' wages and a message. Sinda was ready to move to Alcoa or Abram's Creek.

Willard and Len went home the next weekend to decide on arrangements. Burl and Melva looked for a house to rent. When the farm sold, there might be money to buy another small farm, but it would have to sell first.

Noah placed a sign in Tipton's Mercantile advertising for a house to rent. Sinda would need enough land for Old Spot and her two milk cows to graze. The boys planned to help by planting a garden.

The home came from an unexpected source. Mrs. Lindsey owned fifteen acres of mountain and bottomland and, next to her on a separate plot, was an empty house with a small barn. If they could rent the house, she was glad to let them farm her land. All she wanted was some vegetables out of the garden to can.

This sounded like an excellent plan until Melva and Burl saw the fence around the grazing acreage. And the house next door needed quite a bit of work to make it livable. The barn was in better shape than the house. Still, the fence was fixable. Sinda's strong boys could make short work of it. The house was a different matter.

Noah inquired around and found out the house was owned by a Maryville man who had worked briefly at the slate factory in Chilhowee.

The Southern Slate Company operated along Abrams Creek, mining green, purple and black slate for construction purposes. Before the railroad, the company stacked the slate along the banks of the Little Tennessee River for transport by barge downstream. Since the quarries and property changed owners many times, as a labor source, this industry wasn't dependable,

When the quarry closed, the owner of the house abandoned his home. The only way to contact the man was to go to Maryville and look him up. Since Noah was a good negotiator, he decided to take on that responsibility, but he needed to wait until Sunday afternoon to go. Burl, Willard, Len, and Melva were at a stalemate. They couldn't do anything until Noah returned.

On Monday, Melva went to Alcoa to open the store. When Burl came that afternoon, he teased her about not looking anything like Noah. As they rode to

Chilhowee, they stopped at the rickety house they hoped to fix up for his mother.

"It needs a new roof before anything else is done to the place," said Burl.

"Yes, and all the broken window panes need to be replaced. I wonder why he didn't rent it and let someone keep it up. Seems a shame to let your property run down like this." Melva was headed around to the back of the house. She pumped water from the cistern. It looked useable. "Where's the spring and the springhouse?" she wondered out loud.

"Let's walk up the hollow behind the house." Burl went first.

These sources of water needed cleaned out and some work done on them, such as a new door on the small, stone shed over the spring, but they were serviceable. Melva observed, "The children will haul water farther than at Six Mile. I guess they'll grumble about that."

Holding hands, Burl and Melva walked back to their mounts. Burl stopped for a moment and turned to face her. He shook his head and said, "I'm uneasy to raise this subject, but getting this house repaired and moving Mama will take some time, especially since the work will need to be done in the afternoons and on Saturday afternoon—and maybe even Sunday. I was thinking, we may have to postpone our marriage for a little while."

She stood on tiptoe and gave him a quick peck on the lips. "I was thinking the same thing. I don't want to postpone our wedding," she stood looking at her future husband. "But I want your mother settled in the best surroundings we can provide for her."

Following the example of her father and mother, she intended to be of assistance as much as possible. After all, this was Burl's mama. They rode on to the big house at Chilhowee and ate supper with Nan and the other children.

After dinner on Tuesday, Noah came to Alcoa with news on the house.

"Hi, Melva," he called upon entering the door with his empty money sack in hand.

Melva went around the counter and gave her father a hug. "How was your trip to Maryville? I wish I could have gone."

"I enjoyed it. I stayed at the Blount Hotel in the same rooms we stayed in. Do you remember it?" Noah was behind the counter, checking the safe. He hadn't been able to collect the money since he didn't come on Monday.

"Yes. Did you see Mr. Anderson and give him my note for Juliet?" Melva corresponded sporadically with John's daughter since coming back to Chilhowee.

"I did. He's the one who helped me find the owner of the house. Thinking we could find his address at Blount State Bank, John checked their files but he wasn't a customer there. So, John picked up the phone and called Maryville National. He talked to the other bank president. Within a few minutes, we had an answer and drove out to the man's house in Friendsville. By the way, the owner knew Betty Jo's husband, Robert."

"Sometimes, it's a small world. What did you find out about the house?"

"He said it needed work when he lived in it. He planned on doing a little at a time as he got the money.

His job at the slate company wasn't to his liking, so he moved back to Friendsville. Anyway, if we fix it up, Sinda can have it rent-free for one year."

"Oh, that's wonderful." Melva clasped her hands together.

"He'll come to the store next Saturday on the train with a lease for someone to sign. I guess Burl will need to do that."

Noah had accomplished the impossible.

It took six weeks for the boys, Melva, Noah, Nan, and Mrs. Lindsey to get the house fixed up and the fence repaired so Sinda could move. Noah provided some of the supplies without charge, while Nan and Mrs. Lindsey cooked more than one meal for the workers. By August 1st, all was ready. The Bertrams provided two large wagons and Jake. Noah sent his wagon and horses. Sinda had a farm wagon which Old Spot could pull, and Mrs. Simerly offered a wagon and a horse. It took two days for the men to load Sinda's belongings onto the wagons.

After they were finished, Burl went over to the Bertrams to see D. Boone. He came at Burl's whistle, ambling up to the fence so Burl could scratch behind his ears. He and Johnny would pull one of the heaviest wagons, while the new team of mules would pull the other.

Burl headed for the barn and down the row of familiar stalls. He was headed for one particular one. A low, *I know you* whiney greeted him, and a dark, chestnut colored head stuck over the stall door. Two big brown eyes watched the man's figure as he walked down the aisle. Burl sidled up to the door, acting like he didn't know her, his back turned in her direction.

Dark Queen nudged him with her velvety nose as if to say, *Don't you ignore me!*

Burl turned around, "Oh, there you are Queen. How's my girl doing? Do you still love me?" Between the pats and the nudging, the two renewed their acquaintance. Horses are like elephants, they never forget, especially the fact that someone loves them.

Thursday, August 7, was moving day. The men arose before light and harnessed the mules and the horses by lamplight. As soon as the sun came up, the wagons moved out. Burl felt like saying, "Wagon's ho," as they left, like they did on wagon trains out west. The plan was to get over the mountains before the hot sun was high in the sky. In August, the lowlands were hot and muggy. It would be cooler on the higher peaks.

Moving Sinda's belongings over Chilhowee Mountain wasn't an easy task. The road was steep with switchbacks. The old timers used to say *"you meet yourself going and coming"* around the steep curves. They weren't far off. The teams of horses or mules and a wheel brake provided stopping power up and down the mountain. Once over the top, there were very few places to rest until you got to the valley floor.

Not long after dinner, the wagons pulled into the yard of Sinda's new home.

The house wasn't as big as the last one, but she didn't need a large one now. Sam Duggan and the rest of the surveying crew, along with Milton and Mathew were there to help unload. They worked continuously to set up beds and place furniture where Sinda wanted it set. Not long afterward, food began arriving. Noah came with a box and Mrs. Lindsey brought a cake and bread. Everyone was starved. They sat around eating a picnic on the front porch. As they ate, their dangling legs swung freely, keeping time with each bite they chewed.

Tomorrow, the wagons would be driven back over the mountain. The children would be gathered from Mrs. Simerly, who had graciously offered to keep them for the night. On Saturday, the Whiteheads would be settled in their new home.

Meanwhile, Burl and Melva had put their names on a list for a home in Alcoa. They received notice of its completion on August 5th. As soon as Sinda was comfortably settled, Burl and Melva could get married.

They decided on August 23rd. This was a Saturday. They had two weeks to get their house ready to move into.

Noah and Nan gave Melva her bedroom furniture. The young couple sent to Maryville for a new couch and everything else was bought used or was a hand-me-down from their parents and friends. Melva's hope chest could be moved with her bedroom furniture. The contents provided them with supplies for the kitchen and linens for the bedrooms. One bedroom would be empty until they had enough money ahead to purchase furniture for it.

August 23, 1913, dawned cool and sunny.

Burl had stayed in the barracks until their wedding day. Now he was moving the rest of his belongings into the house. It was still early as he walked out on the porch of his new home. He looked down into the valley and across to the Little T. He had to admit that he was nervous.

The ceremony was planned for just before noon. Buddy Whitehead, who was a Justice-of-the-Peace in

Happy Valley, was to perform the service. Afterwards, Nan and Sinda were providing a meal for those in attendance.

Although wedding ceremonies in the mountains weren't elaborate, several people were to attend this one. Jorge and Josten Bertram came from Six Mile. Juliet came from Maryville, and Mrs. Lindsey was invited, along with Sam Duggan and his crew. Even Cal McMurray and the train engineer were coming. Rita and her husband arrived early to help Nan.

Then there were the rest of the Whiteheads and the Tiptons. Almost thirty people would stand in the yard or crowd onto the porch where the ceremony would take place.

Upstairs, Melva sat at a dressing table in one of the extra bedrooms. She was applying powder and rouge to her face. Lydia, sitting on the bed, watched every move. Melva checked the hair pins holding her heavy mop of hair for the hundredth time. Pulling and pushing, Lydia was sure the pins never changed positions. As Melva dressed, she placed her personal items into her suitcase. Her coral suit dress, the one she bought in Maryville, lay on the cluttered bed and her black patent shoes sat nearby.

At the age of almost nine, Lydia was remarkably quiet while Melva completed her toilette. She was losing her sister, playmate, and friend. Melva looked over at her petite, innocent sister and smiled, remembering Lydia's comment about not liking husbands when they sat high above the valley. That seemed like ages ago. Melva thought about the reversal of roles within a family. Now Lydia played big sister to

Joyce, who already followed her around like a puppy dog.

What goes around comes around, she thought.

"Lydia, go look out the window and see if Burl is here."

Lydia jumped up and walked over to look. The open window allowed the curtains to blow in the soft morning breeze. Outside the muffled sound of voices were heard.

"No—but I see several wagons down at Father's store. People are walkin' up the flagstone path to the house and the train is comin' in the distance."

At that moment the whistle of the arriving train was clearly heard as it echoed in the valley. It would get louder as the train neared.

"Juliet will be on the train. When she arrives, I want you to go down and bring her up here." Melva had asked Juliet Anderson to stand with her when she got married. Betty Jo and Robert were in Friendsville at a church and family function and wouldn't attend.

"Okay." Lydia headed for the door.

"No! No! Not now. Wait and watch for her to get off the train. Then you can go and meet her."

Lydia stood for a minute at the door. "Somethin' smells good."

"The two mothers are cookin' up a feast for everyone." Tables for holding food were placed along the wall in the downstairs hall. Chairs were scattered throughout the house and on either end of the porch so guests could sit while eating. "Are you hungry, Lydia?"

"Yep, a little," Lydia truthfully admitted as she came back inside the room and returned to her place at the window.

Melva had waited until the last moment to get dressed. Now the time had come. She pulled on her undergarments including her girdle, attaching her hose to the garters, and straightening the seam at the back. Stepping into her skirt, she pulled it to her waist, buttoning it securely. Her black patent shoes slipped on easily. She bent over to lace them up. She wondered briefly where Burl was but then he was never late. He would be there. Several minutes went by.

"There she is with Mr. McMurray and the engineer," exclaimed Lydia. It was just a short walk from the depot to the house.

"Run on downstairs and meet her. Remember, her name is Juliet," she called after Lydia's disappearing figure.

Melva put her jacket on and buttoned it up. There was nothing special about her wedding clothes but their beautiful color. Plain cut, the suit fit every curve of her figure. I do have a nice figure, she thought, turning to catch a glimpse of it in the mirror of the dresser. She drew a deep breath. She would be glad when the ceremony was over.

"Hello, you must be Juliet," she heard her mother say downstairs. That meant her mother was dressed for the ceremony. "Melva's upstairs getting ready."

The sounds of footsteps on the stairs ended when Lydia appeared in the doorway, munching on something and towing Juliet by the hand.

The two ladies hugged each other.

"I'm so glad to see you. Did you like your train ride?" asked Melva.

"Oh, yes! That's the first time I've ridden the train by myself. When we came out at the Little T and headed this way, the river took my breath away. I didn't realize it was so wide, and the water moves so fast." Juliet's smile lit up her face and, with her blond hair she brought a radiance or glow when she entered a room.

"I'm glad you liked it. I always discover something new when I ride into Maryville. Do I look like I'm going to be married?" asked Melva.

"You look marvelous. I love the coral suit, but you're missing something," said Juliet, looking at Melva intently.

"What!" exclaimed Melva quickly looking in the mirror. She couldn't see anything wrong.

From her pocket, Juliet pulled out a small box. Inside was a set of beautiful coral earrings. Not pierced, because Melva hadn't put holes in her ears, but the screw-on type.

"I guessed you'd wear this outfit, and Mama and I wanted to buy you something. Do you like them?"

Melva thought they were beautiful. After giving her friend a hug, she sat down at the dressing table, and Juliet placed her gift on Melva's ears.

"Melva, here comes Burl," Lydia called from the window.

Juliet rushed to the window. She had never seen Burl before.

"Which one is he, Lydia?" she asked.

"He has on the felt hat. He's riding a big red mule," Lydia explained. "And he's leading Johnny," she exclaimed. The big mule was D. Boone sent over by the Bertrams for Burl to use at the wedding. "Johnny has a side-saddle strapped on his back." He was Melva's transportation home to Alcoa.

"Wow, Melva," said Juliet, "Burl is handsome."

"There's Buddy Whitehead," said Lydia. "He's shaking hands with Burl and Father." Lydia was giving a blow-by-blow description of the goings on.

"It's time to go downstairs," said Melva. She was so nervous she was shaking. When she got to the bottom of the stairs, she could hardly smile at her future husband. He came over to speak to her privately. "You look a little like the day you fainted. Take several deep breaths and think about," Burl looked around the room for the most outrageous find he could shock her with, "Pineapple!" he finished.

"What?" Melva laughed as he pointed to a tray of cut, juicy cubes on a tray. Ordered especially for the wedding, the cubes were part of the food the attendees would eat. "Pineapple, indeed!" After a good laugh, Melva felt better.

The ceremony wasn't long, thank goodness. When Mr. Whitehead pronounced them man and wife, Burl kissed Melva on the cheek. Everyone crowded around and congratulated the newlyweds.

Then Noah got everyone's attention and announced that a buffet was provided for their guests. Noah motioned for Melva and Burl to go first. The newlyweds went into the house, and everybody followed.

꒳ **Chapter Twelve** ꒳

Postscript and Finish

*For thou shalt eat the labour of thine hands: happy
shalt thou be, and it shall be well with thee.*

Psalms 128:2 KJV

Exactly one hundred and five years later, I look at a
picture taken on my grandparents' wedding day on
August 23, 1913. The couple sit on a pair of red mules.
Burl Whitehead rides the largest one that I've named D.
Boone. Melvina (Melva) Lucinda Tipton Whitehead sits
sidesaddle on the smaller animal—Johnny, of course.

The handsome man riding beside her never had a
chance once Melva made up her mind to marry him,
not that there weren't other suitors for her hand. It was
love at first sight, and Burl Whitehead might as well
have proposed at that instance.

One thing could be said about Burl's family, they
weren't rich. Thirteen children were born to his
mother, Lucinda (Sinda) Hall Whitehead. When her
husband James Alford died suddenly, the family
worked hard to make a living. Sinda's sons were
strong, muscular men—hard workers.

Until James Alford died the family lived on the
family farm at Six Mile, as everyone called it, in the big

farmhouse beside Six Mile Creek. Burl's whole life up to this time, along with his brothers, was spent in tending the fields around the house, schooling, when he could go, consisted of reading, writing and figuring, and the rest he learned at his mother's knee.

All the Whiteheads were tall people, most way over six feet and Burl was no exception. Lanky, blue-eyed with curly light, brown hair, handsome in a sober way, it was no wonder that Melva immediately claimed him for her very own.

He was just the opposite of his lively, young wife, although each possessed a strong sense of right and wrong — morals instilled in them by their parents. Burl sat stiffly, unsmiling on his big, red mule his folded hand on his hip and the reins held loosely in his other hand. It was as if he were saying, "Let's get this over with," or, "Enough of this fooling around."

Working horses and mules, was his vocation and early on he would make much of his living in this fashion. A dedicated worker, he had calloused hands with long, strong fingers. His reputation on the job was as one who understood the animals he worked with. Resilient and sturdy as the trees he sawed or the mules he worked, he would be a dependable, trustworthy husband. Melva had immediately sensed this about him.

Knowing him later in his life, I can imagine the trepidation he might have felt about his coming wedding night, for he was a modest man, and intimate things were best kept to oneself, not that he was unknowing about such things.

The slim young lady, looking back at me from the picture, was well-formed and certainly attractive. She had straight, dark brown hair, partly concealed by a knit, winter style hat. Why this type of hat toward the end of August? I don't know, unless an unexpected cold front, typical of this month arrived during the night before her wedding. Her snapping brown eyes and square face, with pointed chin, (what you can see of it because an ear of the mule obscures it) shows just a hint of a smile as she travels on the rocked, dirt road to her new home.

Newly married, she sits sidesaddle on the big red mule, borrowed just for this occasion by her new husband for he wasn't a man rich in money. She's typical of the young brides of the day, those living in the foothills of the mountains, where it wasn't unusual for girls to marry at the ripe, old age of fourteen. So, by that standard she is a little older, having passed her seventeenth birthday.

Always a child encouraged by her parents to think and stand on her own, she would use these talents as the wife of Burl Whitehead. The life of a woman whose husband's expertise involved the love of horses, mules, forests, and mountains would not be easy. There would be times together, and there would be times apart, but if Melva had anything to do with it, all times would be good.

Their journey today took them to Alcoa, soon to be renamed Calderwood, and a rental house on Cedar Lane where they started their married life. Burl's work with a surveying team, clearing timber for the proposed extension of the rail line from Chilhowee to Alcoa and then Tapoco, was contracted by the Bertrams through the Aluminum Company of America. This would be their home for eight years until their first three children are born. Maddie was born in December 1914. Earl was born in September 1916. Georgia May was born in February 1918.

∽

The marriage of Burl and Melva was not the end but the beginning. Read on.

❧ Chapter Thirteen ❧

Time Passes in the Newest Whitehead Household

Who can find a virtuous women? for her price is far about rubies. The heart of her husband doth safely trust in her.

Proverbs 31:10-11a KJV

If the Tiptons and the Whiteheads had moved en masse to the developing city of Alcoa, they would've made a small community of their own. As it turned out, most of the two families lived there for short periods of time. Sinda became a resident when Elmer and Tom joined their brothers on the surveying crew. Noah and Nan eventually lived there on weekends.

Two members of the family did not live at Alcoa. Fast becoming the friend and confidant of W.B. Townsend, D.H. continued to work at the bank. But Henry, like his father, went into politics. In 1914, the Quarterly County Court, the same body that Noah served on as Squire, elected Henry Tipton as Register of Deeds. He was twenty-three years old and in the beginning states of crippling arthritis.

Studious and detail oriented, he emulated his father. While growing up, Henry was self-consciousness about his ears. They stuck out prominently from his head. Melva wondered if this hang-up wasn't the reason she always found him reading by the sitting room window, out of the hustle and bustle of the household. Confronting the public at his bank teller job and now as a county servant required mustering a good amount of courage on his part.

～

After their marriage, life for Burl and Melva evolved into a normal routine in Alcoa. For the first time in her life, Melva let someone other than her father or mother make important decisions affecting her life. Burl was a good man and totally reliable. If he hadn't been, they would've fought like cats and dogs. As it was, Melva lost some of her feistiness and settled down to married life.

Melva continued to help her father until her first pregnancy forced her to quit. On December 13, 1914, Maddie Whitehead was born. This little one was the most beautiful baby, Melva ever laid eyes on. She had a head of black hair, brown eyes, and ten fingers and ten toes. Melva thought to herself, Burl and I make beautiful babies.

Her grandparents fell in love with her immediately, as did most everyone who saw her.

"The baby's really growing, Melva," said Nan one day when her daughter visited her at Chilhowee in the late summer of 1915. Nan bounced little Maddie on her knee, making her smile and laugh.

"Yes. I tell Burl she eats almost as much as he does." Melva laughed contentedly. She'd dreamed married life would be like this. During the time when she waited for Burl to state his feelings, she had begun to wonder if he really was the one. Mrs. Lindsey had cautioned her not to be impatient, and she'd done just that. Melva decided she would always listen to her heart and never doubt again. It spoke the truth. Love required an ear to your heart. "Where's Joyce"?

"She's at Rita's, playing with her nephews, or should I say ordering them around." Nan laughed. "Rita and James will bring her home around dark."

"Give Maddie a few years and Joyce can play with her niece."

"Yes, she can. Your father will be home shortly to eat dinner. You're staying to eat with us, aren't you?" Nan handed Maddie to her mother so she could check on her boiling potatoes and finish preparing the meal.

"Oh, yes. I'm not planning on heading back to Alcoa until late afternoon. I want to stop by Mrs. Lindsey's, and I need to get the buggy back to the commissary before the sun sets. Burl will be in from his work about that time." Melva intended to stop at the widow's house so she could see Little Maddie. She loved her as much as Nan.

"I'll fix enough food so you can warm your supper in the oven. No cooking for you tonight."

"Have D.H. and Henry been home lately?" asked Melva. She hadn't seen D.H but twice after the marriage. She missed her brother.

"D.H. hasn't been home since he came to visit you after the baby was born. Now Henry's been here at least twice. I'll tell you a secret. Henry's been seeing Lila Lowe. I think it's gettin' serious. Probably won't be long until he asks for her hand." Lila's father was the man from whom Noah purchased the store before moving his family from Cades Cove. "Henry's comin' again this weekend," Nan nodded knowingly.

"Henry couldn't find a sweeter wife. I think she's perfect for him."

Lila's personality immediately made her a friend of everyone she met. She'd certainly liven up Henry's stuffy life.

Melva laughed. "I've always liked Lila." Being four years older than Lila, they weren't best friends at school. Lila was closer to Matthew's age.

"Are Rita and James well?" This couple had two little ones and one on the way.

"The babies are fine. James' latest bout with pneumonia left him weaker than normal. I'm worried about him, but Rita says he's getting better. She should know. She lives with him.

"Have you heard from Ellie?"

"No. Not for a while. D.H. checks up on her from time to time."

Noah walked in the door at that moment and kissed Nan on the cheek.

"Well, look who's here," he said walking over to Maddie, picking her up and raising her high in the air. Maddie giggled at her grandfather, so he did it again. "You're a cutie, little girl," he said to the baby. With his foot, he drew up a kitchen chair and sat down, so he could bounce her on his knee.

Melva chuckled at being totally ignored. "It's good to see you too, Father."

"Ah, Melva, I've seen you for over eighteen years. I haven't seen this little one a year as yet. You'll have to forgive me." Noah continued to tweak Maddie's nose and love-poke her stomach. The baby was giggling nonstop.

Nan and Melva looked at a husband and father reduced to childlike gibberish and actions by his granddaughter. They joined in the laughter.

When everyone could breathe, Noah asked, "Melva, have you been to the store at Alcoa this week? How do you like the fresh paint? Milton did a good job, and the postal area is greatly expanded. Any more residents and a regular post office must be built."

"I think it smells like when you opened the first commissary and I worked the counter." Milton had stayed with her in Alcoa on the days he was painting. She had enjoyed her brief visit with him.

While he was working on sprucing up the store, Burl reminded Milton of his promise to take him to his surveying job in the mountains. So, they loaded up one morning, when the paint needed the day to dry. Seventeen-year-old Milton spent the day chopping limbs off trees, cutting trees down and snaking logs out of the surveyor's path using the red mule, Johnny.

"He'll be going back to the Academy this fall. I'm going to miss his help this summer. Milton loves to work with his hands. Painting the store and moving the counters proved to be fun. Now he wants to paint the Chilhowee store." Almost as an aside, he added, "Nan and I think he'd make a good builder of houses. Thought I'd talk to John Walker. He builds the majority of the big mansions in Maryville," Noah added.

"Let me have Maddie, Father. I'll change her diaper and see if I can rock her to sleep so we can eat in peace." Melva returned and helped her mother dish up the food.

They moved to the dining table. Noah gave the blessing on the food.

"Have you seen Betty Jo lately, Father?" asked Melva.

"She was in last week, I think. She and Robert are moving to Maryville. He's found work closer to home. She asked about you."

"I'd like to see her before she leaves. Would you tell her that?"

After the meal, Noah headed back to the store. Melva and her mother walked to the parlor, took off their shoes, and stretched out on the room's divans. With pillows for comfort each took a nap.

When Melva woke up, her mother was in the kitchen. Nan had cut two pieces of apple pie. The two women shared some quiet talk until Maddie cried from her grandmother's bedroom. Nan went to get her granddaughter.

"I think she's hungry," Nan said, handing the baby to her daughter.

Melva breastfed her child while Nan prepared a small amount of mashed potatoes and mashed up green beans from dinner. With Joyce's baby spoon, she fed Maddie the rest of her food.

"Mother, it's time for us to go home," Melva said, picking up her belongings and stuffing them into a bag to place in the covered buggy. "Albert will need the buggy to drive home to Abram's Creek after he quits work." Noah had bought this carriage for the specific use of Melva and his employee to use on trips between the two towns.

Melva kissed her mother goodbye. She got into the buggy. After Nan handed Maddie to her, she placed the baby between her knees, on a padded seat Burl had specifically made for his daughter. This allowed Melva to keep a close eye on her while driving.

~

Mrs. Lindsey was sitting on the front porch fanning herself when Melva arrived.

"I wondered if you'd stop. I saw you ride by this morning," said the widow."

"I went to Mother's to spend the day." She handed the baby to the widow, secured the horse's reins, and dismounted. "How are you gettin' along?" Melva walked up the steps to the porch.

Maddie was sitting in Mrs. Lindsey's lap while the elderly lady cooed over her.

"I could be better. My arthritis keeps workin' on me, and I move slower these days. I thank the Lord I'm alive and kickin'." Mrs. Lindsey laughed at Maddie's antics. "How's Burl?"

"He's workin' hard as ever. I suppose you miss Sinda since she moved to Alcoa," said Melva.

"Sure do. Those garden vegetables were so tasty. They come by to see me and check on Old Spot and the cow." The animals were left in Mrs. Lindsey's pasture to keep the weeds down. Mrs. Lindsey milked the cow and sold some of the milk to her neighbors. "I don't know how much longer I'll be able to milk the cow. It's so hard to get up off the stool."

The two friends sat and talked several more minutes. Finally, Melva was ready to leave.

"I have something for Maddie," said Mrs. Lindsey. She disappeared into the house, coming out with a pink dress she had hand sewn. The bodice was cross-stitched and the rest of the dress trimmed with delicate lace. It was lovely.

Melva was shaking her head at Mrs. Lindsey. "You shouldn't have done this, but it's certainly pretty."

"A pretty dress for a pretty little girl," said Mrs. Lindsey, tweaking Maddie's cheek.

"She'll be wearing it the next time you see her," said Melva who hugged Mrs. Lindsey goodbye. The sun was going down beyond the Chilhowee Mountains and a golden glow bathed the forest as Melva headed for Alcoa. Melva sighed. Life was perfect.

～

If life was perfect for Melva Whitehead, it was not for the burgeoning community of Alcoa. Mr. I.G. Calderwood, well-known to the Aluminum Company of America, was tapped to became superintendent of the final construction at Alcoa, and the first dam, Cheoah. His first act was to force the extension of the railroad, from Chilhowee to Alcoa, in February 1916.

When Southern Railway, the parent company of the Tennessee Carolina Southern Railroad lagged behind on their promises to extend the spur to the developing city above Chilhowee, an ALCOA representative boasted it could be built in six weeks—trees were cut and the grade was mostly ready.

Mr. Wells, the Southern representative countered, "I suppose, since you want it built in six weeks, you can build it in that time yourself."

The ALCOA representative let out an oath, "We *can* build it in six weeks!"

"Then build it and send us the bill," Mr. Wells said with a grin on his face.

The contract was signed.

Soon every store within two hundred miles of Alcoa was stripped of all materials usable for building a railroad. Later, an invoice was placed on the desk of the Southern Railway's representative in Washington, D.C.

With Mr. Calderwood's supervision, the workers finished the six miles of track in less than six weeks!

The commissary construction was finished in March, coinciding with the railroad's extension. The stocked goods, purchased from Noah's old store, were moved into the new building. After the stock was relocated, the post office was expanded in the old location with new, numbered metal cubbyholes and new counters with cages for two workers. Noah was out of business in Alcoa.

~

The city multiplied rapidly with the slow addition of about one thousand men from throughout the south, mostly black men needing work. Every day the train brought more. With the increase in the population of Alcoa, another problem presented itself whereby Noah could help.

Mr. Calderwood was a man who didn't touch alcohol and hated to see his worker's drink. He tried to prevent the consumption of alcohol in Alcoa, but with a short walk into the mountains, moonshine was readily available. Snuck in undercover, it often caused fights within the unruly element of the city. Brawls broke out over gambling debts and name calling.

To combat this rowdy behavior Calderwood approached Noah, asking for his assistance. As a Justice-of-the-Peace, Noah could arrest anyone causing a disturbance. The store owner didn't more than head back to Chilhowee, until he turned around to help with security at Alcoa.

Because most of the ruckus didn't happen during the week, Noah and Nan decided to live in Alcoa on weekends. Mr. Calderwood provided an empty house for them to use.

They left for Alcoa at noon on Friday, leaving the closing of the store and the Saturday business in the capable hands of a well-trained clerk.

Along with a hired assistant, Noah patrolled the streets of Alcoa on Friday afternoon, Saturday, and Sunday with a brief visit to Chilhowee for church and the preparing of dinner. Noah and Nan went home on Monday morning, in time to open the store. Lydia was eleven at the start of their stay. She and Joyce, then a young child of eight, played with Mr. Calderwood's daughter and the children of the other residents.

A building, designated as a holding area, served as a makeshift jail. Unless the infraction involved a criminal act, most of its inhabitants were held until they sobered up or cooled off. Of course, Noah used these opportunities to counsel each man on the error of his ways. Soon there were two buggies of people traveling to church on Sunday morning.

～

While Noah and Nan were at Alcoa, Earl Whitehead was born in September 1916. He was a blue-eyed, blond, curly-haired charmer. His only problem developed after he was a month old — he had the colic.

To Melva it seemed exactly as the sun went down, he started crying — screaming was the best word. She rocked him. She walked the floor with him. She tried to feed him. Nothing worked. For five months, she, Burl, and Nan consoled and pampered the youngster. His little mouth quivered, his hands flailed the air, until he was so exhausted, he couldn't cry on.

Maddie would wander over and look questionably at her big brother. Tears would well in her eyes, and although she didn't know the reason, she would cry quietly for him. Sometimes, Melva joined them both.

Nan came to help Melva during the week. Dog-tired from the weeks work, Burl was willing to help on weekends. During the night, when his wife awoke alone in their bed, she'd tiptoe to the living room. With Earl in his warm blanket, tucked safely in the crook of his father's arm, they would be sleeping together in the big wooden rocking chair. Melva never disturbed them. She always walked silently back to the bedroom.

～

"Melva, there's war in Europe!" exclaimed Burl, coming in the front door and waving a newspaper in the air. Europe was a seething caldron of ethnic friction and alliances. All it needed was a spark to ignite the fire of war.

"What's happened?" responded Melva, coming quickly from the kitchen, wiping her wet hands on her apron.

Burl was upset. He threw the paper onto the couch.

"You remember some fool shot the Archduke of Austria," he said, sitting in a chair because the long walk uphill left him breathless. "Now Great Britain's joined the fight."

Melva retrieved the paper to read the headlines while her young husband caught his breath. War! For a young family, this was a terrible word and it threatened to upset Melva's idyllic life.

"President Wilson says we aren't going to get involved," said Melva, "He hopes for a *'peace without victory,'* whatever that means."

"It means another alliance or truce for the countries to break. Mark my words," Burl was breathing easier, "we'll be in it next." For the following two years a distant cloud hung over life in the Little T valley.

~

At first, surveying and planning at Alcoa was done at a leisurely pace, but with the war in the Balkans threatening to plunge Europe into a major conflict, the mood changed and completion dates for the dams and the plant moved briskly ahead.

Aluminum products, light and easy to carry, would be needed if the United States entered the conflict. The construction on ALCOA's first reduction plant near Maryville, had started in 1913, four years ago.

In January 1917, British cryptographers deciphered a telegram from German Foreign Minister Arthur Zimmermann to the German Minister to Mexico, von Eckhardt. It offered the states of Arizona, New Mexico, and Texas to Mexico in return for joining the German cause. This message helped draw the United States into the war and thus changed the course of world history.

On April 6, 1917, Woodrow Wilson announced the Declaration of War on Germany. Although his reelection campaign talked about the fact that he'd kept America out of war, he could no longer ignore the torpedoing of American ships. When the German's strategy changed, and they decided that anything floating on the water was fair game, something had to be done.

The armed forces of America were meager. To build them up quickly, it was necessary to sign up young fighting men so they could be evaluated, drafted into the services, and trained. Every able-bodied man signed up for the draft. D.H. and Henry signed up. Henry was immediately turned down because of his crippling arthritis.

Burl and his brothers signed the papers, and Willard was quickly called on to serve in the Army. Melva waited anxiously to see if Burl's call would come.

~

Every day, Melva walked the concrete sidewalk down from Strawberry Holler to the post office to get the mail. Normally she loved the trip, greeting other residents on Cedar Lane and watching the changing seasons on the big maple, sourwood, and dogwood trees which grew in the neighborhood.

Sinda always came over to sit with the children, giving her daughter-in-law a chance to get out of the house into the fresh air.

Sometimes Maddie would stand at the door. "Me go. Me go." She would repeat until her mother relented, and they would walk hand-in-hand to the post office or the commissary.

But today, Maddie was taking a nap along with her brother.

Earl was no longer colicky. He was crawling all over the house, saying "mama" and "dada," sleeping through the night, and growing like a weed.

"I hope the mail has come," she said, waving to Sinda, who stood on the porch waving back.

She turned and immediately her old friend, a singing mockingbird on the top of a power pole started chastising her. "Not today, buddy. How about some beautiful, uplifting music," she suggested to the gray bird. The bird danced and flitted around on the pole's top but didn't change its tune.

Melva realized her get-up-and-go had definitely gone today. She approached the building saying in large letters, United States Post Office, Alcoa, Tennessee.

She opened the door. "Hi, Mr. Campbell," she greeted the postmaster.

"Good afternoon, Melva. I was just getting ready to put up the W's. Let me check—no there's not any mail for you today."

Melva stood looking around the store. It seemed strange to visit the place she'd worked in only a few years ago. Now, its walls were filled with banks of metal, numbered cubbyholes, where mail was deposited each day. Two counters with cages where customers could purchase stamps or mail special letters or parcels stood where the cash register always sat.

Melva didn't recognize the place, except the wood stove still remained exactly where it always was. She wanted to go over and hug the old iron heater but didn't.

"How many customers do you have now?" she asked.

"I think there's close to two thousand here in Alcoa and more coming. Of course, some of these are families and some are brothers, like the Whiteheads, so I don't have that many cubbyholes to fill. Still, it takes a while to place all that mail in slots." Mr. Campbell continued to sort mail into the boxes. The W's were at the end, so he kept poking his head around the corner to talk to her.

"I can't imagine so many people here." Melva shook her head and shrugged her shoulders.

"There's talk about puttin' another row of post boxes down the middle of the room. They'll remove the stove and patch the ceilin' and roof if they build 'em."

There goes the stove, Melva thought. She had her hand on the door knob when Mr. Campbell called her back.

"Here's one for you. It wasn't in the correct order." He handed the official government letter to Melva, observing the uneasy look that suddenly appeared on her face. He'd seen many of these same envelopes before, summing the men from Alcoa. "I hope it isn't bad news," he said simply

~

Melva wanted to immediately tear into the envelope, but she needed a secret place to find out what was inside. She wished she could walk to her overlook, the same place where she and Lydia had sat and talked before Betty Jo was married. She could look out over the serene valley to the Little T. Every time she was anxious, this scene calmed her.

Putting the envelope into the pocket of her skirt, she walked up the hill past her home. She'd find another secret place here in Alcoa. Waving at her neighbor, Mrs. Long, she kept walking until she reached the steps of the Baptist church. She sat down. From here, over the rooftops of the houses and buildings below, the Little T could be seen in the distance. This was the place. She felt safe here — safe enough to tear open the envelope and read its contents.

Burl wasn't going! Melva felt as if she would crumple into a pile on the church steps. She put her head on her knees. Her arms hung limply at her sides, her hand clutching the letter. Tears dropped with her relief, wetting the wooden steps.

Several minutes passed before she read the rest of the letter. The government classified the building of Cheoah and Santeetlah Dams a priority. They needed aluminum and processing aluminum required electricity. Her husband was exempt. He could serve his country by staying at home.

～

D.H. wasn't so lucky. Bank tellers weren't on the exemption list.

Everyone was gathered in the parlor at Chilhowee. D.H. stood there dressed in his new olive-drab tunic, looking very handsome. It was time to say goodbye. Noah approached his eldest son. Melva thought she saw tears in his eyes.

"Son, I'll be praying for you *every day*," he said as he shook D.H.'s hand. Suddenly, he drew his son to his breast and gave him a hug. Noah left the room, heading for the back door.

The affectionate embrace of father and son caused open sobbing among the sisters present. Ellie, Rita, Lydia and Melva were standing in the room to say goodbye. Of course, Lydia was crying the loudest because her sisters were crying. To quiet her, Melva put her arm around her twelve-year-old sister and gave her a hug.

Milton was turning nineteen. Taller than his brother, he walked over and shook his brother's hand. He'd be the next one to sign up for the draft.

"I may be joining you soon," he said.

D.H. and Milton's brother, Matthew, was going to boarding school in Maryville and didn't make the going away dinner.

Nan was in the kitchen with Joyce, cleaning up after the noonday meal. She'd already said her private goodbye. So far, her children were all alive and healthy. She was praying quietly as she often did at the kitchen sink, *"Lord, bring D.H. back whole and safe. Protect him from the evils of war and strengthen him in this time of testing. May his eyes and ears be open while he's in the line of fire and his heart full of love and longing for you. What more can I ask of you – "* Her tears fell in the dishwater.

Melva knew her goodbye was coming. She ached all over. D.H walked out to the porch with her. He wanted this time to be private as much as she did.

"Sister, what can I say? I'm going to miss you."

"Oh, D.H., I don't want anything to happen to you." Melva was crying. She'd tried to keep back the tears, but now they were flowing freely. Had it come to this? Was she going to lose her brother in some foreign country and never see him again?

"Go ahead and cry it out. You'll feel better. Let's sit in the front porch swing for a few minutes." Holding her hand, D.H led her over to the swing. Its movement quieted her crying. He looked over the familiar valley, where he'd played and worked. This scene was one he wanted to remember while he was away.

"Do you know how long you'll be gone?" asked Melva, wiping her eyes with a handkerchief.

"I don't have any idea. As long as it takes, I suppose. I'll probably see the Eiffel Tower and the Rhine River while I'm over there." D.H. threw this in, hoping this would take some of the anxiety off the goodbye.

Melva smiled. She recognized what her brother was doing. He stood up and walked to the porch steps. She followed him. The train would be leaving shortly, and he needed to be headed toward the depot. He could see Cal McMurray standing at the train steps ready to call, "All aboard."

"Take care of beautiful Maddie and Earl. Don't feed Burl too much. He doesn't need to grow any bigger," D.H. teased, as Melva put her arms around him.

"Please be careful. I love you, brother." She'd never said this to her brother before. That fact was always understood.

"I'll be okay. I love you too," said D.H., walking down the steps and on to the gate. He opened the latch and stepped down to the road. "I'll write." He waved and ran for the moving train. Cal McMurray pulled him aboard.

Two long years would pass before she saw him again.

∼

The United States took its time entering the conflict, even after war was declared. Troops must be trained and ferried to Europe. Finally, they were poised and ready to fight. But U.S. commanders weren't interested in integrating their men into the British or French Army. They wanted their units to fight alone. General John J. Pershing finally decided to let one-third of the

American forces fight on the front line with their counterparts. The rest needed more training.

In February 1918, Georgia May Whitehead was born. She had brown eyes set in a round face and straight brown hair. When she smiled, her whole face shone with light. Her mother often thought the word *angel* when she looked at her.

Melva had her hands full with two children in diapers. Burl was working so far away in the mountains, that he didn't come home until the weekends. Melva needed help with the children, so she asked Nan if Lydia could come and help when school let out for the summer. This proved to be a perfect solution. Eight-year-old Joyce was the only child left at the Tipton home in Chilhowee. Nan's nest was almost empty.

In the year 1918, a severe strain of influenza swept around the world. Thousands of soldiers died on the battlefield. D.H.'s letter didn't arrive until the next year. He wrote,

> *Dear Sister,*
>
> *I hope this letter finds you well. I am in France completing training for moving to the front lines. We still don't have a specific time for doing this. General Pershing says we will go when we are ready.*
>
> *I can tell you that much of France looks like the valleys and coves of home, maybe not as many tall trees. The only exception is the clusters of villages present in the countryside. They are tight knit, and there is no room for growing vegetables except in plots as big as a postage stamp.*

We have been busy burying the dead because of an outbreak of the flu. I hope this doesn't reach the States. If it does, watch out. It is deadly. I have buried so many men, I can probably get a job as a grave digger when I come home. That's a bad joke, isn't it?

I know Maddie is growing like a weed, and I would like to see Earl, also. Tell Burl we'll go fishing when I return. I sure can't wait to get home.

Your affectionate brother,
D.H.

D.H. didn't know about his new niece.

The war was over almost as soon as it started for the American troops. Fighting had virtually ceased by the end of 1918.

∾

Early in 1919, the Eighteenth Amendment was ratified by the states and added to the United States Constitution. Prohibiting the manufacturing and sale of alcoholic beverages, the change made the liquid more valuable and in demand. A multitude of stills sprang up in the hollers of the Appalachians, far enough back in the mountains where the government men couldn't find them. This was not true for I.G. Calderwood.

Mr. Calderwood often walked the streets and mountains around the new city. On one of his many trips into the mountains, he came close to a still in full operation and being tended by its owner. The owner fled at the sound of Calderwood's approach, and, taking his rifle with him skulked into the woods, peering back at his still, and the advancing man.

Shots rang out. Three of them hit Calderwood, a big, strong man, who weighed over two hundred and fifty pounds. Calderwood walked back to Alcoa where his wife dressed his flesh wounds. He called Noah, who rode from Chilhowee to check on him.

"Flesh wounds! I don't believe it," exclaimed Noah. "Most mountain men I know are good shots. They supplement their diet with wild game, and some of those animals are shot under difficult circumstances. With three shots, you should be good'en' dead."

"Why do you think I'm not dead?" Calderwood asked.

"I believe you've been given a warning? Stay away from my still."

"We can't let this moonshiner get away with this."

"No, we can't." Noah called in the sheriff of Blount County. The peacekeeper and his deputies located the still and the moonshiner. After a gun battle, the sheriff arrested the culprit.

Calderwood rested for a few days, letting the wounds heal and then returned to work, telling Noah, "I guess you'll be out of work again pretty soon. We'll need fulltime peace keepers since our city is growing so rapidly."

Noah nodded. He agreed.

~

The Treaty of Versailles, ending the war, was signed in the middle of 1919. The Americans were coming home. Millions of people lost their lives in a war that gained nothing for the aggressors, although the land mass of Europe and Asia was redefined.

The first ALCOA dam, Cheoah was completed this same year. Its flood gates were closed, and it began to fill with water. Until it could supply the electricity critical to their smelting plant's operation, ALCOA bought private power from Ocoee River dams. These were located several miles south of Maryville.

When it was completed, Cheoah was the highest overflow dam in the world with the largest hydroelectric generating units.

After the Cheoah dam was finished, the railroad rails were extended northeast to Tapoco so work could begin on Santeetlah Dam. This dam wasn't scheduled to be completed for nine years.

～

In December, 1919, Lydia at fourteen, eloped with Leonard Whitehead.

Noah Tipton was livid. Without thinking through the situation, he saddled up his horse, and headed for Alcoa with the intention of bringing his daughter back home.

Riding up to Melva's door, he dismounted and charged straight into the house. Melva had never seen her father so angry in her life.

"Where is Lydia?" he exclaimed, glowering at Melva.

"I don't know for sure," Melva stammered. "She may be at Sinda's house."

"What do you know about a wedding with Leonard Whitehead? He's almost old enough to be her father. I've come to get her." Noah's anger was lessening somewhat.

"I was as surprised and upset as you are, Father. I didn't even know Lydia liked him that much." Melva said lamely, gesturing with her hands. Melva wanted to fall through a hole in the floor. To be chastised by her father in this manner was the worst thing she could imagine.

"You should've kept better watch on her. I'm going over to Sinda's. Where does she live?"

"It's too late. They were married yesterday by a Justice-of-the-Peace. She walked from Sinda's to tell me. They were going to a house Len rented somewhere. I was so shocked and irritated, I didn't ask where. Sinda may know." How could she explain to her father the dismay and anger she'd felt when she realized exactly what these two had done.

"Already married." Noah sat down in a chair at the kitchen table, putting his head in his hands. Melva talked calmly and rationally to her father. Noah kept shaking his head.

"Her mother and I are terribly disappointed with her actions. And Leonard ought to know better than to marry someone so young." Leonard was twenty-seven.

Maddie stood at his knee. "Grandpotter, is you angry?" she asked, looking up at him with her mother's deep brown eyes.

Noah picked her up. She snuggled in his arms. Concerned at his discomfort, she patted him on the shoulder, just as her parents did her, when she was unhappy. Noah melted. His anger disappeared. "Yes, grandfather's angry but not at Maddie." Still he was so upset, he couldn't enjoy his grandchildren, including Earl, who toddled around the room. Georgia May was asleep in her crib.

"I'm sorry I was so angry," he said to Melva. "I shouldn't have jumped at you." Noah stood up to leave. "I need to talk to Lydia and Len soon — the sooner the better." Noah was no longer angry, but he was still displeased.

He hugged his daughter, kissed Maddie, shook hands with Earl, and said goodbye. "Next time I won't be so ill-mannered." Noah smiled at Melva and opened the door. He turned and said, "Remember, I still want to see them. Make sure they know this."

On the ride home, he thought about the situation. First, he needed to pray.

"Father, does aging cause a human to be more impulsive? I'm sorry for acting so brash — for being so hasty. Please forgive me." Noah hesitated and then continued, "Oh, and I'll probably need your divine help when Lydia and Len come to visit. Thanks in advance."

By the time he arrived in Chilhowee, he'd decided to give the newly married couple the same gift he'd given his other married children — some money to help them get started. Since they were already wed, he would support them in their new life together.

Joyce was playing on the front porch. She came running to greet him. As his last child, he was determined she'd get an education before she got married.

～

In the meantime, Alcoa's name was changed to Calderwood, after the superintendent of the finished Cheoah Dam. The new city of Alcoa, which surrounded the ALCOA smelting plants that were being built, was now located beside its sister city of Maryville.

～

D.H.'s home coming was a happy one. He was now twenty-nine years old. For a few calm weeks he helped his father in the Chilhowee store. He knew he must make up his mind about future employment, but for now he wanted to rest.

The year 1920 ushered in the start of the roaring twenties. The spread of automobiles and use of telephones increased. The radio boomed the news of the world in many living rooms. Even in the mountains of East Tennessee, industrial and economic growth, demanded changes in lifestyle.

～

D.H. decided to travel to Townsend, Tennessee, and take advantage of W.B. Townsend's offer of a meal at Wonderland Hotel at Elkmont. He asked his father to go with him.

The day was cold as they boarded the train at Chilhowee. They were bundled up in overcoats, gloves, scarves, and hats. At Maryville, they changed trains and headed up Little River on a ride that would soon become familiar to D.H. The train made several stops — one at the Kinzel Springs Hotel, where several people got off, and some boarded for the short trip to Townsend. The train started again with a jerk.

"D.H., I need to bring your mother up here," Noah said, looking at the impressive two-story, white-framed building.

"I think mother would enjoy having others wait on her for a few days. But you could give her this same privilege closer to home with a stay at Montvale Springs Hotel."

"Have you been there?"

"No. The owner comes into the bank. I've seen pictures."

The train blew its whistle. The men looked out the windows as the engine pulled into the station. Several stores lined the town area, including a movie theater. There was a boardwalk and, in the distance, a church steeple.

Dressed in a business suit, W.B. Townsend waited on the depot platform, hat in hand. The wooden structure was much, much bigger than the one at Chilhowee and bustling with activity.

The first thing you saw and heard after leaving the train was the impressive number of buildings and distant noise associated with the Little River Lumber Company.

Mr. Townsend escorted Noah and D.H. through the massive operation, taking his time to explain each step thoroughly. D.H. asked several good questions. He was interested in the mechanics of the operation. This included the new band sawing process, as opposed to a circular sawing of the wood, and the flow of materials—from the mill pond to the railcar. They visited the covered storage area where the sawn boards were sorted into bins, according to kind and size before walking to the new concrete dam built across Little River.

"Doesn't look anything like Cheoah," observed Noah, grinning. He'd taken the train at the invitation of Mr. Calderwood to see the completion of the massive structure above the old town of Alcoa.

"No. This one's not high," laughed Townsend. "We use ours to back up water so we can have the mill pond for holding logs," explained Townsend.

"Did you divert the river to build it?" asked D.H. as they walked away, imagining the labor and equipment needed in the dam's construction.

"Yes. We moved a lot of dirt. Are you men getting hungry?" Mr. Townsend asked as they stood by the rail spur, watching the finished product being loaded onto flat cars.

"I could eat anytime," Noah offered.

As they walked back to the depot, W.B. finished his explanation. "The sawn wood will go to Knoxville, then north to New England, and west to the developing frontier. Some of the fancier woods are shipped as far as Europe."

"Imagine, Father, walking into a building in London or Paris which has cherry-wood or walnut from the Appalachians."

"Excuse me for a minute, gentlemen." W.D. had a brief conversation with the agent at the depot, who picked up a phone and made a call.

Within minutes a Studebaker bus, fitted to run on the train tracks, pulled up to the depot.

"Gentlemen, we are clear to travel the rails."

D.H., Noah, and W.B. boarded the mechanical marvel for the ride to Elkmont and their dinner at the hotel. A cloudy Little River glistened in the rays of the noon sun. The ride, which snaked along its banks, was smooth on the rails put down by the lumber company. Although the area had been logged, short trees were beginning to reclaim the forested area. Some were six feet high.

The bus continued to penetrate into the uninhabited area, crossing a stream, and turning upriver to Elkmont. Townsend kept up a running commentary. He kept pushing information at them. Noah began to think he had an ulterior motive.

"You'd think the land was unoccupied, but people lived just about everywhere they could put a house foundation in the ground—even here in this area. And the footing often consisted of a pile of rocks."

The Wonderland Hotel was only a few steps away when they exited the bus. A stylish young woman with a small child stood at the landing. The men took off their hats as they approached her.

"Uncle, I didn't expect to see you here," said the smiling, attractive woman. She was holding the young girl by the hand and getting ready to ride the bus back to Townsend.

"Mayme, I'd like you to meet Noah Tipton and his son D.H. We're headed to eat dinner at the hotel." Turning to the Tiptons he said, "This is my niece, Mayme Townsend, and her daughter."

"I'm very pleased to meet both of you," said Mayme, extending her gloved hand. "I hope you enjoy your meal. They do have delicious food here at the hotel." She helped the girl onto the bus and started to step in.

"Would you like to join us for lunch?" asked W.B.

She turned back to look at her uncle and said, "I can't stay. I promised Aunt Margaret I'd come and help her with some clothing. She's sorting it to give away at church Saturday."

"Ah, I see. I'll probably see you at home later." Mayme, newly divorced, was staying with her uncle.

The men proceeded toward the hotel with W.B. continuing his remarks on the community. Mayme stood by the Studebaker bus, watching them go.

D.H. turned around to take a second look.

She waved.

~

Wonderland Hotel sat in a manmade glade with a manicured, green lawn in front. Unlike the denuded forest the group had just ridden through, massive trees surrounded it. Beyond the leafless trees, tennis courts were visible. Although the air was cold, the sound of rackets hitting balls was clearly heard.

"The horseback riding stables are far enough away not to offend delicate nostrils, and we have many trails in the mountains, both for riding horses and walking."

The Little River Lumber Company operations had progressed up Little River and its tributary Jakes Creek. The clear whistle of the steam engine working the logging sections could be heard at the hotel.

"We have several thousand acres to cut along Jakes Creek."

"Isn't it hard cutting the trees and snaking the logs off the steep hillsides?" D.H. asked.

"Hard and dangerous, but we have a good crew — most of them from this area. Our workers are used to cutting trees. We have many who can walk up to a huge oak or maple, go around it, and predict the exact spot where the tree will fall."

The conversation continued. Before the meal was over, W.B Townsend offered D.H. a job in the office of his business. D.H. accepted.

Back in Townsend, the three men went to the hub of the wood-sawing operation. The white-framed building sat in a grove of trees. The building housed the paperwork end of the Little River Lumber Company. There was a reception area out front with a desk and typewriter on top and three separate offices.

W.D. pointed out his work area on the left. D.H's was in the middle, and his male assistant was to the right.

"You'll be working outside much of the time, estimating board feet of lumber, checking on shipments, and solving problems with men and equipment. In here, you pay bills, make invoices for our customers, and *make sure* they pay us. You'll also supervise the receptionist and your assistant. You can set up the office as you please."

This was D.H.'s dream job. He didn't want to return to the bank, although John Anderson was a wonderful boss.

On the way back to Chilhowee, Noah observed, "It isn't like John Anderson needs you, although I'm sure he'd hire you back in a minute. The Tiptons have supplied him with plenty of good tellers."

For ten years, one Tipton or another worked for Blount State Bank. After his graduation, Matthew started as an employee. He loved working with numbers and was an aggressive worker. John Anderson compared him to a sponge. He soaked up every bit of information he heard and applied it correctly the next time the same situation occurred.

John knew he'd finally found the Tipton he needed as his assistant in the banking business. He would groom Matthew to take over as President after he retired.

Milton never worked at the bank. Without his father's help, he sought work in building structures — any kind. He found it, working as an engineer for the construction company building houses for Alcoa. Like all the men in the Tipton family, he was interested in learning every facet of his job. His dream was a business of his own.

Henry Tipton loved working for the county as Registrar of Deeds. He had turned into an outgoing person who loved meeting people. But the crippling arthritis was advancing rapidly. His health was deteriorating at an alarming rate. Lila, increasingly alarmed, wondered how long he'd be working in the courthouse.

Chapter Fourteen

A New Page in Melva's Life

Wait on the LORD: be of good courage, and he shall strengthen thine heart: wait, I say, on the LORD.

Psalms 27:14 KJV

Calderwood was bulging at the seams. The town was heavily integrated with three thousand black and white men from all over the south — actually from just about every state. ALCOA paid good wages. The living conditions were better than most of the men could afford at home.

The one drawback was being away from their families. The new town of Alcoa, next to Maryville, helped to remedy some of the homesickness. A whole city of new houses was springing up along with the smelting operations being built. Whole familial units were housed close enough for a train ride home.

At Calderwood, a school was built and teachers hired and a Baptist church was established. There was a small hospital with a doctor and nurses — everything anyone could want to raise a growing family. But the work grew farther and farther away from Calderwood, necessitating longer traveling times back and forth.

Burl came home only on weekends. By then, he was exhausted, and his lack of face time with Melva and his children was a strain on the home.

Although Calderwood was growing, Burl's work was rapidly coming to an end. The crew was finishing up surveying and cutting the backwaters of Cheoah. They could've gone on to help with surveying for Santeelah Dam, but there were crews already working in the area. By next year, he would need to decide on whether to move his family to North Carolina, keep working for the Bertrams at Six Mile, or try something else. He was leaning toward the something else, but another possibility or kind of work hadn't presented itself to him.

~

D.H.'s job kept him busy in Townsend, but something earth-shattering happened in August, which caused him to ring his sister on the phone.

"Have you heard?"

"Heard what?"

"Women can vote!"

"I can't believe it's finally happened!"

"Melva, don't you have a radio?"

"No. We need food and clothes worse'n we need a radio."

"I'll get you one and send it to you."

~

Six-year-old Maddie started school in the fall of 1920.

"Maddie, time to get up. This is a school day," Melva called.

Movement and sounds from her nearby bedroom, meant a trip to the bathroom and clothes being put on in a hurry. She bounced into the kitchen to eat her breakfast.

"Hi, Mama."

The morning meal consisted of hot oatmeal or leftover biscuits with scrambled eggs. Maddie ate quickly.

"Slow down. You'll get to school on time," Melva admonished her.

"Mrs. Griffiths said she was giving a surprise to the student who came to school first today." Getting up from the table, she gathered her pencils and paper, placing them in a cloth bag her mother had sewn for a carry bag. Hurrying, she pulled on her coat, gloves, and woolen hat, and went down the front porch steps to the concrete sidewalk.

She stood impatiently, shifting her weight from one foot to the other.

She didn't walk to school by herself. An older child, Lois Lane, went with her. Lois was the daughter of her next-door neighbor. Melva gave her twenty-five cents a week to look after her daughter on the walk to school.

Maddie waved a come on, hurry gesture as Lois appeared from the Lane house and walked toward her.

"Maddie, it's cold today," Lois said, walking up to her charge. She looked up at Melva on the porch and smiled.

"Yes, Lois. Be careful. There may be ice on the sidewalk this early in the morning," Melva cautioned. The sun's rays were just barely glowing over the mountains.

Earl came out on the porch in his nightclothes, dragging his blanket.

"Bye, Sister," he managed, while rubbing his eyes with his fist.

"Earl, my goodness. You'll catch your death of cold." Melva took her barefoot child by the hand and led him back inside the house. "Are you hungry, sweetheart? Mama has biscuits and honey." She picked him up, wooling him around, until he laughed. "My, you weigh a ton." Out of breath, she put him on a chair, and pulled it to the table.

"Mama, I'm big boy."

"Yes, you are. Can I tell you a secret? Remember, if it's a secret, you can't tell anybody," she said, shaking her head and putting eggs and biscuits in front of him.

Earl's eyes got big as he nodded. "Earl not tell," he promised.

"You're going to have a little brother or sister next year."

"Oh, Mama. Earl knows," he grinned.

Melva put her hands on her hips in mock astonishment. "How?"

"I heard you and grandmother talking." He stopped for a second. "And, I hear Georgia May whinin' in your bedroom."

"You have big ears."

Melva poked him in the ribs as she passed.

"No. I don't," he called as she went to get Georgia May from her crib.

∾

Maddie loved school. She couldn't wait to get up in the morning, put her clothes on, and walk down the hill to the frame building.

Mrs. Griffitts was the first-grade teacher. She made learning very interesting and told stories about growing up in the mountains and Maryville and read out of storybooks. They did numbers and ABC's and learned to write their names.

Maddie never got an unsatisfactory grade or a satisfactory one. She always brought home cards with excellent on them, and this included deportment.

～

Early in 1921, the people in the Tipton and Whitehead families boarded the train at Calderwood and Chilhowee. They headed to Townsend, Tennessee for the wedding of D.H. Tipton and Mayme Townsend. Everyone was invited.

D.H.'s brother Henry would not be there. He'd resigned his position as Registrar of Deeds because of his health. He was in constant pain and was no longer gregarious or social. Lila was asked to fill the rest of his term in office.

Tom LeQuire, one of Nan's older cousins, attended the wedding with his wife. They lived in another part of Blount County, in a farming community called Prospect. After the wedding, he approached Noah to say hello.

"Noah, how are you?" Tom asked, drawing near to shake his hand.

"Nan and I are tolerating the middle years well. How about you?"

Tom was much older than Nan. "Having trouble with my bones these days. Can't move around like I did at twenty. Shoeing horses is awful hard. I'm looking for someone to take over and run my business on shares."

Melva was all ears. "Burl did you hear that?" she whispered. He was standing near, carrying Georgia

May. She held Earl's hand. Maddie stood by her grandfather, hanging on to every word.

"Yes. Do you think I should approach him?" Burl whispered back.

"Sure. At least get all the details."

Tom and Burl spent about an hour discussing the business, housing, and what the move would entail. With his children married and gone, Tom and his wife would move out of the two-story, frame building where his family had always lived.

"My wife has a hard time climbing the stairs," he explained.

If they moved, this would be the Whitehead's home.

Tom also suggested, "With Melva's experience in the grocery business, you could run a store in one of the front rooms on the ground floor, along with the blacksmithin' business in a shed to the side of your house."

Burl and Melva discussed the move. Both wanted to establish their independence and to be business owners. This seemed to be the perfect solution to both ideas. It was especially attractive since Burl wouldn't have to build an operation from scratch.

Tom suggested the family ride the train to the Hubbard depot and visit Prospect on the way home. This suggestion cinched it. Burl and Melva would check it out.

∼

A drizzling rain came down the day Melva and Burl moved to Prospect. Most of their worldly goods were wet by the time they arrived, necessitating drying them off or hanging to dry. Melva grumbled under her breath and wondered if the difficult beginning of this move would extend through the rest of their stay. Her question was soon answered.

The move to Prospect didn't turn out like the couple expected. Within six months, Tom LeQuire died from an unknown ailment. His wife moved in with their oldest daughter, who lived several miles away.

The Whiteheads were left with no relatives, and making friends turned out to be difficult. The business lagged in income, and there was no extra money to stock a grocery store. With five people to feed and one on the way, the young family needed to make another decision.

On his many trips to Maryville, D.H. could make a detour at Hubbard, swing by to check on his sister, and have dinner with the couple. Melva could hear the automobile coming down Prospect Road, and she would set another plate at the table.

"Where's Burl today?" he asked, coming in the door of the Prospect house.

"He's down at the Bertrams for the week." Melva said this as she lifted Georgia May to a seat at the table. Earl had no trouble climbing on his chair. "They had a problem with a horse, and he went to tend it."

"When's the baby due. Looks like you're ready. Who's going to help you?"

"Burl's goin' to swing by Parham Street in Maryville and bring his sister, Lou, to help on his way back. She'll stay several days until I can take care of myself. I'll be glad to see her. It's sorta lonesome here."

The two sibling's chitchatted as they ate the noon meal. Talking about serious things started as soon as Earl and Georgia May left the table to play.

"Melva, tell me the truth. Is this job at Prospect working out?"

"We're scrapin' by. That's all. There's not enough business to make any money ahead, especially with the baby comin' and all. We've about used our savings."

"When Burl comes back, tell him there's a new line openin' up at Elkmont, and I'd like for him to run it. At least, until something else opens up closer to your home. I've had him in mind all along."

Melva nodded. "Would you like some tomatoes and Hickory Cane corn outen the garden? We have plenty. If you have time, I could pick you a mess of beans." Melva struggled to get up from her chair. D.H. went to help her.

"You're not in any shape to pick beans." D.H. laughed.

"Oh, they're stuck beans—Kentucky Wonders. I don't have to bend over."

"Let's pick some. Mayme will be happy. She loves fresh vegetables—especially your beans."

"I've canned more'n three hundred quarts of good winter eatin', and there's some more to come." Melva grabbed three paper pokes from a cupboard.

"That's hot work in the summertime." D.H. followed her from the house on the short walk to the acre patch. "Looks like the apples and pears are ripe for jelly and preserves."

"They are. Guess Lou will help me there. I told Burl to tell her to bring jars, and I'll give her some to take home."

Burl's garden was one of his prize accomplishments. He worked the soil in the cool of early morning or just before the sun went down. The dirt was fine without clumps. The rows were in perfect alignment, and the hoed crop was without weeds, looking heavy and delicious.

"Melva, you do have a good husband. The best. We need to find him a job he likes. One where he can make enough money to support and feed his family."

Melva didn't answer for a few minutes as they filled their bags with the garden crop—red tomatoes, green beans, and white corn in shucks.

"Burl's proud. He wouldn't appreciate knowin' we were nosin' around on his behalf. That don't mean we can't look."

"I'll keep my eyes and ears open. Here comes Maddie."

Prospect School was across the road from the Whitehead home with the Baptist Church and cemetery alongside.

"Hi, Uncle D.H." Maddie was grinning as she walked over the gravel road. She skirted his vehicle and gave her uncle a hug. He dug into his pocket and promptly put a dime in her hand. This was his trademark to his nieces and nephews—a dime for a hug. He got lots of them—hugs that is.

"How was school today?"

"Oh, we aren't in school. I went to church to straighten up for the revival tonight."

"I see. Are you going? Does your mama go with you?"

Maddie nodded. "I go, but Mama doesn't go with me. I like the singin', and the preachin' reminds me of Hill Top at Chilhowee."

"I can imagine." D.H. laughed. He hadn't been to church since his wedding. He continued, "Melva, guess

I'd better be gettin' on into Maryville. Mayme will think I'm runnin' around on her."

Melva looked at him, wondering why he'd make such a statement. Was Mayme jealous?

~

Burl stayed a week at the Bertram's farm. He came home with a job offer—in Bluefield, West Virginia. "It's only for a month, Melva. I'll be supervising the cuttin' and loggin' of a new railroad bed. Willard's goin' with me. There'll be plenty of money. Enough for a small nest egg. Here's the down payment." He dug into a pocket and pulled out a fist-full of money.

"You'll miss the baby's birth, and D.H. has work in Elkmont. You could work closer to home," she protested.

"I gave my word."

Melva knew there was no need to henpeck her husband. He always kept his word.

Burl was gone a week when Edie was born. She had beautiful blond hair like her brother Earl. Because she was a small baby, Melva told her mother the baby just popped out. Maddie, Earl, and Georgia May came into the room to see their new sister.

"She's red, Mama," Earl said with his face close to Edie's face. He was checking to see if she had two eyes, a nose, and mouth.

"Son, she'll be the prettiest color of faded red tomorrow or the next day."

Georgia May climbed upon the bed. "She's no bigger than my doll-baby."

"No, God love you. But one of these days she'll run and play with you. You just wait and see."

"Mama, can I hold her?" asked Maddie.

"Sure, for a few minutes. She'll be hungry, and I'll need to feed her."

"When are you goin' to have a brother to play with me?" Earl asked. Dolls weren't his thing.

Melva laughed, but she didn't answer the question.

D.H. called to check on her. "Can't stop on the way to Maryville," he informed her. "I'm pickin' up a visitor at the depot. Be sure and tell Burl I plan on coming to listen to the World Series with him next month. I think the Giants and the Yankees will play. Babe Ruth will be on base for the Yankees."

"Bring Mayme," suggested Melva, before they hung up the phone.

Lou stayed till Burl arrived from West Virginia. She went home as he went to Six Mile to receive his pay.

❧ Chapter Fifteen ❧

Another Move

As arrows are in the hand of a mighty man; so are children of the youth. Happy is the man that hath his quiver full of them.

Psalms 127:4-5a KJV

Months and years passed as the Whitehead family continued to work through the scrapes and bumps of life. Burl started work at Elkmont, riding his horse to Hubbard, leaving it at the local blacksmith shop, and catching the train to Townsend. During the week, he stayed in the barracks at Elkmont, and came home on weekends. He and Melva dreamed of a time when he could stay at home during the week.

One weekend in 1924, he loaded his household into the family wagon and made several trips to the crossroads at Hubbard. Closer to Maryville, their new two-story home sat below the railroad tracks which went to Townsend. His blacksmith shop sat across Tuckaleechee Pike from the home and on the same side of the tracks as the house. He'd bought the former owner out. Saunder's Grocery faced his shop on the upper side of the tracks, a little down from the Hubbard train depot.

The curvy, rocked road, or Tuckaleechee Pike, came from Maryville and ran along Little River on the opposite side of the stream from the railroad. It passed the beautiful Chilhowee Inn at Walland. On a hill above the Inn and the town of Walland, the newly constructed Walland School looked out over the Schlosser Tannery, Little River, and the many houses located below. The road continued to hug the river bank, passing swinging bridges which crossed Little River. These accessed farming areas on the other side, and numerous houses where flat land presented itself to farm. This was the road D.H. drove when he visited Melva on the way to Maryville. Besides Walland and Kinzel Springs, the Hubbard intersection was the next busiest intersection on the road.

～

Work was still hard, but making ends meet was easier with work at Little River Lumber Mill and blacksmithing on the weekend. He and Melva were content.

In the same year as the move, Clyde was born at Hubbard. Earl rejoiced. He had a little brother to play games with. Maddie was ten, a beautiful, curly haired, brown-eyed young lady who still made excellent on her grade cards. Earl loved sports like his father—baseball and basketball. On weekends, the family drove the wagon to Hubbard School and joined other families, shooting hoops, and hitting balls on the school's dirt ball fields.

Georgia May started school and took after Melva, sewing and cooking. Like her sister, Maddie, she lacked the coordination to play sports. Full of life, Edie was three and toddled around the house with Georgia

May's old doll. Georgia May had decided she was too old for dolls since she'd started to school.

Melva was beginning to hope her quiver was full.

～

Traveling day and night between Maryville and Townsend, the train rumbled into the Hubbard depot, stopping to load and unload freight and workers. The laborers were going to and from the Little River Lumber Mill or the Aluminum Company of America in Alcoa. The sound of the train whistle reminded Melva of living at Chilhowee and Calderwood. Besides the train, buses rolled through, corresponding to the three shifts worked at the aluminum company, some coming and some going. Life was not dull at Hubbard.

Automobiles traveled the road. D.H. wasn't the only one driving a car to stop at Hubbard. Mayme had her own car, and Margaret Townsend often stopped to visit with Melva, bringing her a pie or other baked goods. Melva was shocked when Burl bought a rattletrap car, their first, from one of the neighbors. Realizing no one within several miles sold gas, he put in a gas pump, and sold gas to the people driving the road.

Other visitors were bands of gypsy's in covered wagons. They stole from Saunder's Grocery Store across the railroad track and from the Whitehead garden. Melva watched them like a hawk.

～

The family inherited the former blacksmith shop owner's pet dog. The dog hid in the shrubbery and refused to load up with the family as they left.

Old Shep, a Collie mix, took up with Burl, following him to the blacksmith shop on the weekends. He liked the tobacco Burl kept stashed where Melva couldn't see it.

"Here feller. Here's a chew." And Burl would cut one for himself and a small one for Shep, wagging his finger and admonishing the dog, "Don't you tell'er."

Old Shep was the family watch dog, especially when his master was working at Elkmont. He slept on the doorstep and barked at anything which moved. Between the train whistle, road traffic, and the barking, Melva didn't get much sleep. At least, until she got used to all the new sounds.

Shep loved to eat. His second love was running cars and the train. This proved to be his downfall.

When the family used the adjective 'old' that was because the dog was old. Arthritis or some other ailment had caused his hind legs to be stiff, and stopping on a dime was sometimes not possible. Old Shep had several close calls when running cars. His final close call was with the train.

The Saturday day was bright and sunny, and Burl was working at shoeing a horse in his shop and talking with the owner when he heard the train whistle and its creaking arrival at the depot. Old Shep had started barking at the sound of the whistle. He continued and ended with a strange, loud yelp.

Burl went running from his shop, and Melva ran from the house on the other side of the road. Looking pitiful, Old Shep pulled himself across the ground with the two legs he had left. His two back ones were gone.

"You doggone stupid dog," Burl said in a hushed tone. He looked up at Melva, who stood on the front porch with the children. Drawing in a breath and letting it out in a huge rush, he said, "Melva get the rifle and bring the bullets."

Melva went back into the house and brought the gun. "Are you going to shoot him?"

"Don't have any choice. Put him out of his misery." Burl loaded the gun. "I don't relish doin' this. Go back in the house. Take the children."

When he could no longer see Melva and the children, he reached down to rub the dog's head. "Sorry, fella. You've been a good dog." Burl raised the gun to his shoulder and fired one bullet.

Later, the family visited the spot where Old Shep was buried beside the blacksmith shop. Some of the children brought flowers. Burl brought a small chew of tobacco.

~

There were times when Melva thought her sixth sense was working overtime. During the summer, the children loved playing under the cool shade of a huge oak tree. The green monster and its twin sat in the front yard of the Whitehead home. Melva would place an old quilt on the ground under its branches and scatter toys around the edges.

Since Maddie served as chaperone, she could go back to the kitchen to cook or can fresh vegetables without interruption. As long as she heard the squeals and laughter of her children through the open front door, she knew they were safe.

Melva propped open the kitchen door with a chair. A slight breeze blew through the house, taking some of the suffocating stove heat generated by her cooking outside the room. Beads of sweat popped out on her forehead. She bent her head and swiped at it with her green-checkered apron—one she'd made with ruffles around the edge. Jars of freshly canned red tomatoes sat on the countertop. When cool, they'd be placed into the cellar beneath the house. On the stove, she stirred some green beans, cooking for supper, walked to the sink, and prepared to wash up pots and pans.

From the kitchen window, the open backyard, trail to the spring, and Burl's garden were clearly visible. An old shed with her husband's garden tools sat near the beans and tall corn. As she washed the dirty dishes, she could see the blue expanse above the distant trees. All day, clouds with dark underbellies flitted across the sky. About three in the afternoon, the wind began to blow. Maddie came into the kitchen.

"Mama, the wind's gettin' up. There's a storm coming."

"I've been watchin' out the window. The clouds are thicker—darker."

Suddenly, a strong wind gust blew through the house. The kitchen door slammed shut with enough force to knock a key off a nail beside it and sling the wooden chair onto the floor with a BANG. Melva stood still only a moment. She ran for the front door. Maddie followed on her heels.

The oak tree had several dead, black limbs in its upper branches. The lower green boughs, whipped by the wind, swayed wildly! Clusters of leaves with small twigs attached flew through the air, reaching the railroad tracks and beyond.

Taking in the whole situation in a glance, Melva jumped off the porch, heading for the quilt. She called to Maddie. "Hurry! Get Earl and Georgia into the house. I'll get Edie and Clyde." She scooped up Clyde and grabbed Edie's hand, pulling the young child in the direction of safety.

The group made the front porch. The wind blew dust in their eyes.

A loud crack, the sound of broken branches, and one of the upper bare limbs came crashing to the ground. Splitting into several pieces, the parts became projectiles, shooting across the yard.

"Mama, one of us would've got kilt," said Earl, his blue eyes as big as saucers.

A flash of lightning hit the ground somewhere in Hubbard. The children covered their ears and hurried into the house as loud, angry thunder shook the earth.

Defying the elements, Melva stood outside, looking at the limb. It was as big around as her thigh. Another flash of lightning and round of thunder.

The first drops of rain were as big as quarters. She ran for the quilt and toys. Hurrying back through the front door, she watched as the sky dropped buckets of wet stuff. Almost instantly, Tuckaleechee Pike turned into a creek, flowing with muddy water. The new stream ran down the road to a one-lane, concrete bridge and poured into Crooked Creek.

The adrenaline rush was over, and her hot work-period of the day was finished. Her children were safe. It was cuddle time. She went to Burl's big rocker and sat down to rest with baby Clyde nestled in the hollow of her arm. Toddler Edie sat on her knee and leaned back on her chest, while the others pulled small chairs nearby, each touching her somewhere, needing the comfort of her presence.

"That was a close call," Maddie whispered in her nother's ear. The storm continued to blow outside the house's safe walls.

"Yes, sweetheart," Melva whispered in return. Too close, she thought as she dozed off. She awoke to the smell of burnt beans.

🦋 **Chapter Sixteen** 🦋

A Final Home

*The LORD is my shepherd; I shall not want. He
maketh me to lie down in green pastures: he leadeth
me beside the still waters.*

Psalms 23:1-2 KJV

In 1928, Herbert Hoover ran for President of the
United States on the pledge of *"a chicken in every pot and
a car in every garage."* This was the same year the
Whiteheads made the final move of their household
goods.

The change took them closer to town and added a
new family member, Jip, a small, short-haired dog
whose tail never stopped wagging. Jip's coat was white
with a brown spot or two, and he ruled from a bed next
to the stove in the kitchen—his black nose stuck in
every household happening.

Maddie had graduated as the second highest in her
Hubbard School class and would start Everett High
School in the fall. There was no way she could walk to
Everett from Hubbard, and her father's old car would
never make so many trips.

Without Burl knowing the transaction, D.H.
arranged for them to move into a house in Union

Community. He paid part of the cost and schemed with the owner not to tell the family. The house needed lots of repairs, and D.H. knew his brother-in-law could manage them.

Not only did he make sure his sister had a home with garage and wash area, barn, chicken coop with chickens, outbuildings, orchard, flower garden, and several acres, but because of his wife, Mayme, they soon had a brand-new car to replace the rattletrap Burl drove.

Most of the elite in Maryville went to Knoxville to buy clothes at Miller's Department Store on Gay Street. They drove the curvy Maryville Pike through Rockford and Tipton Station to Vestal, crossing three large bridges on the way.

The first bridge was over Little River, the same stream which came from the Smoky Mountains through Townsend. The second one at Vestal was a rough, wooden bridge over the railroad on the outskirts of the city. The other was the steel-girded Gay Street Bridge, funneling you straight into the downtown area.

Most of the customers went early and stayed through the dinner hour, so they could have soup and sandwiches at noon in the store's cafe, and a piece of the store's famous coconut cake with coffee. Mayme was no different. Although she had farther to drive, she went regularly with friends from Maryville. Once or twice, she took Melva and treated her to coffee and cake.

From time to time, Miller's had contests to draw customers into the store. They gave away some expensive prizes. One promotional included a new car.

Mayme and D.H. didn't need a new car. But she liked participating in the contests, and she'd collected a shoe box full of coupons over three months.

"Is this another of your fool dreams?" exclaimed D.H., standing in the cutting-edge kitchen of their home in Townsend. Mayme often had dreams associated with traumatic happenings in her life and the world.

She'd dreamed Lindberg was successful in soloing the Atlantic and that Babe Ruth bested his yearly home run record to sixty. Both men accomplished these goals.

"Yes, I dreamed I won the car, and I even wrote down the number of the ticket." Mayme held out a piece of paper with some numbers written on the white page. "Will you call for me?" It wasn't that Mayme couldn't call on her own. She was a bit nervous about picking up the phone and dialing the number. What if her dream was true? Mayme had an eye tic, and the twitch was doing double-time.

D.H. looked at the black markings and placed the paper on the countertop next to the telephone. "Not likely, Mayme. Just forget it," he said. Opening the kitchen door, he headed for work, mumbling under his breath.

Mayme completed her housework and went to the kitchen. She couldn't wait any longer. Looking up Miller's number in the telephone book, she dialed it. A few minutes later, she burst through the office door of Little River Lumber Mill. She took two steps forward and stopped to get her breath.

D.H. could see the door clearly from where he sat. He hurried into the reception area. "What is it?" he asked, taking her arm and leading her to a chair as she gasped for breath. "Did you run all the way here?"

"I told you." Mayme stopped to take another breath. "I won!"

"The car?"

"Yes!"

D.H. sat down beside her, rocking back and forth in his chair. He shook his head. "This is hard to believe." He started laughing. "We don't need another car."

"No. We know someone who does."

"You're right. The one they drive is put together with wire, iron bars, bolts and screws, and anything else Burl can find layin' around in his blacksmith shop."

"Should we tell them?"

"No. Let's have some fun. When we get the automobile, we'll drive to their house, put the keys and a note on the seat, and leave."

"I'd like to be a bird in one of those tall oaks in their front yard when they realize what's happened."

Melva later joked with Mayme as they sat having dessert and coffee at Melva's dining room table. "We have the car in the garage and chickens in the hen house. Hoover's goin' to come up with another slogan if he wants me to vote for him."

Mayme laughed. "You know, D.H. is dabbling in county politics, don't you?"

"No, but I wouldn't be surprised if he did. He's a chip off the Tipton block, and he's got the disposition for gettin' votes."

"Oh, he's not running, at least not now. He's campaigning for Carringer for Sheriff. He says the man will win. He'd like to put in a word for Burl to be a deputy."

"Why would he do that?"

"Because your husband would make a good one." Mayme paused a moment. "There's something else I can tell you, but you mustn't tell a soul."

"I won't tell."

"There's talk of a national park in the mountains, and if that happens the mill may close. This means Burl will be out of a job."

"That'll be a blow to Townsend and the men who work there."

"Yes. If this happens, Uncle W.B. and D.H. will make sure the change is as easy as possible. They'll try to find jobs for the workers—ALCOA is a possibility."

The two women sat in silence, each mulling over the possible changes a national park would make in their lives.

Melva broke the silence. "Mayme, maybe D.H. *should* introduce Burl to Carringer. They could talk, and—" She threw her hands wide in a you finish the sentence gesture.

"Good idea. I'll mention a meeting to D.H."

"Now, I'll tell you a secret. I'm going to have another child." Melva got up and took the empty dessert plates and forks to the kitchen.

"Oh, Melva. That's wonderful," exclaimed Mayme, turning in her chair.

"If it's a girl, I intend to name it Mayme," said Melva as she returned.

Mayme stood up and hugged her sister-in-law. "I'd be honored, Melva," she said with tears in her eyes.

～

Carringer was elected Sheriff.

Two months after he took office, Burl was hired as a Blount County Sheriff's deputy.

One other exciting thing happened just after the election. D.H. arrived with two men from Townsend. Roped inside the truck's bed was a large, white appliance — a Frigidaire refrigerator. Melva's mouth flew open.

"Sister, we need to take away your icebox," D.H. said. The men removed the cold stuff, placing it on the kitchen counter, and tugged the wooden box with its water drain and pan to the back porch. D.H. held the screen door and the icebox and its parts soon rested in the yard. "Now boys, the refrigerator."

"What are you goin' to do?" stammered Melva.

As the men unloaded the refrigerator from the truck, D.H. explained, "It isn't new, but the Townsends bought the newest model and asked me to take charge of their old one. I thought you needed it."

"It looks like brand new." Melva watched the men as they went up the back steps, through the screen door, and placed it on the linoleum exactly where the icebox had been. "There's no electricity — no box to plug the cord into."

"We'll take care of that. The men will run a line to it."

Within an hour, the men were gone, and the electric icebox was humming in her kitchen. She walked over and ran her hand over its metal surface, tracing the metal logo on the front — Frigidaire. Opening one of the side-by-side doors, she felt to see if it was getting cold inside. Dashing tears, running down her face, she arranged the cold items into the interior.

The ice cube trays, she filled with water, and carefully placed the metal pans in the freezer section.

Burl would never bring ice blocks home from Maryville again, unless they made ice-cream, which he loved in the crank freezer. She picked up the phone to call her brother and thank him again.

~

Tragedy first struck the Noah Tipton family in 1928. Bill Garland, Ellie's husband, died.

On a walk through his mountainous property, he'd stumbled upon an illegal moonshine still. The owner, a next-door neighbor, was there. Rather than destroy the still because the man was poor with several children, Bill asked him to move the contraption of vats and coils from his property.

"Just don't leave it here. Move it by next Sunday, because I'll be back up here to check."

When Ellie needed salt, sugar, or spices, she sent him to a small market on Six Mile Road. On the next Saturday, Bill was in the store, when his moonshiner neighbor showed up on horseback. Bill and the owner watched as he dismounted and opened the door. From the smell preceding him as he entered the store, he appeared to have been testing the swill he'd made. Invited outside to discuss the situation, the man pulled a gun and shot Bill Garland two times. He fell backwards and died instantly. Bill was forty-eight years old with eight children.

Sheriff Carringer and his new deputy, Burl Whitehead, were called to the scene. As soon as Burl shut the door on the patrol car, he recognized the form on the ground as his sister-in-law's husband.

"What's wrong, Burl?" Carringer asked. "Do you know the man?"

Burl nodded. "Melva's sisters' husband, Bill Garland."

Bill's overalls clearly displayed two holes in the bib, and his body was resting in a pool of blood. Bending over, Carringer checked for a pulse. "No need to call for an ambulance. Tell the garage to send a wagon and gurney. We'll take him to the hospital for the coroner to check over. It's obvious he died of a gunshot wound." The sheriff headed for the door of the building. "Come on in the store when you get finished and bring your pad of paper."

Burl was the solid rock in the Whitehead family, but his hand shook as he called in the sheriff's orders on the car radio. He'd seen dead bodies before, but none of them were Melva's relatives. Who would tell Ellie her husband was gone and wasn't coming back? He called Noah from the market and went straight to the point. "Noah, I have some bad news. Bill Garland's been shot. He's dead."

"What on earth happened?" Noah's voice sounded the shock he felt.

"We don't know for sure, but we know who shot him. The sheriff and I are goin' to arrest him. There's a witness, and it looks like cold-blooded murder. Bill wasn't armed."

"Are you goin' to tell Ellie?"

"I was hopin' you would. I think that would be best."

"Nan and I'll head that way immediately. The buggy's already hitched up. Will you call as soon as you know what happened?"

"Yes, or come by." Burl added, "If you find out anything from Ellie as to why this happened, call the sheriff's office and leave a message."

"What will Ellie do with so many babies to raise?" Noah didn't expect an answer to his question. "What will happen to the body?"

"He'll be taken to Blount Hospital to be examined by the coroner and then to the funeral home."

"I'll let Ellie know." The phone went dead. As Noah walked out the door a verse from the Bible ran through his mind. He repeated it out loud. *My grace is sufficient for thee: for my strength is made perfect in weakness.* Ellie's life was changing dramatically. Would she continue in her faith in Christ or give up with eight children to raise? Noah shook his head and headed for the house.

～

The case was open and shut. After the trial, the deceased effects were offered to Bill's family. Ellie refused the package. Burl took the bag home and pulled the overalls out. He placed them on a curved wire he'd made and hung them in the washroom at the end of the garage—a clear reminder to his children of the outcome from making and drinking alcohol. No one touched them or moved them for twelve long years. Finally, they disappeared. No one knew where they went.

As D.H. had helped Melva, he pitched in, and with Noah's help, Ellie raised her children. In later years, she married again.

Chapter Seventeen

Life Goes On

Yea, though I walk through the valley of the shadow of death, I will fear no evil: for thou art with me; thy rod and thy staff they comfort me.

Psalms 23:4

The year, 1928, was an eventful one in the Whitehead family.

Melva's younger brother Matthew got married. The work on the second dam above Chilhowee, named Santeetlah, in North Carolina, finished on schedule. The Calderwood Dam would be completed two years later.

⁓

During the summer and sometimes at Christmas, Melva sent Maddie to Chilhowee. Along with her Aunt Joyce, she became the upstairs maid, helping her grandmother by pulling sheets, making beds, and dusting the furniture. She mopped, swept the floors, and carried drinking water to the rooms. Their help allowed Nan to cook delicious meals and welcome her extensive guest list—some who came year after year. Work within the home was accompanied by laughter and secrets known only to them.

Maddie wasn't the only grandchild who assisted. Other cousins joined in and soon they became a web of first-class buddies, exchanging telephone numbers and visiting each other during the year. The train could take each cousin within walking distance of the home.

While Maddie was there the first yuletide season, something else happened. She confessed her belief in Christ at Hill Top Primitive Baptist Church. She called her mother and father to tell them, and they promised to come when she was baptized the following Saturday.

On that cold winter day, she and a cousin stood on the bank of Abram's Creek, looking at the flowing, dark-green water. Maddie pulled her long, wool coat around her and whispered, "Iris, I'm already shiverin' and gettin' in over my head will be like jumpin' in a glass of iced water."

"I wish the wind weren't blowin' so hard. Mama will be harpin' on catchin' my death of cold," Iris whispered back and pulled her red scarf tighter over her ears. She looked over at her mother, Rita, who stood next to Melva. "I wish this was over with," she said truthfully.

"Do you think Preacher Oliver will be as long-winded as he is at church?"

"If he is, he'll turn into an icicle before he gets done with the five of us." She smiled at Maddie. Three others stood nearby.

Preacher Oliver waded into the water up to his hips. "Please come on in and stand behind each other."

Outer clothes, shoes, and socks were shed and handed to family members who shook in the cold air. Quickly, each one was put under the water in Abram's

Creek near the spot where Maddie's grandfather passed on his way to see John "Jack" Tipton in Cades Cove for the last time.

"I baptize you in the name of the Father, the Son, and the Holy Spirit," proclaimed the preacher, whose terse proclamation surprised all who witnessed the event.

Maddie heard the gurgle of the water close over her ears. Upright, she waited for Iris. She was the last one to go under.

Maddie poked Iris as they helped each other climb the stream's small bank. "Preacher's lips are almost the color of the creek water," she whispered, looking back.

The girls were taken to a home nearby to dry off, change clothes, and warm up by the fireplace.

Back in the Whitehead's new car, Burl, Melva, Noah, Rita, Iris, and Maddie left for Chilhowee and a sumptuous feast prepared by Nan.

~

Burl and Melva's last child, Don, was born at Union in April1929. With his addition, they had six handsome, strong children—three boys and three girls.

Life settled into a routine of getting up in the morning, fixing breakfast, and sending the children off to school. Burl worked shifts at the sheriff's department. Depending on the scheduled time he worked, Melva had to milk the cow in the barn, feed the chickens, and collect the eggs or slop the hogs. She did this accompanied by Clyde and Don.

Clyde, at five, was old enough to get into trouble, nosing into the bins and stalls filled with corn, hay, or animals. Don, in a makeshift manger made by his father and filled with straw, usually slept while she completed her chores.

The months rolled along. There were days when Melva needed to get out of the house. She took Clyde's hand and carrying Don, she walked down her circular drive. Sweet peas bloomed between the drive and woven wire fence on the right. She turned and walked toward town, the Henry Lawson Store, and a bag of penny candy. They passed the homes of friends, calling to them on their front porch or stopping to say a few words.

Jip did not stay at home. He was always underfoot, smelling at bushes, wagging his tail, and licking hands. He was king of the road and everyone loved him. Clyde would run and get him if a car came down the gravel road, and the little band stood still until it passed.

Most food was grown in the big garden behind the house or picked from the fruit trees. These staples, canned in glass jars or dried and put in cotton sacks, were stored in the cool, musty-smelling, hand-dug, dirt cellar, along with potatoes, carrots, cabbage, and onions dusted with lime.

Slowly the repairs were completed to the house and the yard put in order. A new well allowed the family to enclose a porch as a bedroom and build indoor plumbing with running water in the kitchen and a bathroom. No longer was a dark, hot, or cold trip down a weedy path to the outhouse necessary, although it wasn't torn down immediately and sometimes came in handy.

Water from a gutter downspout filled the concrete and bricked cistern. Pumped out, it was heated and used to wash clothes in the room behind the garage, where the bloody overalls hung.

In the fall, when she couldn't catch a ride, Maddie, with her buddies, walked two miles to Everett High School, leaving Earl, Georgia, and Edie at Union School about one-half mile from their home.

In October, the stock market crashed. The Whitehead family was safe and secure in their home, giving away any excess to others less fortunate. Burl went to work for the Maryville Police Department, and Melva was content to watch her children grow up.

∾

In 1932, Joyce Tipton, youngest of Noah and Nan Tipton's children, graduated from Maryville College. The year before, Fred Kimmel and friend, from New York State had come to Chilhowee to go hiking and camping in the wilds of the mountains. Fred had stayed longer than he planned, because of a beautiful, tall young woman he met while renting rooms at the Tiptons.

Professing his love for her, he proposed. She accepted, and he asked Noah for permission to get married. Noah had sent his daughter to Maryville College for three years. He would say yes to the marriage, if Fred would wait until Joyce graduated.

Melva went to the wedding a week after Joyce finished school. Noah and Nancy's nest was empty.

∾

The next year with D.H.'s help, Maddie started to the same college, sewing in the maid shop to buy books and pay for other expenses.

That same year, Franklin Delano Roosevelt was inaugurated as President of the United States. He'd said in his inauguration address, *"The only thing we have to fear is fear itself."* It turns out that fear wasn't the only thing Melva had to be concerned about.

Looking back many years later, Melva called 1934 the year of death. In January, James Garland, Rita's husband, died of pneumonia.

Then the unthinkable happened!

Chapter Eighteen

Death Knocks on the Door

My God, my God, why hast thou forsaken me? why art thou so far from helping me, and from the words of my roaring?

Psalms 22:1 KJV

Melva sat in her favorite living room chair staring straight ahead. Her life trudged on in a series of automatic responses. She arose in the morning, cooked breakfast, cooked dinner, cooked supper, and went to bed or to sit in her chair in the living room. She felt lifeless — neither happy nor sad. A smothering sensation, as if someone had kicked her in the stomach, came and went. She pulled in air and let it out in a slow rush, sighing and sighing and then sitting as still as death — not moving until the ache in her body necessitated movement.

Jip came in, took one look, dropped his tail, and flopped down at her feet, his big eyes staring at his beloved master until he snoozed from boredom.

After the trauma and loss of the previous days, the world revolved around her, but she wasn't a part of it. Coming out of her shell meant facing the events of those days or was that weeks? The children walked around the house talking in hushed tones and doing most of her chores, those not included with cooking.

Burl, who hurt deeply inside, could not console his wife. As a last resort, he called D.H., hoping Mayme might persuade her to go into town—or anywhere. Burl wanted her out of the house, back into the real world.

"There's no change?" asked her brother upon receiving the call.

"No. I'm at my wit's end," Burl exclaimed. "Could you have Mayme call her?"

"Yes," replied D.H. "I'll go tell her right now."

She refused to go, spiraling down into a deeper depression.

~

Days passed.

Mechanically, Melva picked up a newspaper from the stack laying on a table beside her chair. Burl placed the latest under the stack after he was finished. She turned it over and over. Unfolding the paper, she looked at the print, not comprehending what she read. Only the headlines jumped out at her. Sales for the Easter Parade, the Republican Primary, a famous singer to appear at Maryville College, and something about buildings burning were stories making the headlines.

After a cursory glance through the first paper, she placed it on the floor at her feet. Slowly the pile on the table decreased, until she was close to the bottom. Picking up the final papers, the family Bible appeared in its normal resting place. She opened the next newspaper. A familiar name appeared among its sheets.

Obituary

Georgia Whitehead, age 16, daughter of Mr. and Mrs. Burl Whitehead, Route 6, died Tuesday from measles and pneumonia. Funeral Service was at Union School House this morning at 10:00, burial in Grandview Cemetery. Georgia was the second in this family to die within two weeks from measles. A brother, Earl Whitehead, an Everett High School student and member of the basketball team, died about two weeks ago.

Her heart constricted and, suddenly, everything came flooding back. Putting her head in her hands, she moaned, remembering the day Earl came home from school complaining —

"Mama, I don't feel so good. I think I'll go and lie down on the bed." Melva was immediately concerned. Her tough son was never sick. He was a senior member of the school's basketball team, and they were in the midst of playing the final games for the championship. There was a game that night.

"What seems to be wrong?" asked Melva, following him into his bedroom.

"I feel achy, and my nose is running," he said, coughing dryly.

She felt his forehead. He did feel a little warm. Melva went to get the thermometer from the metal medicine cabinet in the bathroom. Later, when she checked it, his temperature was elevated but nothing to be really concerned about.

Still, she suggested, "I don't think you should play in the tournament tonight. You might be coming down with something."

"It's probably just one of your winter colds, Mama. Besides, the team needs me. John will pick me up so we can catch the bus at Everett. We're playing Walland High School, and that's a big game for us," said Earl managing a smile, dead set on going. "Just let me rest a little while."

Against her better judgment, Melva waved goodbye to Earl and John from the front steps. Later, she heard the car coming back up the drive and went to the porch to turn on the light. John came into the house, and Earl went straight to his bedroom.

John whispered to Melva so Earl couldn't hear, "He's sick. Almost didn't make it through the game. You've heard that measles is going around school, haven't you?"

No. Melva hadn't heard. "When did they start?" she asked John.

"Maybe two weeks ago. A young boy in our English class had them first. I think there have been eight or ten cases since then." Neither Earl nor Georgia had said anything about this sickness. They both went to the same school. "By the way, we won the game."

After John left, Melva went into the room where Maddie, Georgia May, and Edie slept. Georgia May was in a small bed toward the door. Farther into the room, the other two slept together.

"Georgia May," Melva spoke quietly, "did you know about the cases of measles at the high school?" She heard rustling from the other bed.

"Yes, I heard about them, but there's some bug or sickness infecting the students most of the time. I didn't think anything of it," said Georgia May. "Why?"

"I'm wondering if Earl might have them," said Melva. "I'd better go and check on him." She started down the short hallway to the boys' room, picking up the thermometer from the bathroom.

Sitting up in bed, Maddie called after her, "Mama, some of the students at Maryville College have the measles." Maddie, a sophomore at the school, had overheard the conversation. Edie was still sound asleep.

Clyde, who was ten, slept with Earl in an adjoining room, while five-year-old Don slept in a tiny room near his parent's bedroom.

Earl's fever had spiked. It was one hundred-four degrees. Alarmed, Melva went to get the Bayer aspirin and alcohol out of the medicine cabinet. "Clyde get up. Go to the living room." The sleepy-eyed boy stumbled out of the room.

"Maddie," Melva called from Earl's bedroom, "Get some quilts and make Clyde a bed on the living room couch or floor."

Melva gave Earl two aspirin and pulled the coverlet over his body. He immediately pushed the bedspread off. It was too late to call the doctor, but she could swab her son with alcohol. This might cool him off. She sat in a chair placed close to the bedside and started the process. Jip came and lay down at her chair. Burl would be home soon.

After working the afternoon shift with the Maryville Police Department, Burl arrived at ten-thirty. All was quiet in the house, except the tap, tap of Jip's toenails on the linoleum floor as he ran to meet Burl in the kitchen. Melva heard them both from the bedroom. She headed for the kitchen. Her husband was cleaning out his black lunchbox and emptying his thermos, an after-shift ritual.

"I'm so glad you're home." She kissed him. A kiss before he left and one when he returned was a habit since they were married over twenty-one years ago.

"Is something wrong?" She was usually in bed and asleep when he arrived.

"Earl's sick. He's runnin' a high fever, and I think it may be measles. I've given him aspirin and swabbed him with alcohol. I'll call Dr. LeQuire in the morning. Why don't you go and say hello? He's awake."

Melva started cleaning the bowls in his lunch pail.

Burl walked to their bedroom, pulled off his coat and removed his gun, holster, and tie.

Melva appeared in the doorway. "Be careful, Clyde's in the living room on the floor. He wanted to camp out."

Burl followed her back to the kitchen. His next footsteps were in the direction of Earl's bedroom. When he felt Earl's forehead, the boy was hot but not burning up with fever. The aspirin was working.

Earl stirred. He gave his father a weak smile.

"How do you feel, son?" his father said quietly.

"Not so good," was the weak reply. "Every part hurts."

"Get some sleep tonight. Maybe you'll feel better in the morning." Burl left the room and joined Melva in the kitchen. She emptied the coffee from his thermos.

"I don't like the looks of him. Do you want me to sit up tonight?" asked Burl. "I don't mind." He often stayed up all night when he and his friends went hunting.

Melva was okay with that, but Burl snored loudly when he slept, and she was afraid Earl wouldn't rest. "No, I'll stay with him. You get some rest. Besides, Maddie's had the measles, she can help me sit with him."

Melva was a light sleeper. She would know every movement her son made. "Maybe, you can sit in the morning, after you're finished at the barn, and before you go to work." Burl had plenty of work around the small farm to keep him busy. He still shod horses and worked his bellows in the blacksmith shop not far from the house.

That night, she lay down beside Earl with her hand on his arm. At least twice she gave him medicine and swabbed him with alcohol. He shivered when she touched him. The next morning, after the children left for school, she called Dr. LeQuire's office. He came straight out. Dr. LeQuire was a cousin of Nancy Tipton and knew the Whiteheads well.

"Melva, how are you? Where's our patient?" Melva ushered him into Earl's bedroom.

Dr. LeQuire took Earl's temperature, listened to his heart and lungs, and looked into his mouth. Then he checked the skin along his hairline and behind his ears.

They went outside the room to talk.

"Melva, you're probably right in your guess. I think he may have the measles, but he's in the first stage. His lungs are clear. There's a hint of a rash on his head. If he develops a rash on his face and body, we'll know for sure."

"What can I do to help him?" asked Melva.

"Exactly what you've been doing. Give him aspirin and alcohol baths. Feed him clear soups and maybe some crackers. With a high fever, he isn't likely to have an appetite, so don't worry if he doesn't eat very much. He may be nauseous. The fever will start down in a couple of days, and the rash will disappear in about a week. I'll come back and see him in the morning." Dr. LeQuire started out the door. "Oh Melva," he said, "Measles is very contagious. No one should go into that room and wash everything he comes in contact with. We don't want the rest of the children coming down with this disease."

Melva felt much better. At least there was a probable diagnosis. Earl lay quietly in the bed, unusual for such an athletic young man. Although listless because of the high fever, he managed a smile when she teased him. He was worried about the basketball team. How were they doing? Melva kept him informed by reading the scores in the paper, and John White visited but stayed in the living room.

The next morning, on his way to the office, Dr. LeQuire came by to see his patient. Earl had a visible rash on his face, and it was spreading down his body.

"He's definitely got the measles. Keep on taking care of him as you're doing. I'll be back in the morning." There was nothing else to be done. Two days passed.

On the fifth morning, Dr. LeQuire realized Earl had a more serious problem. When he listened to his lungs, he heard a rattling sound and the fever wasn't abating. Melva stood anxiously by, waiting for the doctor's comments. She could tell by the grim look on his face something was wrong.

"What is it, doctor?" she asked.

"I don't like mentioning this word, but he may be getting pneumonia. That's not a good development, but Earl's in good physical condition. His body will fight the infection." All the good doctor could do was monitor the situation. If a bacterial infection attacked Earl's lungs, the medical field didn't have an effective treatment. Whatever happened would depend on the type he developed.

"I'll come back at noon and check on him."

Melva hovered over her son. After five days of worrying and continuously running her household, she was on the verge of exhaustion. No one could tend her precious son like she could. Maddie stayed out of school to help. Burl and the others assisted with other chores, but Earl was her responsibility. This was the first time in her life she felt completely helpless. She needed to pray, but why should God answer her prayers when she'd refused to acknowledge him in her life? He might not be close enough to hear her prayers. Instead, she called her mother and asked her to contact the members of Hill Top Primitive Baptist to start praying for her son. She called everyone she could think of to intercede for him.

At noon, Earl's breathing was a lot worse. Still the doctor was reluctant to diagnose his problem. He would come again after office hours. At four o'clock, when he listened to the young man's breathing, he was sure that Earl had pneumonia. The swiftness with which it was invading his lungs meant it was the worst kind.

"I'm sorry, Melva. It's not good news. He has galloping pneumonia—the worst kind. There's no medicine to help him. I'm afraid the results are in God's hands." Dr. LeQuire rubbed the back of his neck with his hand—a feeling of inadequacy flooded him. This day, he preferred another profession.

Did she hear the doctor right? He couldn't help her son. Melva's shocked countenance alarmed the physician. He pulled up a chair and sat beside her to calm her.

"I wish there was more I could do, but the medical profession hasn't discovered a medication to combat this infection." Before he left the room, he said, "I'm hoping and praying for a miracle." Then he promised to return in the morning. She was welcome to call him at home in the meantime.

"Oh, God, please don't let him die." These whispered words burst from the depths of her heart as she sat looking at her beautiful son. While listening to his labored breathing, she leaned over and smoothed the curly, blond hair back from his face. He was hot to the touch. Earl opened his eyes and looked at his mother.

"Mama, is it bad?"

Melva couldn't answer. The tears running down her face answered for her. Earl closed his eyes and went back to sleep. She was sure he didn't understand the magnitude of his problem. Maddie, standing outside the open door, had heard the doctor's comments. She cried silently and prayed for God's mercy.

Each night, Melva had slept with Earl, so she could feel the least movement. Tonight, the lack of sleep might catch up with her. She left the room and talked to Maddie.

"Maddie, I need you to stay with Earl tonight. Can you do that for me?" During his illness, Maddie hadn't gone to school. She'd stayed home, helping her mother in the kitchen, tending Clyde and Don, and sitting at Earl's bedside when her mother had other chores to do. How could she refuse?

"Do you mean sleep beside him?" asked Maddie.

Melva nodded in assent.

The responsibility of staying with her brother sat as a burden on Maddie's shoulders that afternoon. She imagined all sorts of scenarios, but she couldn't refuse her mother. At bedtime, Earl smiled at her when she came into the room. His blue eyes were clouded with fever. She never saw them again. That night she lay fully clothed on her brother's bed. His labored breathing shook the whole bed, keeping her awake.

Burl came to the room at ten-thirty. "How is he?"

"He's breathing really hard," she said.

"Do you want me to sit with you?" asked Burl.

Maddie wanted to say yes—instead, "No, I'm okay," and she realized this was true. Whatever happened during the night, her brother would not be alone. She turned over on her side and put a protective arm over her sleeping sibling. In the early morning, that's the way Melva found them.

Dr. LeQuire came three times that day. He was there when Earl passed away before midnight.

Earl's funeral was attended by the entire basketball team. They sat in a place of honor reserved for them at Union School House and served as pallbearers during the service. Hundreds of students and family friends came to the house and funeral to pay their respects. The circular drive filled with cars.

Then the impossible happened. Eight days later, Georgia came home from school complaining—

Melva didn't have the strength to relive the horror of the second bout with measles and pneumonia. As a last resort, Dr. LeQuire rushed Georgia to the hospital in Knoxville. The frenzied trip was to no avail. Georgia May, her Sweet Peach, was gone.

Melva threw the final newspaper in the floor. She arose and walked around the room. Paced was a better word for it. Thoughts and emotions flooded her heart, mind, and soul. Then she started crying. The horrible, sobbing and groaning came from the depths of her hurt. Don hearing these strange sounds came running into the room.

Grabbing her around the knee and looking up at her, the concern showing in his face, he asked, "Mama, are you okay?"

Melva picked him up and hugged him tightly to her chest. "Yes, son. I think I'm going to be okay. Go and play." She put him down and patted Jip on the head.

Chapter Nineteen

The Last Secret Place

He that dwelleth in the secret place of the most High shall abide under the shadow of the Almighty.

Psalms 91:1 KJV

The dam had broken. Emotionally exhausted, Melva walked back to her chair and sat down. Confronting the dreadful reality of her tragedy would not be easy. As a strong-spirited woman, she would survive, but why did this awful thing happen? Why did these two beautiful children die? What kind of God would take them from her? Why? Why? Why, indeed? The tears came again, just as they would for many days to come. Then there was the nagging but suppressed thought that in some way she might be responsible.

Though her tears she saw the words, Holy Bible, shimmering in gold leaf. The Bible, the same one given to her by her father and mother, rested on the table beside her chair, placed there mostly for show. She'd packed and unpacked it wherever the family lived. No one ever picked it up to read except for Maddie, who took it to church each Sunday. Resisting an urge to look at its pages, she headed for the kitchen to start supper.

Several days passed. Much to her family's relief, she was back to her old routine, but the "Why" questions nagged at her constantly. When Melva relaxed in her favorite chair, one look in the table's direction and at the book it held, brought back her need to find these answers.

Why Melva didn't move the Bible to a less conspicuous place only she could say. Although its removal would have been noticed by the rest of the family. Would they somehow guess the book disturbed her?

One morning when all of the children were at school and Don was playing, she sat down in her chair. Always before when something distressed her, she headed for her secret place to confront the problem. When Betty Jo was upset because she didn't marry her brother or when Grandpa Jack died, she'd gone to her secret place overlooking Chilhowee to calm down and think. When Burl might have been drafted into the armed services and their young family torn apart, she looked for a secret place to open the government letter. At Alcoa, she'd found it on the steps of the church, overlooking the Little T. She looked at the Bible, picked it up, and held it in her hands. What answers were in its pages? She needed a secret place now, but not today. She would wait until she was alone in the house. When she went to face God and ask her questions, she didn't want any distractions.

～

Around her farm, there was a barn, chicken house, corn crib, Burl's blacksmith shop, garage, vegetable patch, and the orchard with her flower garden. Melva took an old quilt and went outside. She looked around. In the early summer sun, the first flowers of the season bloomed beneath the apple trees. She headed in that direction and found a place between the hydrangea, larkspur, and bachelor buttons.

Under an apple tree, she spread her old quilt amid the pink and blue of her favorite flowers. Until she solved her problem, this would be her secret place.

On this day, and not long after sunrise, Burl loaded up the children and headed toward the Bertram's pond to go fishing. She'd have the day to herself, since he wouldn't come home until supper. She went inside and picked up the Bible, returning to the quilt.

The first thing Melva noticed was a marker that Maddie had placed among its pages. The pencil marks on the piece of paper said Psalms 6:6-7. Melva read, *I am weary with my groaning; all the night make I my bed to swim; I water my couch with my tears. Mine eye is consumed with grief.* Why would Maddie mark such a depressing passage? Did she place the note there hoping for her mother's help? Then Melva remembered, while in the fog of her depression, a conversation she'd overheard between D.H. and her daughter.

~

"You're going back to school, young lady."

"No, Uncle. I've lost so much work being out over three weeks, I'll never catch up. Besides, somehow school doesn't seem so important right now. I need to help Mama with the children and the house chores," said Maddie in tears.

"Your mother will make it," said D.H. with more conviction than he felt. "I'm not going to let you give up your dream. You're a good student." Maddie, close to finishing her sophomore year, had walked almost two miles to school and then back each day. This was after working in the maid shop. The job, sewing clothes, helped pay for her schooling, and she still made good grades.

"It's no use. I don't feel like going."

"Okay, I'll make a deal with you. I'll pay someone to drive you to school and pick you up. I'll give you the money so you won't have to work the rest of the year. You can concentrate on completing your work and finishing your sophomore year. Is that a good arrangement?" D.H. held a handkerchief out to her. These days, he always carried a hanky from the neat stack Mayme kept at home.

Maddie looked at him. He'd overcome her main objections. Surely, she could work hard and pass this year. Hopefully, her teachers would understand, she thought, as she dabbed at her tears with the handkerchief.

"I'll try really hard, Uncle," agreed Maddie, giving him a quick kiss on the cheek. When Uncle D.H. made a promise, he always kept his word. The following Monday, Maddie's ride showed up at the door.

~

Melva instantly realized that her daughter and probably the rest of the family were going through the same crisis she'd gone through. Maddie needed her mother. But Melva couldn't help herself, much less her daughter. When her family came home, she would apologize to Maddie, to Burl, and the rest.

Melva thought about the passage from Psalms. King David, whom God loved, had problems that depressed him. David poured out his tears in the darkness of his bedroom, calling upon the God he worshipped. Why didn't God solve his problems? Then David asked the question and gave the answer. Why should God care?

What is man, that thou art mindful of him? And the son of man, that thou visitest him? Because, *God hast made him a little lower than the angels, and has crowned him with glory and honor.* Man *has dominion over the works of thy hands; thou hast put all things under his feet.*

If the omnipotent God put his greatest creation over his most important design, He must attach enormous worth to humankind. Melva was beginning to understand that she was important to God. Because she was important to Him, she wasn't worthless. Since Melva could remember, she'd been proving her importance by her mischievous spirit. Did those acts cover up a feeling of worthlessness? Did her value come from them and her need to control every situation? Sadly, she admitted it did. Tears trickled down her cheeks. This wasn't the reason she'd opened the Bible. She wanted her "Why?" questions answered.

Melva turned the pages of the Bible. In Psalms 24 she read, *The earth is the Lord's and the fullness thereof; the world, and they that dwell therein.* Georgia, while in the Knoxville hospital, talked about the earth belonging to God, his love of the world and of the people living there. She quoted a bible verse Melva had heard often and passed off as meaning nothing to her. The verse from John said, *For God so loved the world, that He gave His only begotten Son, that whosoever believeth in Him should not perish, but have everlasting life.* Georgia knew she was going to die. She knew the steps involved in her death, and she prepared to accept them. Where did she find the inner strength to face death, this final separation from her beloved earthly family?

"Mama, the Lord said, *'Fear thou not; for I am with thee – I will strengthen thee – I will help thee.'* I'm not dying. I'm just going to another home."

Melva chuckled as she recalled Georgia's love of her earthly home. Once, during the summer, when she went to stay with Grandmother and Grandfather Tipton, Melva received a telephone call.

"Mama, I want to come home."

"You've only been at Chilhowee for two weeks," said her mother. Georgia was supposed to stay the summer and help around the house.

"Mama, I want to come home," was the reply – this time said more forcefully with a hint of a tear.

"Let me talk to Mother," said Melva. There was a short silence, and then she heard Nan's voice.

"What's wrong with Georgia?"

Nan laughed quietly. "She's homesick. She's got the worst case of homesickness I've ever seen."

"Don't you think she'll get over it?" asked Melva.

"I don't think so. She sits around sighing most of the day and she's practically quit eating. I think Noah needs to bring her home. To tell you the truth, Melva," Nan was whispering into the receiver, "she's already got her bags packed."

Now Melva was laughing. "Tell Father to bring her home then and to drive carefully." Noah was now an automobile owner and a terrible driver, according to his wife.

Later that afternoon, Georgia came bouncing through the door with a big smile that lit up her whole face. She was home. Now God was blessed with that same smile, because Georgia May was in Heaven. Melva was sure of that. Georgia's strength must have come from her faith in Jesus Christ. Melva felt certain this was the reason for her calmness as she faced death.

Before Georgia lapsed into a coma, she and her mother shared a quiet time together.

"Mama, this isn't your fault. God didn't pick on you."

How did her daughter answer the very question revolving around in Melva's mind? "He loves you and Daddy. Will you promise me to go to church on Sunday?"

There wasn't a church nearby, but several people interested in forming one met in the Union School House. Last summer, a group from Maryville College came to conduct Sunday School and enlisted Maddie's help. When their time was up, Maddie continued the classes and a Baptist minister came to conduct a worship service. Maddie, Earl, Georgia, and Edie walked there on Sunday mornings to attend.

As she looked into her daughter's fever-glazed eyes, Melva said, "I'll try to go." Melva excused her untruth as necessary to console her daughter.

"No, Mama. Promise me!" said Georgia May. She started coughing and threw up spots of blood on her pillow.

Melva had promised, but so far, she hadn't gone. She intended to, but taking the first step was the hardest.

Melva continued her reading in Romans. *For the wages of sin is death; but the gift of God is eternal life through Jesus Christ our LORD.*

What was sin? She was sure that lying to her daughter probably was. But Melva wasn't a bad person. Many of her acquaintances could testify to that. Her family could also confirm her willingness to help them. She obeyed the government, helped her neighbors when they had problems, and offered her home to those in need, whether they were family or not. She was respectful to those around her. It didn't matter if they were rich or poor. She wasn't wasteful with her possessions, mending clothing, eating leftovers, and giving away the excess of her goods. Although she could get upset, she never held a grudge for long, apologizing when necessary. When did she sin? Couldn't she go to Heaven on the basis of her own merits? She was a good woman. She continued to read with Maddie's penciled notes in the margins.

By one man's disobedience (Adam) *many were made sinners, so by the obedience of one* (Jesus Christ) *shall many be made righteous.* And in another place, she read, *For all have sinned, and come short of the glory of God.* There it was! The Bible plainly stated she was a sinner. God said she was a sinner. This profound truth took Melva's breath away and shook her to the core.

Melva remembered a quote she'd memorized in school, *"All means all, that's all, all means."* For several minutes she sat thinking about what she'd just read. Then she went back and read the last part of the first verse, *many shall be made righteous.* What did that mean? Righteousness would not be available to everyone? Why?

She found the answer in a familiar passage that her father often quoted; *I am the way, the truth, and the life: no man cometh unto the Father, but by me.* Her father always explained that to believe in Jesus meant believing in his virgin birth, sinless life, death, burial, and resurrection. Becoming righteous and going to Heaven was only possible through faith in Jesus; all of Him. And faith was vital for eternal life — a gift given freely by God, was the result. It was plainly clear. This was the answer. Her biggest sin was not lying to her daughter but in her failure to acknowledge Christ — all of him, and this oversight meant death with no hope of eternity. Eternity, she read, would be filled with God's love — perfect love. Wasn't that what humans searched for their whole life?

The unfathomable aspect of being a Christ-follower was faith. How could a person let go of the tangible and believe in the intangible? Believe in the unseen rather than the seen. Much of the Bible must be understood by faith. For a controlling person, who always touched, saw, felt, and smelled the world around them, this was a huge amount of belief to swallow. Was Jesus who he said he was?

Melva looked at her watch. She needed to start supper. Her family would be home soon and hungry after the sausage biscuits they'd eaten for lunch. She folded the Bible with regret. Her study was interesting and brought back many truths learned in her younger days. She promised herself she would continue to read the Bible at her earliest chance. After her Bible session, she felt calmer than she had in days, but her encounter with God's word hadn't answered her questions, it had created more.

$\sim$

Mama, Mama," called Don as he slammed the screen door coming into the kitchen. "Look what I caught!"

He held up a small catfish for his mother to see. "I caught it all by myself," he said proudly. Fishy water dripped over Melva's clean floor, but instead of scolding her blond-headed son, she picked him up, fish and all.

"I see. Was it hard to pull in?"

"Oh, yes. I tugged and tugged and the fish pulled on my line. I was scared." Don was beaming—all fear gone.

"After pulling in such a big fish, I'm sure you're hungry."

"Can we fix my fish, can we?" asked Don, looking at his dad.

"No," said his father coming in the door, smiling at his happy son. "We have to skin the catfish first. We'll clean it up with the rest of our catch and fry all of them tomorrow night. Come on. Let's take it out to the bench under the pear tree. We'll work on them after supper."

As they disappeared from sight, Melva heard Don tell his father that he "wanted to eat his fish." Burl promised to keep it separate.

～

Several days passed before Melva was able to visit her secret place in the garden. As she spread her quilt, she looked toward the mountains. The deep V she saw in the distance indicated the gap through which the Little River flowed and the railroad traveled to Townsend. Scattered, white puffy clouds slowly made their way to the rounded hilltops, and at times a slight breeze ruffled the leaves on the apple trees. She sat for several moments as it caressed her face and bare arms. She guessed it would rain tomorrow.

Turning over, Melva opened the Bible to the exact place where she'd stopped reading earlier. Why should she believe in this Jesus man? Was Jesus who he said he was? She followed Maddie's notes and scriptures to answer the questions.

He fulfilled the prophecies of the Old Testament. Christ was born in Bethlehem of a virgin, He became a prophet, who entered Jerusalem in triumph, but after healing thousands, He was rejected by His own people. Betrayed by His disciple, Judas, Christ remained silent during His trial and conviction. Mocked, beaten beyond recognition, and condemned to death, He underwent crucifixion and died. According to what she read, He was the Perfect Lamb who shed his blood as the final sacrifice and died for **all sinners and all sin**. What a heavy burden hung from the nails driven in his cross!

Coming from Jesse and King David, He became the restorer of Israel, Light to the Gentiles, and the Corner Stone of the future church. In the New Testament, Christ said He fulfilled the Old Testament prophecies. He said he was the Son of Man and the Son of God. Messiah, Christ, Teacher, and Master were his names. He emphatically stated, he had the authority to forgive as Lord and Savior.

Melva turned over, lying on her back. Through the apple leaves, she saw the sky clearly as she pondered what she'd read. She was stained with sin and Christ came to blot out those sins. Before she thought through this subject, Melva fell asleep.

"*Melva, I have chosen you, why haven't you chosen me?*"

Melva sat straight up, completely awake. Looking around, she saw no one in her presence. She was certain the voice was audible.

"Melva, I have chosen you, why haven't you chosen me?" There it was! The question avoided her entire life. Tears ran slowly down her face.

She looked up at the sky as the gentle breeze ruffled the pages of the bible behind her. She needed to make a decision, one she could no longer put off.

Returning to her stomach position, Melva found the wind-blown pages rested in Jeremiah, where she read, *Can any hide himself in secret places that I shall not see him? saith the LORD. Do not I fill heaven and earth?*

WHAT! Melva read the passage again. There wasn't a secret place! God was everywhere! He was telling her specifically and personally that she was never alone and that He had chosen her. Now she must choose Him.

The breeze blew and another page of her Bible fluttered in the wind. She read these words over and over and personalized them...*And I will give **you** a heart to know me, **Melva**, that I Am the LORD: and **you** shall be my **disciple**, and I will be **your** God."*

Burying her face into the quilt, Melva sobbed uncontrollably. She cried out to God, pouring out the anger, hurt, and sadness of the last months. When she finally quieted down, she asked God to forgive her of her denial of Him.

She was not a pretty sight. But neither was Jesus when He hung on the cross. God accepted her right then, runny nose, red eyes, and disheveled hair. She sat up on the quilt. A great burden lifted from her shoulders. She felt light as a feather. The Ruler of the universe wanted her as His child. She felt like dancing and did there among the hydrangea, larkspur, and bachelor buttons, her face and hands lifted to the sky.

For thirty-eight years, Melva looked for a *secret place* to mull her problems. In that place she was alone and no one shared her anxiety, loss, or problem *or so she thought*. The means to control the situation or a problem was the answer she sought. Now, she realized there were no secret places, and God was always in control. God was present everywhere, just waiting to be discovered, and she had found him here in her last earthly secret place. *He was her secret place*, a source of comfort and joy. She didn't need to control one single thing. He knew the perfect solution to everything in her life.

❦ Chapter Twenty ❦

The Last "Why" Question

Take my yoke upon you, and learn of me; for I am meek and lowly in heart: and ye shall find rest unto your souls.

Matthew 11:29 KJV

The sting of Earl's and Georgia's death was gone, buried in God's loving arms. Her love for them would make her sad at times, but she would never cry again because they had died.

When man killed God's Son on a cruel cross, showing Him no mercy, God did not turn against his peculiar people. A Sanhedrin zealot unmercifully killed Christ-followers after Christ's death, including Stephen. They didn't die in vain. Because of their glorious deaths, Paul, the most famous apostle's conscience was pricked. He quit kicking against the Holy Spirit's urgings, and he was converted. The disciples suffered terrible deaths because of their stand for Christ, glorifying God.

Why did Earl and Georgia die? Melva didn't find out. She understood that physical death wasn't easy. It was a time of suffering, but it was also a preparation for a future in Heaven in a deathless eternity, full of perfect love and joy, for those who believe in Christ.

Melva rested in this thought and knowledge. Her children were there, playing perfect basketball and without homesickness, and she would be going to see them. They would never be separated again. She determined in her heart to do everything in her power to see that her immediate and extended family went too. She would be a prayer warrior for them, just as her mother and father were for her.

Why did Earl and Georgia die? Melva didn't find out. She was sure the reason would be apparent in the future. Meanwhile, in the present, Melva comforted herself with this verse from Isaiah. *For my thoughts are not your thoughts, neither are your ways my ways, saith the LORD.*

Who can know the mind of God?

No man, when he hath lighted a candle, putteth it in a secret place, neither under a bushel, but on a candlestick, that they which come in may see the light. Luke 11:33 KJV

~

The following Sunday, Melva went to church with her children.

Recent History

If you travel to Chilhowee these days, there's nothing left of the early times. Chilhowee Lake, backed up by the dam, covers most of the area with a road running beside the water.

The famous 129 Dragon, a curvy road loved by motorcyclists, starts where you leave the lake and winds several miles toward North Carolina. This road passes the turnoff for the old town of Alcoa (Calderwood) where you can access the Calderwood powerhouse and the area of the construction town as the ALCOA dams were being built.

At Calderwood, the ruins of a church and its cemetery are visible on a hill above the upper end of Chilhowee Lake. Concrete sidewalks grown-up with weeds can still be walked on in some areas.

Due to problems at Chilhowee Dam, the lake was drained for several years. In the bottom were the clear remains of the Tipton Mercantile Store, the barn, and fields where acres of corn were planted.

Once again, I could walk where my ancestors had been one hundred years ago! Reba Rhyne

Ms. Rhyne may be reached at rebarhyne@gmail.com.